What the critics wrote about

Behind the Scenes at the Museum

'A début novel of astonishing confidence and skill . . . Acutely observant, overflowing with good jokes, it is the work of an author who loves her characters and sets them playing with gleeful energy'
Spectator

'Good grief, I can hardly believe it – a first novel which actually made me laugh, a first novel written so fluently and wittily that I sailed through it as though blown by an exhilarating wind: a first novel with a touch so light I only felt its truth and sadness after I'd finished it'
Margaret Forster

'A many-layered account of an ordinary family's life, written with an extraordinary passion . . . Atkinson's prose is rich, satisfying and self-assured, but never over-indulgent, and always surprising. Packed with images of bewitching potency, this is an astounding book'
The Times

'Really comic, really tragic, bracingly unsentimental . . .
What a triumph! What a joy!'
Boston Globe

'Impressive and entertaining . . . Quirky and colourful . . . Overall, it is ambitious and assured, its whimsical nature cloaking a tragic, but delicately rendered, revelation'
Yorkshire Post

'Remarkable . . . A multigenerational tale of a spectacularly dysfunctional Yorkshire family and one of the funniest works of fiction to come out of Britain in years'
New York Times

'If you tot up the deaths and other family tragedies in this feisty first novel, it seems almost rude to find it so amusing and delightful . . . anyone who thinks that all the sassy new writing by women is coming from North America should check out this gem from Yorkshire'
Independent on Sunday

'Beautifully written . . . hers is an irrepressible voice, frank, funny and sad, that will find echoes in all of us . . . Kate Atkinson maintains a pleasing balance between the tragic, the comic and the ridiculous'
Sunday Express

'A remarkable début novel . . . witty and original . . . this is the start of a long, successful writing career'
Daily Mirror

'The deceptively naïve tone of Kate Atkinson's first novel masks an unsettling complexity of vision, its artless depiction of childhood concealing acute feeling . . . the sense of the strain and the trivialities of everyday family life is always vivid . . . precise and powerful images penetrate the light, witty surface of the narrative, suggesting the raw emotion beneath'
Times Literary Supplement

'Has the best qualities of traditional storytelling'
Penelope Fitzgerald

'Scoundrels, malcontents, misfits, and cheats. Every family has them, though seldom are they handled with the winsome wit and wisecrackery that make *Behind the Scenes at the Museum* such a smart and funny read'
Washington Times

Also by

KATE ATKINSON

Human Croquet

A multilayered, moving novel about the forest of Arden, a girl who drops in and out of time, and the heartrending mystery of a lost mother.

'Brilliant and engrossing'

Penelope Fitzgerald

Emotionally Weird

Set in Dundee, this clever, comic novel depicts student life in all its wild chaos, and a girl's poignant quest for her father.

'Achingly funny . . . executed with wit and mischief'

Meera Syal

Not the End of the World

Kate Atkinson's first collection of short stories – playful and profound.

'Moving and funny, and crammed with incidental wisdom'

Sunday Times

Featuring Jackson Brodie:

Case Histories

The first novel to feature Jackson Brodie, the former police detective, who finds himself investigating three separate cold murder cases in Cambridge, while still haunted by a tragedy in his own past.

'The best mystery of the decade'
Stephen King

One Good Turn

Jackson Brodie, in Edinburgh during the Festival, is drawn into a vortex of crimes and mysteries, each containing a kernel of the next, like a set of nesting Russian dolls.

'The most fun I've had with a novel this year'
Ian Rankin

When Will There Be Good News?

A six-year-old girl witnesses an appalling crime. Thirty years later, Jackson Brodie is on a fatal journey that will hurtle him into its aftermath.

'Genius . . . insightful, often funny, life-affirming'
Sunday Telegraph

Behind the Scenes at the Museum

Kate Atkinson

BLACK SWAN

TRANSWORLD PUBLISHERS
61-63 Uxbridge Road, London W5 5SA
A Random House Group Company
www.rbooks.co.uk

BEHIND THE SCENES AT THE MUSEUM
A BLACK SWAN BOOK: 9780552996181

First published in Great Britain
in 1995 by Doubleday
an imprint of Transworld Publishers
Black Swan edition published 1996

A CIP catalogue record for this book
is available from the British Library.

Addresses for Random House Group Ltd companies outside the UK
can be found at: www.randomhouse.co.uk
The Random House Group Ltd Reg. No. 954009

The Random House Group Limited supports The Forest Stewardship Council (FSC), the leading international forest certification organisation. All our titles that are printed on Greenpeace approved FSC certified paper carry the FSC logo. Our paper procurement policy can be found at www.rbooks.co.uk/environment

Typeset in 11/15pt Giovanni Book by Falcon Oast Graphic Art Ltd.
Printed in the UK by CPI Cox & Wyman, Reading, RG1 8EX.

36 38 40 39 37 35

For Eve and Helen

With thanks to my friend Fiona Robertson
for all her help

CHAPTER ONE

1951

Conception

I EXIST! I AM CONCEIVED TO THE CHIMES OF MIDNIGHT ON THE clock on the mantelpiece in the room across the hall. The clock once belonged to my great-grandmother (a woman called Alice) and its tired chime counts me into the world. I'm begun on the first stroke and finished on the last when my father rolls off my mother and is plunged into a dreamless sleep, thanks to the five pints of John Smith's Best Bitter he has drunk in the Punch Bowl with his friends, Walter and Bernard Belling. At the moment at which I moved from nothingness into being my mother was pretending to be asleep – as she often does at such moments. My father, however, is made of stern stuff and he didn't let that put him off.

My father's name is George and he is a good ten years older than my mother, who is now snoring into the next pillow. My mother's name is Berenice but everyone has always called her Bunty.

'Bunty' doesn't seem like a very grown-up name to me – would I be better off with a mother with a different name? A plain Jane, a maternal Mary? Or something romantic, something that doesn't sound quite so much like a girl's comic – an Aurora, a Camille? Too late now. Bunty's name will be 'Mummy' for a few years yet, of course, but after a while there won't be a single maternal noun (mummy, mum, mam, ma, mama, mom, marmee) that seems appropriate and I more or less give up calling her anything. Poor Bunty.

We live in a place called 'Above the Shop' which is not a strictly accurate description as both the kitchen and dining-room are on the same level as the Shop itself and the topography also includes the satellite area of the Back Yard. The Shop (a pet shop) is in one of the ancient streets that cower beneath the looming dominance of York Minster. In this street lived the first printers and the stained-glass craftsmen that filled the windows of the city with coloured light. The Ninth Legion Hispana that conquered the north marched up and down our street, the *via praetoria* of their great fort, before they disappeared into thin air. Guy Fawkes was born here, Dick Turpin was hung a few streets away and Robinson Crusoe, that other great hero, is also a native son of this city. Who is to say which of these is real and which a fiction?

These streets seethe with history; the building that our Shop occupies is centuries old and its walls tilt and its floors slope like a medieval funhouse. There has been a building on this spot since the Romans were here and needless to say it has its due portion of light-as-air occupants who wreathe themselves around the fixtures and fittings and linger mournfully at our backs. Our ghosts are particularly thick on the staircases, of which there are many. They have much to gossip about. You can hear them if you listen hard, the plash of water from Viking oars, the Harrogate Tally-Ho rattling over the cobblestones, the pat and shuffle of ancient feet at an Assembly Rooms' ball and the *scratch-scratch* of the Reverend Sterne's quill.

As well as being a geographical location, 'Above the Shop' is also a self-contained, seething kingdom with its own primitive rules and two rival contenders for the crown – George and Bunty.

The conception has left Bunty feeling irritable, an emotion with which she's very comfortable, and only after much tossing and turning does she succumb to a restless, dream-laden sleep. Given free choice from the catalogue offered by the empire of dreams on her first night as my mother, Bunty has chosen dustbins.

In the dustbin dream, she's struggling to move two heavy dustbins around the Back Yard. Now and then a vicious tug of wind plasters her hair across her eyes and mouth. She is growing wary of one dustbin in particular; she suspects it's beginning to develop a personality – a personality uncannily like that of George.

Suddenly, as she heaves hard at one of the bins, she loses control of it and it falls with a crash of galvanized metal – CCRASH KERKLUNCK! – spewing its contents over the concrete surface of the yard. Debris, mostly from the Shop, is sprawled everywhere – empty sacks of

Wilson's biscuit mix, flattened packets of Trill, tins of Kit-e-Kat and Chappie that have been neatly stuffed with potato peelings and egg shells, not to mention the mysterious newspaper parcels that look as if they might contain severed babies' limbs. Despite the mess, the dreaming Bunty experiences a flush of pleasure when she sees how tidy her rubbish looks. As she bends down and starts picking it all up she becomes aware of something moving behind her. Oh no! Without even turning round she knows that it's the George dustbin, grown into a lumbering giant and now towering over her, about to suck her into its grimy metallic depths . . .

Somehow, I can't help feeling that this dream doesn't augur well for my future. I want a mother who dreams different dreams. Dreams of clouds like ice-cream, rainbows like sugar-crystal candy, suns like golden chariots being driven across the sky . . . still, never mind, it's the beginning of a new era. It's the 3rd of May and later on today the King will perform the opening ceremony for the Festival of Britain and outside the window, a dawn chorus is heralding my own arrival.

This garden bird fanfare is soon joined by the squawking of the Parrot down in the Pet Shop below and then – DRRRRRRR-RRRRIINGG!!! The bedside alarm goes off and Bunty wakes with a little shriek, slapping down the button on the clock. She lies quite still for a minute, listening to the house. The Dome of Discovery will soon be echoing to the exultant cries of joyful English people looking forward to the future but in our home it's silent apart from the occasional chirrup and twitter of birdsong. Even our ghosts are asleep, curled up in the corners and stretched out along the curtain rails.

The silence is broken by George suddenly snorting in his sleep. The snort arouses a primitive part of his brain and he flings out an arm, pinioning Bunty to the bed, and starts exploring whatever bit of flesh he has chanced to land on (a rather uninspiring part of midriff, but one which houses my very own, my personal, Dome of Discovery). Bunty manages to wriggle out from under George's arm – she's already had to endure sex once in the last twelve hours (me!) – more than once in a day would be unnatural. She heads for the bathroom where the harsh overhead light ricochets off the black-and-white tiles and the chrome fittings and hits Bunty's morning skin in the mirror, making ghastly pools and shadows. One minute she looks like a skull, the next like her own mother. She can't make up her mind which is worse.

She cleans her teeth with some vigour to dispatch the taste of George's tobacco-fumed moustache and then – in order to keep up appearances (an important concept for Bunty, although she's not exactly sure who it is that she's keeping them up for) – she paints on a shapely ruby-red smile and grins at the mirror, her lips retracted, to check for mis-hit lipstick on her teeth. Her mirrored self grins ghoulishly back, but in Bunty's 35mm day-dreams she's transformed into a Vivien Leigh-like figure pirouetting in front of a cheval mirror.

Now she's ready to face her first day as my mother. Downstairs, step by creaking step she goes (in daydreamland a great curving plantation staircase – Bunty, I am discovering, spends a lot of time in the alternative world of her daydreams). She's being very quiet because she doesn't want anyone else to wake up yet – especially Gillian. Gillian's very demanding. She's my sister. She's nearly three years old and she's going to be very surprised when she finds out about me.

Bunty makes herself a cup of tea in the kitchen at the back of the Shop, relishing her few moments of morning solitude. In a minute, she'll take George up a cup of tea in bed – not from altruistic motives but to keep him out of her way that bit longer. My poor mother's very disappointed by marriage, it's failed to change her life in any way, except by making it worse. If I listen in on her airwaves I can hear an endless monologue on the drudgery of domestic life – *Why didn't anyone tell me what it would be like? The cooking! The cleaning! The work!* I wish she would stop this and start daydreaming again but on and on she goes – *And as for babies, well . . . the broken nights, the power struggles . . . the labour pains!* She addresses the front right burner of the cooker directly, her head wobbling from side to side, rather like the Parrot in the Shop beyond. *At least that's all over with . . .* (Surprise!)

The kettle whistles and she pours the boiling water into a little brown teapot and leans idly against the cooker while she waits for it to brew, a small frown puckering her face as she tries to remember why on earth she married George in the first place.

George and Bunty met in 1944. He wasn't her

first choice, that was Buck, an American sergeant (my grandmother had a similar struggle to get married during a war) but Buck had his foot blown off fooling around with a land mine ('Anything for a lark, these Yanks,' Bunty's brother Clifford remarked with distaste) and got shipped back home to Kansas. Bunty spent some considerable time waiting for Buck to write and invite her to share his life in Kansas but she never heard from him again. So George got the woman. In the end, Bunty decided that George with two feet might be a better bet than Buck with one, but now she's not so sure. (Buck and Bunty! What a wonderful-sounding couple they would have made – I can almost see them.)

If Buck had taken Bunty to Kansas think how different all our lives would have been! Especially mine. In 1945 George's father died by falling under a tram on a daytrip to Leeds and George took over the family business – Pets. He married Bunty, thinking that she'd be a big help in the shop (because she'd once worked in one), unaware that Bunty had no intention of working after her marriage. This conflict will run and run.

The tea's brewed. Bunty stirs the spoon round the insides of the little brown teapot and pours herself a cup. My first ever cup of tea. She sits down at the kitchen table and starts daydreaming again, moving beyond her disappointment over Kansas and her ham-tea wedding to George to a place where a flimsy veil moves in a summery breeze and behind the veil is Bunty dressed in gauzy white organza with an eighteen-inch waist and a different nose. The man at her side is unbelievably handsome, remarkably like Gary Cooper, while Bunty herself bears a passing resemblance to Celia Johnson. A huge cloud of orange-blossom threatens to engulf them as they clasp and kiss passionately – then suddenly, an unwelcome note of reality interrupts our reverie, somebody's pulling at Bunty's dressing-gown and whining in a not very pleasant fashion.

Here she is! Here's my sister! Climbing up on Bunty, all arms and soft legs and sweet bedtime smells, crawling her way up the Eiger of Bunty's body and pressing her sleepy face into Bunty's chilly neck. Bunty unclenches the little fists that have fastened on to her hair, and deposits Gillian back on the floor.

'Get down,' Bunty says grimly. 'Mummy's thinking.' (Although what Mummy's actually doing is wondering what it would be like if her entire family was wiped out and she could start again.) Poor Gillian!

Gillian refuses to be ignored for long – she's not that kind of child – and hardly have we had our first sip of tea before we have to attend to Gillian's needs. For breakfast, Bunty cooks porridge, makes toast and boils eggs. George can't stand porridge and likes bacon and sausage and fried bread but Bunty's stomach is a little queasy this morning (I'm privy to all kinds of inside information). 'So if he wants it he can get it himself,' she mutters, doling out a bowlful of (rather lumpy) porridge for Gillian. Then she fills a second bowl for herself – she thinks she might manage a bit of porridge – and then a third bowl. Who can that be for? Goldilocks? Not for me surely? No, indeed not – for here's a surprise – I have another sister! This is good news, even though she looks a little on the melancholic side. She's already washed and dressed in her school uniform and even her hair – cut in a straight, rather unbecoming bob – is brushed. She is just five years old and her name is Patricia. Her plain little face has a somewhat dismal air as she regards the porridge in her bowl. This is because she hates porridge. Gillian is gobbling hers down like the greedy duck in her Ladybird book *The Greedy Duck*. 'I don't like porridge,' Patricia ventures to Bunty. This is the first time she's tried this direct approach over the porridge, usually she just turns it over and over with a spoon until it's too late to eat it.

'Pardon me?' Bunty says, the words dropping like icicles on the linoleum of the kitchen floor (our mother's not really a morning person).

'I don't like porridge,' Patricia says, looking more doubtful now.

As fast as a snake, Bunty hisses back, 'Well *I* don't like children, so that's too bad for you, isn't it?' She's joking, of course. Isn't she?

And why do I have this strange feeling, as if my shadow's stitched to my back, almost as if there's someone else in here with me? Am I being haunted by my own embryonic ghost?

'Mind the shop, Bunt!' (Bunt? This is even worse.)

And then he's gone. Just like that! Bunty fumes to herself – *He might at least ask. 'Would you mind, Bunty, minding the shop for me.' And of course I would mind, very much. But I'd still have to do it, wouldn't I? 'Mind' – why was it called 'minding'? What kind of a mind did you need for standing behind a shop counter?*

Bunty doesn't like the promiscuity of behind-the-counter contact. She feels that she's not really selling dog food and kittens and the occasional budgerigar, but that she's selling herself. At least, she thinks, when she worked for Mr Simon ('Modelia – Ladies' Quality Fashions') it was sensible things they were selling, dresses and corsets and hats. What was sensible about a budgerigar? And, what's more, having to be polite to everyone all the time wasn't *normal*. (George, on the other hand, is born to it, chatting away, making the same remark about the weather twenty times in one morning, scraping and grovelling and smiling and then ripping off his mask as soon as he comes backstage. The children of shopkeepers – me and Chekhov, for example – are scarred by having witnessed their parents humiliate themselves in this distressing way.)

Bunty decides that she's going to have to say something to George, point out that she's a wife and mother, not a shop assistant. And another thing, where does he go all the time? He's always 'slipping out', off on mysterious errands. There are going to be some changes if Bunty has her way. She sits behind the counter clicking her number nine needles as if she's a tricoteuse at George's guillotine when she should be knitting my future – tiny little things, lacy shawls and matinée jackets with pink ribbons threaded through them. Magic red bootees to see me on my journey.

The Shop Cat – a fat, brindled tabby that spends its days squatting malevolently on the counter – jumps up on her lap and she swiftly knocks it to the floor. Sometimes Bunty feels as if the whole world is trying to climb on her body.

'Shop!' George returns. The budgerigars rise up and flutter in their cages.

Shop! Why 'Shop!'? George and Bunty always say this when they come in at the Shop door – but it's supposed to be what the customer says, not the shopkeeper. Are they addressing the shop in the vocative case ('0 Shop!') or naming it in the nominative? Reassuring it of its existence? Reassuring themselves of its existence? Pretending to be a customer? But why pretend to be the thing you hate? 'Shop!' I fear, like the thing it signifies, will remain an eternal, existential mystery.

But now we are freed from our enslavement to the counter (Bunty has just sold the Shop Cat, but she doesn't mention this to George. Poor cat.) and we can go and discover the world beyond the Shop. First we have to go through the ritual of dressing Gillian so that she'll be able to survive in the alien atmosphere outside the Shop. Bunty doesn't trust the month of May so Gillian has her liberty bodice securely strapped to her still cherub-new skin. Then a petticoat, a thick red woollen jersey knitted by Bunty's never-idle fingers, followed by a Royal Stewart kilt and long white cotton socks which cut her fat little legs in half. Finally she puts on her pale powder-puff-blue coat with the white velvet collar and a little white woollen bonnet tied with ribbons that slice into her double chin. I, on the other hand, am free-floating, naked and unadorned. No mittens and bonnets for me yet, just the warm, obliging innards of Bunty's unconscious body, which is still unaware of the precious package it's carrying.

No-porridge Patricia has already been hurried up the road to school by George a couple of hours ago and is at this moment standing in the playground drinking her little bottle of milk and going through the four-times table in her head (she's very keen) and wondering why no-one ever asks her to join in their skipping games. Only five and already an outcast! Three-fifths of the family are now walking along Blake Street towards Museum Gardens, or rather Bunty walks, I float and Gillian rides her brand new Tri-ang tricycle which she has insisted on riding. Bunty feels there's something indulgent about parks, something wasteful – holes in existence filled with nothing but air and light and birds. Surely these are spaces that should be occupied by something useful, like housework?

Housework must be done. On the other hand, children are supposed to play in parks – Bunty has read the childcare section in her *Everything Within* book ('Bringing up Baby') that says so – therefore, some reluctant time has to be given over to fresh air so she pays a precious sixpence at the gate of the Museum Gardens and guarantees that our fresh air will be exclusive.

My first day! All the trees in Museum Gardens are in new leaf and high above Bunty's head the sky is solid blue; if she reached out her hand (which she won't) she could touch it. Fluffy white clouds like lambs pile into each other. We are in quattrocento heaven. Swooping, tweeting birds dance excitedly above our heads, their tiny flight muscles at full throttle – miniature angels of the Annunciation, avian Gabriels, come to shout my arrival! Alleluia!

Not that Bunty notices. She's watching Gillian, who's riding round every twist and turn in the path, following some magic tantra all of her own. I'm worried that Gillian might get trapped amongst the flower beds. Beyond the park railing a broad calm river can be glimpsed and ahead of us lie the pale fretworked ruins of St Mary's Abbey. A peacock screeches and launches itself off its perch on the Bar Walls and down onto the grass at our feet. Brave new world that has such creatures in it!

Two men, who we will call Bert and Alf, are employed cutting grass in the park. At the sight of Gillian they pause in their work and, resting on their huge mower for a minute, regard her progress with unalloyed pleasure. Bert and Alf fought in the same regiment in the war, danced to the music of Al Bowlly at the same dances, chased women (women very like Bunty) together and now they're cutting grass together. They feel there might be a certain injustice in the way their lives have turned out, but somehow the sight of Gillian reconciles them to such things. (Bonny and blithe and good and gay, for Gillian was indeed born on the Sabbath day and still had some of these qualities in 1951. Unfortunately she soon lost them.) Clean and new as a pin or an unwrapped bar of soap she represents everything they fought the war for – our Gillian, the promise of the future. (Not much of a future as it turned out, as she gets run over by a pale blue Hillman Husky in 1959 but how are any of us to know this? As a family we are genetically predisposed towards having accidents – being run over and blown up are the two most common.)

Bunty (our mother, the flower of English womanhood) is irritated by the attention of Bert and Alf. (Does she actually possess any other emotion?) *Why don't they just cut the bloody grass,* she thinks, disguising her thoughts with a bright, artificial smile.

Time to go! Bunty has had enough of all this idleness and we need to go shopping in other people's shops. She prepares for a scene with Gillian, for scene with Gillian there will surely be. She manages to extricate her from the flower beds and get her on the straight path of life, but Gillian, who doesn't know she's wasting valuable time, continues pedalling slowly, stopping to admire flowers, pick up stones, ask questions. Bunty maintains a Madonna-like expression of serenity and silence for as long as she can before her impatience suddenly boils over and she yanks the handlebars of the tricycle to hurry it along. This has the disastrous effect of tipping Gillian onto the ground, where she lands in a neat little blue-and-white heap, sucking her breath in and screaming at the same time. I am dismayed – will I have to learn how to do this?

Bunty hauls Gillian to her feet, pretending not to

notice that her tender palms and knees are grazed. (Bunty's attitude to pain, or indeed, emotion of any kind, is to behave as if it sprang from a personality disorder.) Bunty, only too well aware that we are being observed by Bert and Alf, puts on her don't-be-a-fusspot smile and whispers in Gillian's ear that she'll get some sweets if she stops crying. Gillian immediately rams her fist into her mouth. Will she be a good sister? Is this a good mother?

Bunty walks from the park with her head held high, dragging Gillian with one hand and the tricycle with the other. Bert and Alf return silently to their mowing. A slight breeze ruffles the new leaves on the trees and discovers a discarded morning newspaper on a bench. A front-page photograph of the Skylon tower flutters in a beckoning way – like a city of the future, a science-fiction Oz. It's of no great interest to me – I'm squirming around uneasily in a wash of vicious chemicals just released by Bunty as a result of the tricycle tantrum.

'Well, now, darlin', what can I get you?' The butcher's voice bellows around the shop. 'Nice bit of red meat, eh?' He winks salaciously at my mother, who pretends to be deaf, but everyone else in the shop titters with laughter. Walter's customers like him, he behaves as a butcher in an Ealing comedy might behave, a bluff parody of himself in his stained blue and white apron and straw boater. He's a Cockney and this alone represents something dangerous and unknown for those of us in the spiritual heartland of Yorkshire. In Bunty's private animal lexicon (all men are beasts) he is a pig, with his smooth, shiny skin, stretched tightly over his buttery, plump flesh. Bunty, at the head of the queue, asks for a bit of steak and kidney in her most neutral tone of voice, but nonetheless the butcher guffaws as if she's said something highly *risqué*.

'Somefin' to get the ol' man goin', eh?' he roars. Bunty dips down to fiddle with Gillian's shoelace so that no-one can see the embarrassment flaring in her cheeks.

'For you, gorgeous, anyfin',' Walter leers at her and then suddenly, unnervingly, he draws a huge knife from somewhere and begins to sharpen it without his eyes ever leaving Bunty. She remains bobbed down next to Gillian for as long as possible, having a pretend conversation with her, smiling and nodding, as if what Gillian had to say was of extraordinary interest. (Whereas, of course, she never took any notice of anything any of us said – unless it was rude.)

The butcher begins to whistle the Toreador song from *Carmen* very loudly and makes a dramatic performance out of weighing a heavy, slippery kidney in his hand. 'You should be on the stage, Walter,' a voice from the back of the shop declares and the rest of Walter's customers murmur in agreement. Bunty, now vertical again, has a disturbing thought – the kidney, now being tossed from one hand to the other by Walter, bears an odd resemblance to a pair of testicles. (Not that 'testicles' is a word she's very familiar with, of course, she belongs to a generation of women which was not very *au fait* with the correct anatomical vocabulary.)

Walter slaps the kidney down on the slab and slices it, wielding his knife with astonishing dexterity. His admiring audience give a collective sigh.

If she had her way, Bunty would go to a different butcher, but Walter's shop is near ours and not only is he therefore a fellow shopkeeper, he is also a friend of George, although little more than an acquaintance of Bunty. She likes the word 'acquaintance', it sounds posh and doesn't have all the time-consuming consequences of friendship. Acquaintance or not, Walter is hard to keep at arm's length, as Bunty has learnt to her cost on the couple of occasions he has cornered her behind the sausage-machine in the back of his shop. George and Walter do each other 'favours' – Walter is doing one now, in full view of the shop, performing a sleight-of-hand with the steak that will give Bunty far more than she's due on her ration coupon. Walter also has a reputation as a ladies' man so Bunty isn't at all happy about George keeping company with him. George *says* that kind of thing's disgusting, but Bunty suspects that he doesn't think it's disgusting at all. She prefers George's other shopkeeping friend, Bernard Belling, who has a plumbing supplies business and, unlike Walter, doesn't conduct innuendo-laced conversations in public.

Bunty takes the soft paper package of meat, avoiding Walter's gaze and smiling stiffly instead at the inside cavity of a dead sheep behind Walter's left shoulder. She walks out, saying nothing, but inside a silent Scarlett rages, tossing her head indignantly and swirling her skirts as she flounces out of the butcher's shop, damning him to hell.

After Walter we go to Richardson's the bakers, and buy a large floury-white loaf but no cakes because Bunty believes shop-bought cakes are a sign of sluttish housewifery. Then we go to Hannon's for apples, spring cabbage and potatoes, on to Borders' for coffee, cheese and butter which the man behind the counter takes from a tub and pats into shape. By this time I think we are all a little weary and Bunty has to nag Gillian into pedalling up Gillygate and along Clarence Street towards our final port of call. Gillian has gone a funny lobster colour and looks as if she wishes she had never asked to bring the tricycle. She has to pedal furiously to keep up with Bunty, who's getting very annoyed (I can tell).

At last we reach Lowther Street and the squashed terraced house where Nell lives. Nell is my grandmother, Bunty's mother, Alice's daughter. Her entire life is defined by her relationship to other people –

Mother to: Clifford, Babs, Bunty, Betty, Ted.

Daughter to: Alice.

Step-daughter to: Rachel.

Sister to: Ada (dead), Lawrence (presumed dead), Tom, Albert (dead), Lillian (as good as dead).

Wife to: Frank (dead).

Grandmother to: Adrian, Daisy, Rose, Patricia, Gillian, Ewan, Hope, Tim and now . . . ME! Bunty's stomach rumbles like thunder in my ear – it's nearly lunch time, but she can't face the idea of eating anything. My new grandmother gives Gillian a glass of bright orange Kia-ora and to us she gives arrowroot biscuits and Camp coffee which she boils up with sterilized milk in a pan. Bunty feels like throwing up. The smell of sawdust and rotting flesh seems to have been carried on her skin from the butcher's shop.

'All right, Mother?' Bunty asks without waiting for an answer. Nell is small and sort of two-dimensional. For kith and kin, she's not very impressive.

Bunty notices a fly crawling towards the arrowroot biscuits. Very stealthily, Bunty picks up the fly swatter that my grandmother always has handy and skilfully bats the fly out of existence. A second ago that fly was alive and well, now it's dead. Yesterday I didn't exist, now I do. Isn't life amazing?

Bunty's presence is getting on Nell's nerves and she shifts restlessly in the depths of her armchair wondering when we're going to go so she can listen to the wireless in peace. Bunty is experiencing a wave of nausea due to my unexpected arrival and Gillian has drunk up her Kia-ora and is taking her revenge on the world. She's playing with her grandmother's button box and chooses a button, a pink-glass, flower-shaped one (see *Footnote (i)*) and, carefully and deliberately, swallows it. It's the nearest thing she can get to the sweets our forgetful mother promised in the Museum Gardens.

* * *

'Bloody Parrot!' George holds his bitten finger up for inspection. Bunty tut-tuts indifferently. (Injury, as I said, is not really her forte.) She's up to her elbows in suet and flour and her stomach is heaving again. She watches George in disgust as he picks up one of the fairy cakes we've spent half the afternoon making, and swallows it in one bite, without even looking at it.

The afternoon has been a bit of a disappointment. We went shopping again but only for some dun-coloured wool from a shop kept by a timid old woman who made me appreciative of Walter's shopkeeping-as-performance technique. I hoped we might visit a florist and celebrate my arrival with flowers, a garland or two, a bouquet of joy and roses, but no. I keep forgetting that no-one knows about me.

We went and picked up Patricia from school, but that wasn't very interesting either and her day seemed rather boring, viz:

'What did you do today?'

'Nothing.' (Said with a shrug of the shoulders.)

'What did you have for dinner?'

'Can't remember.' (Shrugs again.)

'Did you play with any friends today?'

'No.'

'Don't shrug like that all the time, Patricia!'

Bunty chops up the blood-glazed kidney, the idea of testicles never far from her mind. She hates cooking, it's too much like being nice to people. Here she goes again – *I spend my entire life cooking, I'm a slave to housework* –

***chained** to the cooker . . . all those meals, day after day, and what happens to them? They get eaten, that's what, without a word of thanks!* Sometimes when Bunty's standing at the cooker her heart starts knocking inside her chest and she feels as if the top of her head's going to come off and a cyclone is going to rip out of her brain and tear up everything around her. (Just as well she didn't go to Kansas.) She doesn't understand why she feels like this (Go ask Alice – see *Footnote (i)* again) but it's beginning to happen now, which is why when George wanders back into the kitchen, takes another fairy cake, and announces that he has to go out and 'see a man about a dog' (even tapping his nose as he does so – more and more I'm beginning to feel that we're all trapped in some dire black-and-white film here), Bunty turns a contorted, murderous face on him and lifts the knife as if she's considering stabbing him. Is a torch being put to the great city of Atlanta?

'I have some business to do,' George says hurriedly, and Bunty thinks the better of things and stabs the steak instead.

'For heaven's sake, what's wrong with you, what do you think I'm doing – meeting another woman for a riotous night on the tiles?' (A clever question, of course, as this is exactly what my father-of-a-day is going to do.) Will Civil War rage in the kitchen? Will Atlanta burn? I wait with bated breath.

No, it's saved for another day. Phew, as Bunty's brother Ted would say if he was here; but he isn't, he's in the Merchant Navy and is being tossed on the

South China Seas at this moment. Bunty loses interest in the skirmish and returns her attention to her steak and kidney pudding.

Well, my first day is nearly over, thank goodness. It's been a very tiring day for some of us, me and Bunty in particular. George isn't home yet but Bunty, Gillian and Patricia are fast asleep. Bunty is in dreamland again, dreaming of Walter, who's fumbling with her buttons with hands of pork and kneading her flesh with fingers that look like sausages. Gillian is snoring in her sleep, in the middle of a Sisyphean nightmare where she must pedal endlessly uphill on her tricycle. Patricia is deep in sleep, her pale face drawn and her panda clutched to her chest. The spectral wraiths wander at will making puny efforts to create domestic disorder – souring the milk and sprinkling dust on the shelves.

I'm wide awake too, turning somersaults and floating in the ocean of Bunty. I tap my tiny naked heels together three times and think, there's no place like home.

Next morning George is in an uncharacteristically good mood (his night on the tiles – with Walter – was satisfying) and he prods my sleeping mother awake.

'How'd you like breakfast in bed, Bunt?' Bunty grunts. 'How about a bit of sausage? Black pudding?' Bunty moans, which George takes to mean 'yes' and he saunters off down to the kitchen while Bunty has to run to the bathroom. For a second she thinks she sees Scarlett smiling in the bathroom mirror in full Technicolor, but the image disappears as she vomits. Leaning her hot, prickling forehead against the cold tiles, a terrible idea forms in Bunty's head – she's pregnant! (Poor Bunty – throwing up every single morning at every pregnancy. No wonder she was always telling us that she was sick of us.) She sits abruptly down on the toilet and mouths a silent Munch-like scream – it can't be (Yes, yes, yes, Bunty's going to have a baby! Me!). She throws the nearest thing (a red shoe) at the mirror and it breaks into a million splintery pieces.

I'm hanging like a pink-glass button by a thread. Help. Where are my sisters? (Asleep.) My father? (Cooking breakfast.) Where's my mother?

Still, never mind – the sun is high in the sky and it's going to be a beautiful day again. The crowds will be flocking into the Exhibition Halls and the Dome of Discovery, craning their necks at Skylon and the shimmering emerald city of tomorrow. The future is like a cupboard full of light and all you have to do is find the key that opens the door. Bluebirds fly overhead, singing. What a wonderful world!

Footnote (i) – Country Idyll

THE PHOTOGRAPH IS IN A SILVER FRAME, PADDED WITH red velvet with an oval of glass in the middle from behind which my great-grandmother regards the world with an ambiguous expression.

She stands very straight, one wedding-ringed hand resting on the back of a *chaise-longue*. In the background is a typical studio backdrop of the time, in which a hazy Mediterranean landscape of hills drops away from the *trompe-l'œil* balustraded staircase which occupies the foreground. My great-grandmother's hair is parted in the middle and worn in a crown of plaits around her head. Her high-necked, satin dress has a bodice that looks as trimmed and stuffed as a cushion. She wears a small locket at her throat and her lips are half-open in a way that suggests she's waiting for something to happen. Her head is tilted slightly backwards but she is staring straight at the camera (or the photographer). In the photograph her eyes look dark and the expression in them is unfathomable. She seems to be on the point of saying something, although what it could be I can't possibly imagine.

I had never seen this photograph before. Bunty produced it one day as if by magic. Her Uncle Tom had just died in the nursing-home and she had been to collect his few belongings, all of which fitted into a cardboard box. From the box, she took the photograph and when I asked who it was she told me it was her grandmother, my great-grandmother.

'She changed a lot, didn't she?' I said, tracing the outline of my great-grandmother's face on the glass. 'She's ugly and fat in that photograph you've got – the one taken in the back yard at Lowther Street with all the family.'

This was a photograph Bunty had with '1914, Lowther Street' written on the back in watery-blue ink and it shows my great-grandmother with her whole family gathered around her. She sits, big and square, in the middle of a wooden bench and on one side of her sits Nell (Bunty's mother), and on the other is Lillian (Nell's sister). Standing behind them is Tom and squatting on the ground at Rachel's feet is the youngest brother, Albert. The sun is shining and there are flowers growing on the wall behind them.

'Oh, no,' Bunty said dismissively. 'The woman in the Lowther Street photograph is Rachel – their stepmother, not their *real* mother. She was a cousin, or something.'

The woman in her padded frame – the real mother, the true bride – gazes out inscrutably across time. 'What was she called?'

Bunty had to think for a second. 'Alice,' she pronounced finally. 'Alice Barker.'

My newly discovered great-grandmother, it appears, died giving birth to Nell, shortly after which my feckless great-grandfather married Rachel (the unreal mother, the false bride). Bunty had a vague, handed-down memory that Rachel came to look after the children and act as a poorly-paid housekeeper. 'Six children without a mother,' she explained in her death-of-Bambi's-mother voice. 'He had to marry someone.'

'Why didn't you ever tell me this before?'

'I forgot,' Bunty said defiantly.

The forgotten Alice stared straight ahead. Carefully, I removed the photograph from its frame and more of her artificial sepia world was revealed – a large parlour-palm in a brass pot and a thick curtain draped across a corner of the set. On the back of the photograph, in printed copperplate, it says *J.P. Armand. Travelling Photographer*. And in faded pencil underneath, the date – *20th June, 1888*.

'Twentieth of June, 1888,' I told Bunty, who snatched the photograph back again and scrutinized it carefully.

'You would never have noticed, would you? The way she's standing behind that couch hides it.'

'What? Noticed what? Hides what?'

'My mother was born in 1888. On July the thirtieth. Alice is eight months pregnant in this photograph. With my mother, Nell.'

Does that account for that impenetrable gaze? Can she feel her own death coming, sniffing around her sepia skirts, stroking her sepia hair? Bunty was still inspecting the photograph. 'She looks just like you,' she said, her tone accusing, as if the lost Alice and I were fellow members of a conspiracy, intent on stirring up trouble.

I want to rescue this lost woman from what's going to happen to her (time). Dive into the picture, pluck her out –

Picture the scene –
A hundred years ago. The door of a country cottage stands open on a very hot day in summer. In the yard outside, two small boys are kicking and wrestling in the dust while a pretty girl of about nine years old, older than the boys, sits on a stool by the back door, apparently oblivious to the noise her brothers are making. This is Ada. Her long, pale gold hair falls in a mass of curls and is held back from her face by a ribbon which is limp with the heat. Around her feet a few chickens scratch aimlessly. She is crooning to a doll lying cradled in her arms and her face has assumed an expression of maternal piety rarely seen outside the Nativity. A farm dog sleeps in the shadow of a barn across the yard, and a black cat sits on a wooden plough lapping up the blistering heat and occasionally washing itself in a random, lazy way. Beyond the fence are fields, some with cows, some with sheep. Some empty. On the south side of the cottage a garden has been dug out of the unpromising chalky soil and rows of undersized cabbages and carrots can be seen, wilting in

the dry earth. By the door of the cottage, marigolds and cornflowers droop in the bleaching glare of the sun.

The whole effect is as if someone had taken an idyllic rural scene and set it slightly off-key – the sun is too hot, the light too bright, the fields too arid, the animals too thin. The cottage, although charmingly pastoral from the outside, has a suspicious gingerbread and walking-stick candy air about it. Who knows what's inside?

Suddenly, without modifying her Madonna-like expression in any way, the girl picks up a stone and throws it at her brothers, hitting the younger, Tom, on the head. They jump apart in a state of genuine shock and run yelling into the field, united in mutual disgust at their sister's behaviour. Ada remains impassive, returning her gaze to the doll-baby. The sun stands at midday, white-hot with anger. In the kitchen of the cottage a woman is making bread, slamming down the dough onto a wooden table, picking it up, slamming it down again, picking it up, slamming it down. A child of, as yet, indeterminate sex is sitting underneath the table, hitting wooden blocks with a wooden hammer. (So it's probably a boy.) It has the same angelic curls as its eldest sister.

The woman, flushed with the heat from the kitchen range, pauses every now and then to straighten her back and run her hand across her forehead. She kneads the small of her back with her fists. She has a toothache. Her belly, swollen with the next child, keeps getting in the way of the breadmaking.

This woman is Alice. This woman is my

great-grandmother. This woman is lost in time. This woman has beautiful fair hair that is scraped and pinned into a sweaty bun. This woman has had enough. This woman is about to slip out of her life. One of those curious genetic whispers across time dictates that in moments of stress we will all (Nell, Bunty, my sisters, me) brush our hands across our foreheads in exactly the same way that Alice has just done. A smudge of flour powders her nose.

Alice is thirty-one years old and pregnant with her seventh child (she has already lost one – William, Ada's twin, dead of some unknown fever at three months). Alice came from York originally. Her mother, Sophia, had married a man much older than herself and her father was delighted at the good match she had made, especially as her elder sister, Hannah, had caused a shameful scandal by running away with a man who had been court-martialled out of the navy. At the time his daughters' fortunes couldn't have seemed more different – one living amongst wealth and privilege, the other in dishonour and poverty. Sophia's husband's money had come from buying and selling railway land, vast profits made quickly and, as it turned out (before he hung himself), fraudulently. So while Alice had been born in a gracious house on Micklegate, with a sunlit nursery and more servants than were necessary, by the time she was fourteen the family's fortunes had tumbled and the family's name was disgraced. Alice had been the only child, doted on by her mother, but Sophia never recovered from the scandal of her husband's death, her mind wandered and she ended up taking so much laudanum that she accidentally killed herself.

Poor Alice, brought up to play the piano and look pretty, was an orphan and – worse – a schoolteacher by the time she was eighteen, with nothing to her name except her mother's clock and a silver locket that her grandfather had given her when she was born.

She was twenty-one when she met her husband. She had been in the village of Rosedale almost a year, having taken the position of head teacher at the local school. It was a small rural school with one other teacher and a big wood-burning stove. The children were culled from the local farms, most of their parents were farm hands and attendance was poor as the children were often needed to work on the land. Alice hated teaching and missed the urban charms of York, so different from the green dales. She had begun to slide into a state of melancholic gloom when destiny trotted up behind her one Saturday afternoon in May.

My great-grandmother had gone out walking along the country lanes. It had started off as a beautiful day, the wild lilac and the hawthorn that lined the lanes had just blossomed, and everything smelt fresh and new – which only succeeded in plunging her further into melancholy. Then, as if to match her mood, a thunderstorm boiled up from nowhere and my great-grandmother, equipped only with her stout boots and no umbrella, was woefully unprotected from the rain. She was half drenched when Frederick Barker bowled up in his dog-cart and offered her a lift back to the school-house.

He owned a small farm locally, a flat, fertile strip of land at one end of the Rosedale valley with a pretty honey-coloured farmhouse, a herd of Devon Reds and an orchard where his father William had espaliered peach trees along one wall, although the fruit they produced was hard and sour. My foolish great-grandmother was charmed, although by what we can never be sure – his easy banter perhaps, or his solid-looking farm or his peach trees. He was twelve years older than she was and courted her assiduously for a whole year with everything from curd cheese and peach jam to logs for the school-room stove. There came a point sometime during the spring of the following year when she couldn't avoid the choice any longer – to go on teaching (which she loathed) or accept Frederick's offer of marriage. She chose the latter and within a year she had given birth to the twins – Ada and William.

During his courting of Alice, Frederick struggled to show only his better side, but once he'd secured her in marriage he was relieved to be able to reveal the less savoury aspects of his character. By the time William was being carried in his tiny coffin-cradle to the cemetery Alice knew what everyone else in Rosedale had known for years (but never saw fit to tell her) – that her husband was a sullen drunkard with an insatiable appetite for gambling on anything, not just horses, but dog fights and cock fights, how many rabbits he could shoot in an hour, how many crows would take off from a field, where a fly would land in a room. Anything.

Eventually, inevitably, he lost the farm, land that had been in his family for two hundred years, and moved Alice and the children – Ada, Lawrence and brand-new baby Tom – across to Swaledale where he got a job as a gamekeeper. There have been two more children since then and another one on the way. Not a day passes when Alice doesn't imagine what life would be like if she hadn't married Frederick Barker.

Alice cuts up the dough, shapes it, puts it in the tins, covers the tins with damp cloths and places them to prove on the range. It won't take long in this weather. Underneath her white apron she's wearing a thick, dark-grey serge skirt and a washed-out pink blouse with pink glass buttons shaped like flowers. Daisies. She can feel the sweat trickling down her skin beneath the blouse. Alice has dark-blue shadows under her eyes and a buzzing noise in her head.

She takes off her apron, rubs her back again and moves dreamily towards the open doorway. Leaning against the doorpost she reaches out a hand towards her daughter, Ada, and gently strokes her hair. Ada shakes her head as if a fly had landed on it – she hates being touched – and resumes her tuneless lullaby to the doll-baby while the true baby, Nell, begins to thump Alice from the inside. Alice rests her unfocused eyes on the marigolds by the back door. And then – and this is the really interesting bit of my great-grandmother's story – something strange begins to happen to Alice. She's about to enter her own private wonderland for she suddenly feels herself being pulled towards the marigolds on a straight, fast trajectory; it is automatic and entirely beyond her control and she has no time to think as she is sucked on her giddy journey towards the heart of a flower that looks like the sun. As she accelerates closer and closer to it, every detail of the flower becomes clear – the layers of elongated oval petals, the maroon pincushion of the central stamens, the rough, hairy green of the stems – all speed towards her and then engulf her so that she can actually feel the surprisingly velvet texture of the petals on her skin and smell the acidic perfume of the sap.

But then just as the whole world begins to fizz and hum alarmingly, the floral nightmare ends. Alice experiences a cool rush of air on her face and when, with an effort, she opens her eyes, she finds herself floating in a forget-me-not blue sky, some thirty feet above the cottage.

The oddest thing is the silence – she can see Lawrence and Tom shouting at each other from opposite corners of the field, but no noise rises towards her. She can see Ada singing to her doll, but no tune falls from Ada's lips and, most peculiar of all, she can see herself – still by the cottage door – speaking to Ada, but although her mouth is clearly forming words, no sound issues from it. The birds – swallows and swifts, a skylark, two wood-pigeons, a sparrow-hawk – are equally voiceless. The cows below are dumb, as are the sheep sprinkled on the fields. The air is visibly alive with insects of every kind yet their wings remain silent.

What the world has lost in sound, it has gained in texture and Alice floats through a shimmering, vibrating landscape where the colours that were previously washed out by the sun have been restored with a vivid, almost unnatural depth. The fields below are a plush quilt of emeralds and golds and the hedgerows between them are shooting with dog roses, yarrow, nettles, honeysuckle – the perfume mingling and rising until the heady scent reaches Alice and sends her reeling off in the direction of a river that flows like silver between a dark-green border of trees.

Alice is enjoying herself, floating like thistledown on the wind, wafted from one place to another – one minute wreathed in the smoke from her own cottage, the next hovering over the home farm and marvelling at the chestnut-bronze plumage of the rooster. Everywhere she looks, the world is opening out and unfolding. Alice experiences a huge fullness of the heart. Looking at the corporeal Alice she has abandoned down below, a thought shapes in her mind –

'Why,' thinks my floating great-grandmother, 'I have been living the wrong life!'

With these magic words she accelerates again, away from the ground, upwards into the thin brilliant air towards where it is darkening into indigo.

Then, suddenly, sound returns to the world. A noise imposes itself on Alice's consciousness. It's the steady *creak-creak* of an old cart's suspension and the sound of horses' hooves moving slowly on a dry track.

After a few seconds the source of this noise becomes visible and a horse and cart, loaded with mysteriously-shaped objects, moves slowly across the edge of Alice's visionary landscape. The cart makes an odd, intrusive silhouette on the brow of the hill and Alice follows the movement of this creeping two-dimensional caravan with irritation. It continues to plot its resolute course on the hill track, a course which will inevitably bring it to the cottage.

Sure enough, it curves away from the brow of the hill and progresses along their own track. Already the countryside is beginning to lose its colour. Alice's children have also seen the horse and cart and stand quietly watching as it by-passes the home farm and moves inexorably towards the cottage. The man driving the cart tips his hat at the boys as he passes them in the field but they return his greeting with scowls. The cart passes through the open five-bar gate and turns into the yard. Ada stands up, half in fear, half in excitement and the doll-baby drops unheeded to the ground.

Alice knows a threat when she sees one. She can feel herself being pulled back, and tries to resist, screwing up her eyes and concentrating on returning to the silence when – the child under the kitchen table (whom we'd forgotten about) chooses this moment to hit his finger with the wooden hammer (yes, it is indeed a boy) and lets out a bloodcurdling yell that would bring the dead inquisitively out of their graves let alone a mother back from an out-of-body experience.

His brothers rush whooping into the house to see if

there is any blood, the dog in the yard wakes up and starts barking in a demented way and the child in a cradle in the corner of the kitchen that we hadn't even noticed, wakes up with a start and adds its screams to the chaos.

Poor, hypomanic Alice finds herself being sucked back into her life, through the bluebird-blue sky and the molten-gold marigolds, until she's thrown back against the kitchen doorpost. Slam! The invisible baby Nell kicks in sympathy with the howling child under the table who, when Alice picks him up to try and comfort him, tangles his fingers in her hair and pulls three pink glass buttons from her blouse.

Finally, as the culmination of this cacophony, the horse and cart arrive in the yard of the cottage rendering the dog hysterical. A lanky, foreign-looking man with a hooked nose and a whiff of Edgar Allan Poe about him – the old-fashioned frock-coat, the melancholy hands – dismounts and approaches the open door. With a theatrical sweep he removes his hat and makes a low bow. 'Madame,' he announces, straightening himself, 'Jean-Paul Armand at your service.'

He was a magician, of course, the mysterious shapes in his cart were his strange props – the collapsible Mediterranean back-cloth, the ornate brass plant-pot holding a palm with stiffened-cotton leaves, the velvet drapes, the extraordinary camera – only the *chaise-longue* wasn't provided by him, but was dragged by Ada and Lawrence out into the back yard. 'The light's better there,' he explained.

'Nothing to pay until I return with the photographs' was how he ensnared Alice who, in an uncharacteristic burst of optimism, believed she would indeed somehow acquire the money in the intervening period. So the children were scrubbed and brushed and generally transformed. Albert's tears (the child under the table) were assuaged by a barley-sugar twist from Mr Armand – he always had a pocketful with him to persuade his small, recalcitrant sitters. He took photographs of Alice's children in different permutations – Ada with Albert on her knee; Albert, Tom, and Lawrence together; Ada holding the real baby Lillian (the neglected child in the crib) instead of her doll, and so on. Lillian hasn't celebrated her first birthday yet and just succeeds in slipping it in before her mother disappears from her life for ever.

Alice has crammed her overblown figure into her best dress for Mr Armand and brushed and pinned up her hair in plaits. The weather is far too hot for the dress and she has to stand for a long time in the heat while he messes around under the black canopy which makes Alice think of the carapace of a beetle. Perhaps her enigmatic expression is merely the result of the heat, the waiting, the kicking. Mr Armand thinks she is beautiful, an unexpected rural Madonna. When he returns with her photographs, he thinks, he will ask her to run away with him (he is eccentric).

Flash! An explosion of chemicals and my great-grandmother is consigned to eternity. 'Lovely!' Mr

Armand says in the parlance of photographers down the ages.

The fate of the three glass buttons was as follows –

The first one was found the same evening by Ada and thrust into the pocket of her pinafore. Before the pinafore was washed she transferred it to a little box of treasures and trinkets she kept (a length of red ribbon, a piece of gold wire found on the way to school). When Alice was finally lost for ever Ada took the button out of the trinket box and threaded it on silk floss and wore it round her neck. Months later, the evil stepmother Rachel tore the offending button off Ada's neck, infuriated at the sight of her defiant, tear-stained face. Try as she might, Ada could not find the button and sobbed her heart out that night as if she had lost her mother a second time.

The second button was found by Tom who carried it around in his pocket for a week along with a conker and a marble, intending to return it to his mother, but before he could he lost it somewhere and then forgot all about it.

The third was found by Rachel, during a vigorous cleaning session not long after she moved into the cottage. She prised it out from between the two flagstones where it had lodged and placed it in her button box, from where, many years later, it was transferred to my grandmother's button box, a presentation tin of Rowntree's chocolates – and from there to Gillian's stomach of course, and from there – who knows? As to the fate of the children – Lawrence left home at fourteen and nobody ever saw him again. Tom married a girl called Mabel and became a solicitor's clerk and Albert died in the First World War. Poor Ada died when she was twelve after a bout of diphtheria. Lillian led a long, rather strange, life and Nell – who on this hot day is unborn and has all her life ahead of her – will one day be my grandmother and have all her life behind her without ever knowing how that happened (another woman lost in time).

CHAPTER TWO

1952

Birth

I DON'T LIKE THIS. I DON'T LIKE THIS ONE LITTLE BIT. GET ME out of here somebody, quick! My frail little skeleton is being crushed like a thin-shelled walnut. My tender skin, as yet untouched by any earthly atmosphere, is being chafed raw by this sausage-making process. (Surely this can't be natural?) Any clouds of glory I might have been trailing have been smothered in this fetid, bloodstained place.

'Get a move on, woman!' an angry voice booms like a muffled fog-horn. 'I've got a bloody dinner party to go to!'

Bunty's reply is inarticulate and indistinct but I think the general gist of it is that she's just as anxious to get the whole thing over with as our friendly gynaecologist. Dr Torquemada, I presume? The midwife angel sent to preside at my birth creaks with starch. She raps out her orders – 'PUSH! PUSH NOW!'

'I am bloody pushing!' Bunty yells back. She sweats and grunts, all the while clutching onto something that looks like a small shrunken bit of mammal, a furry locket round her neck (see *Footnote (ii)*). It's a lucky rabbit's foot. Not very lucky for the rabbit, of course, but a talismanic charm of some potency for my mother. I've gone off her actually. Bunty that is, not the rabbit. Nine months of being imprisoned inside her hasn't been the most delightful of experiences. And recently there's been no room at all. I don't care what's out there, it has to be better than this.

'PUSH, WOMAN! PUSH NOW!'

Bunty screams convincingly and then all of a sudden it's over with and I slip out as quietly as a fish down a stream. Even Dr Torquemada is surprised, 'Hel-lo, what have we here?' he says as if he wasn't expecting me at all. The midwife laughs and says, 'Snap!'

I'm about to be shipped off to the nursery when someone suggests that Bunty might like to have a look at me. She takes a quick glance and pronounces her judgement. 'Looks like a piece of meat. Take it away,' she adds, waving her hand dismissively. I suppose she's tired and emotional. She didn't specify what kind of meat. Rolled brisket? Spring lamb? Hand of pork perhaps or something unnamed, raw and bloody. Well, there you go – nothing surprises me any more. After all, I'm surely not a novelty – she's already produced pale Patricia and cross-patch Gillian from her loins, and I'm so well behaved in comparison with the latter. Gillian was born angry, bustling out of the womb, little arms and legs angling furiously while she screamed her head off, just in case nobody had noticed her. Fat chance.

My absent father, in case you're wondering, is in the Dog and Hare in Doncaster where he's just had a very satisfactory day at the races. He has a pint of bitter in front of him and is just telling a woman in an emerald green dress and a 'D' cup, that he's not married. He has no idea that I've arrived or he would be here. Wouldn't he? In fact, my gestation has neatly spanned the old and the new, for I've arrived just after the King's death, making me one of the first babies born into the new Queen's reign. A new Elizabethan! I'm surprised they haven't called me Elizabeth. They've called me nothing. I'm 'Baby Lennox', that's what it says on my label anyway. The midwife, who has red hair and is very tired, carries me through to the night nursery and deposits me in a cot.

It's very dark in the night nursery. Very dark and very quiet. A dim blue light shines in one corner, but most of the cots are just black coffin-like shapes. The darkness stretches out to infinity. Space winds whip through the icy interstellar spaces. If I reached out my tiny, wrinkled fingers that look like boiled shrimp, I would touch – nothing. And then more nothing. And after that? Nothing. I didn't think it would be like this. It's not that I expected a street party or anything – streamers, balloons, banners of welcome unfurling – a smile would have done.

The midwife goes away, the neat tip-tapping of her black lace-up shoes on the linoleum of the corridor gradually fades and we are left alone. We lie in our cots, wrapped tightly in white-cotton cellular blankets, like promises, like cocoons, waiting to hatch into something. Or little baby parcels. What would happen if the little baby parcels lost their labels and got mixed up? Would the mothers recognize their babies if they pulled them out of a baby bran tub?

A rustling of starched wings and the red-haired nurse reappears with another baby parcel and puts it down in the empty cot next to me. She pins a label on its blanket. The new baby sleeps peacefully, its top lip curling with each small inhalation.

There are no more babies this night. The night nursery sails on into the cold winter night freighted with its delicate cargo. A milky vapour hangs over the sleeping babies. Soon when we're all asleep, the cats will creep in and suck our breath away.

I will disappear in this darkness, I will be extinguished before I've even got going. Sleet spatters in gusts onto the cold glass of the nursery window. I'm alone. All alone. I can't stand this – where's my mother? WAA! WAA! WAAAAAAAAAAAAAA!!! 'The little bastard's going to wake them all.' It's the red-haired nurse, I think she's Irish. She's going to save me, she's going to take me to my mother. No? No. She takes me to a little side room, behind the sluice. A kind of cupboard, really. I spend my first night on earth in a cupboard.

The maternity-ward ceiling above our heads is painted in apple-green gloss. The upper half of the walls are magnolia and the lower half of the walls look like minced-up mushrooms. I would prefer a celestial ceiling of azure with golden, fiery-edged clouds, and peeping out from the clouds I want smiling, fat, rosy cherubs.

Bunty's settled in well in the maternity ward. The mothers all lie beached on their beds complaining all the time, mostly about their babies. We're nearly all being bottle-fed, there's an unspoken feeling that there's something distasteful about breast-feeding. We're fed on the dot, every four hours, nothing in between, no matter how much noise you make. In fact the more noise you make the more likely you are to be relegated to some cupboard somewhere. There are probably forgotten babies all over the place.

We're fed by the clock so that we don't become spoilt and demanding. The general feeling amongst the mothers is that the babies are in a conspiracy against them (if only we were). We can scream until we're exhausted, it won't make any difference to the ceremonial feeding ritual, the time when all the little baby parcels are fed, winded, changed, laid down again and ignored.

I am nearly a week old and still nameless, but at least Bunty now takes a cursory interest in me. She never speaks to me though, and her eyes avoid me, sliding over me as soon as I enter her field of vision. Now that I am outside my mother, it's difficult to know what she is thinking (nor am I any longer privy to the fertile inner world of her daydreams). The nights are still the worst time, each night a dark voyage into uncertainty. I do not believe that Bunty is my real mother. My real mother is roaming in a parallel universe somewhere, ladling out mother's milk the colour of Devon cream. She's padding the hospital corridors searching for me, her fierce, hot, lion-breath steaming up the cold windows. My real mother is Queen of the Night, a huge, galactic figure, treading the Milky Way in search of her lost infant.

Sometimes my grandmother, Nell, comes to visit in the afternoon. Hospitals make her nervous, reminding her of death, which she feels she doesn't need any reminding of at her age. She perches on the edge of the hard visitor's chair like a sickly Pet Shop budgerigar. She already has several grandchildren who all look alike to her so I can't blame her for not being very interested in me. George brings Gillian and Patricia. Gillian peers mutely at me over the side of the cot, her expression inscrutable. George doesn't have very much to say. But Patricia, good old Patricia, touches me with a wary finger and says, 'Hello, Baby,' and I reward her with a smile. 'Look, she's smiling at me,' Patricia says, her little voice choked with wonder.

'That's just wind,' Bunty says dismissively. I am not very happy, but I have decided to make the best of things. I've been given the wrong mother and am in danger of embarking on the wrong life but I trust it will all be sorted out and I will be reunited with my real mother – the one who dropped ruby-red blood onto a snow-white handkerchief and wished for a little girl with hair the colour of a shiny jet-black raven's wing. Meanwhile I make do with Bunty.

Bunty's sister, Babs, comes to visit, all the way from Dewsbury, with her twins – Daisy and Rose. Daisy and Rose are a year older than Gillian and are spotlessly clean. They're exactly alike, not a hair nor a fingernail to choose between them. It's uncanny, almost frightening. They sit on their chairs in complete silence, their dainty little legs dangling above the bile-green linoleum. Bunty lies in queenly splendour under her lily-white sheets and salmon-pink bedspread. Daisy and Rose have hair the colour of melted lemon-drops.

Bunty knits continuously, even when she has visitors. She's knitting my future in the colours of sugared almonds. 'Elizabeth?' Auntie Babs suggests. Bunty grimaces.

'Margaret?' Auntie Babs tries. 'Anne?'

They could call me 'Dorothy', or 'Miranda', that would be nice. 'Eve' would have a certain resonance. Bunty's ack-ack eyes search the ceiling. She takes a deep decisive breath and pronounces the name. My name.

'Ruby.'

'Ruby?' Auntie Babs repeats doubtfully. 'Ruby,' Bunty confirms decisively. My name is Ruby. I am a precious jewel. I am a drop of blood. I am Ruby Lennox.

Footnote (ii) – Still Lives

THIS IS THE STORY OF MY GRANDMOTHER'S CONTINUALLY thwarted attempts to get married. When she was twenty-four, Nell became engaged to a policeman, Percy Sievewright, a tall, good-looking man and a keen amateur footballer. He played for the same Saturday league team as Nell's brother, Albert, and it was Albert who had introduced the pair of them. When Percy proposed, down on one knee and very solemn, Nell's heart had buoyed up with happiness and relief – at last she was going to be the most important person in someone's life.

Unfortunately, Percy's appendix burst and he died of peritonitis not long after they'd set the date for the wedding. He was only twenty-six and the funeral was one of those wretched ones that rubs the grief raw instead of pouring balm on it. He was an only child and his father was dead so his mother was beside herself, sinking into a faint at the graveside. Nell and Albert and another man ran forward and lifted her up from the soaking-wet grass – it had been raining for two days and the ground was like mud – and then Albert and the other man stood one on either side of her like pillars and supported her for the rest of the service. The raindrops that were clinging to the black net of Mrs Sievewright's veil trembled like little diamonds every time her body convulsed in anguish. Nell felt her own grief was dull in comparison to Mrs Sievewright's. The lads from the football team carried the coffin and Percy's fellow policemen formed an honour guard. It was the first time Nell had seen grown men with tears running down their faces and it seemed especially awful to see a uniformed policeman crying. Afterwards, everyone kept saying what a grand bloke Percy was and Nell wished they wouldn't because it made it worse somehow – knowing he *was* a grand bloke and only being his fiancée and not his widow. She knew it shouldn't make any difference, but it did. Lillian sat next to her at the funeral tea and kept squeezing her black-gloved hand in dreadful, mute sympathy.

Nell thought her life was over, and yet to her surprise it carried on much as before. She'd been apprenticed to a milliner in Coney Street when she left school and her days were still spent curling feathers and swathing chiffon as if nothing had happened. It was the same at home, she was still expected to wash pots and darn stockings while Rachel, her stepmother, watched her from the rocking-chair that she was growing too fat for and said things like, 'Employment is nature's physician' which was the epigraph to her *Everyman's Book of Home Remedies*. Nell kept her face turned away from her stepmother and tried not to listen because she was afraid if she did she would hit her with the big, cast-iron stew-pot. Now that she no longer had Percy to rescue her it seemed as if she would be trapped in the little house on Lowther Street for ever. To have been 'Mrs Percy Sievewright' would have given her a shape and identity that seemed to be denied to plain Nell Barker.

Nell was surprised at how quickly Percy faded from everyday life. She got into the habit of visiting Mrs Sievewright every Friday evening, knowing that she was the one person who could be relied upon not to forget Percy, and the two of them would sit over a pot of tea and a plate of bloater-paste sandwiches, talking about Percy as if he were still alive, imagining a life for him, that now would never be – *Just think what Percy would have said about that . . . Percy always liked Scarborough . . . Percy would have loved to have had sons* . . . but they couldn't conjure him back, no matter how hard they tried.

Sheepishly, because he thought it might seem a bit daft, Albert knocked and came into Nell's bedroom one evening and gave her the team photograph that they'd had taken the previous year, the year they'd almost won the challenge cup. 'And we would have done if Frank Cook hadn't missed that shot, daft bugger-excuse-my-language. Jack Keech sent him a perfect cross, it was an open goal,' Albert said, shaking his head in disbelief, even now, a year later. Nell asked, 'Which one was Frank then?' and Albert told her the names of all the players and stopped abruptly when he came to Percy, and finally said, 'Death's awful when it happens to somebody young,' which was what he'd heard someone say at the funeral and not what he thought at all because Albert didn't really believe in death. The dead had just gone away somewhere and were going to come back sooner or later – they were waiting in a shadowy room that no one could see the door to, and being ministered to by his mother, who was almost certainly an angel by now. Albert couldn't remember what his mother had looked like, no matter how hard he screwed up his eyes and concentrated. But that didn't stop him missing her, even though he was nearly thirty years old. Alice, Ada, Percy, the lurcher he'd had as a boy that fell under a cart – they were all going to jump out from the waiting-room one day and surprise Albert. 'Well, night-night, Nelly,' he said finally, because he could tell from the way that she was staring at the photograph that she thought the dead were gone for ever and weren't hiding anywhere.

Nell found it strange looking at Percy in the photograph because in real life he had seemed so distinctive and different from everybody else, but here he had the same vague, slightly out-of-focus features as the rest of the team. 'Thank you,' Nell said to Albert, but he'd already left the room. Frank Cook looked like anyone else, standing in the middle of the back row, but Jack Keech was recognizable, he was the one crouched down at the front with the ball. She knew he was a good pal of Albert's but it was only when Nell came home from work one evening and found the pair of them together in the back yard that she recognized Jack Keech as the man who had helped them with Percy Sievewright's mother when she'd collapsed at the graveside.

The sun trapped in the back yard at Lowther Street was hot even though it was only May and Nell paused for a second on the threshold, feeling the warmth on her face. 'There you are, Nell,' Albert said as if they'd both been waiting for her. 'Brew up a pot of tea, there's a good lass – Jack's fixing the bench.' Jack Keech looked up from wrenching out a nail and smiled at her and said, 'Tea'd be grand, Nell.' Nell smiled back and went into the house without saying anything and filled the kettle.

She put the kettle to boil and then walked back to the stone sink under the window and rested her hands on the edge and watched Albert and Jack Keech through the window. While she waited for the kettle she moved her toes up and down inside her boots and felt her ribcage moving as she breathed and when she put the back of her hands up to her cheeks she could feel how hot they were.

The bench was an old wooden one that had been in the back yard ever since they moved into the house. There were several slats missing from the back and the arm had begun to come away. Jack Keech was kneeling on the paving-slabs of the yard, sawing a block of clean, new wood with a stubby saw, and through the open door Nell could smell the resin from the pine. A lock of Jack's thick, dark hair kept falling over his forehead. Albert was standing over him laughing. Albert was always laughing. His angelic blond curls had never gone away and his baby-blue eyes looked too big somehow under the sweep of pale gold lashes so that he still didn't look grown up. It was hard to see how he was going to stop looking like a boy and start looking like an old man, never mind all the years in between.

There was always a flock of girls after Albert but there was never one he chose to be special. His brother Tom was married and away from home but Albert said he didn't think he'd ever get married and both Lillian and Nell agreed that this was a daft thing to say because you could see that he'd make a grand husband, and in private they agreed that if he wasn't their brother they would have married him themselves.

The way things were going they'd probably all end their days together anyway. Neither Nell nor Lillian seemed capable of catching a husband, they'd both had broken engagements, Nell's broken by death and Lillian's by an act of betrayal, and one day Rachel would die and leave them alone. 'If only . . .' Lillian would say as she plaited her hair at night in Nell's room, and Nell, pressing her face into her pillow, wondered, for the millionth time, why their mother had been taken away and they had been given Rachel in exchange.

Nell rinsed the teapot with hot water from the

kettle, swirling it round and round before emptying it down the sink. Jack Keech had taken his braces down so that they hung around his waist and had rolled up the white sleeves of his shirt so that she could see the muscles in his forearm flexing as he sawed the wood. The skin on his arms was the polished walnut colour that came from working outdoors. Albert looked like a guardian angel standing over him and Nell watched both of them, holding the teapot to her breast and wishing that this moment would go on longer.

When she went out again with the tray of tea and plate of bread and butter, Jack was marking off a piece of wood with a pencil and with a tremendous effort Nell said shyly, 'It's very good of you, mending the bench like this,' and he looked up and grinned and said, 'That's all right, Nell.' Then he straightened up for a minute and, rubbing the small of his back, said, 'It's a nice yard you've got here,' so that both Albert and Nell looked round in surprise because neither of them had ever thought of the back yard in Lowther Street as being 'nice'; yet now that Jack said so you could see how sunny it was and Nell wondered how they could have lived here for five years and never really noticed the dusty-pink clematis that was climbing all over the wall and the back door.

'Jack's a chippy,' Albert said admiringly (although Albert was a train driver which Nell and Lillian agreed must be a wonderful thing to do). Jack knelt down again and started hammering a nail in and Nell found the nerve to stand and watch him for nearly a whole minute and all she could think about was what high, sharp cheekbones he had, like razor-clam shells.

Jack didn't stop and drink his tea until he'd finished, by which time it was cold. Nell offered to brew a fresh pot but Albert said he fancied a beer and suggested the Golden Fleece. Jack gave Nell a rueful smile and said, 'Another time, maybe,' and she could feel a blush rising up from her chest to her cheeks, so that she had to look away quickly while Albert helped Jack to pack up his tools.

Nell was left alone to deal with Rachel when she came back from a temperance meeting at the church. She was in a foul mood because no one had put the tea on to cook and they ended up eating bread and butter without speaking because Lillian didn't come in until later and said she was working a late shift (she worked at Rowntree's) which Nell knew wasn't true. Albert didn't roll in until past midnight; she heard him pause and sit on the bottom stair to take his boots off so he wouldn't wake anyone and then creep up to his room.

The next time Nell saw Jack was a few Sundays later when he stopped in with Frank to pick up Albert for the football team's annual outing. Frank was wearing a tweed cap and carrying a fishing rod (they were going to Scarborough). Frank was a draper's assistant but neither Albert nor Jack ever let on to Frank that they thought being a draper's assistant wasn't much of a job, especially when they could see that he knew that well enough for himself without being told.

* * *

Jack leant against the back yard wall and smiled a lazy smile at no-one in particular. He had a straw boater on and Albert laughed and said, 'He looks like a real toff, eh, Nelly?' and gave her a wink so that she didn't know where to look. Underneath the hat his black hair was slicked back from his forehead and he was so clean-shaven that Nell wanted to reach out and touch his skin just above where it met the whiteness of his collar. She didn't of course, she could hardly bring herself to even look at him as they stood in the yard, waiting for Albert. 'We'll miss the train if he doesn't hurry,' Frank said, and Lillian said, 'Here he comes!' as they heard their brother's boots on the stairs, and then Lillian smiled at Jack with her cat-green almond eyes and gave Nell an invisible prod in the back and hissed, 'Go on, Nellie – say something,' because she knew how sweet her sister was on Jack.

But then Albert came out and said, 'Come on, we're going to be late,' and all three turned to go and were half-way along the lane at the back of the house before either Nell or Lillian remembered the lunch they'd packed for them. Lillian shouted, 'Wait!' so loudly that an upstairs window across the way shot open, the sash rattling, and Mrs Harding looked out to see what the fuss was about. Nell ran back into the kitchen and grabbed Tom's old haversack off the kitchen table and ran back out into the lane.

The packed lunch had been the subject of much discussion between Lillian and Nell because originally they were only going to do enough for Albert, but then it struck them that Frank didn't have any family so maybe he wouldn't make himself a good lunch – if any at all – and then they thought about Jack and decided it wouldn't be right to leave him out, and in the end Lillian laughed and said they were going to end up making lunch for the whole football team if they weren't careful. Eventually, inside Tom's old knapsack they placed – a dozen ham sandwiches wrapped in a clean tea-towel, six hard-boiled eggs in their shells, a big piece of Wensleydale, a slab of parkin, a bag of cinder toffee, three apples and three bottles of ginger beer (even though they knew there'd be crates of beer going with the lads). Needless to say, Rachel knew nothing of this largesse.

Jack broke away from the other two and walked back towards Nell and, taking the haversack from her said, 'Thanks Nell, that was right good of the two of you, we'll think about you when we're sitting up on the Front eating this lot.' Then he gave her his boyish, cheeky smile and said, 'Maybe one evening next week you'd like to walk out with me?' and Nell nodded and smiled and kicked herself because he must think she was a deaf-mute for all she ever said anything to him, and eventually she managed to say, 'That would be nice,' with a tremulous little smile.

She almost ran back to Lillian at the gate and the two of them stood, framed in pink clematis, watching the three men walk to the top of the cobbled lane where they all turned and waved. The sun was behind them so you couldn't see their faces, but Lillian imagined their smiles and she had to put her hand to her mouth and blink away the tears that had formed because she was thinking what fine young men they were and how afraid she was for them, but all she said was, 'I hope they're careful if they go out on a boat.' Nell said nothing, she was thinking how sad Percy Sievewright's mother would have felt if she'd been here at that moment, seeing his three pals going off to Scarborough and knowing Percy couldn't go with them.

Nell didn't know whether she'd never loved Percy properly or whether she simply couldn't remember what it was like to love Percy, but either way, what she felt now for Jack seemed nothing like anything she'd known about before. Just the thought of him made her feel hot and alive and she prayed every night that she'd be able to carry on resisting him until their wedding-night.

She kept on visiting Percy's mother, although she changed the night to Monday because she saw Jack on Friday nights now. She didn't tell Percy's mother that she was in love with someone else because it was hardly a year since Percy had died and they continued to talk about him over the endless cups of tea – only now he felt like a person they'd invented between them rather than a man who had ever been flesh and blood. If she looked at the photograph of the football team it was with a sense of guilt because her eyes skimmed over

Percy's lifeless face and fixed on Jack's impudent smile.

Albert was the first to join up. He told his sisters it would be 'a bit of a lark' and a chance to see something of the world. 'A bit of Belgium, more like,' Jack said sarcastically, but nothing would have put Albert off and they hardly had time to say goodbye to him properly before he was on his way to Fulford Barracks to join up with the 1st East Yorkshires and be transformed from a train driver into a gunner. They had a photograph taken though, that was Tom's idea. 'Whole family together,' he said, perhaps having a premonition that there would never be another time. Tom had a friend – a Mr Mattock – who was a keen photographer and he came one sunny afternoon and posed them all in the back yard at Lowther Street, with Rachel, Lillian and Nell sitting on the newly mended bench, with Tom standing behind and Albert bobbed down in the middle at Rachel's feet, just like Jack in the team photograph. Tom said what a shame it was that Lawrence wasn't with them and Rachel said, 'He might be dead for all we know.' If you look very closely at the photograph, you can see the clematis growing along the top of the wall, like a garland.

Frank joined up the day that Albert crossed the Channel – Frank knew he was a coward and was terrified other people would find out as well so he thought he'd join up as quickly as possible before anyone noticed. He was so scared that his hand wouldn't stop shaking when he was signing his papers and the commissioning sergeant laughed and said, 'I hope you've got a steadier hand when it comes to shooting the Hun, lad.' Jack was standing right behind Frank. The last thing Jack wanted to do was fight a war, privately he thought it was all a piece of nonsense – but it seemed wrong to let Frank just go off like that, so he went along with him and signed his name with a flourish. 'Well done, lad,' the sergeant said.

Lillian and Nell went to the station to wave them off but there were so many people crowded onto the bunting-decked platform that they only got a glimpse of Frank at the last minute, waving at nobody in particular from a carriage window as the train passed beneath the vaulting cathedral arches of the station. Nell could have wept from disappointment at not seeing Jack amongst this flag-waving, kit-toting mêlée and she was only glad that she'd given him that lucky rabbit's foot the previous evening when they had said their fond farewells. She'd clutched onto his arm and started crying, and Rachel, moved to disgust, said, 'Leave off that noise,' and thrust the little rabbit's paw into her hand and said, 'Here's a good luck charm for him,' and Jack laughed uproariously and said, 'They should make them standard issue, eh?' and tucked it into the pocket of his jacket.

They had letters, they'd never had so many letters in their lives – letters from Albert, cheerful letters about what a grand lot the lads were and how busy they were kept. 'He says he's missing home cooking and he's picking up a bit of the lingo,' Lillian read out for Rachel's benefit, because Albert never once sent her a letter, even though she went around telling everyone that 'her son' was one of the first from the Groves to join up, which amazed Lillian and Nell because although Rachel disliked all of her stepchildren, she disliked Albert the most.

Nell got letters from Jack, of course, not quite so cheerful as Albert's letters, not as long either; in fact Jack wasn't much of a letter writer at all, and generally never got beyond, 'I'm thinking about you and thank you for your letters,' in his blunt handwriting. They even got letters from Frank, because, 'Of course, he has no-one to write to,' Nell said. His letters were the best of the lot because he told them all sorts of silly little things about his fellow soldiers and the daily routine so that they often laughed out loud when they read his funny, spidery scrawl. Strangely, none of them – Frank, Jack or Albert – ever wrote much about the war itself and battles and skirmishes seemed to pass with little apparent involvement from any of them. 'The battle of Ypres is over now,' Albert wrote cryptically, 'and we are all very glad.'

Nell and Lillian spent a lot of time replying to these letters; they sat every night under the bead-fringed lamp at the front parlour table, either knitting blankets for the Belgian refugees or writing letters on special lilac notepaper they had bought. Lillian developed an uncharacteristic passion for maudlin postcards and bought whole sets like 'The Kiss Goodbye' that she sent off indiscriminately to all three men, so that none of them ever ended up with a full set. And then there were parcels to send containing peppermint lozenges, knitted woollen mufflers and tenpence halfpenny tins of Antiseptic Foot Powder from Coverdales in Parliament Street. And on Sundays they often walked all the way over to Leeman Road to see the concentration camp that had been built to house the aliens and Lillian used to take apples to throw over the wire because she felt so sorry for them. 'They're people just like us,' she said sorrowfully, and as one of them was Max Brechner, their butcher on Haxby Road, Nell supposed Lillian was right, but it did seem odd to be taking fruit to an enemy that was trying to kill their own brother – although Max Brechner, who was sixty if he was a day and got out of breath if he walked a few yards, hardly seemed like the enemy.

The first person they knew that came home on leave was Bill Monroe from Emerald Street and he was followed by a boy from Park Grove Street and one from over on Eldon Terrace, which seemed unfair as Albert had joined up before any of them. There was a big to-do one day because Bill Monroe hadn't gone back when he should have done and they sent in military policemen to take him back. His mother barred the front door with a broom handle and had to be lifted out of the way by the military policemen, one at each elbow, and Nell, who happened to be walking home from work along

Emerald Street at the time, was reminded of Percy's funeral.

She had a further shock when an ordinary, civilian policeman appeared from nowhere and for a second Nell thought it was Percy. For a ridiculous moment she wondered if he'd come back to ask her why there was a little pearl and garnet ring on her engagement finger instead of the sapphire chips he'd given her which were now wrapped in tissue paper and put at the back of her drawer.

Bill Monroe was hauled off eventually and Nell didn't linger on the street. She felt embarrassed for him because she'd seen the look of terror on his face and thought how awful it must be to be such a coward – and how unpatriotic as well – and she was surprised how many women came up to Mrs Monroe, who was raging and shouting and crying on her doorstep, and told her that she'd done the right thing.

Frank came home after the second battle of Ypres; he'd been in hospital in Southport with a septic foot and was given a few days' leave before going back to the Front. It was odd because before the war they'd hardly known him yet now he seemed like an old friend and when he came knocking at the back door they both hugged him and made him stay to tea. Nell ran out and got herrings and Lillian cut bread and put out jam and even Rachel asked how he was doing. But when they were all sat round the table, drinking their tea from the best service, the one that had gold rims and little blue forget-me-nots, Frank found himself unexpectedly tongue-tied. He had thought there were a lot of things about the war he wanted to tell them but was surprised to discover that the neat triangles of bread and jam and the prettiness of the little blue forget-me-nots somehow precluded him from talking about trench foot and rats, let alone the many different ways of dying he had witnessed. The smell of death clearly had no place in the parlour of Lowther Street, with the snowy cloth on the table and the glass-bead fringed lamp and the two sisters who had such soft, lovely hair that Frank ached to bury his face in it. He was thinking all these things while chewing his bread and casting around desperately for conversation, until with a nervous gulp from the gold and forget-me-nots he said, 'That's a grand cup, you should taste the tea we get,' and told them about the chlorinated water in the trenches. When he saw the look of horror on their faces he felt ashamed that he'd ever wanted to talk about death.

They, in turn, told him about Billy Monroe and he tut-tutted in the right places although secretly he wished he had a mother who could somehow – anyhow – prevent him having to return to the Front because Frank knew he was going to die if he went back to the war. He listened politely while they told him about all the things they were doing – they showed him their knitting – they'd stopped knitting for the Belgians and now they were knitting socks for soldiers, and Nell told him about her new job, making uniforms, where she'd just been made a forewoman because of her experience with hats, and Lillian was working as a conductress on the trams and Frank raised both eyebrows and said, 'Never!' because he couldn't imagine a woman conductress and Lillian giggled. The two sisters were so full of life that in the end the war was left more or less unspoken of, except, of course, to say that Jack was well and sent his love and that he hadn't seen Albert at all but he was a lot safer behind the big guns in the artillery than he would be in the trenches.

And Rachel, the toad in the corner, unexpectedly spoke up and said, 'It must be dreadful in those trenches,' and Frank shrugged and smiled and said, 'Oh it's not too bad really, Mrs Barker,' and took another drink from his forget-me-not cup.

Frank spent most of the rest of his leave with one or other of the girls. He took Nelly to the music-hall at the Empire and Lillian took him to a meeting at the Educational Settlement but it was a bit above his head. They were all Quakers and conchies and socialists and they kept on about negotiating an end to the war. Frank thought they were a load of slackers and was glad he was in uniform. 'Do you think you should be mixing with folk like these?' he said to Lillian as he walked her home and she just looked at him and said, 'Frank!' and laughed. More enjoyable was when all three of them went to see *Jane Shore* at the New Picture House in Coney Street which had just opened and was really grand with its one thousand tip-up seats.

When he had to go back to the Front he felt worse

than he had done leaving the first time and he could hardly bear to leave Nell and Lillian behind.

Lillian and Nell had plenty to occupy them after Frank went back. They worked long hours and they still had Rachel to contend with, although even she wasn't as bad as their fear of the Zeppelins. They bought dark blue holland from Leak and Thorp's for the windows and were obsessive about the blackout, especially as poor Minnie Havis next door had to go up before the magistrates for leaving a light showing. Tom came to visit regularly, although he hardly ever brought his new wife Mabel. Lillian said Mabel was a wet piece of dough, although Nell quite liked her. Somebody asked them if their brother was a slacker and they were outraged, but secretly Nell thought it wasn't very brave of him getting an exemption like that. Lillian said wasn't it enough that they had one brother that might get killed? and Nell threw a cushion at her because she never, never thought Albert was going to get killed and it seemed dreadfully bad luck to say something like that. Tom helped them fix the holland blinds at the windows and laughed off the idea of a Zeppelin attack. He believed in them after his hand got blown off though, and they went to see him in hospital and at least now no-one could accuse him of being a slacker, not with his hand like that. Nell was just about to write a letter to Albert telling him about all this excitement when he surprised them by turning up on the doorstep on leave. All Rachel said was, 'More mouths to feed,' but then she'd never liked Albert.

They were convinced Albert had grown when they saw him; neither of them remembered him being so tall. He had fine lines round his eyes and would have slept all the time when he was home, if they'd let him. When they asked him questions about the war he always made some joke and never told them anything. They were greedy for Albert, they would have spent every minute with him, just looking at him, they were that happy to have him home. Albert had always looked after them and now they wanted to look after him and they hung around his neck and stroked his hair as if he was their baby not their great strapping brother. When he went, they waved him off at the station and they were still standing on the platform, looking at the empty rails, ten minutes after he'd gone. As long as they were still standing there they felt as if they hadn't let him go and they had to tear themselves away to go home, where Rachel said, 'He's gone then, has he, the light of your life?'

Frank thought it was probably the noise that got to Jack in the end. For three days and three nights the barrage never stopped and as the guns seemed to get louder, so Jack seemed to get quieter and quieter, although he didn't go mad with it like some chaps, he was just too quiet. Funnily enough, the noise didn't bother Frank so much any more, he thought it was because he'd got used to the constant booming of the howitzers although in fact he'd gone deaf in his right ear.

It wasn't the noise that bothered Frank anyway – it was death, or rather, how he was going to die, that worried him. There was no doubt he was going to die; after all, he'd been out here nearly two years and the odds were piled high against him by now. Frank had begun to pray his way through the war. He no longer prayed that he wouldn't die, he just prayed he would see it coming. He was terrified of dying without any warning and prayed that he might at least see the mortar that was coming for him so he would have time to prepare himself. Or anticipate in some magical way the sniper's bullet that would take his brain out before his body even knew about it. And please God, he begged, don't let me be gassed. Only a week ago nearly a whole battalion in a trench that ran parallel to this one, a Pals' battalion from a factory in Nottingham, had been taken by a low-level tide of gas that rolled quietly along towards them and took them before they realized what was happening. Now they were all quietly drowning to death in some field-hospital.

The night before the attack nobody could sleep. At four in the morning, when it was already light Frank and Jack lolled against the sandbagged wall of the trench while Frank rolled a cigarette for each of them and one for Alf Simmonds who was ducked down on the firing-step above them on sentry duty. Then Jack sucked on his spindly roll-up and, without looking at Frank, said, 'I'm not going,' and Frank said, 'Not going where?' so that Jack laughed and pointed in the direction of No Man's Land

and said 'There, of course – I'm not going there.'

Alf Simmonds laughed as well and said, 'Don't blame you lad,' because he thought it was a joke but Frank felt sick because he knew it wasn't.

It was silent before the order came. The guns had stopped and there was no laughing or joking or anything, just the silence of waiting. Frank watched the clouds pass over in the blue sky above, little puffs of white that were floating above No Man's Land as if it was any other bit of countryside and not the place where he was going to die very shortly. The new lieutenant looked as green as the grass that didn't grow there any more, you could see the beads of sweat as big as raindrops on his forehead, they'd never had a lieutenant quite as nervous as this one. Or as mean. Frank suspected it wouldn't be long before a sniper got this one, and not necessarily the enemy's either. The men were still missing Malcolm Innes-Ward who'd been with them for six months before he was shot through the eye. He was helping drag a wounded man back from No Man's Land when a sniper got him. The private helping him was killed as well and the wounded man died of gas-gangrene anyway, so it had all been for nothing.

Jack had got on well with Malcolm Innes-Ward, they'd spent long hours in his officer's dug-out talking about politics and life and Jack had taken his death particularly hard. Innes-Ward and the noise, that's what had done for Jack, Frank decided.

When the order came to go over the top it was more

like a relief than anything and everyone scrambled up the ladders and over the parapet until there were only three of them left – Frank, Jack and the new lieutenant. Frank didn't know why he hadn't moved, it was just a momentary hesitation really – he wanted to make sure that Jack was coming with him – but then the new lieutenant started screaming at them and waving his gun around, saying he was going to shoot them if they didn't go over, so that Jack said, really quietly, 'Officers generally lead from the front, sir,' and before Frank knew what was happening he was looking down the barrel of the new lieutenant's Lee-Enfield. Then Jack said, 'You don't have to do that, sir, we're going,' and he half-dragged Frank over the top, and before they were even over the parapet Jack was yelling 'Run!' at him, which Frank did, because now he was more frightened of being shot in the back by the new lieutenant's rifle than he was of being blown up by the enemy.

Frank was determined not to lose sight of Jack, convinced for some reason that if he could keep with Jack his chances of dying were lessened. He fixed his eyes on the regimental badge on the back of his jacket and the scrap of material tied as neatly as a girl's hair ribbon on his webbing, but within seconds Jack had disappeared and Frank found himself advancing alone through what seemed like a wall of fog, but which was actually the smoke from the big guns which had started up again. The fog seemed to go on and on for ever but Frank kept on walking even though he didn't come across Jack, or any other soldier, for that matter – living or dead.

It was only after quite a long time that he realized what had happened. He had died – it must have happened when he'd first lost sight of Jack, probably a sniper's bullet and now he was no longer advancing across No Man's Land but was walking through Hell and that's what Hell was going to be for Frank – to trudge for ever across No Man's Land towards the enemy trenches.

Just as Frank was trying to adjust his thinking to this new idea his foot slipped and he was half-falling, half-sliding down the side of a muddy crater, holding his rifle above his head and screaming at the top of his voice because this was one of the pits of Hell and it was going to be bottomless.

But then he stopped falling and sliding and screaming and realized that he was about two-thirds of the way down the side of a huge crater. Down below was thick, muddy-brown water and in the water a body floating face down. A rat was swimming round the body, executing slow, lazy circles and Frank was suddenly reminded how he and Albert had taught themselves to swim one sweltering hot day. It had been years ago, although now it could just as well have been another lifetime. They'd been on Clifton Ings and the Ouse had been that same thick colour as the water in the shell-hole. Jack had been ill with measles and it had just been the two of them that day. Frank closed his eyes and pushed himself back into the soft mud of the side of the crater and decided that the safest place to be was in the past.

Frank concentrated hard until he could feel the heat of a childhood sun on his skinny, nine-year-old shoulders and smell the cow-parsley and hawthorn along the banks of the Ouse. Now he could feel what the water was like when you first stepped into it, the shock of the cold and the strange feeling of his toes splaying out into the mud at the bottom. And he could feel the itchy hemp of the rope that they took it in turns to tie round each other – one splashing out into the river while the other one stood guard, ready to haul him back if he started to sink. And the willow tree in full, silvery-green leaf that trailed in the water like a girl's hair.

Frank stayed in his crater for several hours recreating his first swimming lesson with Albert until by the end of the day they could both make it nearly half-way across the river. Exhausted but triumphant, they lay down on the hard, dry earth under the willow tree until the water evaporated off their skin and Frank remembered he had pieces in his jacket pocket (this was before his mother died) and they sat and ate the squashed squares of bread and strawberry jam. When they finished, Albert turned his jam-smeared face to Frank and said, 'This has been a right good day, eh, Frank?'

He thought he might have fallen asleep because he looked up suddenly and found the gunsmoke fog had cleared and the sky was a pale blue. Standing above him on the lip of the crater was Albert, laughing and smiling, and Frank's first thought was how perfectly like an angel Albert was, even dressed in khaki and with his blond curls crammed under his cap. There was a thin line of blood and grease along the golden skin of his cheek and his eyes were as blue as the sky above, bluer than the forget-me-nots on the tea-service in the front parlour of Lowther Street.

Frank tried to say something to Albert but he couldn't get any words to come out of his mouth. Being dead was really just like being trapped in a dream. Then Albert put up his hand as if he was waving goodbye and turned and disappeared, dipping down over the horizon of the crater. Frank felt a terrible sense of despair when Albert was lost to sight, as if somebody had torn something out of him, and he began to shiver with cold. After a while he decided the best thing to do would be to try and find Albert and so he dragged himself out of the crater and set off in the general direction of Albert's disappearance. When, some time later, he staggered into a dressing-station and announced to a nurse that he was dead the nurse merely said, 'Go and sit over in that corner with that lieutenant then,' and Frank walked over to a sandbagged wall where a subaltern on crutches was leaning, staring at nothing with one eye – the other one was bandaged. Frank reached into his pocket and found to his surprise that he still had his tobacco so he rolled up two cigarettes and gave one to the lieutenant. After he'd helped him to light it (the young subaltern was having terrible difficulty with his monocular vision) the two dead men stood in silence inhaling their cigarettes with dizzy pleasure as daylight faded over the first day of the Battle of the Somme.

* * *

Lillian was taking fares on a tram in the middle of Blossom Street when she felt a sudden cold shiver pass right through her body even though it was a hot day. Without even thinking she pulled her ticket machine over her head and left it on a seat, rang the bell and stepped off the tram, to the amazement of her passengers. She marched up Blossom Street and down Micklegate. Breaking into a run before she'd even reached Ouse Bridge, she was running as if the dead were at her heels until by the time she finally turned into Lowther Street and saw Nell waiting for her, sitting on the doorstep, her hair had lost all its pins and she had great stains of damp sweat on her blouse. She hung onto the little wooden front gate, holding her heaving sides and retching for breath, but Nell just sat there, not moving, leaning against the doorpost with her face tilted up towards the sun. She hadn't run home, she had left the dusty airless basement where uniforms were being stitched all day long and had strolled slowly along Monkgate, for all the world as if she was out for a Sunday prom. They were locked out because Rachel was shopping and neither of them ever remembered a key, and for a minute they just looked at each other, astonished by the strength of their homing instincts.

Lillian was the one who finally broke the silence, 'He's dead, isn't he?' she gasped, swinging the gate shut behind her and walking slowly up the path until she sank down next to Nell on the step. After a long time, when the sun had moved right over the roof and headed for the next street, she said, 'He'll be in heaven now.' Nell looked up in the thin brilliant air as if Albert might show himself amongst the host of angels but there was nothing, not even a cloud, not even a swallow gliding on a slow thermal.

By the time they opened the telegram that Lillian read aloud to Rachel, 'Regret to inform you that Albert Barker was killed in action on July 1st, 1916. The Army Council sends its sympathy,' both Lillian and Nell had already been in mourning a week.

A mortar had taken out Albert's gun emplacement; the shell had landed right on top of the heavy howitzer sending the bodies of the gunners flying outwards so they landed in a star shape around what was left of their gun. The only mark on Albert had been a line of blood and grease on his sun-burned cheek and he had a beatific smile on his face like a child that's just seen its mother in a crowd, and you would have wondered what had killed him until you lifted him up and saw that the back of his head was missing.

It seemed strange to Frank that Albert looked perfectly all right but was dead and Jack, who was covered in blood from head to foot so that he looked like one of the martyrs of the early church, was alive. That all three of them should turn up at the same dressing-station that day seemed perfectly natural to Frank at the time – the coincidence was, after all, no stranger than the fact that the only corpse he had seen all day (apart from the soldier at the bottom of the mud crater who'd been there several days) was that of Albert. Jack didn't speak to Frank; in fact Jack passed right by the dead Frank without seeing him, the blood still streaming down his face.

When Frank had fallen down his crater Jack had in fact still been only a few yards in front of him. Jack had just kept on walking; he walked all the way across No Man's Land, mortars exploding around him and machine-gun bullets tracing past his head until – to his great surprise – he found himself right up against the barbed-wire fencing of the German trenches. Even then he didn't stop but just walked right through the wire as if anaesthetized and carried on until he came to the next barbed-wire barrier. He wasn't even surprised at the sight of all this wire, even though they had been sending shells over for days to destroy it. Suddenly, unexpectedly, Jack found himself in a German trench and he walked along it until he came to a neat little dug-out and thought how much better constructed this was than Malcolm Innes-Ward's dug-out. Jack had forgotten that Innes-Ward was dead and half-expected to come across him round the next corner. He didn't though, instead he'd found the dug-out and huddled in the dug-out were three German privates, young boys. One was very blond, one was very tall and one was very stocky and Jack laughed because they reminded him of a music-hall act he'd seen at the Empire before the war when three young men, who looked just like the German privates, had danced and sung a song that Jack couldn't remember now. They'd done a funny routine where they kept passing a top hat from one head to another and the audience had loved them. What was the song? Jack wished he could remember. He stood there laughing, half-expecting one of them to produce a top hat, but no-one moved so in the end Jack raised his Lee-Enfield and fired off the clip. In turn, each private flung his head back and then slid down the sandbagged wall of the dug-out and the last one had such a look of surprise on his face that Jack laughed again and thought that wasn't a bad routine either. He turned and walked away from them, knowing that he'd never remember the song now.

Jack had leave after the Somme, it was the first time he'd been home for nearly two years. His injuries had almost healed, they'd been surprisingly superficial lacerations and his hands and face were now covered in thin scars like threads that made Nell rather proud because they certainly weren't the marks of a coward. In fact, Jack had been given a medal for his bravery in killing the three Germans, and Nell was disappointed that he wouldn't wear it when he walked out with her. She nagged him a few times about it until he turned and looked at her with such a peculiar look in his eye that she was almost frightened.

He was difficult the whole time he was on leave. He walked round to the house in Lowther Street every day, but he hardly ever said anything, just sat at the table, sullen and morose, so that Nell nearly lost her temper with him for being so inconsiderate towards her. He talked to Lillian though. Lillian had joined the local branch of the UDC and had been going to all kinds of lectures and Rachel told Jack that she was an alien-lover, just like Arnold Rowntree, but Jack just laughed. Jack and Lillian seemed to agree about most things and Jack even said that he thought conchies were brave so that Nell almost dropped her tea-cup. She was irritated at the sight of the two of them, sitting there with their heads together talking about goodness knows what. For the first time in her life, Nell found herself disliking her sister.

Nell and Jack almost got married that leave; they discussed getting a special licence; Jack was only home for a week, but somehow the days went quicker than they'd expected. Jack was reluctant – not because he didn't love her, he said, but because he didn't want her to be a widow. Nell could hardly say that she'd rather be a widow than a bereaved fiancée for a second time, so she didn't argue.

Just before Jack went back to the Front they went to see *The Battle of the Somme* at the Electric Cinema in Fossgate. Nell was looking for Albert, convinced that his smiling face would pop up on the screen, even though she would have had a dreadful time coping with it if he had. All the Tommies were smiling and laughing as if the war was a great joke. 'A lark,' that's what Albert had said. Of course, they were smiling for the camera, you could almost hear the cameraman saying, 'Give us a smile, lads!' as the columns trudged past on their way to the Front. They all turned and waved and smiled as if the Somme was no more than a day's excursion. The film showed a lot of preparation – the troops on the move, the barrages of guns. You saw the guns firing and in the distance you could see little puffs of smoke like clouds. Because there was no sound, the Somme seemed like a very peaceful battle. Nell watched as the big guns were loaded up by men in shirt-sleeves and braces and a little lump formed in her throat because she remembered the day Jack had fixed the bench in the yard.

Then there were a lot of shots of German prisoners being offered cigarettes by British Tommies, and of the walking wounded of both sides limping through trenches, but there wasn't very much of the actual battle in between. In one shot you saw men being given the order to go over the top and they all went except one man who got to the top of the parapet and then slid gently down again. There was a shot of dead horses and the caption said that two dumb friends had made the final sacrifice, but on the whole the battle of the Somme didn't seem to have many dead and you were left wondering where they were. (So in some ways, of course, it reflected Frank's experience of the Somme.)

Even Nell felt it was an unsatisfactory account and when the lights went up and people started shuffling out of their seats, both Jack and Nell sat there a little longer and Jack leant across and said in a very quiet voice, 'It wasn't like that, Nell,' and Nell said, 'No, I expect it wasn't.'

And then Jack was gone, not to the Front but to Shoeburyness. Frank was mystified – somehow or other Jack had got himself attached to the new dog training school down there and was going to become a handler in the Messenger Dog Service.

Jack didn't hear the guns any more. They were still there, he just didn't hear them. At night he lay in bed with Betsy at his feet and found the little dog's regular breathing made his own sleep easier to come by. Sleeping with the dogs was strictly against the rules, they were supposed to be confined to their kennels at night, but Jack found that the more careless he was about rules these days, the easier they were to break. Betsy was his favourite, a devoted little Welsh terrier that would have gone through the fires of Hell for him. He loved the other two as well, but not quite the same way he loved Betsy. Bruno was a German Shepherd, a big phlegmatic dog. Jack and Bruno understood each other, they both knew they were going to die and because of that they kept a mutual, respectful kind of distance between them. In some of his less lucid moments Jack found himself believing that the spirit of Malcolm Innes-Ward had come back in Bruno. Sometimes he sat on the ground outside the kennels at night with Bruno, in the same way that he sat with Innes-Ward, and had to stop himself from rolling up a cigarette and passing it to the big, polite dog.

His third dog was Pep, a little Jack Russell, who was the fastest and the best messenger dog of all.

Pep enjoyed his runs; the war was a game to him; he would shoot back with a message in the little canister round his neck, 'More ammo needed in such and such a trench' or whatever, and bounce and roll along with his little feet hardly touching the ground, skirting shell craters, leaping over obstacles, often doing whole somersaults and rolling up and back on his feet, heading straight for Jack's arms and leaping right up to shoulder height. Pep had been somebody's pet. Jack had seen the letter that came with him – 'We have let Daddy go and fight the Kaiser, now we are sending Pep to do his bit, love Flora.' A lot of the dogs had been pets. Jack had seen them coming into Shoeburyness by the van load after the initial appeal. Some of them came from the Dog Homes that were overflowing with unwanted dogs because of rationing. But some of them came straight from families. Jack wondered what those families would have thought if they could have seen the way the dogs were selected for training. He'd found it hard enough himself to stomach. The dogs were only fed once a day – they could all see the food being laid down for them but just before they were set free from their kennels, the handlers had to throw grenades into a pit nearby. Of course, the grenades made a terrifying racket and at first not a single dog would venture out for the food. By the third or fourth day, the dogs were starving and the bold ones, the ones that would eventually go to the Front, sneaked out along their own version of No Man's Land to the dishes and wolfed the food down as quickly as possible before dashing back to the shelter of the kennels. And the odd thing was that within only a matter of a few days these dogs were straining on their leashes to get out there as the first grenade was thrown.

The unsuitable dogs were sometimes sent back, the lucky ones back to the Dog Homes or their owners, but more often than not they were simply shot. Jack had sleepless nights thinking about some of these dogs – one little dog haunted him still, a gentle spaniel the colour of chestnuts called Jenny, petrified out of her wits by the grenades and eventually shot behind the parade ground. Even now, back at the Front, Jack could see the little dog's big, soft eyes turned to him in disbelief at what was happening to her. When he remembered Jenny, he'd reach down and feel Betsy's warm coat and in forgiveness she would roll over and push her wet nose into his hand.

Jack knew that Frank felt he'd betrayed him. The dogs were an easy number, the kennels were far enough behind the lines to be safe, at least a lot safer than the firing-trench, an opinion voiced frequently and vociferously by Frank to anyone who would listen. He often wondered how Jack had swung it until Jack told him it was Innes-Ward's brother who'd got him the job. 'You're a jammy bugger,' Frank said when he came upon Jack one time. Frank was in a support-trench but followed Jack up to the firing-trench where Jack was taking Bruno to help lay a telephone line. The dog had the reel of cable strapped to its back and trotted off, its ears up, its tail wagging, for all the world as if it was going for a daily run in the park. Part of the line stretched across a corner of No Man's Land and Jack lay flat on his belly across the parapet whistling encouragement to Bruno, all the while trying to ignore Frank, who wouldn't shut up. 'I'm going to die,' Frank was telling him over and over again. Frank was back from the dead and had to worry about dying all over again. His faith in the imminence of his death was unwavering now, 'I'm going to be blown to pieces while you and those bloody dogs are going to be all right. Then you'll go home and marry Nell and everything'll be grand for you and I'll be cold slime in the earth and you know why? Because you're a lucky bugger and I'm not.'

Jack was concentrating on the big dog as it accelerated the last few yards towards him.

'You'd be more worried if a sniper got that bloody dog than me,' Frank hissed as the heavy dog bounded over the parapet and Jack hugged it and said, 'Good lad, Bruno,' and gave it food from his pocket. Jack said nothing because there was nothing he could say, for it was true. Bruno meant more to him than Frank.

Frank continued to hover belligerently by his side, waiting for Jack to say something that would make him feel better. But the only thing that would make Frank feel better was knowing he wasn't going to die and there wasn't much Jack could do about that. He took the reel of cable off Bruno's back and put it in his haversack. Then he lifted the flap on his jacket pocket and took out something small and oddly shaped and put it into Frank's hand. For a second Frank thought it was a dog's paw until he looked at it and saw it was too small for a dog. 'Rabbit's foot,' Jack said, 'for luck,' and then he turned on his heel and said, 'Bruno,' and dog and man had walked up the trench and taken a right-angle before Frank could think of anything to say.

Jack thought a lot about what Frank said; part of him felt ashamed that he didn't care about anyone much any more, and another part felt set free by the certainty of death. The idea of going back home and marrying Nell, becoming a father, growing into an old man, was so absurd, so unlikely, that it made him laugh. He could see it – coming home from work, Nell rushing around in an apron putting tea on the table, digging an allotment in the summer evenings, taking his sons to a football match – he could see it all right, but it wasn't going to happen to him. It would have been no life with Nell anyway; he'd liked her at first because she was so soft – soft and quiet and gentle – but now that softness seemed like stupidity. If he thought about a woman now it was Lillian. Lillian had a bit more life about her – with her lovely slanting eyes, like a cat, and the feeling you got that secretly she was laughing at everything as if she knew what a piece of nonsense the world was. He thought about other people too, of course, lying awake in the darkness. He thought about Malcolm Innes-Ward and he thought about the little dog Jenny and the baffled look in her trusting eyes. But most of all he thought about Albert.

He thought about Albert and a hot day a long time ago when they'd been swimming in the Ouse. Albert flopped on his belly on the bank, glistening with the water like a fish and said, 'Frank and I taught each other to swim here, just at this spot,' and Jack sat up and looked at the skin on Albert's back that was more beautiful than any woman's. Albert laughed a muffled laugh because his face was buried in his arms. Jack said, 'What's funny?' as he looked at Albert's shoulder blades quivering with laughter. You could easily imagine that at any minute the little nubs of wings would push through the satin skin over his shoulder blades and Jack had to stop himself leaning over and stroking the bones where the wings would sprout and said again, 'What's funny?'

But Albert leapt up and dived back in the river and Jack never did discover what had made Albert laugh. Maybe it was just happiness. Albert had an extraordinary capacity for happiness. When they parted company, Albert to go up Park Grove Street, Jack to continue along Huntington Road, Albert shouted after him, 'We had a right good day, didn't we?' and afterwards, after Albert was dead, Jack realized that Albert collected good days the way other people collected coins, or sets of postcards.

Frank wasn't even surprised when he heard that Jack was dead. He heard the whole story from a mate of his who'd seen it happen. Pep, the little Jack Russell, had been sent back with a message from the front-line trench, saying they needed more magazines for the Lewis guns, and he'd gone at his usual hop, skip and a jump pace, little stumpy tail making his whole body wag, when he'd been caught right at the top of a bounding arc. He fell to the ground, his back leg splintered by shrapnel, making a horrible squealing noise and all the time trying to scrabble back to his feet and carry on running. Jack was shouting and yelling at Pep to try and get him back, but the poor little dog was too badly injured. By all accounts there was a real hail of bullets overhead, but Jack started crawling out to the dog, still calling encouragement to him all the time. Perhaps he was thinking of little Flora who'd sent her pet to do his bit. He hadn't reached Pep before a hand grenade went off behind him, ripping him to pieces, while the dog howled frantically. Mercifully, one of the British snipers managed to hit the little dog. That sniper was Georgy Mason who told Frank the story and he said that if that dog had howled for one more minute he would have put the bullet through his own brain.

Frank didn't know what happened to Bruno, but Betsy was a sad case, she wouldn't work with any other handler and for a while kept running up to the front-line and back to the kennels racing around looking for Jack. Then after a while she just slunk about, or lay on the ground moping so that everyone tripped over her and cursed her. Eventually a lieutenant took her out and shot her because no-one could bear to look into her sad eyes any more.

Frank led a charmed life once he had the rabbit's foot

and had no more trouble with death until 1942. He came home after the Armistice and married Nell who had already put away her little pearl and garnet ring alongside Percy's sapphire chips and never really looked at them again until she took them out nearly thirty years later to give to the twins, Daisy and Rose, for their christening presents.

The wedding was a small church one. Nell wore lilac and Lillian wore grey and Frank was reminded of pale, fluttering moths when he saw them together in their pearl-buttoned gloves and big hats with floating veils. He wished he could marry both of them, not because he loved Lillian (she was too clever, too mocking), but just so he could keep her safe as well. It seemed important to try and keep everyone who was left safe. When he and Nell leant out of the railway carriage window that was steaming them away on their honeymoon (they went to the Lakes, neither of them could face Scarborough somehow) Frank looked at the little wedding-party standing on the platform waving them off (Rachel, Lillian, Tom and Mabel and Percy Sievewright's mother) and thought he saw his old friend death hovering in the background and was sure for some reason that he'd come for Lillian. Later, of course, he realized it was for Rachel, who dropped dead just as the train had rounded the bend in the track.

Frank seemed to put the Great War behind him pretty well. He was determined to lead the most undramatic and ordinary life possible where the only problems would be from a teething child or greenfly on the floribunda rose he fancied growing by the front door of the house in Lowther Street. Memories of the war had no place amidst this kind of domestic harmony. There was a moment though, one day not long after Barbara, his first daughter, was born, when Nell had sent him looking for a pin and, rummaging through a drawer in the dresser, he came across the photograph of the football team. He felt a shiver like iced water going down his spine because when he looked at each member of the team in turn he realized that out of the whole lot there was only one still alive, and that was him. He looked at Percy and almost laughed – it had seemed so tragic when Percy died and now death seemed such a commonplace. Frank threw the photograph away, tearing it into little pieces first, because he knew that every time he looked at the faces of Albert and Jack he would be reminded that they should be alive, not him. When he came back downstairs again and Nell discovered he had forgotten all about the pin, she was irritated with him but tried not to let him see. Finding and keeping a husband had been a fraught business and she didn't want to have to go through it again.

Frank and Nell had five children altogether – Clifford, Babs, Bunty, Betty and Ted. When Clifford was born he already had a cousin. Lillian's son, Edmund, was born in the spring of 1917. Lillian wouldn't say who the father was, even when Rachel tried, unsuccessfully, to throw her out of the house. For a while Nell feared the baby would be born with thick, black hair and cheekbones like razor-clams. That would have been bad enough, but it seemed so much worse somehow when he turned out to have golden curls like an angel and eyes the colour of forget-me-nots.

CHAPTER THREE

1953

Coronation

IN HER BIG, WHITE DRESS THE QUEEN LOOKS LIKE A BALLOON that's about to float up to the roof of Westminster Abbey and bob about up there amongst the gilded arches and roof bosses. To prevent this happening people keep weighing her down with cloaks and robes, orbs and sceptres, until she's so heavy that bishops and archbishops have to help propel her around. She reminds me of the wind-up Chinese doll that Uncle Ted has brought Patricia back from Hong Kong – both glide over the carpet without revealing their feet and wear an expression of grave serenity. The difference between them is that the wind-up doll doesn't have any feet, just little castors, while we must suppose the brand-new Queen's feet really are her means of locomotion across the deep, crimson pile of the carpet. The colour of the Coronation carpet is also a supposition, of course, as the Coronation is taking place, in miniature, in various shades of grey on the little Ferguson set in the corner of the living-room Above the Shop.

The television set is George's gift to Bunty, a consolation for having to bring up her family Above the Shop instead of a normal home. We cannot claim to have the first television set in the street, that honour must go to Miss Portello of Hapland, the children's clothes shop. But we are the runners-up and, more importantly, the winners in the family, for no-one on either George or Bunty's side of the family have yet acquired this most desirable of objects.

Bunty is torn two ways – she is naturally proud of the television set and must show it off, and what better occasion than a coronation? At the same time she can't stand having all these people in the house. The sandwiches! The pots of tea! Will it ever stop? She is buttering scones in the kitchen, heaping up a great pile of them like cobblestones. She's been saving her butter ration for weeks for the Coronation baking, storing it in the fridge, along with what she's managed to prise out of her mother, Nell, and her sister-in-law Auntie Gladys. She has baked an exotic array of goods, for 'The good cook knows that nothing will repay her skill so well as attractive cakes, whether nut brown from the oven or daintily decorated,' – this according to Bunty's Bible, *Perfect Cooking*, the 'Parkinson Gas Stove Cook Book'.

As well as the scones, she has also produced plates of ham sandwiches (ham courtesy of Walter, the philandering butcher), 'Coconut Madeleines', 'Lamingtons' and 'Little Caramel Pastries' (*Very Special!*), not to mention 'Piccaninnies' (*from Australia*) and 'Dago Cakes' – these last two presumably in honour of all our little Commonwealth friends. They all have the slightly rancid aftertaste of butter that has been stored for too long in Bunty's brand new Frigidaire (*Nothing smaller is big enough!*), another consolation prize from George. She has also made sausage rolls and Auntie Gladys has brought an enormous pork-pie and Auntie Babs has brought two fruit flans – big cartwheels, one of overlapping tinned peaches and maraschino cherries, the other of tinned Bartlett pears and grapes. These arouse much excitement and envy. Bunty thinks her sister hasn't got enough to do if she can spend time making such perfect, flawless circles. She should try having as many children as Bunty has, Bunty thinks, adding one last scone to the pile. Bunty has so many children she doesn't know what to do.

'It's like the Black Hole of Calcutta up there,' she says to George as he passes through the kitchen, looking for more brown ale. 'And there are too many children,' she adds, as if there were a quota for such events.

There *are* rather a lot of us. I'm one of them, weaving myself in and out of grown-up legs like a dog at an agility trial. Here there and everywhere, I don't know how I move so fast – one moment I'm standing by the television set, the next I'm hurtling through the passage to the kitchen. If you blinked you'd almost think there were two of me. Perhaps I'm on castors like the Chinese doll – but then I'm very advanced for my age. People are always eyeing me doubtfully and saying to Bunty, 'She's very advanced for her age, isn't she?' 'Too clever for her own good, that one,' Bunty confirms.

Our own Coronation guest list is not as long as the Queen's. For a start we have no Commonwealth friends to invite, although Auntie Eliza is reputed to be friendly with a couple from Jamaica – one of the many taboo subjects drawn up on a separate list by George (Auntie Eliza is George's sister-in-law, married to his brother Bill). We are also, amongst other things, forbidden to talk about Auntie Mabel's operation, Uncle Tom's hand and Adrian's weediness. Uncle Tom isn't our uncle, he's Bunty's and Auntie Babs' uncle, and has been invited here today because he has nowhere else to go – Auntie Mabel is in hospital having her unmentionable operation. (Uncle Tom's hand is a wooden replica of the one that was blown off long ago.) Adrian is our cousin – Uncle Clifford and Auntie Gladys' only son – and we're not sure if he's weedy or not as we know no other ten-year-old boys to measure him against. He has brought his boxer-dog, Dandy, with him and I think the size of Dandy's tightly-bunched testicles sticking out from behind his back legs is also a forbidden subject. Dandy is just the right height to knock me over, which he does regularly, causing much hilarity for Gillian and Lucy-Vida.

Lucy-Vida is our cousin, Auntie Eliza and Uncle Bill's daughter (Bunty would much rather she didn't have to invite this side of the family). Auntie Babs has also brought her husband, Uncle Sidney, with her, a mild, cheerful man who we hardly ever see. The Coronation audience are constantly dividing and re-dividing into different parties and factions, the most common of which is that age-old favourite – men and women. Everyone is related in some way (unfortunately) to each other except for Dandy the Dog and Mrs Havis, Nell's next-door neighbour who has no family (imagine!) of her own.

Gillian is in her element – a ready-made, captive audience ensconced in the living-room. Her only rival is the television set itself so she spends a lot of time trying to obliterate it by dancing in front of it and showing her knickers under her white, smock-bodice frock that is all petticoats and flounces and has come straight out of the window of Hapland. Our cousin, Lucy-Vida, she of the string-hair and long stick-legs, treats Gillian like a pet and whenever she gets too annoying for the grown-ups says things like, 'Come here, our kid,' in her thick Doncaster accent. Lucy-Vida is Gillian's heroine because she goes to dancing-class. She has magic feet that just *cannot stop* tapping so that her presence is constantly signalled like that of a little blind girl.

There is a sigh of discontent from the majority of the living-room audience (not from Uncle Ted who has a fondness for little girls, especially when they show their knickers) as Gillian breaks into 'The Good Ship Lollipop' (hard to believe, but true. She gives a new meaning to the word 'cute'). She is the only one in my generation to have inherited the cherub gene – like Ada and Albert before her she has a headful of bubbling blond curls. She does not yet know that the price exacted for this unearthly splendour is, generally speaking, an untimely death. Poor Gillian!

Lucy-Vida is rewarded with a toffee for ushering Gillian away and teaching her the five basic ballet positions out in the hall. Meanwhile, back at the television set, the young Queen is being 'Girded with the Sword' and Patricia is helpfully supplementing Richard Dimbleby's reverent commentary with snippets from the *Daily Graphic Coronation Gift Book for Boys and Girls*. We learn that it 'signifies an act of beautiful symbolism, the power of the State placed at the service of God.' Her squeaky voice stumbles over the word 'symbolism' – she is only seven years old after all, although top of the class in Reading and generally regarded as quite precocious in her learning – but she picks herself up and tells us that 'the Jewelled Sword' was made for George IV's coronation, thus precipitating an argument amongst one section of the grown-ups about George IV's position in the chronological order of kings – clearly he came after Georges I, II and III, but did anybody come before him? Someone proposes Queen Anne as the bolster between Georges Three and Four, but then a fresh argument brews up as to who exactly George IV *was* 'when he was at home' anyway. Uncle Bill claims he was 'the fat git that built Brighton', while Uncle Clifford staunchly maintains that he was 'the one that lost America'. (They should ask the house ghosts, for whom it's all just like yesterday.)

Patricia is brought in to adjudicate – rather a heavy burden for a child of her tender years, I fear – but she is an ardent Royalist and has already committed half of the entire royal family tree to memory, starting with

Egbert (827-39). Unfortunately, she has only reached Edward II and cannot help in the matter of the mysterious Georges.

Other members of the party (Nell, Mrs Havis and Auntie Gladys) are already launched on the remaining Georges (V and VI) and an orgy of nostalgia is occasioned by the appearance of Bunty's *George V – Seventy Glorious Years* book and the discovery that Patricia's *Daily Graphic Book*, having of necessity been published before today's Coronation, is actually full of pictures of George VI's coronation, 'The old king,' as everyone fondly calls him as if England is one big fairy-tale country full of goose-girls and wicked queens and 'old kings' who suck on pipes and wear slippers embroidered with golden crowns.

The Georges I to IV contingent are also the Brown Ale contingent – a conspiracy of husbands on the Watneys composed of Uncle Sidney, Uncle Clifford, Uncle Bill and George, and a token bachelor, Uncle Ted.

Coronation memorabilia begins to pour out of every nook and cranny now – my father's Edward VIII Coronation jug, an item commemorating an event that never took place thus giving it a curious philosophical value, not to mention Ena Tetley's George VI Coronation teaspoon, now in Bunty's possession and which is, of course – technically speaking – stolen property (see *Footnote (iii)*).

Patricia, being a school-age child, has the biggest and best trawl of loot and is hauled onto centre-stage to shyly but proudly display her 1) Coronation mug, 2) Coronation coins in a plastic wallet, 3) Coronation medal (identical to the one the new queen will pin to Prince Charles's little chest later in the day), 4) Coronation toffees in a splendid purple and silver tin, 5) the aforesaid *Daily Graphic Coronation Gift Book for Boys and Girls* and, last but by no means least, 6) a Union Jack flag. For patriotic reasons, she is dressed in her school uniform – brown and yellow gingham dress, a brown blazer and a brown beret. Like Gillian in her Coronation-white, I am also in my best frock for the event – a lemon taffeta with Peter Pan collar and short puffed sleeves. Lucy-Vida is dressed in one of Auntie Gladys' weird home-made creations. Whenever Lucy-Vida visits from the wilds of South Yorkshire she appears to be on her way to a fancy-dress party. Auntie Eliza's flying needle stitches her one and only into a vast array of net and tulle, frills and furbelows so that on the stalks of her thin legs Lucy-Vida looks like an exotic flower blown wildly off course.

We are all familiar with the fact that Auntie Eliza is 'common', about as common as you can get, according to Bunty. We know this has something to do with the fact that her blond hair has coal-black roots and she is wearing immense rhinestone earrings and we suspect it also has to do with the fact that – even on Coronation Day – she is not wearing stockings and her legs are dimpled and mottled and brazenly display their blue-cheese veins. (Not to mention the fact that she is welcomed into the Georges I-to-IV faction where her raucous laughter spills over the men and reconciles them to the existence of women.) Auntie Eliza's hands seem to be permanently occupied with drinks and cigarettes and if she ever does have a spare one it's usually to be found grabbing any passing child so that she can deposit a wet and sloppy kiss on its cheek – unusual behaviour in our family, to say the least.

Auntie Eliza has brought all the little girls a present – home-made, crêpe-paper flower coronets, just like the ones that the Queen's Maids-of-Honour are wearing. She even leads us in a little Coronation ceremony of our own, with us all lined up on the stairs where she fixes them to our heads with uncomfortable kirby grips. I am strangely moved by this event and the pain of having our scalps lacerated by the grips is lessened by Auntie Eliza's contribution to the festivities – a sticky paper bag of Barker and Dobson's Fruit Drops. Poor Adrian looks on glumly, one cheek bulging with a Fruit Drop, unhappy about being exiled from our paper-flower kingdom on account of his sex. 'Never mind, kid,' Lucy-Vida says solicitously. 'I'll teach you the splits if you like,' and Adrian cheers up considerably.

On the whole we rather like Auntie Eliza – even the sober Patricia will sit on Auntie Eliza's knee and confide some of her less important secrets (her favourite school lesson, her favourite school dinner, what she wants to be when she grows up – answers: maths, none, a vet).

Daisy and Rose play little part in anything – small and perfect, they are a self-contained world. They are dressed identically, they finish each other's sentences (when they condescend to speak, that is, for they have their own private, secret language), and they look at you with the kind of cool, level gaze that would get them bit-parts in *Invaders from Mars*. Adrian is too young for the Brown Ale group but not particularly welcomed by the mainly female coterie who worship the 'old King' and who've now been joined by Auntie Babs and are embarked on a lively homage to the Queen Mother ('the old queen', you would suppose, but nobody calls her that). 'The Queen Mother' – it's an interesting phrase, isn't it? The Queen of the Mothers, the Mother of all Queens. Bunty would like to be a Queen Mother. 'Queen Bunty, the Queen Mother.' Then I would be Princess Ruby, which is rather lovely, isn't it? Certainly a lot livelier than Princess Gillian or Princess Lucy-Vida.

The Queen Mothers are on sherry, brown and treacly lethal cough mixture. Auntie Babs takes one downstairs to Bunty who is brushing a tray of sausage rolls with milk. 'Oh, I thought *I'd* been forgotten about,' Bunty says archly, taking the sherry and sipping it delicately. 'You're missing the Coronation,' Auntie Babs tells her, and Bunty gives her one of her best looks, the one that says, 'And who else is going to skivvy around doing all the work?' without her ever needing to even move her lips.

'It's the anointing with holy oil!' Patricia's voice squeals excitedly from upstairs, and Auntie Babs manages to persuade Bunty to leave the sausage rolls unanointed and come upstairs for what is, in the *Daily Graphic*'s words, 'really the most solemn and important part of the ceremony'. So solemn and important that the Queen disappears inside a scrum of bishops, and her anointing is not witnessed Above the Shop.

'That's a lovely television set,' Auntie Gladys says appreciatively to Bunty when Babs leads her back into the room and Bunty glows a little and simpers, 'Thank you,' as though she had been a handmaiden to Logie Baird in another life.

'Nice bit of walnut veneer,' Uncle Tom says and everyone murmurs in agreement. 'That's a grand dress you're wearing, Bunty,' Uncle Bill says suddenly, and Bunty flinches slightly because she doesn't like Bill (an antipathy based entirely on the fact that he's George's brother) and if her brother-in-law thinks it's a 'grand dress' – a man with no taste whatsoever (this much is true) – then Bunty thinks there must be something far wrong with it. It *is* a ghastly creation actually – a peculiar thing, knitted in stripes of brown and yellow with a faint lurex thread running through so that she looks like a party-going wasp.

'Now comes the moment for which all the peoples of Britain, the Commonwealth and Empire have been waiting,' Patricia reads.

'The Supreme Moment,' Uncle Ted says peering over her shoulder. His hand rests lightly on the back of her school blazer in a way that you might say was avuncular, but on the other hand, you might say was not. Anyway, he's chosen the wrong person because Patricia can't stand being touched and she succeeds in wriggling free very quickly.

Gillian bounces back into the room at this moment, desperate to show everyone her pirouettes, and flashes in front of the Ferguson just as the crown is being perched on the Queen's head so that a resounding shout goes up of, 'God Save the Queen!' and 'Get out of the bloody way, Gillian!' Her lip pouts and trembles, her angel curls quiver with distress and Lucy-Vida stretches out a maternal hand and says, 'Come along, pet – you come with me,' and they both flounce off to do important things with their dolls. Neither Patricia nor I have a doll. Patricia doesn't want one, although she often borrows Gillian's to play schools with. Patricia plays schools a lot and she is a very strict teacher, believe me – I know because I have to stand in for a doll occasionally.

I have to admit, I would quite like a doll, even if they do all seem to have hard, sculpted plastic hair and unkind expressions. Gillian's dolls have names like 'Jemima' and 'Arabella'. Patricia has her panda ('Panda' – no fancy nomenclature for our Patricia) to which she's very attached, and I have a teddy bear ('Teddy') that is closer to me than a relative. I already have an astonishingly mature vocabulary list of ten words: Teddy is on my list of vocabulary, along with: Mummy, Daddy, Pash (Patricia), Gug (Gillian), Gamma (Nell), Bye-bye, Shop!, Dotty (an all-purpose word that covers everything else) and – the most important word of all – Mobo.

Instinctively, I know where Mobo is at the moment – in the Back Yard. Bunty is in the kitchen again, putting the sausage rolls in the oven, and when Teddy and I totter towards the back door, she obligingly lets us out. I take a deep breath and – there he is! The light of my world! The Mobo horse is perhaps the most handsome creature ever manufactured by man. All of five-and-a-half hands to his withers, he is made from dappled grey and white tin, with a permanently scrolled mane and plumed tail. His eyes are friendly, his back is firm and he has a scarlet saddle, scarlet reins and scarlet pedals (also of tin). In the sunshine of the Back Yard (we are having much better weather than the poor Queen) he looks magnificent, you can almost see his nostrils flaring and his hoof about to paw the ground. Patricia, in her kindness and Coronation zeal, has decked him out with tartan ribbons and he looks as splendid as any horse that has trotted up the Mall that day.

He was bought for Gillian (that was *her* consolation for having to put up with me), but Gillian is now too big for him and I am his official rider. This makes no difference whatsoever to Gillian who guards him fiercely and never allows me anywhere near him unless forced to. But Gillian is inside with Lucy-Vida and here is my steed, roaming in the Back Yard, unguarded, unfettered and for a brief moment in space and time – all mine!

By a continuous and relentless incantation of 'Dotty-dottydottydottydottydottydottydottyMobo!' I force Bunty into helping me mount my heart's desire and happily ride off at a canter around the Back Yard. Well, not strictly speaking, a canter exactly. Mobo's means of locomotion are his pedals. When you sit on him, you press down hard with your feet and he moves along in a jerky, awkward fashion. I pump and pedal and lurch and pretend I'm pulling a golden coach for at least ten minutes before our nemesis appears.

A cold wind suddenly blows as the kitchen door is flung open dramatically and a dark shadow falls across the yard. The shadow is not merely dark, it contains the squid-inky evil of hatred, jealousy and murderous inclinations – yes, it's our Gillian! She comes barrelling across the yard like a waddling torpedo, securely locked onto her target, accelerating all the while so that when she finally reaches the Mobo she can't stop but continues – knocking him and me over and somersaulting over his back and landing on her frilly-knickered bottom on the hard paving slabs. The Mobo is sent skidding across the back yard, deep, unsightly scratches scored along his metal flanks. He lies panting on his side while I lie still looking up at the June sky and wondering if I'm dead. There is a throbbing bruise on the back of my skull but I'm too shocked to cry.

Not so our Gillian, who is screaming loud enough to wake the dead and even brings Bunty out to see what the matter is. Gillian's grief-stricken response almost elicits sympathy from Bunty. 'You should be more careful,' she tells her – which may not sound very sympathetic, but it's about the nearest she can get. Lucy-Vida buzzes around, executing a mournful tap – tap-tap-TAP, tap-tap-TAP, and helps Gillian to her feet, lamenting all the while about the state of her frock – smears of Coronation-red blood have indeed sullied Gillian's pristine whiteness and her torn and tattered coronet is round her neck like a flowery noose. 'Ee, poor kid,' Lucy-Vida sympathizes in her lush tones. 'Come with me, we'll get you cleaned up,' and off they go, hand in hand, while Mobo and I are left to the ministrations of Dandy who licks and cleans us up as best he can with his hot, slobbery dog's breath that smells vaguely of stolen sausage-rolls.

The rest of the day is a bit of a blur – I suspect I have concussion. Certainly when I next remember wandering back into the living-room it's to meet a scene of genteel debauchery. The Brown Ale crowd are clearly drunk and playing poker in a corner of the room. Above their heads, Patricia's Union Jack has migrated to the picture-rail where it droops over our framed Polyphotos, thirty-six tiny black and white photographs in each frame – thirty-six of Patricia, thirty-six of Gillian and, for some reason, seventy-two of me, so that it seems that Bunty does indeed have too many children, hundreds of miniature little girls all spitefully gobbling her up.

The Queen Mother clique has been joined by Uncle Tom and they are all wearing paper hats that they've produced from heaven knows where and are reminiscing about VE Day and street parties and Auntie Betty who is so far away across the Atlantic and reminds us of her existence by still sending us food parcels. The Queen Mother clique is also well acquainted with the sherry bottle by now and Bunty's hostess duties have led her to wear a pirate hat and orchestrate a game of 'I-Spy' which has its participants gripped in hysteria. Adrian and Dandy are in the Back Yard playing throw and fetch, although who is doing what isn't always entirely clear. Uncle Ted is upstairs with Lucy-Vida and Gillian playing a game called, 'Surprise!' The alcohol level Above the Shop is reaching critical levels and I'm quite relieved when Bunty looks at me, clasps her hand to her mouth in horror and says, 'They're not in bed yet!'

However, I fear our mother has drunk too deep of the sherry barrel to do anything about this; her pirate hat is already tilted rakishly over one eye and she is having to use the support of Auntie Gladys' broad back to stop her from sliding off the arm of the sofa.

Auntie Eliza clucks like a grown-up version of Lucy-Vida and, abandoning the 'I-Spy' ('I spy with my little eye something beginning with "T S"', answer – you've guessed – Television Set) gathers up children like a sheepdog and herds them up the stairs to bed. Auntie Eliza's bedtime routine is more slovenly than Bunty's. With Bunty, we have to line up in regimental fashion in the bathroom and scrub and brush and scrape until we're almost rubbed away but a quick wipe with a flannel over the grubbier bits seems to be all that is expected by Auntie Eliza before we're packed off to our light, summery bedrooms. Lucy-Vida and Gillian share a bed, top-to-toe like sardines. The twins have landed up in George and Bunty's bed – heaven only knows what Bunty will think about *that* when she abandons the gun-deck of her pirate sloop and staggers up to bed. Adrian is bedded down in a kennel somewhere with Dandy. It seems the whole world is going to stay over and sleep in the Shop tonight. Nobody volunteers to share Patricia's bedroom – even at seven, her lust for privacy is monumental and off-putting. Perhaps she roosts upside down, like a bat, her panda clinging on underneath one wing.

Hours later I wake suddenly, sit bolt upright in bed, and remember that Teddy is down in the Back Yard somewhere, carelessly abandoned in the wake of the equine disaster.

My bedroom looks over the Back Yard, so I go to the window to see if I can spot him. The sky is a magical dark blue colour, full of stars that look like Auntie Eliza's earrings, and (considering how late it is) the yard is surprisingly full of life. Mobo remains on his side, perhaps he's asleep – I hope so, although Patricia's coronet placed at his head looks suspiciously like a wreath. Teddy is in the bed of marigolds that runs along one wall, his arms and legs spreadeagled like a dead soldier. Standing guard over him is Dandy, whose black eyes glisten in the dark. Leaning awkwardly against the back gate is George, locked in a thrusting embrace with an unseen woman, his trousers unbecomingly around his ankles. One bare, unstockinged leg pokes out from behind him and in a hoarse giggle a voice says, 'Come on, pet, that's the way.' I suppose I must leave Teddy in this dubious company and rescue his dew-spangled body in the morning.

There is a tap-tap-tapping noise coming from Gillian's bedroom. Perhaps Lucy-Vida sleep-taps.

Patricia is sitting up in her narrow little bed and reading by the light of her Bambi-and-Thumper nightlight. She has reached the final chapter, Chapter VII of the *Daily Graphic Coronation Gift Book for Boys and Girls*, the one entitled 'The New Elizabethan Age'. This chapter outlines the duties of all the boys and girls who 'will be the grown-up citizens of a new Elizabethan age' in a country which is 'still the leader of western civilization'. The exhortations of this chapter do not fall on stony ground. Patricia will join the Brownies and attempt to win every badge possible before graduating to the Girl Guides; she will go to Sunday School; she will work hard at school (despite this relentless group activity she will remain strangely friendless). And she will stick by her principles. The *Daily Graphic*'s blueprint for the future cannot, however, help Patricia with the twin strands of alienation and dejection which form her personal DNA, but its text is stirring, its exhortations noble –

'You will have to grow up and when you have left childhood behind you must behave as a responsible man or woman. This may sound rather frightening, but you know as well as I do that although as a nation we have sometimes made mistakes we have never lacked courage.'

How proud we all are on this day! How we look forward to our magical journey into the future as citizens of a brave new world. Patricia falls asleep, royal benedictions on her lips. 'God bless the Queen,' she murmurs, 'and God bless all the peoples of the United Kingdom,' and an echoing murmur from the household ghosts vibrates on the evening air. They are celebrating in their own ghostly way, by the light of sooty flambeaux and greasy candelabra. They are dancing spectral minuets and gavottes – the 'York Maggot' and 'Mrs Cartwright's Delight', learned perhaps from Mr Rochefort, the dancing master in rooms over the Sycamore Tree. They have seen much happen within these ancient city walls, sieges and air-raids, fires and massacres, the rise and fall of empires. They have witnessed the coronation of the Roman Emperor Constantine a stone's throw away and the degradation of the great Railway King, George Hudson. They have seen poor Richard of York's head spiked on the city gates and the valiant Royalists besieged within them. Yet still they summon the strength to join Patricia in one last ragged, yet valiant, cheer – glasses are raised in a toast, horns are blown and the great eagle of the Ninth is held aloft. *God bless us all!*

Footnote (iii) – Business as Usual

THE SECOND WORLD WAR FOR BUNTY WAS NOT SO MUCH a matter of getting a husband as a personality.

At the outbreak of war Bunty was working in a shop called 'Modelia – Ladies' Quality Fashions'. She'd been there ever since leaving school two years before and quite liked the unchallenging nature of each day, although she daydreamed furiously about all the exciting things that were going to happen to her in the future – like the charming, unbelievably handsome man who would appear from nowhere and sweep her away to a life of cocktails, cruises and fur coats.

Modelia was owned by Mr Simon but it was run by Mrs Carter. Mr Simon called Mrs Carter his 'manageress' and Bunty's father said he'd never heard it called *that* before. Bunty wasn't entirely sure what he meant by this, although there was no doubt that there was something slightly racy about her employers – Mr Simon was foreign for a start, Hungarian even, although when the war broke out he became very vocal about his British nationality. He was short and had a shiny bald head and was always immaculately dressed, with a big, gold fob-watch looped across his waistcoat. 'He's a Jewboy, isn't he?' Clifford, Bunty's brother, asked when Bunty first got the job and Frank nodded and rubbed his thumb against his fingers.

Bunty couldn't stand Clifford or his opinions. He was a cocky little so-and-so, Bunty and Betty agreed behind his back. 'Jewboy' was an odd word that didn't really suit Mr Simon at all – he was never mean and he certainly wasn't a boy and, if anything, reminded Bunty of a well-dressed seal.

He adored Mrs Carter, or Dolly, as he called her when there were no customers in the shop, and the amount of hand-kissing and eye-gazing that went on made Bunty feel quite uncomfortable sometimes. She couldn't recall ever having seen her own mother and father do more than exchange a slight peck on the cheek. Clifford said that Mr Simon had a wife 'locked up in the nut-house', and that was why he didn't marry Mrs Carter, although there was more 'how's-your-father' went on in Mrs Carter's flat above the shop (according to Clifford) than happened next door, where newly-weds Maurice and Ena Tetley could be heard exercising their bed-springs through the wall of the bedroom that Bunty shared with Betty. Bunty and Betty had many a late-night whispered discussion about what exactly Maurice could be doing to Ena to produce such a noise.

Bunty liked both Mr Simon and Mrs Carter, especially Mrs Carter who was a large woman about the same age as Bunty's mother but without the drab patina that Nell had acquired over the years. Mrs Carter was blonde – very blonde – and wore her hair in big rolls and laid her make-up on 'with a trowel' according to Frank. She also possessed a huge bosom that looked as though it would burst if it was pricked with a pin. She was a real mother-hen to Bunty, though, cluck-clucking around after her and saying things like, 'How's our little Bunty, today?' and giving her discreet hints about her appearance so that Bunty no longer wore ankle socks, flat shoes, and the bob that she'd had from the age of five to fifteen, but was quite the thing nowadays in heels and stockings and even lipstick. 'Our young lady,' Mr Simon said approvingly when Mrs Carter made Bunty do a twirl for him in her first grown-up frock.

Nell wasn't a great one for compliments, she didn't like people getting above themselves. Nell had adopted the philosophy that, generally speaking, things tended always to get worse, rather than better. This pessimistic outlook was a source of considerable comfort to her – after all, unhappiness could be relied upon in a way that happiness never could. Nell preferred the extremities of her family – the eldest and youngest, Clifford and Ted – Ted in particular, which was strange, Bunty and Betty agreed, because he was the most obnoxious little weasel that ever lived. Babs had managed to gain a little prestige within the family from being the eldest girl and from being a no-nonsense, practical sort and Betty had found a place as Frank's baby, but poor Bunty was stuck right in the middle with nothing to mark her out as special.

* * *

'Where's our little Bunty, then?'

'I'm in the back, Mr Simon, brewing up. One for you?'

'Yes please, dear!'

Bunty was currently trying out a personality based on Deanna Durbin, which involved adopting a sweet and kind-but-plucky sort of persona. It went down very well with Mrs Carter and Mr Simon but was totally overlooked at home.

'I've got my sugar through here, Bunty!' Mrs Carter's ladylike tones cracked into indecorous Yorkshire when she tried to shout.

'Rightio!' Bunty yelled back.

The shop was deserted. It was a Sunday and Bunty had offered to come in and help with the stocktaking. They sat round the wireless with their cups and saucers on their laps, listening to a programme called 'How to Make the Most of Tinned Food' while they waited for the Prime Minister to make his 'statement of national importance'. When Mr Chamberlain said *I have to tell you that no such undertaking has been received and consequently this country is at war with Germany* a little shiver ran down the back of Bunty's neck. Mrs Carter sniffed noisily; she had lost a husband in the Great War and her son, Dick, was just the right age to be killed in this one.

'Well, so,' Mr Simon said, raising his cup and giving a little cough, 'I think we should have a little toast.'

'A toast?' Mrs Carter repeated dubiously.

'Yes – to the fighting bulldog spirit. Britons never

shall be slaves and good riddance to Mr Adolf Hitler!'

'Hear, hear!' Mrs Carter and Bunty chorused – Bunty the more enthusiastic of the two – raising their tea-cups. 'Rule Britannia!' Bunty added in a very plucky way.

Bunty had great hopes for the war; there was something attractive about the way it took away certainty and created new possibilities. Betty said it was like tossing coins in the air and wondering where they would land – and it made it much more likely that something exciting would happen to Bunty and it didn't really matter whether it was the unbelievably handsome man or a bomb – it would all mean a change in one way or another.

Clifford was called up and Frank went round the house saluting him and calling him 'Trooper Cook' and seemed to have quite forgotten how unpleasant a war could be. Clifford was very smug about it all. Sidney, Babs' fiancé, got his call-up papers at the same time as Clifford and the wedding was arranged with what would have looked like indecent haste before the war.

When the bridal couple came out of the church Mrs Carter and Mr Simon were among the well-wishers on the steps and Mrs Carter handed Babs a little sprig of white heather which she took with a look of slight distaste and Bunty heard Clifford say 'What's that blowsy tart doing here?' and Bunty went hot and cold and looked at Mr Simon to see if he'd heard; but he kept smiling benignly at everyone and when he spotted Bunty he gave her a little wave.

The reception took place in the same church hall that

Mrs Sievewright had chosen for Percy's funeral-tea and consisted mainly of all the men getting very drunk on a syrupy milk stout that was definitely from under someone's counter but nobody seemed to know whose. 'Mum's the word,' the normally quiet and sober Sidney said, before downing a pint in one, to shrieks of encouragement from the wedding guests. Babs was furious. 'You've got to indulge us,' Frank laughed, leaning heavily on Sidney for support, although Sidney was so drunk that it was a miracle that he was still vertical.

'Why?' Babs snapped in her best matronly manner. Babs was only eighteen but had some very old ways.

'Because,' Frank said darkly, 'we're all going to die.'

'You're not, you silly old fool,' Babs hissed at him and Bunty thought that if she'd said that to her father, he'd have slapped her face. Sandy Havis from next door came up and tried to whirl Babs off in a dance but she stalked away, saying, 'Dance with Bunty instead, I've got better things to do,' and headed off in the direction of Clifford in a vain attempt to get him to impose sobriety on the gathering.

'What about it then, Bunty?' Bunty liked Sandy Havis; when she was little he used to push her around in her pram and he had such an open, cheerful manner about him that he endeared himself to most people. He wasn't at all handsome, quite the opposite – he had bulging thyrotoxic blue eyes and a ridiculous shock of sandy hair, hence his nickname – his real name was Eric. He launched Bunty on an energetic two-step – the music was provided by an old wind-up gramophone and a selection from Sidney's eclectic record collection. Sandy had always reminded Bunty of a nice dog – trustworthy, loyal and endearingly eager to please – so it was a bit disconcerting to be enveloped in the swamp of his beery breath and find him trying to nibble various bits of her and all at about sixty miles an hour around a makeshift dance floor.

When the record finished Bunty was sweating with exertion and was keen to get Sandy off the floor before the music got going again. Misinterpreting her prodding and pushing, he circled one arm very tightly around her waist and started moving the fingers of the other one up and down her ribs as if she was a piano. By the time she'd managed to push him into the corridor that ran the length of one side of the hall he was quite carried away with his rib-playing and kept saying, 'Can you recognize that tune, Bunty? Eh? Eh?'

'No Sandy, I can't,' Bunty said firmly, trying to twist away from his drumming fingers. He was surprisingly strong, Bunty remembered Sandy had been a champion swimmer at school. 'Go on, guess, go on,' he urged.

'"Putting on the Ritz"? "The Blue Danube"? "The Yellow Brick Road"?' Bunty hazarded at random. 'Yes! Yes! Yes!' Sandy shouted. Sandy was on leave from the Merchant Navy and, unbeknown to Bunty, had vowed that he was going to have a woman before he went back on his ship the next day, so he didn't have much time left. 'This is my sister's wedding,' Bunty said indignantly when Sandy put his tongue in her ear. 'This is a church hall,' she tried when he started investigating her groin with his knee. Finally, she bit him on the hand, very hard, so that he leapt back in astonishment and, shaking his hand as if to cool it down, he looked at her admiringly and declared, 'What a tiger!' Bunty rushed back into the heated mayhem of the reception, but his words lingered on in her mind. She rather liked the idea of being 'tigerish' and even practised a quiet growl to herself. Her personality shifted up several gears, from Deanna Durbin to Scarlett O'Hara.

Some time later, the remnants of the wedding-party retired to the house at Lowther Street. Bunty had surreptitiously drunk three half pints of stout by this time in an effort to join in the ambience of the occasion and was surprised to find herself – as if by magic – slicing bread in the kitchen. Two well-muscled arms suddenly slid round her waist. Bunty had been planning to flounce and pout the next time he tried anything on (in keeping with her new character), but when Sandy said, 'Hello, Bun, my little cream Bun,' and poked her in the back in case she hadn't got the joke, she started to giggle and Sandy said, 'God, Bunty – you're squiffy!' which made her laugh even more and it wasn't long before he'd persuaded her outside and was pushing her up against the back wall of the house. It was like being at the mercy of an octopus, he had hands everywhere and Bunty kept feebly incanting, 'This is wrong,' until Sandy, in a state of some desperation, said, 'I love you, Bunty, I've always loved you – we'll get married on my next leave,' and Bunty, instantly baffled into thinking this was true love (it happens all the time), let him have his wicked way, comforting herself with the fact that it might be her last gift to him before he died and taking her mind off it by gazing at the almost-dead clematis on the other side of the yard. 'What a woman!' Sandy said as he reached a rapid and rather undignified climax. Bunty felt absolutely disgusted by the whole process, particularly as he banged her head off the drainpipe in his excitement, but at least she had a better idea now of what Maurice Tetley was doing to the bed-springs ('Never!' a wide-eyed Betty said when Bunty told her).

1942 was the most eventful year of Bunty's war. She had left Modelia by now – Mrs Carter and Mr Simon gave her a very emotional farewell and said they didn't know what they'd do without their little Bunty. Mrs Carter gave her a pair of stockings and some lavender cologne and Mr Simon gave her five pounds and a hug which made her blush. They weren't in a very good state with themselves – rationing had meant a drop in business and Mrs Carter's son had been posted as officially missing.

Like Babs, who was stuffing explosive into shell-cases on the Rowntree's floor that had previously produced unlethal fruit gums, Bunty had also moved into war work. Her new job was in a technical instruments factory; before the war they'd made things like microscopes but now they were making things like gun sights. Bunty's job was to check the focus once everything was assembled, and in the beginning she used to pretend she was shooting Germans, *bang bang bang*, but after a while the novelty wore off and she had to struggle to stop herself going cross-eyed by the end of the day.

By the beginning of 1942 Bunty was pretty much fed up with the war. She was sick of Dr Carrot and Potato Pete and Mrs Sew-and-Sew, and would have given anything for a big box of chocolates and a new winter coat and if she met the Squander Bug in the street she was personally prepared to take him round every shop in York. She really wasn't in the spirit of things at all.

There wasn't any romance in the air either. Sandy Havis came home on leave in the February. Bunty had remained faithful to their plighted troth only because there hadn't been anyone else who was interested in her. She saw him come home, duffle-bag slung across his shoulder, whistling in a very jaunty fashion as he pushed open the door of the Havises' back yard, and had to duck down beneath the bedroom window-sill in case he saw her. He looked even uglier than he had done the last time she saw him and it made her flesh crawl to think what she'd let him do at Babs' wedding.

Sandy, who was ploughing the great, grey Atlantic on the convoys, was very put out at Bunty's distant demeanour. Like Frank before him, Sandy was convinced his chances of survival were slim. Unlike Frank, he was right and three weeks after returning to duty his ship went down with all hands and a cargo of Spam. Mrs Havis, naturally, was distraught and Bunty felt pretty bad as well. Betty broke into tears when she heard the news because he was 'such a nice boy' and Nell said, 'They all are.'

The house at Lowther Street was sandwiched between two founts of grief because only the week after they heard the news about Sandy, Ena Tetley on the other side lost her husband, Maurice. She had a baby by then, six-month-old Spencer. She turned very queer after Maurice died. Frank said she'd lost her mind and avoided her but Nell felt duty-bound to call in every day like she did on Minnie Havis.

Ena wouldn't let the baby out of her sight for a minute; in fact she got so bad that she wouldn't even put the baby down in his pram or his cot and wouldn't let anyone else touch him; she just carried him around in her arms all day long and slept with him in her bed at night. She spent a lot of time in the back yard, gazing at the skies, waiting for Spencer's father to come home (Maurice had been the navigator on a Wellington) which was bad enough in daytime but was frightening when she was still there in the dark, the baby crying and coughing in the cold spring air, and someone had to go round and persuade her to go back inside. Even the mourning Mrs Havis was driven to comment that you had to control your bereavement a bit.

Nell, unable to stand it any longer, passed on the detail to Bunty (Babs was living with her in-laws on Burton Stone Lane), and she had to go in every morning before going to work and make Ena a cup of tea and spoon out powdered milk for Spencer's bottle. Spencer was a most unattractive infant, always bellowing with anger and nappy rash. He had red sores around his mouth and a permanent plug of thick, yellow snot in his nose. He smelt bad as well and his nappy was disgusting. Nell told Bunty to change him if he was wet, but he was *always* wet and Bunty felt sick at the very idea and ignored her mother's instructions. Bunty vowed she would *never, ever* have babies. It was a tedious start to the day having to sit with damp-eyed Ena and howling Spencer. Sometimes at work, Bunty imagined she had them in her sights, *bang bang*.

She hadn't seen Mrs Carter for months but decided to visit her and ask her advice about Ena, amongst other things, but the shop was deserted and the curtains drawn in Mrs Carter's little flat above. She rang and rang but there was no answer and when she came down again the barber from the shop opposite said, 'I think she's gone away – her son was killed, you know,' and Bunty felt suddenly very cold because she'd met Dick Carter once and he'd been a good-looking boy with a dazzling smile that had made a fifteen-year-old Bunty blush down to her toes. So no help with bereavement there.

That was about the middle of April. At the end of April, on a Tuesday, Bunty had gone with her friend Vi Linwood to Clifton Cinema to see *So Ends Our Night* with Fredric March and both were agreed it wasn't up to much and they'd have had a better time at the Electric where they were showing *Hellzapoppin*. They walked home through Bootham Park followed by a bright, cold moon. 'Bombers' moon,' Vi said, and Bunty shivered and said, 'Don't say that, Vi.'

The siren had Betty out of bed like a scalded cat. Almost simultaneously a strange, deep, rumbling shook the terrace and Bunty opened her eyes to see a bright white light and for a second she thought it was the moon and then realized it was flares dropping everywhere. They were in the Morrison shelter in the living-room within a minute, Ted carrying their ginger cat Totty and Mrs Havis in her hairnet diving under to join them with her Scottie dog Rex, who everyone hated because he was an ankle-nipper. 'Baedeker raid,' Ted said; and everybody hissed, 'Be quiet,' as if the bombers overhead might hear them. 'Heinkels,' Ted said and Nell said, *'Ted!'* 'Probably a couple of Junkers out front. Called the flying pencil because of—' Betty hit him. 'Somebody should go and get Ena,' Nell said, but then the bombs *really* started thudding down and they had a job to stop themselves from going mad, all squashed in the Morrison like that. There was a terrifying BANG that later turned out to be the doors being blown off their hinges, then an even louder *BANG!!* that turned out to be Ena and Spencer making the ultimate sacrifice.

They came out with the all-clear at dawn and Frank said, 'Well, I've never been so grateful to hear anything in my life.' St Martin-le-Grand destroyed, the roof of the ancient Guildhall turned to ash. The riverside warehouses, the *Evening Press* offices, the Art Gallery, the School for the Blind – all in flames. Not a pane of glass left in the magnificent arched roof of the railway station. The carriage works smashed, trains damaged, schools and houses wrecked – five nuns killed at the Bar Convent School, the emergency mortuary in Kent Street nearly full.

Bunty walked along Bootham on her way to work, the same route she had taken to get to the cinema the night before. There were no windows left in any of the big Georgian houses and the only sound was the eerie noise that tons of broken glass make when they're being swept up. But at the end of Bootham, the Bar stood untouched, and rising up behind it was the great bulk of the Minster, unscathed by the Nazis, and Bunty's heart swelled with pride and wartime spirit and her personality underwent another metamorphosis to become very like that of Greer Garson in *Mrs Miniver*.

A road was closed because of a crater and Bunty took a detour by the street where Modelia was and was shocked to see the little shop – and the flat above – exposed to the air like a doll's house with the front taken off. She could see the gas stove in the kitchen and the display shelves with Mrs Carter's Worcester plates and, down in the shop, a tailor's dummy, headless and legless like a torso, and a couple of frocks hanging on a rail, swaying gently in the breeze. 'Place was empty, they weren't there,' the barber said, sweeping furiously at glass on the pavement. His red and white pole hung above the door, twisted and bent, and there was a sign placed in his glassless window that said, 'Business as Usual. Bombed but not Beaten.'

Not so Ena and Spencer, who were found still in Ena's

bed which had fallen right through the floor into the living-room below and the rescuers said it was tragic to see that little baby curled up in his mother's arms, looking so peaceful (for once). Mrs Havis, Bunty, Betty, Ted, Nell and Frank had all been astonished beyond words when they surveyed the destruction of the next-door house, the all-clear siren still echoing in their ears. 'Phew,' Ted said eloquently.

Nell picked up a silver teaspoon which was lying in the brick dust of their back yard. 'Ena's George the Sixth Coronation teaspoon,' she marvelled. 'Not even bent.' Bunty felt quite uneasy when she remembered that only the previous morning she had grudgingly stirred sugar into Ena's cup of tea with that very spoon.

Watching the grey, dusty bodies of Ena and Spencer being carried from next-door was a sobering experience and around the tea-table that night they all agreed with Frank when he said that, in war, sometimes the ultimate sacrifice had to be made. They were eating potato pie and cabbage from Frank's allotment on the edge of the football pitch and Bunty was playing with the cabbage until Frank said sharply, 'Something wrong with that cabbage, Bunty?' and Bunty shook her head and forced herself to eat a mouthful of the slippery stuff. She didn't like Frank's vegetables because there was generally something lurking amongst the leaves – a dead earwig or a little slug overlooked in the rinsing process. She'd washed the cabbage herself tonight and sure enough there had been the smooth body of a slug, rolling over and over in the water in the sink, and for some reason Bunty thought of Sandy Havis choking to death on oily sea-water in the Atlantic, trying desperately to swim for his life and then rolling down – over and over – into a lost, watery grave. What did you think of when you were drowning? (Nothing in Sandy's case because he was hit on the head by a crate of Spam as he fell into the water.) *So ends the night,* Bunty thought.

'Poor Ena,' Betty said, her eyes filling up with tears. 'Bloody Jerry,' Ted said and Frank clouted him for his language. (Poor York, undefended by barrage balloons and ack-acks and the nearest fighter plane ninety minutes away, even though Churchill, for whom poor Spencer had been named, knew all along, thanks to the Bletchley codebreakers, that the German bombers would be over York that night, guided by a wonderful, clear moon. *Bang bang.*)

Not long after the Great Air Raid there was a surprise visit to Lowther Street. They'd been sitting peacefully round the wireless listening to 'The Brains Trust' when there was a knock at the door and Bunty was sent to answer it.

A tall, young man in officer's uniform stood there, his RAF cap pushed to the back of his head in a casual way so that you could see how curly his blond hair was. He grinned at Bunty and said, 'Hi,' in a very un-English sort of way.

'Hello,' Bunty said with a good deal of national reserve and waited for him to explain his presence. He was really quite handsome with his blue, blue eyes and his hair was lovely – far too good for a man (none of Nell's children had inherited the cherub curls, although both Babs and Bunty made many attempts to emulate them with perming lotions and peroxide).

'Let's see,' he grinned. 'You must be Auntie Nell's daughter?'

'Auntie Nell?' Bunty repeated, trying to work out this relationship. The man stuck out his hand towards her. 'I'm your cousin, Edmund.'

'Who is it?' Frank yelled from the living-room in chorus with, 'Shut that bloody door!' from a female air-raid warden in the street, and Bunty yanked the man into the passage and shouted, 'It's our cousin Edmund!' Nell came hurrying out of the living-room and stood, quite transfixed at the sight of the stranger. He held out his arms and walked towards her, 'Auntie Nellie?' and Nell fell down in a dead faint.

'What the bloody hell's going on, Jerry landed or something?' Frank grumbled, coming into the passage. The man tried again, holding out his hand to shake Frank's. 'Uncle Frank? It's Lillian's boy.'

'Edmund?' Frank whispered, a look of wonder on his face, as if he were witnessing a miracle. Edmund pumped his hand up and down vigorously for a few seconds before they turned their attention to Nell, still prone on the floor. Bunty and Betty helped her into a sitting position and their cousin Edmund squatted on the floor next to her. 'Auntie Nellie?' he said, with a beautiful smile. 'Lillian sends her love.'

Their cousin Edmund was quite something – a handsome, brave bomb-aimer stationed at Croft and delighted to meet his English cousins. Cousin Edmund, Frank said, was the 'spitting image' of Nell's brother Albert, and he laughed and said he'd thought it was a ghost walking in the door when he saw him. Nell hadn't heard from her sister Lillian for twenty years and the last time had been a cryptic postcard from Vancouver saying, 'I am doing well, don't worry about me,' which naturally made Nell worry because she didn't know there'd been anything *not* to worry about. There had been no address to reply to and she'd never heard from Lillian again and so she worried even more. In fact she'd decided her sister was dead and now that she'd discovered she was alive she was furious with her for not keeping in touch. 'She promises to write,' Edmund said. Lillian, it appeared, was married to a man called Pete Donner and was living on a farm on the prairies and Edmund had a 'kid brother', called Nathan.

'Nathan?' Frank asked suspiciously. 'Is that a Jewish name?' and Edmund laughed and said, 'I don't know, sir.' At ten, he got up to leave, saying, 'Mustn't miss the lift back to the base, eh?' which, they all noticed, was a Canadian kind of 'eh?' rather than a Yorkshire one. He wasn't really going back to his base that night, he was going to Betty's Bar where he had a rendezvous with a nice little Irish nurse but he didn't want to say that in front of his English relatives. He promised to return and visit again as soon as he had some leave and he laughed but he didn't tell them he was laughing because he fully expected to be dead before his next leave came up, seeing as he was well into his second tour of duty.

That night, Bunty and Betty had a long whispered conversation about Edmund. Betty declared her intention to marry him, but Bunty wasn't so sure about Edmund – there was something *knowing* about the way he looked at you with those laughing blue eyes as if he could see into you and knew there wasn't very much inside. He made Bunty think of a lion – a great golden-velvet lion. 'What colour would you say his eyes were?' Betty asked. 'Sky-blue? Sea-blue?'

'Forget-me-not blue,' Bunty said, thinking of the saucer that Totty got his food in, with the faded forget-me-nots and scratched gold rim. They both fell asleep thinking about Edmund and grateful to have something to pin all their romantic feelings on.

Edmund, unfortunately, never did come back, he was shot down on his very next sortie.

'Hellish bad luck,' Ted said, and everybody was too upset to tell him off.

Not as hellish as Frank's luck. In December he was walking home and took a short cut down a long narrow alley with high brick walls on either side. Just as he entered the alley, the siren went so he tried to trot along a bit faster but he got out of breath because, although he hadn't told Nell, he'd been having a bit of trouble with his ticker. Then a strange feeling began to take hold of him and as he walked along the alley he was taken back all those years to walking across No Man's Land on the first day of the Somme, and before he knew what was happening, he was in the grip of all those old fears. He clutched his heart – he was going to die – and spoke out loud, 'Dear God, let me see it coming,' just like he had all that time ago in the trenches. He wished he hadn't given the lucky rabbit's foot to Clifford.

He was about half-way along the alley when he heard the whining noise of a sick engine, quite low overhead. Then, suddenly, there it was – shockingly low, one engine streaming black, oily smoke – in the narrow ribbon of sky above the alley, but by then it had already dropped the bomb that engulfed Frank in one last blinding crack of light. Bad luck because it hadn't been aiming at Frank at all, of course. The crew of the Heinkel had overshot their target (the railway yards) and decided they'd better dump their bombs before they tried for a crash landing. They were shot down before they made it and their relatively intact bodies buried in the cemetery. Frank was buried there as well, although the undertaker had to piece his bits together as best he could.

Bunty had *really* had enough of the war by now. Things were made worse by the arrival of Babs, bombed out of Burton Stone Lane and full of her own way of doing things, but improved considerably by her acquaintance with an American, called Buck, who was stationed at Grimsby. They met at a dance – Bunty and her friend Vi had quite a social whirl now; they were out all the time at dances at the de Grey Rooms and the Clifton Ballroom and became regulars at Betty's Bar (which was nothing to do with her sister Betty, of course, Bunty would joke. This was Bunty's only joke) –

where it was the thing for all the forces to scratch their names on the big mirror there, and Bunty was sorry for Edmund because he hadn't been in York long enough to even have a drink in Betty's, let alone scratch his name in the mirror (she was wrong on both counts).

Still, things were looking up – Bunty was being courted by Buck, who was a great big, bear-like sergeant from Kansas and Vi had got herself a Canadian radio operator. Betty, who was just seventeen, was also being courted by a Canadian and spent a lot of time at Uncle Tom and Auntie Mabel's cottage in Elvington because her Canadian (Will) was stationed at Elvington aerodrome. Buck wasn't quite everything Bunty had dreamt of, although, unlike Sandy, he was quite handsome – but not unbelievably so. Whenever things started to get steamy between them he'd say things like 'Aw, shucks,' and look embarrassed and it turned out that he was quite a serious Baptist and had been brought up by his widowed mother who'd instilled good manners and a respect for women in him. Eventually, after much humming and hawing, he asked Bunty to marry him and tied a little piece of thread around her finger and said, 'When I get you back home to Ma, I'll buy you a real expensive ring,' and they all had quite a little tea-party in Lowther Street to celebrate.

It was not long after that he blew his foot off in a stupid accident. 'Anything for a lark these Yanks,' Clifford said so that Betty gasped and Bunty hit him so hard that she hurt herself. He was home on leave, but, thankfully, *they* weren't his home any more as he'd married a girl called Gladys who'd been in the ATS and was now very pregnant with their one and only child. Buck got shipped back to the States to his 'Ma', promising he'd send for his little Bunty but he never did.

Bunty met George towards the end of 1944; he was a corporal in the catering corps and was stationed at Catterick. They had a sporadic kind of courtship and became engaged just before the war finished. She wasn't entirely sure about this, but, with the war now drawing to a close, the possibilities were beginning to fade and all those coins tossed in the air were falling back to earth with a clatter in rather dull and predictable positions.

Not for Betty though; she announced she was going to Vancouver. Betty and Bunty searched the atlas for a map of Canada to see where Betty was going to be living. But they both knew that Betty wasn't really going to Canada, she was going to a new life. 'So are you Bunty,' she said, tapping Bunty's engagement ring, but Bunty didn't really think so.

Clifford was demobbed, unharmed, thanks to the rabbit's foot, and became a slightly nicer person under the influence of Gladys. He gave the lucky rabbit's foot to Bunty on her wedding-day. He reckoned she was going to need a lot of luck with a man like George. Babs and Sidney waited until 1948 before having the twins, Daisy and Rose.

Betty, the war-bride, divorced her husband twenty years later, but stayed in Vancouver and only came back to England for a visit once, in 1975, and, as she reported to her daughter, Hope, once was quite enough, even though it had been nice to see Bunty.

It wasn't until years after the war that Bunty learnt what happened to Mrs Carter and Mr Simon. When the shop and flat were bombed out (the barber was wrong – they *had* been in it) they went to stay with Mrs Carter's sister in Leeds and never came back to York. In the dreadful winter of 1947, while Mrs Carter's sister was marooned in Newcastle on a visit to her daughter, they gassed themselves in her little kitchen. Mr Simon (who suffered a lot for his accent during the war) had lost a son in Dachau – which really surprised Bunty because he'd never mentioned him – and of course, Mrs Carter had already lost her son, so Bunty could see why they'd done it, but she wished they hadn't.

They went to Liverpool to see Betty off on her Atlantic crossing. Like nearly everybody else standing on the quay, Bunty cried as the big ship eased away. Betty was a happy-go-lucky sort, always willing to see the bright side of things, and Bunty didn't realize how much she was going to miss her until she saw her waving from the deck.

In the end, Bunty's war had been a disappointment. She lost something in the war but she didn't find out until it was too late that it was the chance to be somebody else.

Somewhere at the back of Bunty's dreams another war would always play – a war in which she manned searchlights and loaded ack-acks, a war in which she was resourceful and beautiful, not to mention plucky and where 'String of Pearls' played endlessly in the de Grey Rooms as a succession of unbelievably handsome officers whirled Bunty off into another life.

Before her marriage to George, Nell gave Bunty her mother's silver locket. She had meant to leave it, after she was dead, to her eldest, Babs, but Bunty's spirits seemed so low, considering she was about to get married, that Nell gave it to her instead.

Bunty took one other thing to her marriage from the house in Lowther Street – Nell had kept Ena's teaspoon on the mantelpiece as a strange, silent *memento mori*. She didn't seem to regard it as odd when, the night before her wedding to George, Bunty asked her if she could take it with her to her new life. Bunty always polished Ena's spoon regularly and kept it as clean and shiny as a new coin.

CHAPTER FOUR

1956

The Naming of Things

I DON'T THINK THIS IS KANSAS, TEDDY. BUT WHERE ON earth is it? What's that you say, Teddy? Dewsbury? Oh my God, let him be wrong. But he's not – this is Dewsbury, Shoddy Capital of the north.

But why? Why are we in Dewsbury – and worse, not just in Dewsbury but in the attic bedroom of Number Twelve, Mirthroyd Road – the den, the lair, the pod of the twins from hell – Daisy and Rose!

They regard me with their solemn little eyes. They are perched on the edge of the double bed they share while I am installed in the corner by the window on an old camp bed constructed out of green canvas and rusting tubular metal. It's covered in a dark, grey blanket that reeks of moth balls. The guest bed.

But how I got here or why I am here – these are mysteries, for I remember nothing about the journey. In fact, if I think hard – which is not easy to do with the twins staring at me – I can't remember anything much at all. I confirm my existence to myself with a growing sense of panic – my name is Ruby Lennox, I have a mother, a father, sisters. These are not my sisters. Perhaps Daisy and Rose really are an alien life form and they sucked me up on board their spacecraft while I was innocently playing in the Back Yard and are now going to conduct a series of barbaric experiments on me. The twins begin to glow a funny shade of green—

'Ruby! Are you all right?' Auntie Babs squeezes into the bedroom – it's clear that the guest bed is taking up much needed space – and looks at me doubtfully. I can see that the only way for a guest to behave in these circumstances is very politely. 'Yes, thank you, Auntie Babs,' I reply in a clear, firm voice.

'Why don't you play with Ruby, girls?' Auntie Babs says, looking at her offspring. I shrink a little farther into the corner, I'm not at all sure I want to be initiated into their games. Auntie Babs turns back to me with a bright, artificial smile that I recognize because it's Bunty's. I wonder where they got it from? (See *Footnote (iv)*) 'Can you tell them apart yet, Ruby?' she asks. Perhaps they are like those quizzes in Gillian's *Beano* where you have two 'identical' pictures and have to *Spot the Difference!*. Perhaps one twin will have six fingers, no ear and a ribbon in her hair. 'Look up to the ceiling,' Auntie Babs commands one of them and points out a small freckle under its chin. Is that all? Spot the Difference? Hardly any. 'This one is Rose.' Rose stares blankly at the ceiling until Auntie Babs says, 'It's all right now, Rose, you can put your head down.' Rose looks at me as blankly as she did at the ceiling. They have a very limited range of facial expressions. Already I'm beginning to miss the startling variety of emotions that scud like clouds across Gillian's face, or even the sombre, yet subtle, palette that Patricia draws from.

'A game? A toy?' Auntie Babs prompts my little hosts. Reluctantly, Daisy slides off the bed and produces a box of *Fuzzy Felts*. If I have a quick game of *Fuzzy Felts* with them, will I be allowed home? Somehow I don't think so.

I have with me a small suitcase which contains a pair of winceyette pyjamas, a toothbrush and flannel, a pair of ruby-red slippers, five pairs of knickers, a vest, a liberty bodice, two Viyella blouses, a kilt, a corduroy pinafore-dress, a pair of tartan trews, two hand-knitted jumpers (one white, one Fair Isle), a cardigan (bottle-green, round-neck, raglan sleeves), a petticoat and four pairs of socks. Plus, of course, what I was wearing when I arrived – one vest, one liberty bodice, one pair of knickers, one pair of socks, one petticoat, one pair of shoes, one blue woollen skirt with straps, one yellow jumper, one winter coat, one pair of gloves, one scarf, one woollen hat (Tam o' Shanter style). If there was one thing we were good at as a family it was dressing properly for the great outdoors.

Reviewing the amount of clothes, it seems as if I might be in for quite a long stay. On the other hand, there is the anomaly of only one pair of pyjamas – are the clothes really there to impress Auntie Babs while the pyjamas tell the real story? Who knows? Not me. And why am I here? Is this a holiday? It doesn't feel like a holiday. As well as Teddy, I also have with me Gillian's Ladybird book *Puppies and Kittens* which she must have given to me in an extraordinary and unprecedented act of generosity.

I have been here nearly a week. I don't think the twins sleep at night. I think they just lie very, very still. I can't sleep if I think they're awake and if I do drop into sleep it's always to wake in a state of terror. I clutch Teddy tightly under the covers. His hot little body is a great source of comfort to me, I can feel his furry little chest rising and falling with his breathing. The eiderdown that covers Daisy and Rose does not move at all, however, confirming that they do not have normal, human lungs. I have seen the way they look at Teddy and I do not think their intentions are good.

In the dark, the furniture takes on a new malevolence – the bedroom is crowded out with furniture – big, heavy pieces that don't belong in a child's bedroom at all, not just the Arctic waste of their double bed, but the huge, double-fronted wardrobe and matching dressing-table that's big enough to stow a corpse in. In the blackness of night, the furniture-shapes possess a profound ultra-blackness that hints at anti-matter.

Over in the other corner is their doll's house, a big four-storey Victorian one. It has pictures the size of postage stamps and postage stamps the size of dots; it has gilded chairs fit for a fairy queen and chandeliers like crystal earrings and a kitchen table groaning under the weight of plaster hams and plaster-moulded blancmanges.

This doll's house is much coveted by Gillian who has frequently tried to persuade the twins to make a will and leave it to her. I doubt very much that they have. If it were willed to me (which is even more unlikely) I would refuse to accept it. There's something eerie about it, with its microscopic plumbing (tiny copper taps!) and little, little leather-bound books (*Great Expectations*!). I would be frightened – I am frightened – of getting trapped in there and becoming one of the tiny ringletted and pinafored little girls up in the nursery who have to play with teeny-weeny dolls all day long. Or worse – the poor scullery maid, for ever consigned to blacking the kitchen range.

Perhaps the twins, with their galactic powers, will miniaturize me in the night and Auntie Babs will come in this room one morning and find the guest bed empty and the guest bed in the doll's house (much nicer than the camp bed) full of a doll-like Ruby Lennox clutching a teddy bear the size of an amoeba.

The stairs are the worst – both in the doll's house and in Mirthroyd Road. Auntie Babs and Uncle Sidney's house reminds me of Above the Shop, the same thin, tall dimensions and the same abundance of staircases – although in Mirthroyd Road there's really only one room on each floor and to get to the attic bedroom involves a long, long climb up the dark, narrow staircase, which is full of bends and twists and unexpected corners which harbour vast quantities of Unknown

Dread. The amiable ghosts Above the Shop have been replaced by something that crackles with evil.

I am sent to bed first and have to negotiate this treacherous journey entirely on my own. This is manifestly wrong. I have adopted certain strategies to help us in this ordeal. It's important, for example, that I keep my hand on the bannister rail at all times when climbing the stairs (the other one is being clutched by Teddy). That way, nothing can hurtle unexpectedly down the stairs and knock us flying into the Outer Darkness. And we must never look back. Never, not even when we can feel the hot breath of the wolves on the back of our necks, not when we can hear their long, uncut claws scrabbling on the wood at either edge of the stair-carpet and the growls bubbling deep in their throats.

Terrible, apocalyptic images rise before my eyes as we undertake our ascent – images of Teddy being ripped to pieces, torn limb from limb and tossed from wolf to wolf as great gobbets of saliva drop from their jaws. Finally, his little body is held down under a stinking, matted paw and his stuffing is pulled out. He turns his pleading amber eyes towards me—

'Who's that?' A hoarse, thick voice rasps out this question – we are on the landing outside 'Grandpa's' bedroom, not my grandfather (they have both undergone their genetic fate by now – one run over, one blown up) but the twins' grandfather – Sidney's father – who lives in the room beneath ours. 'Just Ruby!' I shout back to him – although I don't think he has the faintest idea who 'Just Ruby' is – and carry on up the stairs. Now we've reached the really tricky bit – getting into bed.

We linger on the threshold of the bedroom for a while – thresholds are safe, but unfortunately you can't stay on them for ever. Also, the wolves that live on the stairs can't cross them (or they'd be all over the house), which is good, but the bed is on the other side of the room, which is bad. There are things living under the camp bed. There are a handful of crocodiles and a small dragon but mainly they are nameless things without clear definition or taxonomy. But one thing is certain – all the things that live under the bed, named, or unnamed, have teeth. Teeth that will snap vulnerable little ankles when they try to get into bed.

Speed is the only stratagem here. Ready, Teddy – steady, Teddy – Go! Little slippered feet patter across the linoleum, little hearts go thud, thud, thud, as we get near the danger zone – two feet from the bed – we launch ourselves onto the camp bed, which nearly collapses, but we are safe. Safe, that is, as long as we don't fall out of bed during the night. I stuff Teddy down the front of my pyjamas, just in case.

I want to go home! I want Patricia. I want *Watch with Mother!* This is still a television-less household and every afternoon I feel a hollow sense of deprivation when I realize that my friends – the biggest spotty dog in the world, Little Weed, Rag, Tag and Bobtail – are playing their games without me. *Time to go home! Time to go home! Ruby and Teddy are waving goodbye! Goodbye!* If only.

I resolve that I will use *Puppies and Kittens* as my escape plan. I will learn to read! I've been trying to read for a long time, I'm due to start school after the summer and I would like to get off to a flying start. I have absorbed as much as I can when I've been roped in to help Patricia play schools (to tell the truth, I don't think she's as good a teacher as she thinks she is) but although I know the alphabet inside out, back to front, and upside down, it makes absolutely no sense whatsoever.

If I learn to read and then to write – because I know one thing leads to another – then I will be able to write a letter to the outside world, to Patricia, and she will come and rescue me from Mirthroyd Road. Auntie Babs is my unwitting ally in this because she gives me Daisy and Rose's old alphabet cards to play with – I am 'under her feet' (not as much as I would be if I shrank to doll's house size) all day long. The twins are at school and Auntie Babs is obviously peeved at suddenly finding herself with a child in the house, especially as she already has 'Grandpa' to look after. This is more evidence that I have been sent as a terrible punishment rather than a holiday; if I was here on holiday she would put herself out to make sure I had a good time. But then again, perhaps not.

Everything runs like clockwork in Auntie Babs' house. For example, there's a strict rota for the bathroom in the morning, with Auntie Babs going first, then Uncle Sidney, then the twins (together) and then me. The order is reversed in the evening. There is none of the bleary-eyed grumpiness that George, Bunty and Gillian taint the morning with. I wouldn't say Patricia was exactly chirpy in the mornings, more phlegmatic and resigned, but that's a great improvement on Gillian who doesn't even speak in the morning and usually communicates via her Sooty and Sweep glove-puppets. Sooty can be particularly unpleasant at the breakfast table.

Auntie Babs is also a slave to housework, I know this because she tells me so. Often. On Monday she does the washing. She has an antiquated boiler that she has to heat up (her domestic appliances are all more primitive than her younger sister's) and the whole house ends up a soapy, sudsy Turkish bath by the time she's finished. She makes me play next to the frightening boiler because I have a croupy cough and tells me that 'I should count myself lucky that's all I have.' Auntie Babs, you notice, has the same cryptic ways of communicating as Bunty. If the Germans had used Bunty and Babs instead of the Enigma coding machine they would probably have won the war. On Tuesday Auntie Babs irons all the clothes she washed on Monday. On Wednesday she does low dusting, on Thursday, high dusting. On Fridays she washes paintwork and floors and sweeps the carpet with her Ewbank. On Saturday she does the shopping. This is exactly the same housework timetable as her fellow housework slave – Bunty!

Meals are regular and wholesome; Uncle Sidney never has to wait for more than two minutes for his tea when he comes home at night. Auntie Babs prides herself on being a good cook and suffers none of the Strindbergian gloom that Bunty experiences when cooking. (Or perhaps it's Ibsenesque – perhaps Bunty is also trapped in a doll's house? Just a thought.) Uncle Sidney is a great encouragement to Auntie Babs' culinary talents. He talks about 'Babs' Yorkshire Pudding' and 'Babs' Onion Gravy' as if they were fellow members of the family – 'Hello, hello, here comes Babs' Shepherd's Pie' – I'm surprised he doesn't ask it if it enjoyed itself at the end of the meal. And Auntie Babs is the Queen of Puddings – every night a new one – treacle sponge pudding, jam roly-poly (which Patricia calls 'dead baby' but I think it best not to mention this at Auntie Babs' table), lemon meringue pie, rhubarb crumble, rice pudding – what will we have on Sunday, I wonder? What will we *do* on Sunday? In our house it's a no-housework day, so presumably it will be the same here.

'Are you ready for church, Ruby?'

Church – this is a novelty: we are a family of heathens for the most part, although Patricia takes herself off to Sunday School every week and would probably have ended up as a nun if she hadn't become so thoroughly alienated. I know what churches are like because Auntie Gladys has taken me to hers (Church of England, straight-down-the-middle) and I'm not averse to the idea. It's a women-only outing – 'Grandpa' hardly ever leaves his room anyway and Uncle Sidney dis-appears on Sundays into the front room and listens to Gilbert and Sullivan records all afternoon.

* * *

This is very unlike Auntie Gladys' church. It's in a basement for a start and you have to go down a spiral stone staircase and along a corridor lined with heating pipes and then you come to a door with a little sign above it announcing, 'Church of the Spirit'. It's very hot in the basement and there is an odd sickly-sweet smell like Parma Violets mixed with Dettol. There are a lot of people here already, chatting away as if they were at the theatre, and it takes them a long time to settle down but eventually a small organ strikes up and we sing a hymn but, as I can't read the words in the hymn book, I have to open and close my mouth in a variety of ways in what I hope is a polite imitation of singing.

Then a woman, who introduces herself as Rita, invites a man called Mr Wedgewood up onto the platform. Auntie Babs leans over to inform me that Mr Wedgewood is a medium for the world of Spirit and will be talking to them on our behalf. 'Dead people,' Rose says (I can see the freckle – she has her chin tilted in a very pious fashion). She's watching me carefully, down her nose, to see my reaction to this information. She can't frighten me. Well, she can, but I'm not going to let her know that. Instead I merely raise my eyebrows in silent but eloquent surprise. I wonder to myself if the dead people will have anything to say to me, but Daisy – who I'm beginning to think can read my mind – says, 'Dead people, you know, don't speak to you if you don't know them.' Given this rule of etiquette I suppose I won't be spoken to because I don't know anybody who's dead (how wrong I am).

Mr Wedgewood then proceeds to ask Spirit to come and talk to us and that's the signal for all kinds of strange things to happen – the dead pop up all over the place – a woman's husband who's been dead for twenty years tells her there's a light at the end of the tunnel. Then there's the father of another woman who 'passed into Spirit' last year and reports to her that he misses going to the cinema. Somebody's mother comes back just to tell her 'how to get rid of that scratch in your coffee table' (linseed oil) and one woman has an entire family of six people materialize behind her chair (to Mr Wedgewood's eyes, anyway) who turn out to have been next-door neighbours who died in a house fire thirty years ago. Clearly, there is no escape from the dead. Their message to their ex-neighbour is to 'batter on', to the end of the tunnel presumably. The world of spirits seems a rather mundane place to me, like a doctor's waiting-room full of people trying to top one cliché with another.

I'm just beginning to droop into sleep in the over-heated atmosphere when I realize Mr Wedgewood is standing at the end of our aisle and looking at *me*. I swallow with difficulty and stare at my feet, perhaps he knows I was only pretending to sing the hymn. But he smiles benignly at me and says *Your sister says not to worry about her* and Auntie Babs gives a little gasp, but before I can work any of this out the little organ strikes up another hymn identical to the last one (all the hymns in the Church of the Spirit are exactly the same

– a phenomenon that, interestingly, nobody seems to notice).

I puzzle over my experiences in church for the rest of the day, even Babs' Roast Beef and Babs' Apple Pie – our guests for Sunday dinner – cannot allay my fears that Patricia or Gillian are dead. I try and bring this subject up with Auntie Babs – to a background accompaniment of 'Willow, Tit-Willow, Tit-Willow' – but she just says, 'Don't try to be clever, Ruby – it doesn't suit you' (I think it suits me very well, actually) and refuses to talk any further about it.

Another week passes. Another week of the housework timetable. Another week of assiduous study of alphabet cards and Ladybird text – I try to copy the words in the book with the alphabet cards, laying them out on the dining-room table like fortune-telling cards, but as there is only one card for each letter, the sentences are inevitably foreshortened – 'Here is a Puppy' becomes 'Her is a Puy' and 'Here is a Kitten' becomes 'Her is a Ktn'.

I have slipped into the routine of Mirthroyd Road, soon I will be transformed into one of them. Already, Auntie Babs is dressing me in their cast-off clothes and trimming my hair to resemble theirs. Soon no-one will be able to tell the difference between us and they will have achieved their aim of taking over the body of an earthling. If I could learn to spell, I could chalk H-E-L-P on the pavement outside the house. What do they really want me for? My telluric powers? Or my teddy bear?

The worst things of all are the nightmares – terrible dreams of drowning, of falling, of being trapped, of flying. Flying dreams are the worst – we're pitched headlong from the top of the stairs onto a vertiginous, non-stop flight over which we have no control. We accelerate faster and faster until we reach the hallway down below when we wake up just before crashing into the stained-glass panels of the front door.

These dreams are bad enough when they take place on the stairs at Mirthroyd Road, but even worse when they are in the doll's house. Its stairs are too narrow to negotiate properly and after a night in the doll's house Teddy and I wake up with bruised elbows and battered ankles. Whichever stairs we're on, we also have to dodge the Unnamed Dread lurking on the landings, or worse – Grandpa shouting out at us like a mad cuckoo clock screaming, 'Who's that?' and I wake up crying, 'It's just Ruby,' but now, even I'm not sure who 'Just Ruby' is.

And then something *really* horrible happens – I begin to walk in my sleep. And now I not only dream about the staircases – I am sometimes shaken awake by Auntie Babs and find that I'm really there! Just Ruby – all alone except for the Unnamed Dread. Once, I wake up and find I am alone in the dark, no Auntie Babs – perhaps I have shaken myself awake? I am standing in front of the doll's house and the dim street light filtering through the attic curtains reveals a complete muddle in its little rooms as if some small creature desperate to find something had ransacked it from top to bottom. Horrors!

* * *

I comfort Teddy by telling him stories, stories that involve a lot of rescuing – Rapunzel, Snow White, Sleeping Beauty, detailed episodes of Robin Hood in which I am Maid Marian, Teddy is Alan-a-Dale and Auntie Babs is the Sheriff of Nottingham. Or sometimes I am the Lone Ranger and Teddy does his passable imitation of Jay Silverheels. Sometimes we are captives on a pirate ship, already teetering on the gangplank as Sinbad's ship hoves into view; sometimes we are stranded in log cabins and are shooting at the Indians outside, sure in the knowledge that the cavalry, Patricia at its head, hair streaming behind her, will rescue us at the last split second. Of course, I realize now we were on the wrong side – if we'd gone over to the pirates or the Indians we would probably have been quite safe.

Sometimes we sit on the fireside rug – a contemporary thing with geometric designs on it in black, red and grey – and pretend it's a magic carpet that's going to take us away from Mirthroyd Road, take us home – but no matter how hard we wish we cannot get it to rise more than a couple of inches above the ground, where it hovers indecisively for a few seconds before flopping back to earth.

Another Sunday comes around. We go to church. This week Rita introduces a visiting medium called Myra, who looks like Alma Cogan, but without the frocks, and Myra gives us a little talk on 'Animals in the Spirit World'. Myra claims that animals as well as people pass over into Spirit, posing many unanswered questions, not least of which is how there can be enough room for everybody. If all living things exist in the afterlife then there must be zillion upon zillion of plankton, amoebas, bacteria, spinning off to the astral plane every day. If not, then where do you draw the line? Domestic pets only? Nothing smaller than a Yorkshire terrier? A wasp? And are they segregated – do dogs float around with dogs, giraffes with giraffes? Puy with Ktn? Does chicken flock with chicken? Bluebird fly with bluebird (birds of a feather)? Or all the birds of the air? And what of teddy bears – is there one section where all the spirit teddy bears are corralled or are they allowed to live with their children? Questions, questions . . .

I devote myself to the alphabet. Teddy and I sit, day after day, on the magic carpet in front of the fire and study its arcane messages – 'A is for Apple', 'B is for Bus', 'C is for Cat', 'D is for Dog'. I understand the meaning all right, it's the form that escapes me. The cards have pictures on them – Apples, Buses, Cats, Dogs, Elephants, Fish, Goats – hermeneutic symbols that drive me into a frenzy. 'I' is for Indian and in the night the hostile tribes gather on the landings, their eyes and beads shining in the darkness, their feathery headdresses forming a barricade behind which huddle the Unnamed Dread. The things that live under the bed crawl out and join them and here and there, a cutlass flashes. We fly past them all on our unstoppable, roller-coaster dreams.

Perhaps the flower-twins, the cabal of two, have bewitched me – put a flying spell on me that dooms me to fly, wingless, every night. Or perhaps they have made a wax doll of me and have slipped it unnoticed into the nursery of the doll's house and practise telekinesis on it at night, throwing it down the narrow little stairs while lying 'innocently' in their beds. When I wake in the mornings they are both lying there, looking at me; their eyes are pinpoints of darkness boring into my skull as they try and probe my brain. I will not let them read my thoughts. I will resist them.

There are so many things I want to ask and nobody who has the answers. One of the twins, chin held down to avoid identification, shows me one of her school books (I'm surprised they bother with language when their telepathy is so advanced) in which Janet helps Mummy bake a cake while John makes a bonfire with Daddy. And I thought 'J' was for Jam! One afternoon, Auntie Babs comes into the living-room and finds Teddy and me sitting on the magic carpet in tears – in front of us a ouija-board of letters spelling the mysterious word P-E-A-R-L. Auntie Babs' face is pinched in fury so that she resembles a Picasso portrait. She picks up the letters and throws them on the fire. Fools that we are – 'P' is for 'Puy' not 'Pearl'.

So the days fly by in the alchemical pursuit of reading and the nights speed past in flight and all the time I try to find the secret spell that will take us out of our mysterious exile and back home. How long have we been imprisoned in Mirthroyd Road? A year? Five years? Two and a half weeks really, but it seems like a hundred years. How will my family be able to recognize me when I return? I have no handy freckle to mark me out as the Ruby Lennox who left them so long ago. Perhaps they will cry 'Impostor!' and refuse to let me back in.

And then suddenly we are free! I come into the kitchen and there is Auntie Gladys talking in a low voice to Auntie Babs, who is buttering bread for a Bread-and-Butter Pudding whose acquaintance I will never make because Auntie Gladys sees me and says, 'I've come to take you home, Ruby.' Both Aunties regard me warily over the bread and butter, as if I were a notoriously unpredictable animal ('T' for Tiger).

Home! Sweet Home. There Is No Place Like It. Keep Its Fires Burning. It's Where The Heart Is. My ordeal is over at last. Patricia is my welcoming committee, standing in the hallway to greet me. 'Hello, Ruby,' she says, a soft, forgiving smile on her face. In the kitchen, Bunty offers me milk and biscuits. Her eyes are rimmed in red and she has a slightly mad air about her. She looks at me, or rather a point slightly to the left of me and with a visible effort says, 'Now, Ruby – we've decided that we're all going to try and carry on and put the accident behind us.' Well, that's fine by me, seeing as I have no idea what 'accident' she's talking about. And anyway no-one appears to be hurt – apart from Teddy who has a small gash in his leg where the wolves took a little of his stuffing and Patricia sews him up very neatly with silk embroidery floss. She will make a very good vet one day.

Before I go to bed that night I harass Patricia into helping me translate *Puppies and Kittens*. I regret ever having doubted her talents as a teacher, for the way she explains it now it all suddenly makes sense and, as if by magic, I am able to unlock The Mysteries – 'Here is a Puppy, Here is a Kitten, Here are Puppies and Kittens.' I am powerful! I have the key to the Temple of Knowledge and there's no stopping me – we get out crayons and form letters. No need for Puy and Ktn any more, now there are enough letters to make all the Puppies and Kittens we want, enough letters to make everything. Slowly, with a red crayon, I create my own hieroglyphics – R-U-B-Y spells Ruby! My name is Ruby. I am a precious jewel. I am a drop of blood. I am Ruby Lennox.

I go to sleep in my own bed for the first time in what seems like a long time. It's strange to be alone in my bedroom and I have a distinct feeling that something – or somebody – is missing. There is a space in the room that wasn't there before, not a vacuum but an invisible cloud of sadness that drifts around, bumping into furniture and lingering at the foot of my bed as if the domestic phantoms had been joined by a raw recruit. The fur on Teddy's neck stands up and he growls nervously.

My night-time perambulations do not stop when I'm home and Bunty often wakes me from my parlous state in order to tell me how annoyed she is at being woken by my ghostly odysseys. But what of the times when she doesn't wake me? Why do I have such unquiet sleep?

Something has changed Above the Shop. Patricia, for example, has definitely taken a turn for the worse, there is a look of troubled confusion in her eyes that's quite distressing to behold. On my first night back, as I race to the end of *Puppies and Kittens* ('Puppies and Kittens are sleeping'), I can see she's trying to say something. She bites her lip and stares at the picture of sleeping puppies and kittens. Then she speaks in an urgent, ferocious whisper – 'Was it Gillian, Ruby? Was it Gillian's fault?' – but I just look at her blankly because I haven't the faintest idea what she's talking about.

And as for Gillian herself – Gillian is being nice to me! She says I can keep her *Puppies and Kittens* and have untrammelled use of Mobo (not much good as I've outgrown him and he's on his way to the knacker's yard. Outgrowing the Mobo is a kind of rite of passage and I can now understand Gillian's feelings when it happened to her.) Furthermore I can borrow Sooty or Sweep – I am even given a free choice and I choose Sweep because he has a voice. Of sorts. For a brief, pleasant period of time, Sooty and Sweep have a friendly relationship, until Gillian's natural animosity reasserts itself and with one last *Izzie Wizzie let's get busy* she breaks Sooty's wand over Sweep's head and reclaims him by pulling him violently off my hand. I don't really care – I still have Teddy and an Alexandrian library of books, in the form of the Children's Section of the York City Library, is waiting to be deciphered by us.

In dreams, Teddy and I fly down the stairs of our own house on the magic carpet – we have perfect control and manoeuvre skilfully on landings, outwitting the wolves who skitter off into the Outer Darkness and neatly avoiding the Unnamed Dread (whose collective name is Fear) and the Sioux and Apache braves who stick out their feet in a vain attempt to trip us up. Ahead of us rides Patricia, dressed in Lincoln Green, on a horse called Silver. Hi-ho! We gather speed at every turn, zoom, zoom, zoooooom, zoooooooooom – we are all-powerful. We reach the last flight of stairs, the scary one, but accelerate triumphantly down and glide along the hallway at the bottom like hypersonic owls. The front door stands open and as we fly towards it, it changes into a rainbow arch and – we are free! We are in the open air, no longer in the street but on the open plains beneath an endless sea of stars. Teddy laughs in exultation and ahead of us Patricia's hair streams out like a banner of gold.

Footnote (iv) – Bonny Birds

FREDERICK LAUGHED AS HE CAME INTO THE KITCHEN. 'Tha's a reet workhoss, lass,' he said, looking approvingly at Rachel's huge backside, tilted towards him as she knelt washing the stone floor. Rachel turned as red as a beetroot but didn't look round from her meditation, moving the scrubbing-brush up and down on the stone flags, up and down, up and down, the muscles on her powerful arms moving as she worked to clean the cottage of the lingering spirit of Alice Barker.

''Appen it's not such a bad little place, eh?' Frederick said. He was carrying a pair of dead rabbits by their ears and laid them down on the draining-board, leaving a thin trail of blood on the newly-scrubbed and bleached wood. 'I'm doing my best, Mr Barker,' Rachel said, feeling the blush spread uncomfortably down her body. Mr Barker, sir, 't'master' – Alice Barker's husband. Alice Barker, the wife. 'And a grand job it is,' he said, and she could hear the sly chuckle in his voice. Rachel smiled, keeping her eyes on the flags. He'd be hers soon enough. She'd take Alice's place – be a second wife, or near enough anyway. She'd have a man of her own, a household to be mistress of, a readymade family. They needed her because they were weak and she was strong. 'I'm off to see to t'traps on Pengill Crags,' he said.

Rachel sat back on her heels and wiped the sweat from her face with the back of her hand. She nodded in the direction of the table. 'I've made snap for you.'

Frederick picked up the bread and cheese that was wrapped in a cloth. 'Tha's a grand lass, Rachel.'

And so I am, thought Rachel. A grand lass, who will set this lot right. And they'd be grateful to her, whether they liked it or not. She was all they'd got in the end, now that their dizzy, idle mother was gone. Their only kin too, for Rachel was no hired servant, but cousin to Alice Barker. Their family tree had been split down the middle, a bifurcated trunk – Alice's mother, Sophia, and Rachel's mother, Hannah, were sisters but Sophia had married up in the world and Hannah had married down and been disowned by her father. So while Rachel had gone into service as a scullery maid at the age of ten, little Alice was still brushing out her blond curls and having piano lessons. And where had all her fancy ways got her? A clarty midden, that's where, Rachel thought, pausing for a moment to look round the kitchen. Hadn't she ever dirtied her pretty, white, schoolteacher fingers in this place? Not to judge by the amount of soot and grease in the kitchen, the lamp-black on the walls, the unswept dust on the floors, the unmended, unpatched linen. Now 't'master' had been forced to send for Rachel from Whitby because he had very carelessly lost his pretty wife.

And as for her children! They were a disgrace, unruly and sullen, ignorant of their Bible, their hems hanging down, their handkerchiefs filthy – if they had them at all, that is. The girl, Ada, had hair that was so tangled that the first thing Rachel had to do was shear half of it. She'd screamed like a stuck pig when she'd seen her curls falling around her feet. She was so like her mother it was uncanny. Those children might resent her now but in another few months they'd be thankful for the order she'd brought into their lives, something clever, silly Alice Barker could never do.

From upstairs came the thin whine of the baby, followed by the more articulate cry of an older child. Rachel ignored both, they were going to have to learn that she wasn't there to dance attendance on them all the time, she had a floor to scrub for a start. Something glinted in the weak November sun and Rachel tweaked it out from a crack in between the flags – a button. Pink glass, fancy like a flower – Alice's no doubt. Rachel slipped it into her pocket, it would go in her button tin. All Alice Barker had in her button tin was an old George IV coin and a violet cachou. That was the kind of woman she was.

A little lead soldier skidded across the flags and Albert clapped his hands and laughed. He was watching her from the passage where he was playing with his soldiers and bricks, tied by makeshift reins to the newel-post of the stairs. 'Aye, you can wipe that smile off your face,' Rachel said, pocketing the soldier as well. Out of all of them, he got on her nerves the most, always trying to suck up, putting his arms around her and kissing her. He was like a little girl, the mirror of his sister and his mother.

Rachel threw the bucket of dirty water out into the yard and left the door open to try and dry the flags, but the sun was already a fading bruise beyond the hill. She went back to the sink and picked up a limp rabbit, and was about to get about skinning and paunching when she stopped and fetched the cleaver that hung by the range and smartly chopped off a paw. It was luck, a rabbit's foot, everyone knew that, and tonight she'd turn a silver threepence under the new moon and, all in all, that should take care of the future, please God. A great clattering of pattens on the cobbles of the yard announced the arrival of the older ones, home from school. They hardly seemed to be out of the house in the morning before they were back in it again.

They all three stood framed by the door, like a sentimental photograph, and then Ada pouted and said, 'Yon bairns are roarin', can tha not hear them?' and, kicking off her clogs, broke free from the frame and marched across the wet floor. When she spotted Albert tied up to the stairs she went pink and yelled at Rachel, 'Tha've got yon poor bairn tied up like a dog, it's you that should be tied up!' and while she was untying him she kept saying, 'Poor wee Bertie, poor wee Bertie, Addie's here,' and when Rachel told her to leave him be she turned to her and said, 'Tha's not Mother, tha canst tell me nowt,' and then smiled that artificial smile that nearly split her face like a big sliver of moon and Rachel picked up a discarded clog and bowled it overarm so that it bounced off Ada's shorn curls. Even that didn't stop her, and she stood there with a heavy Albert hoisted awkwardly in her arms, a patch of blood no bigger than a button staining her hair and her face white with shock, and screamed hysterically, 'Tha's not Mother!' over and over again until Frederick's shadow suddenly darkened the kitchen and he bellowed, 'Frame thissen, yer tyke!' and then he brayed each and every one of them in turn except for baby Nelly. 'Yon childer need a mother,' he said to Rachel when he'd finished. 'Aye, they do that, Mr Barker,' she agreed, trying to look as solemn and righteous as she could so he would appreciate the contrast to her cousin.

A warm September sun washed the cottage like honey. Rachel was in the kitchen, salting beans, snapping them and packing them down in their layers of salt into the big stone crock. She'd grown the round beans herself, and runners too, with scarlet flowers on a vine on the gable-end of the barn that faced south and it had taken off like something from a fairy story. She'd got Frederick to make sure that the night-soil from the privies went on a muck-heap and now she had a real garden going with potatoes and brown onions, rhubarb and carrots, and dark-green crinkled savoys. She'd never have believed she had such a country woman inside her.

This was her kitchen now, her cottage, her life. A stranger chancing by the cottage (a rare occurrence) would never have known about Alice, although they might have queried how a wet lump of dough like Rachel could have produced such a pretty clutch from her loins.

She put up the photographs of the children on the mantelpiece each side of the clock that – like the children – the foolish wife had left behind. These photographs were a queer thing. Frederick never had understood where they had come from. 'T'Frenchman came and took 'em,' Ada said with her surly pout, but was unforthcoming about the details. Two of them were already framed – by 't'Frenchman' presumably – and those were the two that Rachel put on the mantelpiece. One was of the three boys together and the other was of Lawrence and Tom with the baby Lillian. The rest, the unframed ones, were put at the back of a drawer. None of the children ever looked at those photographs on the mantelpiece, they remembered only too vividly that they had appeared on the last day they ever saw their mother. 'I wish there were a photograph of Mother,' Ada said miserably one day and Lawrence said, 'Rachel 'ud throw it in t'fire if there were,' but later Tom took them both upstairs and showed them the treasure he had purloined from the kitchen table on the morning of his mother's death and for a full half-hour the three oldest children exclaimed over the photograph of Alice – the beautiful (albeit ambiguous) expression on their missing mother's face and the plush extravagance of the silver and red velvet frame.

The children were improved a little, in appearance if not in temper – they were brushed and patched and scrubbed, and had their allotted tasks. They read from the Bible and said their prayers and the whole family went to church on a Sunday, Frederick in his smart jacket with the braided trim and a bowler on his head.

The door to the outside was wide open and Rachel could see Albert playing with that stupid little lurcher that Frederick had given to him, he was soft as lard to let him have that dog. Ada was sitting on the grass by the fence telling Lillian and Nell stories, making extravagant gestures with her hands and Rachel knew exactly what kind of stories they were. When she'd sealed the crock of beans she put it on the low shelf in the pantry. The pantry, cool and dark, was the heart of Rachel's new life – the shelves were weighed down with her clever housewifery – jams and pickles and chutney, big glass jars of raspberry jewels and gooseberry globes, a fat leg of ham, a bowl of brown eggs, flagons of rhubarb wine, puddings, both sweet and savoury, wrapped in cloths.

Rachel surveyed her garnerings with satisfaction, unconsciously twisting the gold ring on her finger round and round, trying to loosen it. She knew when he put it on her finger that it was Alice's ring – with a piece put in to accommodate her thick finger – but she hadn't said anything, a wedding-ring was a wedding-ring, after all, no matter how you came by it. 'To make thee respectable,' Frederick said when he put it on her finger, as if that were enough. Rachel had her own harvest to come now, respectable or not, she was so swollen up with this child that he must be a prize-fighter in the making. He was going to be as strong as an ox, she could feel it, not like these spindly, sickly children, never one without a cough or a streaming nose.

Lawrence and Tom clattered across the yard, Albert trailing behind them with his dog. There was not one of them doing anything useful. 'Right, Lawrence, hold back!' she roared, because when they saw her standing in the doorway they had wheeled round like a flock of birds and headed for the field. 'There's jobs to be done, Saturdays aren't just for laiking – the privies need emptying.' Lawrence turned his face on her, tutored into sullenness by Ada's example. 'Now?' It was unfortunate for Lawrence that his mouth turned down in a natural kind of sneer; it infuriated Rachel even more than Ada's false smile.

'Yes, now, Lawrence-me-lad, or you'll have the soil bucket over your ugly head!'

Rachel reached for the leather strap that was hung on a peg behind the door and measured its weight in her hand. 'Are you going to do as I say? Or do I have to make you?' She advanced on him and the rest of the children scattered like chickens, all except for Lawrence who just stood looking at her.

He stood his ground even though he knew what it meant and screamed at her, 'Shift for yerself, yer great stirk!'

He couldn't get away from her because the first thwack from the strap knocked him off his feet and it was all he could do to lie there screaming with his arms over his head and if Ada hadn't sent Tom running for the pump to draw a bucket of water to throw over their stepmother she probably wouldn't have stopped until he was unconscious, even dead maybe. It wasn't just the water that stopped her though, because suddenly, just as she raised her great arm up for a really good blow, she doubled over with pain and clutched her stomach, hissing, 'The baby, the baby's coming.'

Frederick locked Lawrence and Tom in one of the outbuildings for two whole days and nights without food or water to teach them a lesson for that and they missed the arrival of their new brother. ''Appen yon bairn doesn't want to be born,' said Mrs May, who'd come from the village to help with the confinement. 'But there's no going back on t'road once tha've started,' she added with a sigh. She wasn't very taken with this Rachel. Say what you like about Alice Barker, and plenty was said about her after she went, but she always had a pleasant word and her confinements were easy which was a great thing to Mrs May. When she came out of the room she nearly fell over Albert, playing with his soldiers outside the door, 'Art tha going to be a soldier when tha's grown, Albert?' she asked, and the little boy smiled.

'Well, Albert, 'appen tha's got a new brother,' Mrs May told him as a tiny cry came from the room behind them and Mrs May had a sudden memory of handing the newborn Albert to Alice Barker. She could see her as clear as day, lifting out her arms for Albert and saying, 'Welcome, my bonny bird,' and Mrs May had laughed because that was a famous song about a baby that was one too many for a poor household.

Tha'rt welcome, little bonny bird,
But shouldn't ha' come just when tha did

and Alice Barker smiled too because he was one of the prettiest babies either of them had ever seen, like a little cherub in her arms.

'It's as yellow as butter,' Frederick said, when he first saw his new son. 'He,' Rachel said. '*He* and his name is Samuel.' Mrs May had brought spice with her for the children and later, when Albert woke up and wouldn't go back to sleep, Ada gave him a piece of the toffee that was the colour of marmalade and gold and he sat happily on her knee, while she told him the story of Snow White and her wicked stepmother, and many other stories too in which the new usurping mother had to dance for ever in red-hot iron clogs. 'And then their mother came back, and they were all happy for ever after.'

'Mother coming back,' Albert chanted happily, and Ada felt for her mother's little silver locket that she kept hidden in her apron pocket where she could touch it like a talisman because she didn't believe it possible that their mother could have gone and left them for ever.

Rachel sat rocking the big wooden crib back and forth with her foot. They kept the baby in the kitchen by the range like a loaf of bread, but this was one loaf that was never going to rise. Mrs May was a regular visitor right into the winter, bringing other women from the village with her who all had their different ideas as to what to do with an ailing baby like Samuel who was as small as Ada's old doll and almost as lifeless.

In the cold evenings of Samuel's one and only winter they would sit in the kitchen, Rachel on one side with the crib, the children on the other, huddled together on the big oak settle, and between the two factions the lamp threw a pool of yellow light that seemed to make the darkness blacker. Frederick was out most evenings again now, drinking in the village. Sometimes Ada would hold Nell in her arms like a baby and Ada and her stepmother would face each other across the kitchen like rival queens. This night Ada had been forced, after a real set-to, to do something useful and was darning stockings. Every so often she looked up and stared at Rachel as if she was looking at an empty space in the kitchen. 'What are you looking at?' Rachel snapped eventually and Ada smiled that false smile she had, that made Rachel want to swipe at her and said, 'Nowt,' and when Rachel persisted said spitefully 'Nobbut a big, fail fuzzock,' and Rachel knew enough of their stupid broad dialect by now to know that she was an ugly donkey.

Next year, Rachel thought, they would send the girl into service and that would be the end of that. And there would be some kind of justice at work when Alice Barker's daughter was having to black-lead and empty slops. Rachel had grown to hate this place. She felt land-locked and out of her sea-salty element in this green land. She missed the screech of seagulls and the potent reek of fish and boiling whale-blubber and if it wasn't for Samuel she might have packed up and gone home. She wasn't sure which she disliked most – husband or children.

'It's time you were all in bed,' she said without looking at any of them.

'Can we wait for Feyther to come home from t'Fox and Grapes?' Lawrence asked, his voice sliding into a whine that irritated Rachel.

'If I say it's time for bed, then it's time for bed.' Rachel spoke with a heavy measure, stressing every word through her gritted teeth. A cleverer boy than Lawrence might have sensed she was eager for a set-to.

'Why not?'

Rachel moved her foot from the rocker and reached across, grabbing Lawrence by the hair and pulling him into the lamplight, but when she saw him she let go as if his hair had burned her skin and gave a gasp of horror. They all gathered round Lawrence with interest – his face was erupting in vicious little red spots. 'Is it t'plague?' Tom asked, looking up at Rachel, who shook her head in disgust and said, 'No, yer big lump – it's chickenpox.'

The fire in the grate of the range had been well banked and still glowed red even at two in the morning. Ada had listened to the hours and half-hours chiming on the mahogany-cased mantel-clock that had belonged to her mother even before she was married to Frederick. Her mother had loved that clock. Ada crept over to the door and lifted the latch, holding her breath in case it squeaked or rattled. She pulled the door open wide so that a sudden inrush of icy air lifted the edge of the crocheted runner on the mantelpiece and wafted a piece of blue sugar paper off the table. But outside the air was still and cracking with frost. Ada was still flushed and hot with the chickenpox and the cold air felt almost pleasant on her skin.

An enormous, cold moon hung above the fields, turning everything blue beneath it. The hoarfrost on the trees glittered like sparkling sugar-icing. Ada wished on the white moon, the only wish that any of them wished – that Rachel would die and her fat body rot and disappear into the ground. She was like one of the great beasts in the field, only that wasn't fair because the beasts in the field meant no harm and were God's creatures, but Rachel was surely the Devil's own.

Ada took out the little silver locket from her pocket and opened it in the moonshine. The hair coiled in the locket looked no colour in this light. She'd disappeared in the night. She'd kissed each of them in turn at bedtime as usual and in the morning she was gone and in her place was the little silver locket slipped under Ada's pillow in the night by her mother's ghost. The next morning Frederick gathered them round the kitchen table and told them their mother was dead and Ada was left to make the oatmeal while Frederick went into the village to try and find a wet-nurse for baby Nellie, cursing as he left, 'She mun have taken t'bloody bairn wi 'er!' Ada didn't see how her mother could be dead without leaving a corpse behind – but if not dead, where could she be?

Ada shut the door as quietly as she'd opened it and tip-toed over to the crib, 'There Samuel, did tha like that? Nice cowd air to haste you to t'Maker.' The baby made a small snuffling noise. 'Tha'rt a mardy gowk for all tha cosseting, eh?' Then, slowly and deliberately, Ada rubbed her finger across the thick crust on top of one of her chickenpox spots so that it broke and she stamped her foot with the pain of it. She took a deep breath and rubbed her finger round on the pus underneath and then reached down into the cot and rubbed it on the baby's face, like a priest giving a blessing.

'What are you doing?' Rachel came across the flags in her voluminous nightgown like a man-o'-war in full sail bearing down on a hapless victim.

Ada jumped and automatically put the offending hand behind her back. 'Nowt,' she said, smiling hugely.

'Little liar! Don't play the innocent with me – get away from that crib!' Rachel's voice was rising all the time, a familiar prelude to her going berserk. 'If you've laid a finger on that baby I'll rip you limb from limb, do you understand?'

Samuel made a small mewling sound from within the depths of the crib and Rachel grabbed Ada's arm and spun her away from it, grabbing her hand at the same time to see what she was hiding. 'There's nowt there!' Ada shouted, 'Nobbut my hand – I was doing nowt to him – I thought I heard 'im bawlin'.'

'As if you'd care,' Rachel said, turning her this way and that, searching in her pockets, and Ada suddenly remembered the locket and made a frantic effort to corkscrew her body away from Rachel's rummaging hands.

'And what's this, madam?' Rachel held the locket aloft, triumphantly. 'Well, well, I know who gave this to you.'

'My mother gave it me, it's got nowt to do wi' you!'

'Oh, but it has,' Rachel said, laughing as Ada scrabbled for the locket. She gave Ada a hefty shove across the kitchen so that she banged into the settle. Rachel fumbled for the catch on the locket, which sprang open suddenly, and she removed the lock of blond hair that was coiled neatly behind the glass and threw it on the embers where it hissed into nothing. Ada was spitting like a kitten and ready to launch herself at Rachel with her nails but at that moment Frederick pushed his way through the door, his face dark from drink and Rachel turned her anger on him, 'Look at you! You're a disgrace, a shiftless good-for-nothing drunkard. I can see why she left you—' but the rest of the sentence was walloped away by Frederick's vast red fist.

The baby had only been dead an hour but already it seemed to have shrivelled into a deflated thing, yet Rachel nursed her corpse child as if it were still alive. 'Shall I run and get t'parson?' Lawrence offered after they'd sat in troubled and guilty silence for a long age. No-one had even stirred to put a log on the fire.

'I'll go,' Ada volunteered quickly, and slipped and slid across the icy yard in her clogs and stumbled along the track to the village, praying for forgiveness all the way for although he had died of a seizure without a chickenpox spot in sight, there was no doubt in Ada's mind that Samuel had been murdered by her wishes.

Diphtheria. She could hear the word being whispered outside the door. It was a pretty word – *diphtheria,* like a girl's name. Rachel had sent for old Dr Simpson, who smiled at Ada from behind his mutton-chop whiskers and looked down her throat and said, 'A-ha, I see, a-ha,' when he smelt the dreadful odour of her breath and saw, across her throat, the membrane that looked like chamois leather. Then Dr Simpson held her hand and said, 'We'll soon have you running around again, Ada,' and thought how pretty the child was, just like her mother.

When he left the room Ada could hear snatches of his conversation with Rachel, 'You must keep the other children away from her . . . a rapid deterioration . . . in cases like this one . . . be over.' Rachel said something shrill but Ada couldn't make out the words, then there were footsteps going down the stairs and silence broken only by the tick-tocking of her mother's mantel-clock which she'd asked to have in the room and which Rachel, numb and penitent in the face of death, had agreed to. After a minute or two, Ada heard the hooves of Dr Simpson's big bay in the yard below. As he rode off into the glimmering winter light he found himself thinking about Alice Barker's curls, a thought which kept him happy until the bay shied at a hare as they went past the home farm and he nearly lost his seat. Ada listened as the clip-clopping grew fainter and fainter and then the snow began to fall.

Ada could hear the rattling sound in her throat, which may as well have been her death rattle, for she knew that when you heard that it meant you weren't going to get better. The sister of a schoolfriend had died of diphtheria last winter so she knew what happened. Death wasn't such a dreadful thing when you got close to it. The church bells were ringing a muffled peal as if they knew she was coming, although really it was for a local lord who had died a few days ago and was being buried today. Christmas had come and gone without the sick-room even knowing about it. The cold weather that had helped to carry off the infant Samuel had intensified and the ground was as hard as iron and cold as lead. They had dug his grave but they would have to use picks to break the ground for Ada.

There had been a blizzard, 'A white over,' Rachel said, trying to get her to drink barley water but her throat hurt too much to swallow. The light coming through the window was dazzling, reflected off the snow, and it seemed to shiver and wave like water. Albert and Lillian and Nell were playing in the snow outside and their high voices broke the deep silence that snow brings.

It began to snow again, lightly at first, but gradually the flakes got bigger and bigger until they were like the downy feathers off the breasts of soft birds, or angels' wings. Ada was standing outside, her bare feet in the crisp, sugary snow and only her white shift on, but she wasn't cold. She looked around to see where the little ones were but there was no sign of them. When she looked at the trees she could see that the snow-heavy branches were full of white birds and even as she looked at them they all rose in the air at once, with a great *shoosh shoosh* of wings, dislodging feathers that drifted and turned into big, lazy snowflakes. Ada watched them in the air, snowflakes melting on the cheeks of her upturned face. The snowy flock wheeled round and flew back overhead, so that Ada could hear their wings beating through the air and from somewhere far off the noise of muffled bells and, nearer, the tick-tock of her mother's clock and the sound of Dr Simpson's big bay horse, trotting across the yard.

Then the birds described great descending circles in the air as they came down towards her and the next moment without her knowing how it happened she was flying with them towards a bright Arctic sun and there at the heart of it was her mother, her arms outstretched to welcome her.

Lawrence disappeared two years later, slipping out of the house one summer morning to run away to sea. Tom was hysterical, convinced that his brother had been removed by some supernatural force. 'Tha daft bugger,' Frederick said, cuffing him on the side of the head. Tom, however, continued to believe that Lawrence had been spirited away into thin air, infecting the younger children with the idea so that for ever afterwards when they remembered Lawrence they remembered him as a mystery, for they never heard from him again, although he did try to write but the family had moved on by then. He landed up in Hull, his shoes worn out and his stomach shrunk to nothing, and he was standing in the middle of the Land of Green Ginger wondering what kind of a place it was to have streets called names like that when an old sailor took pity on him and took him aboard his tramp steamer. For the next two years Lawrence wandered up and down the east coast and across the North Sea to Holland and Germany before taking a job as a stoker on a boat bound for South America. He stayed on that far-flung continent for some fifteen years before home-sickness drove him back to England. By the time he reached home waters the Great War had begun. Home itself was a place he never reached though, as he was blown up in the North Sea by a German mine just as the English coast was sighted.

A year later, one freezing February night, Frederick died of hypothermia, outside his own cottage door – too drunk to reach up to the latch to let himself in. Rachel decided that she'd had enough of country living after this and decamped back to urban civilization. For preference she would have gone back to the coast but she was offered a position as a cook in York by the vicar's sister-in-law and thought she'd be a fool not to take it. First they rented rooms in a slum in Walmgate, but once she'd got the family back on its feet, they had a decent terrace in the Groves. The children went to church, had clean handkerchiefs, had lost their broad accents and had almost forgotten about the country.

When Nell came back from her Lake District honeymoon and discovered that Rachel was dead and buried ('I saw no sense in spoiling your honeymoon by telling you,' Lillian said reasonably), Lillian had already thrown out most of her things, but not the silver locket which she knew had belonged to their mother because in the one and only known photograph of her, which their brother Tom had, the locket was clearly visible. Lillian gave the locket to Nell because, she said, 'You were just the baby, she never even held you,' and they both wept over the empty locket and other things too. They didn't know, of course, that even as they sat together in the parlour in Lowther Street, crying over the locket, their mother was screaming and throwing a vase across a bedroom in Whitby, a vase which had the misfortune to hit Monsieur Jean-Paul Armand square on the temple so that a maid had to be sent for to bring hot water and cold compresses for the huge bruise, growing like a flower on his head.

CHAPTER FIVE

1958

Interlude

BUNTY AND THE PARROT WENT MISSING ON THE SAME night and it was only later when they were both safely returned that we realized this was a co-incidence and that Bunty had not run away with the Parrot. Or, for that matter, the Parrot hadn't run away with our mother, an idea firmly lodged in my own mind because Patricia had recently been reading the *Tales of a Thousand and One Nights* to me and I imagined the Parrot flying through the skies with Bunty hanging grimly, like Sinbad, onto one of its scaly, reptilian legs. The extreme unlikelihood of the Parrot being the only thing that Bunty would choose to take with her when she ran away from home did not, somehow, occur to our childish minds.

It takes us some time to realize that Bunty is missing at all. She is our living alarm-clock and when she doesn't go off we all simply sleep on. We don't wake in fact until a quarter-past nine when a customer, anxious for his Sherley's conditioners, bangs loudly on the Shop door below, waking all the Pets, who have also overslept, and a furious Patricia who hates being late for anything (Patricia is the kind of girl who arrives at school before the caretaker). The information trickles down the house – Patricia wakes Gillian, Gillian wakes me – by bouncing on top of my sleeping body and screaming that I've purloined her Rosebud doll, Denise (Denise has ousted a dejected Sooty and Sweep from her affections), and I wake George by running into the parental bedroom in hysterical tears, displaying the rapidly blooming bruise on my cheek where Gillian's foot has caught me. This is all too much for George who lurches out of bed in a daze, picks up the clock by the side of the bed, stares at it uncomprehendingly, stares at the empty space on the other side of the double bed where Bunty should be and then flops back into bed and mutters, 'Go and find your mother.'

Not such an easy task, as it turns out. We all three of us play 'Hunt the Mother' for at least half an hour before returning to George to admit our hopeless ineptitude at this particular game. 'What do you mean you can't find her?' He is by this time up and shaving with his electric razor while standing guard at the toaster. Occasionally the Shop bell clangs and he has to go through and serve. Although he has his trousers on, he is still in his vest and pyjama jacket and we can hear the usual sophisticated level of Shop humour being exchanged, 'Overslept then, Mr Lennox? Ha, ha, ha.' 'Well, well, George – find something to keep you in bed, then? Ha, ha, ha.' This last being the unmistakable smutty East

London of Walter, buying a cuttlefish for his mother's budgie. Even this purchase is transformed into an occasion for a lewd joke, but George it appears is in no laughing mood.

'How's Doreen?' Walter asks, making a peculiar gesture as if he was pushing up a large, invisible bosom. George mutters something dark about Bunty. 'Lost the wife?' Walter repeats incredulously, 'You jammy bugger, mate!' The expression on George's face does not reveal jamminess as he casts a glance around the Shop – discovering two things almost simultaneously – an absence of Parrot and a presence of Ruby. 'Get some clothes on!' George says instantly as if I was performing a striptease rather than standing in nightdress and slippers forlornly holding aloft a piece of charred toast.

'Little pitchers,' Walter says, fingering one of his ears.

'What's a pitcher?' I ask Patricia, who, back in the kitchen, is burning slice after slice of toast. 'How the hell should I know,' she says viciously and pushes her hair back from her head before screaming in frustration at the toaster. Gillian fetches a box of cornflakes from the cupboard and pours herself a bowl. '*Bambi*,' she says, sprinkling two huge spoonfuls of sugar on her flakes, '*Snow White, Cinderella* – they're pictures.'

The Shop bell announces Walter's departure and George storms back into the kitchen, 'Where the bloody hell is she?' he asks, looking wildly round at each one of us. 'Perhaps she's left a note,' Patricia says, carefully aiming one of the blacker slices of toast at the waste bin.

'A note?' George repeats. He looks stunned. The idea of Bunty having left us, as opposed to having mislaid herself somewhere about the house, hasn't occurred to him. 'Yes, a note,' Patricia says as she accurately lobs the toast into the bin (she's a relentless goal attack in Queen Anne Grammar School's Junior Netball team). 'You know, a note.'

'I know what a bloody note is,' George says angrily and stomps out again. I sigh and reach for the cornflakes box. They spill everywhere but at least some go in the bowl. Patricia butters a piece of smouldering toast and bites into it with a certain grim enjoyment. We are eating standing up, leaning against whatever kitchen counter is available. This liberation from the dining-room tastes of furtive pleasures and we make quite a good breakfast of it in the end, enjoying not only the burnt toast and over-sugared cornflakes but also some daring eggy-toast-fingers that we make in a joint effort around the frying-pan. This spirit of co-operation doesn't extend to getting to school. Once we've eaten our leisurely breakfast Patricia packs her satchel and says, 'Right, I'm off then.'

'What about me?' Gillian wails, quickly shoving the last piece of eggy-toast into her mouth. (Bunty usually accompanies Gillian and me on our long walk to primary school.)

'What about you?' Patricia asks in just the kind of belittling tone that's guaranteed to drive Gillian mad. 'How am *I* getting to school?' Gillian shouts at her, jumping up and down (there's no 'us' in this, I notice).

Patricia shrugs, '*I* don't know,' she says scathingly. 'It's nothing to do with me – anyway you're nearly ten years old, surely you can get yourself to school?' and with that slight on Gillian's maturity she slings her satchel over her back and disappears. Gillian begins to boil over with indignation but returns to a seething simmer when Patricia suddenly reappears. 'I'll get my satchel,' Gillian says hurriedly.

'Don't bother, I haven't come back for *you*,' Patricia says dismissively. 'I forgot to write a note, that's all.' Patricia is writing a note too? 'Are you running away as well, Patricia?' I ask, horrified. 'No, stupid,' she snaps, 'a note because I'm late.' She tears a page from her French jotter and writes, in a perfect counterfeit of Bunty's handwriting – *Dear Miss Everard, I'm sorry Patricia is late coming into school this morning, I'm afraid our dog was run over. Yours sincerely, Mrs G Lennox.*

'What dog?' Gillian asks – we are both hanging over Patricia's shoulder watching her write. 'We don't have a dog.'

'Yes we do, we've got loads of dogs,' Patricia says, folding the note neatly into a square.

'Yes, but they're *Pets*,' Gillian says, confused. 'And one hasn't been run over. Has it?'

'*Gillian*,' Patricia says, looking at Gillian in disbelief. 'You lie *all the time*, so I don't know why you're getting so worked up.' Gillian *is* getting worked up, her cheeks have gone that funny mottled-pink way – a bit like a trout – that they do when she's about to have a tantrum. 'I'm definitely off this time,' Patricia says, ignoring her and then turning to me she says nicely, 'I'll see you tonight, Ruby,' so I repay this favouritism by going to the Back Yard gate to wave goodbye to her, something Bunty never does. In the background I can hear a wail like an air-raid siren starting, 'I want Mummy!'

Well, 'I want doesn't mean I get,' as 'Mummy' never ceases from telling us. We never do get to school that day but spend our time well away from George, mostly in Gillian's bedroom where she takes it upon herself to run an alternative school – all her pupils sitting on the floor while she sits on her bed. I am forced to cram myself into a desk with Denise. Gillian's main duties seem to be handing out punishments and when I venture to complain that when Patricia used to play schools we had lessons, I am put in the corner for over an hour, only let out to go and forage for something to eat. Even then, I fail to make myself teacher's pet as all I can find are a few cream crackers and half a Soreen malt loaf. Occasionally, George shouts up the stairs and asks us if we're all right to which we shout down a resounding, 'Yes!' because we can't imagine what he would do with us if we weren't.

'Have you been here all day?' Patricia asks in amazement, when she comes in from school.

'Yes.'

'And no sign of Mummy?' (The maternal noun is on the verge of extinction in Patricia's vocabulary – but is rescued for this crisis.)

'No.'

She's disappeared without a trace, not a hair nor

a fingernail left. Perhaps she's dead. Perhaps she's joined the household ghosts, passing through walls and gliding down the stairs. If we had Mr Wedgewood or Myra from Auntie Babs' church they might be able to ask our ghosts if they would be so kind as to have a look around and see if she's there. It could certainly give the Ninth Legion something to occupy their time.

George goes out and brings fish and chips back for tea. He looks very worried. 'The bloody Parrot's gone AWOL as well, you know,' he says, shaking his head in mystification. 'Do you think we should call the police?' he asks, and all three of us stare blankly at him as he has never asked our opinion before about anything. 'Well,' Patricia says cautiously. 'Did you actually *look* for a note?'

'Have I had the time to look for a note?' he asks, very aggrieved, and the search party's dispatched once more. Gillian suggests to Patricia that she forges a note. 'What good would that do?' Patricia frowns. 'It would keep him happy,' Gillian urges and Patricia narrows her eyes speculatively. 'So he wouldn't get mad at us you mean?' I concur enthusiastically with this plan, even though I feel slightly ashamed that we're all more concerned with our own fate than our mother's. The plan collapses anyway because none of us can think of anything that Bunty could write that would make George happy.

We search the drawer in Bunty's bedside table which is very neat and tidy but contains no message for

George. It does contain, however, a little silver locket. 'What's this?' I ask Patricia and she shrugs. 'Oh, it's me!' I say delighted, because when I open up the locket I find two tiny photographs of me, one in each wing of the locket, that look as if they've been cut from the Polyphotos Bunty used to have hanging on the living-room wall. Gillian sits on the bed and looks at the locket over my shoulder. 'Mummy's got a picture of me by her bed,' I say pointedly to picture-less Gillian. 'Oh yeah,' she says sarcastically. 'She's got that there because it's a photograph of P— and Patricia digs her hard in the ribs so that she squeals.

Our attention is diverted by Patricia discovering what we presume to be a genuine note in the drawer of George's bedside table, along with a poppy-red packet of Craven A and some loose change and a pink-and-purple packet of Durex. We mull over George's treasure-drawer for a while, trying to get up the nerve to open the envelope with the word 'George' scrawled cruelly across it.

Gillian suggests we steam it open but going down to the kitchen seems a bit risky until Patricia has the bright idea of using the Teasmade at Bunty's side of the bed and filling the kettle in the bathroom. The Teasmade has not been made up – no water in the kettle, no tea in the pot, which, Patricia says, is evidence that Bunty intended to leave and wasn't spirited away by some unnatural force in the middle of the night. This is possibly true – since she's had the Teasmade Bunty has become as ritualistically devoted to her morning tea-ceremony as any geisha girl, but I still can't bring myself to believe that she would wilfully abandon her own children.

I'm wrong, it appears. We manage to open the envelope but not before Patricia has scalded herself and the envelope itself has become wrinkled and soaked – in the end we just tear it open. 'Read it *out*, Patricia!' Gillian pleads desperately because Patricia's reading the note to herself, very stony-faced. 'What does it *say*?'

Patricia reads out loud, giving an uncanny impression of Bunty as she does so, although the words themselves are oddly stilted as if Bunty had copied them from a book – or, more likely, some film. *Dear George, I have come to the end of my patience and feel I cannot go on in this vein much longer and I think it is better if I spend some time apart from you all. Although you know how much I love the children. You say you are not running around with someone else and I must believe you because you're my husband but as you know life has not really been the same for me since P* – Patricia chokes on the next word and gives Gillian a funny look and there is a short, uncomfortable pause before Patricia resumes – *Well, anyway I am going away for a bit because really I've had enough* (that sounds more like Bunty). *Don't worry about me. As if you would, Bunty.*

We digest this in silence for a while – particularly the bit about how much she loves her children – until Patricia snorts and says, 'What a load of rubbish,' which surprises me because I thought it was rather moving. 'Maybe we don't need to give it to him?' Gillian asks hopefully but Patricia, ethical to the last, says we do, and forges another envelope.

'You haven't opened this have you?' George asks, looking up suspiciously from the note.

'Of course we haven't,' Patricia says, sounding very offended. 'The envelope's sealed, isn't it?'

'Hmmph,' George says, playing for time by staring intently at the note long after it's obvious that he's finished reading it. 'Well,' he says eventually. 'Anyway. Your mother's had to go away suddenly to look after Auntie Babs because she's feeling poorly. Auntie Babs that is. Auntie Babs's feeling poorly, not your mother.'

We all murmur in sympathy for Auntie Babs while looking at each other bug-eyed, hardly able to contain our knowledge of the truth. A little while later, when our hysteria has subsided, Patricia reminds George about our imminent holiday – we had all quite forgotten that we are due to go to Whitby for the Whit holiday. George bangs his head on the door. 'No,' he says. 'No, I don't believe it. How could I forget?' he asks, turning to us all with a pantomime face of amazement. We all three give accentuated Gallic shrugs of incredulity – eyes open wide, palms turned upwards. How can these things be? How is it that without Bunty around to remind us we can't do the simplest things like waking up, eating, remembering we're going on holiday?

'I'll close the Shop,' he says finally, after ringing round everyone he can think of who might take over for a week and finding no-one willing or able. Previously, and only in cases of dire need, Granny Nell has been drafted in for Shop-minding, but Uncle Ted's taken her to the Lakes (*see Footnote (v)*) for the week. Of course, George was supposed to have arranged all this a long time ago – Bunty has told us several times that George is 'getting someone in' so we can have a 'proper family holiday'. We all still have lingering memories of last year's holiday when George managed to wriggle out of a rain-sodden week in Bridlington with us (and yet, curiously, could never be found at home when Bunty phoned – she spent most of the holiday in the call-box. He certainly paid for those calls when she got back). 'What would happen to the Pets if you closed the Shop for a week?' sensible Patricia asks. More banging of head on door. Gillian begins to blubber in a very unattractive way. 'We can't miss our holiday!'

'I don't know,' George says, sounding increasingly harassed. He waves his hand around in the air. 'Maybe you could all go to Babs' or something.'

'No,' Patricia reminds him gently – 'Auntie Babs's ill, remember?' He gives her a madman's stare. 'And what about Lucy-Vida?' Gillian says, her sobs reaching a descant.

'Lucy-Vida? Lucy-Vida? What about Lucy-Vida?' George snaps at her.

'She's supposed to be coming with us,' Patricia says. (Auntie Eliza is going into hospital to have the Stilton cheese veins in her legs stripped.) 'She'll be here in the morning.'

George drops to his knees on the floor and bangs his head on the carpet. It's too much for him, he's 'had enough' – wife and Parrot missing, four little girls to look after, a Shop to see to, a holiday to enjoy – he looks up suddenly. An idea spreads like sunshine across his face. 'Ha!' he says but does not elaborate.

Patricia sits in the front and Lucy-Vida, Gillian and myself sit in the back of our battered '48 Ford Anglia. We are still going to Whitby, to spend the half-term holiday in a self-catering flat, as previously arranged, but instead of heading off to Pickering we execute a curious detour. We pass a sign that says 'Leeds, Mirfield, Dewsbury' and I curl up in horror like a hedgehog. Patricia gives him a sharp, sideways look. 'I thought we weren't going to Auntie Babs'.'

'We're not,' George says smugly.

'Whit in Whitby, Whit in Whitby – that's a funny thing, isn't it?' I say conversationally. 'What could you spend in Filey? File?'

'I wonder if Daisy and Rose are going on the Whit Walk this year,' Lucy-Vida says to no-one in particular. 'I doubt it,' Patricia says gloomily. 'Auntie Babs's poorly, remember.' This last fact has been stated so many times over the last twenty-four hours that we're beginning to believe it's the truth. Lucy-Vida, to whom we have, naturally, told everything, including the colour of Durex packets (although nobody has explained to me what they're *for*), keeps forgetting where Bunty is supposed to be and has to be prompted. 'Oh yes, of *course*,' she says theatrically so that George looks uneasily at her in the rear-view mirror.

Eventually, after what seems like an age, we pull up in front of a small, rather drab, terraced house in Chapeltown. 'I won't be a minute,' George says, leaping from the car and leaning his full body weight against the electric doorbell of the house. The door is opened by an invisible hand and George disappears inside. George has informed us that he's 'got someone to look after us' and speculation is rife as to what kind of person this 'someone' might be. We all have our preferences – Lucy-Vida would like Margot Fonteyn, I want Nana, the dog from *Peter Pan*, and Patricia wants Mary Poppins (a woman whom we long for, to take over our neglected upbringing). Gillian, typically, wants a Fairy Godmother to come and look after her and put the rest of us into an orphanage. We get none of these. We get Auntie Doreen.

'Into the back seat, Patricia!' George commands, as if he was talking to a dog. Patricia slinks unwillingly into the overcrowded back and we stare churlishly at the front-seat interloper. 'Girls,' George says. 'This is Mrs Collier, you can call her Auntie Doreen.'

'Auntie Doreen' twists round in the seat and smiles at us. She's a soft, round, brown sort of woman, older than our mother but with less make-up and hair-dye. She puts out a small, plump hand towards a startled Patricia. 'Now I know you must be Patricia,' she says in the most extraordinary accent we've ever heard, 'because you're the tallest.' Tentatively, Patricia shakes the proffered hand. 'So would you be so good, dear, as to introduce me to the other little girls?' Auntie Doreen shakes each of our hands in turn with a grave formality, saying 'How do you do?' to each of us. George watches his brood like a hawk in the rear-view mirror for any sign of bad manners. When the introductions are over, George says, 'Your Auntie Doreen's very kindly agreed to look after you for the week so that you can have your holiday. What do you say to that?'

'Thank you, Auntie Doreen,' we all chorus dutifully. All that is, except for Patricia, who raises her eyebrows at me and mutters 'What is this? *Little House on the Prairie*?' which is a book she particularly loathes. Patricia's rebellious stance goes unnoticed by George who is already attacking the gear-box to find the always shy and bashful reverse gear of the Anglia. The blasphemy with which he usually addresses the reluctant reverse is noticeably muted in Auntie Doreen's presence.

'This is nice,' she says, as George finally manages to turn the car round and grinds into first. She folds her hands in her lap, ready to enjoy herself. (How extraordinary.)

Once we're on the open road Auntie Doreen takes out a packet of cigarettes and asks George if he'd like one. 'Don't mind if I do,' he says expansively as if she were offering a best Havana cigar and she lights two and passes one to George. The compelling intimacy of this act does not go unnoticed in the back seat and we watch them both with new interest. Is Auntie Doreen perhaps a relative of George's?

The journey to Whitby is incident-free – a rarity for any outing in the Anglia when something is usually run over even if it's only the grass verge. Auntie Doreen and George seem to know Whitby quite well and, on the steep run down into the town, point out various landmarks to each other and with a giggle Auntie Doreen says, 'Do you remember those kippers?' and George throws his head back and laughs and sheds at least twenty years from his back.

Whitby certainly looks like a magical place – from the gaunt, mysterious ruins on the cliff-top to the higgledy-piggledy fishermen's cottages – and Patricia is particularly delighted because, she says, this is where the *Demeter*, sailing out of Varna, ended its voyage.

'The *Demeter*?' Auntie Doreen queries. 'Yes,' Patricia says, 'Dracula's ship, landed in a wild, unnatural storm with all the crew dead – and those cliffs,' she points, knowledgeably, 'must be where he ran up, disguised as a black dog. A hound of hell,' she adds with relish and I shiver, remembering Auntie Babs' stairs. 'Perhaps,' she says, scrutinizing Lucy-Vida who is squeezed between her and Gillian (I am at the end, crushed against the unreliable car door and will probably fall out if we take a particularly challenging bend), 'perhaps Auntie Eliza named you after Lucy Harker? She became a vampire, you know,' she adds with relish.

''Appen she did,' Lucy-Vida says phlegmatically. She's known Patricia far too long to be scared by her.

'My, my,' Auntie Doreen says, without a trace of sarcasm. She turns her head round so she can see Patricia. 'What a glorious imagination you have, Patricia,' and Patricia tries hard to look as if she isn't pleased, but I can tell she is because, sitting next to her, I can feel her glowing pink with heat.

Unerringly, we make our way to the Royal Crescent and, once George has carried the bags up the three flights of stairs to our apartment, he stays only long enough for a cup of tea (all the makings of which we have brought with us in a cardboard box) before saying, 'Right, I'd better get back to the Shop then,' and leaving us all abruptly in the company of a total stranger.

'Well,' says Auntie Doreen, the one word containing more vowel sounds than we knew existed, 'we'd better get unpacked, girls, so we had.' Patricia's curiosity overcomes her usual social reticence. 'Where do you come from, Auntie Doreen?' and Auntie Doreen gives us the benefit of her big swooping, choky laugh and says, 'Why Belfast, Patricia, Belfast.' Patricia disappears with the tea things so Lucy-Vida and I have to look to Gillian for geographical enlightenment. 'It's the capital of Wales,' she says authoritatively.

We are all very taken with the flat; it is completely free of the usual domestic clutter and has just enough of everything – sheets, blankets, pots, cutlery – with the addition of a token ornament or two. The wallpaper is clean and flowery and has not been impregnated with the reek of family dramas and the autumn-leaves carpet and orange curtains of the lounge speak only of holiday good-humour. There is a slight drawback in that there are only two bedrooms and Auntie Doreen gets one of them, leaving we four girls with two double beds in one room. It's least bothersome to let Patricia have one of the beds to herself and for the three of us to squash into the other. To compensate for this crush (which also includes Panda, Teddy, Denise and Lucy-Vida's unclassifiable 'Mandy-Sue' which looks like a black-and-white cat that has suffered at the hands of an incompetent taxidermist) our bedroom has a staggeringly good view, over the Crescent Gardens below, across the Prom, over the Pavilion, and then on, for ever and ever, over a rolling, unbounded North Sea – the edge of the world as we know it.

It takes a couple of days for Auntie Doreen to win Patricia over. Indeed, to begin with, Patricia is downright hostile and even runs away for several hours and is eventually found down on the beach helping the donkey-man lead the donkeys up and down. The donkey-man is quite pleased with himself for acquiring an unpaid assistant, unaware that she is lulling him into a false sense of security in order to carry out her grand plan of liberating all the donkeys. She is brought home in tears (unusually) and cannot be mollified even though Auntie Doreen does not resort to the physical abuse with which Bunty normally placates us. The following day, when we're taking a stroll along the Prom, Patricia falls off it and although it's cleverly disguised as an accident, I think, in retrospect, that this was actually a spontaneous suicide attempt.

She does no more than sprain a wrist and is taken home to be expertly bandaged and slinged by Auntie

Doreen. 'I was a nurse during the war,' she smiles, when complimented on her bandaging. This puts her up several notches in our estimation – we all think a nurse is an excellent thing to be, although none of us is planning to be one ourselves when we grow up. Patricia still has an overwhelming desire to be a vet and save every animal in the world from death; Lucy-Vida is going to be a chorus-girl – she can do breathtaking high kicks and splits with her long legs, actions which reveal grubby underwear that strikes horror in the breasts of Bunty and Auntie Babs. I am going to be an actress when I grow up ('You already are one, Ruby,' Bunty says), and Gillian is simply going to be famous and doesn't care how she achieves it. Unlike Bunty, Auntie Doreen listens to these girlish aspirations with real interest.

Patricia capitulates, impressed by the quality of tender care afforded to her injury by Auntie Doreen – *Does it hurt when I do that, Patricia? Oh, I am sorry . . . You're a brave girl, Patricia, so you are . . .* The contrast with Bunty is unavoidable. There are many other areas where a comparison with Bunty can only work in Auntie Doreen's favour. Her cooking for example – with no fuss whatsoever, she produces big, hearty meals of the stew-and-dumpling variety, 'Heavy food to weigh you down, Patricia, so you won't run away,' she laughs – and, astonishingly, Patricia laughs along with her! Nor does she have any qualms on the pudding front and dishes up apple and rhubarb pies from Botham's or sticky custard slices – in fact anything we care to choose on our daily visits to the shops. (Auntie Babs, Auntie Gladys and Bunty – the invisible Greek chorus in our heads – throw their hands up in horror, exclaiming, 'Shop-bought!' but do we care? No, we don't.) What's more we have fish and chips for dinner *nearly every single day* as well as frequent trips to the Rock Shop and the candy-floss stalls and many, many ice-cream cornets, because, as Auntie Doreen says, adjusting her large, bouncing bosom, 'We *are* on holiday, after all, so we are.'

This is not to say she is generally lax or slovenly. Quite the contrary, there is order and harmony in everything she does and she is as calm and unflappable as the harbour-wall when confronted by the high-tides of Gillian's emotions. She has a strange gift for persuading us into thinking that the mundane tasks of self-catering life – the washing of pots, the making of beds – is yet another occasion for orderly fun and games so that Gillian actually fights to get her hands on the carpet-sweeper before anyone else. 'Ee our Gillian,' Lucy-Vida marvels, 'I didn't know you 'ad it in you, kid.' We have many things in us that we didn't know about and under Auntie Doreen's guidance they struggle to see the light of day. Even my sleepwalking seems to be in abeyance under Auntie Doreen's watchful night-time care. ('It's because she doesn't wake you up that you don't know about it,' Gillian says scornfully. Thank you, Gillian.)

Auntie Doreen orchestrates games on the beach from which no-one marches off in a huff; she organizes little pedestrian expeditions – up the 199 Steps to the Abbey, along the beach to the café at Sandsend – on which we sing things like 'Ten Green Bottles' and 'One Man Went to Mow'. We make sandcastle after sandcastle, their little turrets proudly stuck with paper Union Jacks and rampant-red Scottish lions, and when we've had enough of the sand and sea we dawdle around the quaint streets of Whitby, admiring the funny street names, almost as funny as York street names – 'Dark Entry Yard', 'Saltpanwell Steps' and 'Arguments Yard' (George and Bunty should have lived there).

Auntie Doreen knows more card games than I knew existed in the world (Patricia is overjoyed to learn there are so many different varieties of Patience) and on the rainy afternoons, of which there are several, she actually *enjoys* playing games with us, sitting on the carpet amongst us and passing round chocolate digestives and orange squash. She even manages to persuade Gillian not to cheat, something no-one else has ever been able to do – although Gillian draws the line at not screaming when she loses. Patricia usually just hits her when she does this, but Auntie Doreen leads Gillian away to the bedroom and shuts the door on her and says 'Now then, let the poor child get it out of her system.'

Schooled by the week in Bridlington we have brought a lot of games with us and as well as the ubiquitous rounds of Snap we also play draughts, Ludo, Snakes and Ladders and endlessly exciting games of Buccaneer, on whose azure board, figured with compass-points and treasure-maps, our little wooden pirate ships plough the main, laden with little barrels of rum, small gold bars, tiny rubies (!), and pearls like bird-seed. We are much better at Buccaneer than we are at 'Hunt the Mother'. But our favourite game of all is Astron, a thrilling game in which our little spaceships move on a celluloid grid that is scrolled across outer space. Our spaceships have to dodge hazards – showers of meteorites, asteroid belts, rogue comets and so on – and, before we can achieve our goal (the Heart of the Sun) we must negotiate one last, awful menace – the huge, gaseous Rings of Saturn. The Rings of Saturn are Deadly, we know that because it says so on the Astron board and they're always catching Auntie Doreen's spaceship out. 'Oh, there I go again!' she says with a little scream as she explodes in a cloud of space dust. I think Patricia sometimes plays Astron in her sleep because I've heard her calling out, 'Watch out for the Rings of Saturn, Ruby! – they're Deadly!'

For the first time in our lives we say our prayers before we go to bed. 'Just a short one,' Auntie Doreen says, 'just so God knows you're here,' and, at the end, she makes us add a PS asking God to look after Mummy and Daddy. Auntie Doreen, perhaps because George has never described his family in very great detail to her (he can be very vague himself), is of the belief that Lucy-Vida is our sister. Nobody bothers to tell her that she's actually our cousin as it would hardly make any difference and anyway we rather like having a fourth sister. 'Four of us again,' Patricia murmurs – rather mournfully – when setting the table for breakfast one morning. She has brought *Little Women* on holiday with her (as well as

What Katy Did and *Black Beauty* – from which she reads aloud the more barbaric paragraphs so that we all cry, except for Gillian) and sometimes we play at being the March family – Patricia, naturally is Jo, Gillian is Amy (who else), Lucy-Vida is Meg (not very good casting) and I – much against my will – am forced to be meek and mild Beth. Auntie Doreen, however, makes a splendid 'Marmee'.

Auntie Doreen mentions Bunty quite a lot. She says things like, 'I'm sure your mummy wouldn't want you to do that, Gillian,' and 'I expect your mummy's missing you, Patricia,' although when we ask if she actually knows Bunty she laughs and splutters on her cigarette and says, '*Goodness* me, no!'

Lucy-Vida asks Auntie Doreen if she's got any children of her own and Auntie Doreen's face turns very sad and she says, 'No dear, I had a little girl but I lost her,' and when Patricia says softly, 'What was she called, Auntie Doreen?' Auntie Doreen regards her with bleak eyes and shakes her head. 'I don't know.' How odd not to know the name of your own child! Or perhaps not, as Bunty has to run through all our names before she comes to the right one and I'm always at the end of the list – *Patricia, Gillian, P—, Ruby, what's your name?* Perhaps if Bunty doesn't come back we can have a new mother, Auntie Doreen for preference, a mother that will remember my name.

George arrives on the Friday night and says we'll be going home first thing in the morning. We have fish and chips for supper – we have already had them at dinner-time, down on the pier, and when Auntie Doreen says, 'Well, I don't know about you, children, but I'll be quite happy not to see a chip for a while, so I will,' we all agree heartily with her. Afterwards, we all of us play a raucous game of Pontoon until it's well past bedtime. 'Where are you going to sleep, Daddy?' Patricia asks as she puts the cards back in their box. 'Oh,' George says, borrowing Bunty's smile for a second, 'I'll just sleep here on the settee, Patricia.' So that's all right.

I'm woken early next morning by a posse of screeching gulls outside the window and I wander into the lounge and ensconce myself behind the orange curtains at one of the big windows to have a last look at the sea – as blue and as sparkling as a sapphire. It's the most wonderful morning and I can't believe that today we're not going to go down again and play on the glinting, newly-washed strip of sand that the tide is peeling away from. I've completely forgotten that George is here – there's no sign of him on the settee – not even a blanket or a pillow to remind me – and it's only when I hear his phlegm-fuelled smoker's cough approaching that I remember him. I peek out from within my curtain-hide and see him, in candy-striped pyjamas, scratching his neck as he comes into the room. Then Auntie Doreen comes in, dressed in a shell-pink nylon slip, her blowsy, unsupported bosom wobbling like a blancmange within, and she puts her solid fleshy arms round George's waist from behind so that her hands meet somewhere underneath his vest and he lets out a funny kind of groan. Auntie Doreen laughs and says 'Ssshh,' and George says, 'God, Doreen,' and shakes his head in a baffled, rather sad way. But then Auntie Doreen says, 'Come on Georgie-Porgie, let's get these kiddies up and breakfasted,' and George sighs again and lets her lead him out of the room by his pyjama-cord, like a condemned man on a tumbril.

We drop Auntie Doreen back in Leeds, after lengthy goodbyes and farewell hugs; even Patricia has damp eyes as we pull away. Auntie Doreen's spirit lingers on in the form of rousing choruses of 'One Man Went to Mow' and a round robin version of 'Ten Green Bottles' and in no time at all the familiar bulk of York Minster beckons us on a rapidly approaching horizon. 'Who's looking after the Shop?' Patricia asks (George has missed nearly all of Saturday trading), and George says, 'I closed up for the day,' and we're flattered that he has put his family before Mammon.

We barge into the Shop with our suitcases. 'Shop!' Gillian shouts, not expecting any response, and so stands open-mouthed with shock when she sees Bunty emerging from the back.

'Mummy!' we all gasp in amazement because it seems years since we've even thought about her. 'Bunty,' George says, and adds, somewhat unnecessarily, 'you're back.' There's an awkward silence which should have been filled with us all running towards Bunty and kissing her – or perhaps (a better version), Bunty running towards us – but we remain rooted by the Shop door until finally George says, 'Well, I'll put the kettle on, shall I?' but Bunty says, 'It's all right, I'll do it,' and walks quickly away in the direction of the kitchen as if she'd just come back from a trip to the hairdresser's rather than having run away from us for over a week.

The smile on George's face fades Cheshire-cat like, as he watches Bunty's retreating back, and the moment she's finally out of view he spins round and faces us all, a desperate look on his face, as if he can hear the guillotine blade being sharpened. 'Listen,' he whispers urgently, 'you weren't on holiday with Doreen – do you understand?' We nod our heads, although we don't really understand at all. 'Who were we on holiday with?' Patricia asks, intrigued. George stares at her, an expression of fixed madness on his face – you can actually see the workings of his brain etched on his retina. 'Who?' Patricia prompts insistently, to an accompaniment of the unnerving sound of a guillotine being raised. 'Who, Daddy? Who?'

Bunty's muffled voice drifts from the kitchen. 'By the way, who looked after the Shop all week? It was closed when I got back.'

'What time was that?' George shouts with a forced kind of nonchalance.

'About half an hour ago.'

George breathes a sigh of relief and shouts, 'Walter's mother – I told her to knock off early, she gets a bit tired in the afternoons.' 'Walter's mother?' Not surprisingly, Bunty doesn't sound convinced. Walter's mother is almost as batty as Nell. No doubt, with a little prompting from Walter (Walter owes George a favour), his mother can be convinced that she actually *did* mind the Shop all week.

George bobs down so that he's at eye-level with all of us except Patricia. 'I was with you, in Whitby. *I* was looking after you all week, right?'

'Right,' we murmur in another round robin. Bunty comes through and tells us that the tea's mashed.

'Remember,' George says to us, 'no Doreen.' He taps the side of his nose with his finger. 'Mum's the word.' A wholly inappropriate phrase, given the circumstances.

'Let's have a treat for tea,' Bunty suggests as we sit upstairs, rather stiffly, drinking our cups of tea.

'Oh good,' Gillian says. 'What?'

'Fish and chips, of course,' Bunty says, beaming at us.

I'm woken in the pitch-black of night by something scrabbling at the window. I lie rigid in my bed, wide-awake with horror, imagining a particularly ravenous vampire trying to get in. How long until dawn? A very long time, I discover, and I lie listening to the noises that an old house makes at night – the settling of ancient timbers, the cracking of plaster and the *tramp* and *clank* of thousands of hob-nailed legionary sandals marching up and down the staircases. These are harmless noises compared to the thing trying to get in my window. When it's quite light and the birds have started singing, I pluck up enough courage to peek through the curtain. It's not a vampire at all, but the Parrot, sitting on the window-sill and looking very thin and bedraggled. It has the same expression of defeat on its face as George, as if it had spent the week looking for, and failing to find, South America.

Things quickly return to normal for all of us, including the Parrot. As soon as George and Bunty have their first falling-out, Lucy-Vida, as if by magic, remembers that she is not actually our sister and escapes back to Auntie Eliza and Uncle Bill. The holiday rapidly takes on the quality of myth – faded and tantalizingly beyond recall – as if it had happened to children in a story rather than us. We enjoyed ourselves too much to want to remember. For a while we talked about Auntie Doreen amongst ourselves, but, by and by, she grew as unreal as Mary Poppins herself. Some months later Gillian had even come to believe that we had seen her flying, skimming along the West Pier and circling the green and red lights of the harbour mouth. So sweet did this memory seem to our benighted sister, that we never had the heart to disenchant her.

Footnote (v) – Rain

1958: TED PUT HIS MOTHER'S SUITCASE DOWN ON THE FLOOR of her room in the boarding-house and then lingered, running his finger along the mantelpiece and humming tunelessly. Nell couldn't wait for Ted to go away so she could take off her corset and stockings and lie down on the bed. 'Well, I'm going to unpack, Mother, I'll see you down at the tea table?' Ted said, hovering in the doorway, and Nell looked at him vaguely. What did he want exactly? Nell's youngest child was nearly thirty, yet whenever she looked at him she could only see a little boy. Ted used to be her favourite but now she found him distracting, disturbing, he gave her the impression that she had something he wanted but she hadn't the faintest idea what it might be. She shooed him away with her hands. 'Right then, at the tea table, Ted.'

Ted had just left the Merchant Navy after twelve years and this week in the boarding-house in Kendal was supposed to help him find his land-legs. Nell hadn't wanted to come. She didn't like leaving home any more, not that she ever had left it very much.

Ted closed the door of her room quietly as if she was an invalid and Nell wondered how long she had to go before she died. Death was a terrifying thing and yet more and more Nell found herself thinking that she'd be glad when it was all over.

It was warm in the bedroom although the sash window was open at the top and the nets billowed out gently in the breeze. There was the hard narrow bed, a dressing table, a wardrobe, a bedside table and a clock on the little cast-iron mantelpiece. The clock said ten to four but Nell didn't know if it was right. 'I've been to the Lakes before,' Nell said suddenly as they had driven into Kendal and Ted crashed his gears in surprise because he never thought of his mother having been anywhere farther than York Market on a Friday morning.

'Really? When?'

'On honeymoon.'

'Honeymoon?' While Ted tried to imagine his mother on something as self-indulgent as a honeymoon, Nell was thinking what a strange word that was, *honeymoon*, so soft and sweet, like violet creams and rosewater and that Valentine card that Percy Sievewright had given her that was all covered in lace. Inside he'd written, in his big, round policeman's script, *I am yours forever* and the funny thing was that it was true, for nobody else would want him now, would they?

1919: Nell knew she must be dreaming because she was

no longer in the room in the boarding-house in Kendal that Ted had booked with such a fuss. Now she was in her honeymoon bed in that gloomy hotel Frank had taken her to, overlooking a lake. It was a hot, stuffy night, the last of several. All day long Nell had felt as if the heavy weather was a physical force, crushing the top of her skull down. 'There'll be a thunderstorm tonight, Nelly,' Frank had said to her as if it was a personal promise to cheer her up. But how could she be cheered when he was on top of her like a lead weight, heavier than the weather, pressing her down. Would he do this every night of their married life? Would there be no relief from his thick cotton pyjamas and his prickly little moustache and that other part of his anatomy that she had to turn her eyes away from because it was so embarrassing.

There was a strange buzzing noise in the room and it took Nell a long time to realize that the noise was in the room and not in her head. She gave Frank a little shake to wake him so he could deal with it. He was already snoring very gently by her side. She didn't understand how sleep could come so easily to a person. Lillian was the same; every night she just turned over like a small animal getting comfortable and fell into a sleep as sweet as a baby's, while Nell used to lie next to her, staring at the ceiling and knowing she would take hours to find sleep. She was almost glad when Lillian moved out of their room after Albert died. Without a word of explanation or farewell she'd taken all her things and moved into his room and the only reference

Lillian made to this decision was next morning over breakfast, when she said, 'Oh, Nelly, I wish we hadn't changed his sheets when he went back to the Front.' Rachel had thrown a teaspoon at Lillian and said she was disgusting but Nell knew what she meant, if they could just have touched something of his once more, smelt his scent like dogs trailing something lost.

She pinched Frank on his arm but he brushed her away as if it was her that was the insect rather than the angry little sawmill buzzing at the window. Nell felt for the matches on the bedside table and struggled to light the candle so that she could see what the creature was.

When she saw the insect she gave a shocked little scream and hit Frank hard because, flying across the room – straight towards the honeymoon bed – was a huge monster of a wasp, a great mutant black and yellow thing droning steadily like a Zeppelin. Frank took a few seconds to come to but when he did he said, 'Bloody hell, it's a hornet!'

Nell reached down and picked up a slipper from the linoleum and flapped it around her head. The hornet darted off and did a circuit of the gas light hanging from the centre of the room. 'Kill it! Kill it!' Nell screeched at Frank as he slid cautiously out of his side of the bed and felt for his own slipper. He crept towards the hornet which was still furiously circling the gas light and tried to bat it with his slipper. The hornet made a feint at Frank and he ducked and twitched and held onto his hair and Nell surprised both of them by laughing out loud. 'It's not bloody funny, Nell!' he said crossly, keeping his eyes fixed on the hornet that was going up and down like a lift at the window.

Nell slid down the bed and pulled the covers over her head. He was right, it wasn't funny at all. That hornet really had him worried, he was dancing around the room like a real namby-pamby; you wouldn't think a man could go through the whole of the Great War and still be a coward. Percy would have dealt with the hornet no bother – firmly, like a policeman. And Albert, Albert would have tried to set it free; she could see him as if he were there, turning to her with a big grin. She remembered a time he'd caught a bee, a big bumble, in his cupped hands and turned to her with his lovely smile and said, 'This is a right big lad, Nelly, d'you want to see it?' and then he'd opened his hands and let it go.

She could hear Frank grumbling through the covers. 'You'd think it would be able to see that the bloody window's open,' he said, but she ignored him. And Jack, what would Jack have done with the insect, she wondered? Nell didn't think she'd ever really known him. Sometimes she thought it was just as well he was dead because she couldn't imagine what their marriage would have been like. He would have soon tired of her; she could see the way he'd looked at her on his leave after the Somme, doubtful-like, as if he couldn't believe what a wet dishcloth she was.

Sometimes in the honeymoon bed, when Frank

slipped off her ribbon-decked trousseau nightdress and touched her shoulders and moaned as if he was ashamed of what he was going to do to her, then Nell thought about Jack and his beautiful skin, like polished walnut – skin that would be all rotted away now. Soon there'd be nothing but clean bone left, and that would be the end of Jack Keech. It didn't seem right that a person could cease to exist like that. Like Percy, like Albert. Like their mother.

Frank's voice was triumphant. 'I've killed the bugger, Nelly! Nelly? Why are you crying, what's wrong? It's all right now, lass – I've killed it.' Frank put his arms round her and patted her back cautiously; he had no idea what to do when people cried and certainly didn't know what to do when Nell made a horrible choking noise and wailed, 'I want my mother!' In the distance, the thunder began to rumble.

1958: 'Mother! Mother? Are you all right?' Ted was standing in the doorway, knocking on the doorpost and regarding her uncertainly. 'Aren't you coming down? They've already served the soup – it's brown Windsor. You'll like that. Won't you?' he added doubtfully because Nell didn't look much like a woman who had the soup course on her mind.

His mother sighed and sat up on the bed. 'I'll be down in a minute, all right?' When Ted had gone, Nell got up awkwardly from the bed and struggled back into her corset. She stood in front of the mirror to brush her hair and put a dab of powder on her nose and tried to remember the smell of Jack Keech's skin and the feel of his hair, but it was so long ago now that she couldn't even remember what he looked like. It began to rain, a light summer shower, and the smell of the rain on the new June grass made Nell feel suddenly wretched.

CHAPTER SIX

1959

Snow Feathers

GILLIAN'S LAST DAY. IT'S CHRISTMAS EVE WHEN GILLIAN pays the price of all those golden-blond curls, so there'll never be much chance of forgetting the anniversary of her death. It will put a blight on Christmas this year, and for quite a few Christmasses to come, I bet. We're going to the pantomime this particular Christmas Eve. I like to think this is some kind of compensation for Gillian ('At least she had a good time before she died' kind of thing), but in fact it's the very fact that we're going to the pantomime that kills her.

'Ruby!' This is George shouting up the stairs, competing with the rain hammering on the window.

'RUBY!!'

He doesn't really want anything. I know that tone of voice. He's walked into the kitchen and found Bunty doing her impression of the Martyred Wife (she should have taken it up professionally) and he'll be so irritated by this that he's looking for the nearest person to take it out on. Me.

Although it's cold in the bedroom – there is no heat in any of our bedrooms – I am warm after having just completed a vigorous hula-hooping session in the rather confined space between the beds. Now I'm curled up happily on my pink candlewick bedspread with an old copy of Gillian's *Judy*. My bedspread is the exact match of Gillian's on the other side of the room, except that Gillian's is peach because she got the first choice of colours. I have to share Gillian's bedroom nowadays because Nell has left her house in Lowther Street and moved in with us. This is because, according to George, she's 'not the full shilling', a phrase I don't entirely understand although you only have to spend a couple of hours in her company to see that she is undergoing a metamorphosis of some kind. She gets very confused (so do I but not about things like what century it is), not confused enough to be 'put away' (which is what George wishes for when it's his turn for the wishbone), just serious enough to get on Bunty's nerves all the time. But then what doesn't get on Bunty's nerves?

As you can imagine, Gillian is furious about this new arrangement and in order to placate her I have to creep around pretending I'm not really here. I spend a lot of time placating Gillian and yet Patricia (a teenager now!) spends no time at all on this task. But then Patricia isn't really in the same space-time continuum as the rest of us any more (if this is what being an adolescent's like then I do *not* want to be one).

'RUBY!!'

He isn't going to forget about me, is he? Guiltily, I

unruffle the candlewick. Lying on the beds after they have been made is strictly against Bunty's domestic rules. I think life would be tidier for her if we didn't sleep in our beds at all. She can hardly wait to get us out of them in the morning, yanking back the curtains and tweaking us out from under the covers so that she can eradicate our warm shapes from the sheets as quickly as possible, like an odd form of child cruelty.

Our bedroom (Gillian never uses this plural pronoun. 'My bedroom,' she says pointedly. As if I could forget.) has a carpet on the floor and pink flowers growing on trellises on the wallpaper and a narrow oak wardrobe that smells like the inside of old suitcases. The most important piece of furniture is a kidney-shaped dressing-table with a frill round it that matches the curtains. Gillian regards this as hers as well, even though it was bought for 'us', along with the candlewick bedspreads, after I moved into the bedroom. One of the (many) reasons that Gillian loathes having to share a room with me is because I still walk in my sleep and she's petrified that I'm going to do something nasty to her when she's fast asleep and unable to defend herself. Hah! If only.

I check my face in the dressing-table mirror for signs of guilt, not just over the bedspread – who knows what else I might be doing wrong? You never can tell, not with George and Bunty who have all kinds of unwritten rules; sometimes I think they're running some kind of secret society of Masonic complexity, although not always in full agreement with each other – just to make it even more difficult for their poor children. Some of these rules are well known, others less so, and I'm constantly being trapped unawares by the more mysterious ones. These are revealed haphazardly – only yesterday I learnt that girls shouldn't sit with their legs crossed (this from George) and that the Labour Party is more dangerous than the Catholic Church (from Bunty).

'Ruby! Come downstairs and give your mother a hand!' I bet a 'hand' is the last thing Bunty wants. I go down the stairs very reluctantly, especially the last flight down to the kitchen, where the more truculent of the ghosts plot and conspire their come-back. There is a faint sound of puppies whimpering and kittens snoring in the Shop and underneath that a different stratum of quiet noise as the ghosts get ready for their festival celebrations. These are the last days of living Above the Shop – Bunty already has her eye on a 'nice little semi' out on the wilder suburban shores of Acomb and our progress thither is considerably accelerated by Gillian's death which is the prime cause of the Great (and truly terrible) Pet Shop Fire. So some good will come out of Gillian's death for Bunty. And for me, of course, because I will take full possession of the kidney-shaped dressing-table (slightly smoke-damaged).

I pause outside the kitchen door and listen before going in. It seems peaceful enough. It's important to me that everyone remains in a good mood because of the pantomime. I have been on outings before with George and Bunty when they were fighting, and it's not pleasant, believe me. The fact that we were going at all on Christmas Eve is a source of some confusion. We don't usually go until January but I think Bunty has got it into her head that it shows more style to go on the opening night – Christmas Eve. So really she's responsible for Gillian's death.

Cautiously, I open the door. The kitchen feels warm but it doesn't fool me. Frost glitters everywhere, on the new English Electric washing machine, on the humming refrigerator and the Kenwood Chef mixer. You can almost see the atmosphere in here like thick, cold smoke spreading out from George and Bunty, figures of icy sovereignty in their Kingdom Above the Shop.

'Your mother could do with some help.'

This is clearly an exercise of power on George's part – he can't get any over Bunty, so he's wielding it over the most helpless member of the family – me. Ever since coming back from my mysterious exile in Dewsbury I have been the scapegoat in this house. It is quite obvious from the set expression on Bunty's face that she is doing very nicely without any help, thank you. She is standing at the sink peeling potatoes with demonic fury, every arc and bone of her body stretched taut. (Sometimes I try to imagine Bunty as a child but for some reason this makes me unbearably sad – see *Footnote (vi)*). Raw undercurrents of feeling bubble and break on the surface of her skin. Sparks of bitter static fly from the tips of her baby blond hair. Something particularly horrible is happening between these two, something, we suspect, to do with The Floozy.

George is sitting at the little kitchen table shaking the

icy rain off his moustache like a dog. I wonder why he has been out? He ought to be in the Shop at this time of day. Maybe he was buying last-minute Christmas presents for us all. Maybe he's been having a secret meeting with The Floozy. The Floozy is a new addition to our family life. Only Bunty speaks about her as such, George never refers to her at all but behaves as if Bunty had invented her from an overheated imagination. For example, a typical exchange about The Floozy goes something like this:

BUNTY: (to George) Do you know what *time* it is? Where have you been? (silence) With your Floozy I suppose?

GEORGE: (scathingly) Don't be ridiculous. I've been having a pint in The Punch Bowl with Walter.

BUNTY: I can't imagine what she sees in you – it can't be your looks, and it's certainly not your money. What do you do – pay her?

GEORGE: (mildly) Have you seen *The Evening Press* anywhere?

We, the Innocents, are a bit confused as to what The Floozy actually is, although we know she's *bad*. Patricia says she's a Jezebel but that's the name of the next-door shop's cat, for heaven's sake.

George's face is as cold and wet as the kitchen window and he is making a performance out of putting on his slippers and lighting a cigarette so it will seem he's very busy. George takes up a lot of room. Bunty's always saying that there isn't enough room Above the Shop, usually in the same sentence that she mentions the 'nice little semi', but I think it's mainly George that takes up the room. True, Above the Shop does seem very crowded but I think it's an illusion. Patricia, for example, hardly ever leaves her bedroom nowadays and Nell takes up less space than the ghosts.

It would be better for Bunty if George stayed in the Shop all the time – she could push his meals across the passage to him and he could push his washing back.

'Any chance of a cup of tea, Bunt?'

George is trying to imitate the way he thinks happily married couples speak to each other. He often does this when Bunty is in a bad mood (or at any rate, worse than usual) and it's so patently artificial that all it does is make her even crosser. If we all know this, why doesn't he? Bunty stops peeling potatoes, wipes her hands and sighs noisily. Putting the kettle on the stove, she lights the gas with the same look on her face as the Virgin Mary has, standing at the foot of the cross in the painting in the Catholic church that my new friend Kathleen Gorman has recently introduced me to. (*Nobody*, not even Patricia, knows I have been in there.) I didn't like it, it was full of dripping hearts and pictures of people doing horrible things to other people. Bunty would have liked the Catholic church if she had given it a chance.

'The child can do that,' George says, indicating the abandoned potatoes in the sink.

'No, she can't,' Bunty snaps, much to 'the child's' relief. Bunty looks like she's willing to defend her potato peeler to the last King Edward. She pushes her hair back from her forehead in a centuries-old genetic gesture of suffering. The life of a woman is hard and she'll be damned if anyone is going to rob her of her sainthood. There's a tremendous battle of wills going on in the kitchen, in which I am clearly the hapless pawn. George keeps sizing up for a real ding-dong and then backing down because he doesn't really want to risk the consequences of an argument. He's been in Bunty's bad books since we opened the first door on the advent calendar (or rather since Gillian did, as she has done nearly every day. Patricia has got round this by making her own personal advent calendar out of a cornflakes box). I haven't discussed with anyone this new phase of the Cold War (more of an Ice Age really) between our parents but then Gillian and I rarely 'discuss' anything – she shouts, I ignore her. And Patricia, since entering adolescence, is incommunicado. I don't have the right words anyway – I won't have the right vocabulary for several years.

George stubs out his cigarette and makes a kind of snorting noise in his throat and settles back into his chair to watch Bunty making his cup of tea (well, this is 1959). He clears his throat and spits into his handkerchief just as Bunty puts the cup and saucer in front of him with a glazed expression on her face. This is the expression she wears when she picks up George's socks, handkerchiefs and underpants (wearing rubber gloves) and drops them into a bucket of Dettol to soak before they are allowed to join the rest of our barely-sullied washing in the English Electric.

Bunty reclaims her peeler while I remain hovering in the doorway, uncertain as to whether I'm still needed in my pawn-role. They seem to have forgotten it's Christmas Eve and, despite the mound of mince pies on the dresser, the kitchen is not carolling with the festive spirit. The Christmas cake, I notice, is sitting un-iced on the refrigerator, decidedly naked in its almond paste. This is a bad sign. The cake is a close relative of the Boxing Day trifle, both regarded by Bunty with the kind of reverence that Kathleen's mother affords the Nativity Scene.

'We *are* going to the pantomime tonight, aren't we?' I ask rather recklessly.

'Why else do you think I'm going flat out like this?' Bunty spins round, the potato peeler moving like a dagger through the air, indicating a panorama of mince pies, Christmas cake, potatoes, George.

'*And* I haven't had time to make a pudding.' Her eyes narrow to slits as she looks at George and adds menacingly, 'It'll have to be tinned fruit.' She advances on a tin of peaches, clawing them open with a tin opener and pouring them into a big glass bowl where they swim about like goldfish. George shakes out the evening paper and starts whistling 'Jingle Bells', softly, under his breath.

'Haven't you got anything to do, Ruby?' Bunty asks sharply.

I haven't. I didn't think you needed to have anything to do on Christmas Eve.

'Where's our Gillian?' George asks suddenly. Always Bunty's favourite of course, Gillian has recently managed to make herself extremely popular with George. I suppose if you work hard enough at anything you're bound to succeed in the end.

'Piano lesson,' Bunty replies, turning down the gas under the pan of potatoes.

'On Christmas Eve?' George says, a note of surprise in his voice. You see? I'm supposed to be 'doing something' but 'Our Gillian' isn't. I seem to be dismissed so I go up to the living-room and switch on the television. *Champion the Wonder Horse* is just starting and although my heart thrills automatically to his stirring theme music I have to confess to being a little disappointed that there isn't something more seasonal on. Don't the television people know it's Christmas Eve either? Still, the Christmas tree is beautiful; the lights are switched on and we have some new decorations – big silver glass balls with silver glitter snowflakes stuck on them – a company Christmas gift from a pet food traveller. And the coal fire in the living-room has just been lit so that the room is full of promising smells like coal-dust and pine needles and I begin to cheer up. Nell is asleep in an armchair next to the fire, a piece of tinsel wrapped mysteriously round her finger. Maybe it's to remind her of something? Her personality perhaps?

Gillian bursts into the room, throwing her music case down and sprawling in an armchair, revealing her navy blue knickers. She sighs darkly and rearranges herself, crossing her legs and staring at a spot two inches above my head.

'You're not supposed to cross your legs,' I tell her helpfully. Without speaking she slowly uncrosses them then recrosses them. I wonder if I were to say, 'Listen Gillian, this is your last day on earth, lighten up, for heaven's sake,' she would take any notice? Probably not.

George puts his head round the living-room door. 'Tea's ready,' he announces, glaring into the middle distance of Champion's girth and stirrups. In one smooth movement, Gillian sticks her tongue out at me, uncrosses her legs and turns round and gives George a big, toothy grin. 'Hello, Daddy,' she beams at him. If only she would teach me how to do that before she goes.

The dining-room. A very small room, off the kitchen. There's just enough room for the table, the chairs and the people – George, Gillian, Nell and me are sitting at the table while Bunty makes a lot of noise in the kitchen in case we should forget about her. If only. Patricia wanders in and studies her chair for a long time before she sits on it. I'm fascinated by what goes on in her brain these days. She reveals few, if any, clues. Finally, she sits down. George looks at her briefly and says, 'You took your time.' She screws up her face and tilts her head to one side (an uncanny impersonation of the Parrot) and appears to think hard about this statement before saying sweetly, 'Yes, yes I did take a long time, didn't I?'

No matter how ravaged by adolescence I may become in future years I know I'll never be as daring as Patricia. George looks as if he'd like to hit her. But he can't – not just because it's Christmas Eve, but because Patricia has accidentally met The Floozy and may reveal this encounter to the Snow Queen in the kitchen. George, therefore, treats his eldest child like a ticking time bomb that might go off at any moment. Patricia relishes her new, powerful status.

Nell is trying to cut up invisible food on the tablecloth. Bunty is banging things around in the kitchen, thumping down pots and pans and slamming cupboard doors, like a woman possessed. I know she is trying to say something to George so why doesn't she just speak, for heaven's sake?

But no, nothing as simple as that for Our Lady of the Kitchen, who is pretending to dish out pork chops, mashed potatoes and carrots but is really shooting out steel tension wires from her fingertips. They make little noises as they hit the walls of the bedrooms, the living-room, the front of the Shop, the occasional Pet. Ping! Ping! Ping! Until the whole house is criss-crossed with the metal web of Bunty's thoughts.

She makes an entrance into the dining-room, singing, in a high, tuneless voice, a totally inappropriate Doris Day song ('The Black Hills of Dakota') that indicates that she is pretending to ignore whatever is going on between her and George. This is a special occasion after all – the pantomime, Christmas, not to mention Gillian's death. Bunty circles the dining-table, with the plates held high, as if she is a waitress in an American film. She looks ridiculous.

'Pork's a bit tough,' George says. Why can't he just chew and swallow without comment like everyone else? I hate this. I hate these people at the table. I can see Gillian's doing the same as me, rehearsing expressions of agreement and dismay in case George continues with his carping. Bunty, however, is not in a placatory mood.

'Really?' she says, slicing icebergs with her tongue. 'Really?' she says, daring him to continue. Her eyebrows have risen so far they seem to be hovering above her head. 'Really?' George falls silent under the pressure of Christmas.

'What a wet night it is for going out!' Bunty says suddenly, in a different tone, her 'company' voice. This is her way of letting it be known that she is a very well-behaved person with good manners, unlike the boorish man at the other end of the table, who unfortunately happens to be her husband.

Nobody replies. Everybody's too busy chewing – George is right, the meat is tough, small charred chops that have been grilled by the flame of Bunty's temper. What a shame for Gillian, her last supper and it's a burnt offering. If we had known we could have had Christmas dinner a day early just for her.

Nell's knife skitters off the table and onto the floor. George and Bunty exchange looks over her head as she makes a futile attempt to bend down and reach the knife. Finally, George sighs and picks it up for her, slamming it back down on the tablecloth.

'Can I sit next to you at the pantomime, Daddy?' Gillian asks, turning the full torchlight beam of her smile on George.

'Of course, pet,' he smiles. This is sickening. But George is soothed, so some (reluctant) admiration is due to Gillian, I suppose.

I'm sitting next to Nell, dutifully chewing and saying nothing, but that doesn't make me safe. Bunty turns to me suddenly, like a frustrated cobra. 'If you don't hurry up, Ruby, you'll still be sitting here when *we're* all at the pantomime.' She says this as if she's pleased with herself for saying something clever. *Is* this my real mother? Why does she do this? What kind of enjoyment does she derive from idle threats like this? For one thing we have plenty of time. And for another thing they wouldn't dream of actually leaving me here while they go to the pantomime. Would they?

'Yes,' George says unexpectedly. 'Stop dithering, Ruby, you can't spend your whole life being late, you know.' He's taking sides with Bunty either to mollify her or irritate her, it's hard to say which. I start to eat as fast as I can, but stop in open-mouthed astonishment when Nell, slip-sliding in and out of lucidity, suddenly turns to me and says (in a foreign language, I notice) 'Aye, frame thyself, girl!' For a split second the entire family appears to be staring at me with the kind of look that sparrows give to their poor innocent cuckoo-babies.

Bunty, still chewing, starts whisking the plates away, ignoring the protests of Nell who hasn't managed to start eating anything yet. I think Bunty would prefer it if she could wash up before we'd eaten. She waltzes back in with the cut-glass bowl containing the tinned sliced peaches that are like big smiles, like the enormous, manic smile fixed on Bunty's own face. (An extreme version, this, of the smile of *Footnote (iv)*.) She dishes out the peaches and when Patricia protests that she doesn't want any, tells her that's too bad because she needs the bowl for the Boxing Day trifle. Bunty is the only person in York who knows how to make a sherry trifle properly, and as its sacred properties are not to be interfered with Patricia takes her bowl of peach slices, but not without leaning over towards George and saying in a mock-confidential whisper, 'They say discretion is the better part of valour, don't they?' George looks extremely uncomfortable; he has no idea what Patricia's talking about but he's pretty sure it's got something to do with The Floozy.

George cuts a peach slice in half with his spoon, scoops up a little cream on it and raises it, delicately, to his lips.

'The cream's off,' he pronounces, hardly tasting it at all. His spoon remains suspended on the way down from his sandy moustache, which is the colour of peaches. He stares at Bunty, daring her to contradict him, all thought of festive goodwill abandoned.

On the other side of the table from me, Patricia eats a spoonful of cream and peaches and gags. She nods at me and mouths the word 'Off'. Nell, fearful of starving probably, has already finished hers.

Bunty licks her lips with the fastidiousness of a

cat. 'Tastes all right to me,' she says quietly. She's being very brave, rather like Deborah Kerr in *The King and I*.

George pushes his plate away. 'You bloody well eat it then,' he says, leaving Gillian in a bit of a dilemma, her cheeks stuffed with rancid cream and slippery peaches, not sure which parent to suck up to. She is able to spit her dilemma back into her bowl when Bunty and George's attention is diverted by a loud snore from Nell. She is as sound asleep as a dormouse with her head in her empty dish.

'She's behind you! She's behind you!' Gillian yells with abandon. (She means the wicked witch but I fear that it's sweet death in all her gauzy splendour.)

'Shush,' Bunty whispers, her freshly rose-budded lips pouting primly. 'Not so loud, someone will hear you.'

The absurdity of this statement is not lost on Gillian who can see the whole theatre is in uproar as the witch, an elf, a panda, a cow and a plucky village youth rush about the stage while Hansel and Gretel hide under a pile of leaves. (Why is there a panda? Perhaps to make Patricia happy – she nudges me and says, 'Look! A panda!' a note of rare happiness in her voice.) Undeterred, Gillian continues to shout at the top of her voice. Make the most of it, Gillian, I say.

When they ask for volunteers from the audience to come on stage I sink into my seat as far out of sight as possible, and Patricia has rendered herself completely invisible, but there's no holding Gillian back and before you can say, 'Oh yes she is,' she's kicking up her white kid heels and layers of petticoats and is on stage, charming the panda and singing her heart out.

'Well, really,' says Bunty self-consciously to the woman in the seat next to her (I am in the middle of the Lennox sandwich – George on one end, then Gillian, me, Patricia and, on the other end, Bunty. Nell has been left at home). 'Really, she *is* a one, our Gillian.' Not for much longer.

When Gillian returns to her seat you can see that she's flushed and irritable (her mother's daughter) at having to step out of the spotlight. 'All good things come to an end,' Bunty says, smiling stiffly, keeping her eyes on the stage.

If Hansel and Gretel had stayed lost in the forest for ever, we could have remained trapped with them and forgotten about The Floozy and sour cream and un-iced Christmas cakes. And Gillian wouldn't have died either. But the plot's unstoppable – the witch is burnt to a heap of charred rags and ashes, the wicked stepmother's pardoned, children reclaimed. Hansel and Gretel discover the witch's treasure chest, overflowing with emeralds, diamonds, opals, rubies (!), sapphires, glowing like the bag of boiled sweets Gillian and I are sharing. The Good Fairy sends a shower of glitter from her wand so thick that when I put out my hand I can touch it.

'Well, that's over for another year.' George is out of his seat before the house lights are even up and while we are still applauding he's already standing in the foyer, lighting up a cigarette. Bunty is behaving like a frantic rodent, jumping up and down at the end of the row, urging us to hurry up, while we fumble desperately with hats, scarves, gloves, programmes. Why does she do this? Why does she induce a sense of panic commensurate with an earthquake when it's obvious that we are going to have to queue for ages before the exits clear. Gillian, who is transfixed by the sight of the empty stage, suddenly bursts into tears. Bunty moves along the row, mouthing simpering things to the people crushed in around us, 'very tired', 'too much excitement', 'children, you know', while she secretly pulls viciously on Gillian's hand, hissing under her breath, 'Why don't you just bloody *grow up*, Gillian!'

I feel it's unfortunate for Bunty that these are her last words to Gillian. Not only is it a futile admonishment – the one thing that Gillian is clearly *not* going to do is 'grow up' – but it's not a very nice note to finish on. However, this is Bunty's problem, not mine. My last words to Gillian are – as I hand her a jewel-like sweet – 'Do you want the last red one, or can I have it?' Fairly neutral in the circumstances, and luckily she takes the last red one (this is Gillian, remember) so I won't have to feel guilty about it afterwards.

Outside the Theatre Royal, George is hopping about trying to catch a taxi (our car, we discovered as we started out for the theatre, had a flat tyre – one more coincidence in the conspiracy of coincidences that kill Gillian). The rain is turning to needles of sleet. Patricia is skulking under the arches that decorate the outside of the theatre – terrified that someone she knows might see her out with her family (can we blame her?). Bunty, for some reason, is holding tightly onto my hand as we stand shivering on the pavement. She is making a big mistake, she's hanging onto the wrong child. Gillian is trying to look sophisticated (I can tell from the way she's dangling her white fur muff). She has just spotted a group of her friends from school – she has just finished her first term at Queen Anne's – on the other side of the road. They're all shouting and waving to each other like a bunch of idiots.

I don't see what happens next because Bunty is beginning to panic about not being able to get a taxi, but I suppose Gillian has run out from between the parked cars without looking, because all of a sudden there is a bang and a pale blue Hillman Husky van is lobbing her gently into the path of the taxi George has just succeeded in hailing.

I'm struggling to get away from Bunty but I can't pry her fingers off my hand, she went into a kind of rigor mortis when she saw Gillian flying through the air. People are milling around making a lot of noise but after a while a space clears and we can see George sitting on the edge of the pavement, one of his trouser legs inexplicably rolled up, exposing a beige woollen sock. He's being sick. Then Bunty starts screaming, loud at first, and then the noise seems to get thinner and higher until it rises up, bat-like and starts bouncing off the sodium street lights, the gargoyles on the theatre, the blue light flashing nearer and nearer.

* * *

On Christmas morning I wake up next to Patricia in the otherwise vast emptiness of George and Bunty's bed. Between us huddle Teddy and Panda. It's extraordinary to be sharing a room with Patricia, let alone a bed. I expect that, like me, she feared to be alone when Gillian's vengeful spirit must be stalking Above the Shop, jealously guarding the kidney-shaped dressing-table and the advent calendar and all the other thousand and one things invested with her life-force. At eleven o'clock on Christmas Eve, George and Bunty phoned from the hospital to say that Gillian was dead and then they just seemed to disappear into thin air. Nell was distressed at the idea of having to cope. 'I can't cope,' she whined down the phone to Bunty, but Bunty didn't care.

I think she's coping very well actually, especially with the stocking.

One of her thick, wrinkled sixty deniers lies across the bottom of George and Bunty's eiderdown, looking faintly obscene in the dim winter dawn-light and certainly untouched by the hand of any North Pole elf. I know Father Christmas hasn't put it there because he doesn't exist. Gillian disabused me of this possibility last year, debunking the Tooth Fairy at the same time for good measure. What an iconoclast she was.

The bed gives off an unsettling odour composed of both Bunty's sickly-sweet face powder smell and George's tobacco-and-fish smell and I tentatively nudge Patricia and say, 'There's a Christmas stocking.'

'I know,' she says flatly and I realize that it is she, rather than Nell, who has been playing Santa Claus. Good old Patricia. It must have been doubly difficult for her to undertake this role, for although she's thirteen years old and arguably the most grown-up member of the family, it is Patricia more than anyone who mourns the way magic has drained from our world. No Father Christmas, no Tooth Fairy, no Fairy Godmother – no fairies at all. Our childhood is over, yet we're still waiting for it to begin. I was lying next to Patricia's stiff little body last night and know how desperately she was listening for the clatter of unshod hooves on the roof and the jingle of approaching sleigh-bells.

My stocking for Christmas 1959 contains (in reverse order from the toe upwards) – a sixpence, a walnut, an orange, a pack of Happy Family playing cards, a bar of Fry's Peppermint Cream and a cheap, rather pink, doll wearing a knitted vest and knickers. I've had better.

We lie back on the parental pillows and share the chocolate while we play a rather desultory game of Happy Families. The irony is not lost on us as we survey the families of Mr Bun the Baker and Mr Haddock the Fishmonger, all considerably more complete than that of Mr Lennox the Pet Shopkeeper.

Eventually we go up to Nell's room and kiss her on her leathery cheek. A faint whiff of urine rises up from her sheets. She's wearing an enormous pale-pink bedjacket that dwarfs her. The hands poking out from the ends of the sleeves have purple veins that stand out like wires. She looks at us both warily through rheumy eyes.

'Merry Christmas, Grandma.'

'Merry Christmas, Patricia.'

'Merry Christmas, Grandma.'

'Merry Christmas, Ruby.'

'Merry Christmas one and all!' The tinkling cry goes around the house, like glass bells, as the household ghosts feebly carol and wassail and raise a glass to Christmas.

We make an effort. I switch on the Christmas tree lights and Nell puts an apron on. Patricia makes a brave attempt to clean out the grate and lay a new fire. But when she tries to set a match to it the fire peters out as soon as it's burnt up all the kindling. She hauls through the electric fire from Nell's bedroom and we huddle round the one element that gives off the unpleasant acrid smell of burnt hair. We light the candles of the Angel Chimes so that at least we have some kind of flame to light the festivities.

All three of us look doubtfully at the pile of presents under the tree. 'May as well open them,' Patricia says at last, shrugging her shoulders in that way she has of suggesting she couldn't care less about anything, although of course, she cares terribly. About everything.

I have several presents. George and Bunty have given me a *Girl* annual, a white fur muff (new, not ex-Gillian), a pair of roller skates, a Terry's Chocolate Orange and some pretend jewellery. I think these are surprisingly good presents. Nell has given me a tin of Yardley's Freesia talcum powder and Patricia has given me a brand-new copy of *The Railway Children*, bought from her pocket-money. Meanwhile, from beyond the grave, Gillian has sent me a brown Bri-nylon dog, with a purple ribbon round its fat neck, holding a green and purple bottle of April Violets cologne between its paws. 'That's disgusting,' Patricia says, with no reverence for Gillian's newly-dead condition – but then, although we believed she was dead last night, it's almost impossible to believe that she's still dead this morning. 'Disgusting,' I agree and stuff a whole segment of Chocolate Orange into my mouth.

Patricia and Nell open their presents but the remainder are left undisturbed under the tree, like offerings to the dead. I think Patricia and I should share Gillian's presents but don't say so because I know this isn't the right attitude.

Some time later Patricia and I go looking for Nell and find her in the kitchen trying to do some very odd things to the uncooked turkey. Patricia takes the apron from her and ties it authoritatively round her own waist, telling me to take Nell away and play with her. Sensibly, Patricia does not attempt to cook the turkey, but instead makes a commendable attempt at mashed potatoes, baked beans and corned beef although only after all three of us have lacerated ourselves opening the corned-beef tin. Afterwards we have mince pies and Ambrosia Creamed Rice Pudding. We eat with our plates on our knees in front of the television and enjoy our Christmas dinner more than seems appropriate after the demise of a close relative. Nell recklessly drinks two glasses of rum and then Patricia and I pull the entire box of crackers between us while our grandmother sleeps in the armchair and I take the opportunity to relay to Patricia some facts about the Spirit World, as gleaned during my Dewsbury exile. Patricia is uncommonly taken with the idea of animal afterlife, but less so with the idea of Gillian wandering out there for ever and learning how to get rid of scratches on coffee-tables.

By Boxing Day we have settled into a kind of routine based loosely on television, sleep and mince pies. Patricia has even learnt how to make a pretty good fire. We're grateful to Bunty for keeping her cupboards so well stocked with tinned food. Things look up a lot when we discover the Boxing Day trifle lurking at the back of the fridge, although Patricia is a little queasy about it as she says she distinctly remembers that Bunty hadn't even begun to make it when we left for the pantomime. Who made the trifle? Ghostly cooks schooled in syllabub, flummery, and frumenty? Handy elves? Who knows. We put aside our qualms and devour it at a single sitting and feel sick all night.

We rapidly shed our former lives of orderly routine and good habits and I expect all three of us would have soon reverted to a pretty savage state if Bunty and George hadn't suddenly appeared on New Year's Eve in a flurry of snowflakes. They had the decency to ring the front door bell and look a little shamefaced, aware that they had somewhat abrogated parental responsibility. Gillian wasn't with them, of course.

Where had they been? Patricia and I talked about this

quite a lot. Quite a lot by our standards anyway. From what we could gather they had decamped to Uncle Clifford and Auntie Gladys (thus, no doubt ruining Christmas for Adrian). Heaven knows why, perhaps they wanted to be looked after or perhaps (less likely) they wanted to protect us from the aftermath of the tragedy. They had the funeral and everything without us and although neither Patricia nor myself were sorry to have missed this particular social occasion, it did leave us for a long time afterwards – perhaps for ever – with the feeling that Gillian was, if not exactly alive then not exactly dead either.

They probably had to open a whole new zone in the Spirit World, just for Gillian. For several weeks afterwards, Patricia and I planned a trip to the Church of the Spirit in Dewsbury in the hope of receiving a comforting message from Gillian. *Your sister says not to worry about her,* that sort of thing. Knowing Gillian, she would have kept silent just to spite us (she would be furious at having missed Christmas). These plans faded abruptly after The Great Pet Shop Fire when the Spirit World received such a large new intake that it was easier to forget about the world of the Spirit altogether than to dwell on all those Spirit Pets wandering the astral plane, mewing and whimpering.

Bunty wasn't the full shilling for a while. It was surprising just how much Gillian's death had affected her. I used to see her through her open bedroom door, lying on her back on the bed emitting little yelps, her hands clawing the eiderdown. Sometimes she'd moan, 'My baby, my baby's gone,' as if she'd only had one baby, which wasn't very nice for me and Patricia. At other times, she'd set up a banshee wail of 'Gilliaaaaaan,' which should have been enough to recall Gillian from the region of the undead, yet it didn't. Sometimes you could hear Bunty crying to the night, 'My Gillian, my pearl,' which I thought was very odd, because I'd never heard her call her that when she was alive. And anyway, surely it's me that's the jewel of the family?

She got better after a while. So did the Pets. Patricia and I had forgotten about them for a couple of days and it was only when the dogs started howling in the middle of the night that we realized they hadn't been fed. Thankfully, none of them had starved to death although the knowledge of our neglect hung heavily on our consciences, particularly Patricia's, needless to say. It is hard to look into the eyes of starving puppies and kittens, knowing it's your fault, and not feel that you have been marked down for ever. The Parrot, in the short time left to him, never forgave us. The Great Pet Shop Fire expunged many things (although mostly Pets) but not the guilt.

It is the eve of a new and different decade, the last day of 1959. Our newly-returned parents are now fast asleep in their room downstairs and it is three o'clock in the morning on my Snow White alarm clock. I creep down to the living-room, awake, not sleep-walking. I would rather not be in my bedroom – the sight of

Gillian's empty bed makes me nervous. Dead or not, she's still there – if I stare hard enough at her bed I can see the peach candlewick bedspread rising and falling with her invisible breath.

The mantelpiece clock, always running slow, chimes *One, two, three*. The curtains in the living-room have been left open and outside I can see the snow falling silently. There are great flakes, like goose feathers, and small, curled ones like swansdown and great flurries as if a flock of stormy petrels had shaken their feathers out. As I watch, the sky fills with clouds of snow feathers from every kind of bird there ever was and even some that only exist in the imagination, like the bluebirds that fly over the rainbow. Most of the Christmas tree needles are on the floor by now but I switch on the tree lights anyway. Then I start spinning the glass balls on the tree. If I work very hard at it I can get them all spinning at the same time. Sometimes they bang together and dislodge glitter which falls in a shower of fairy dust all over me.

Footnote (vi) – The Sunday School Outing

THE SUNDAY SCHOOL OUTING TO SCARBOROUGH WAS going to be a splendid affair. Mrs Mildred Reeves, who was in charge of St Denys' Sunday School and its annual outings, was marshalling her helpers at the railway station, well ahead of time. Her assistant teacher, Miss Adina Terry, was already waiting at the ticket barrier with Lolly Paton, the friend she had brought along with her for the day. The eager new curate Mr Dobbs was accompanied by his fiancée, Miss Fanshawe, and together they were standing guard over the large wicker hamper which contained the children's lunch. Nearly all the parents had contributed to the picnic, although unfortunately they had nearly all furnished sweetmeats so that Mrs Reeves and Miss Fanshawe had been making sandwiches (fishpaste and egg) since the early hours.

'What a glorious day!' Miss Terry's friend, Lolly Paton, exclaimed, throwing her arms wide and laughing so that the curate flushed slightly and Mrs Reeves pressed her lips together in disapproval. But Lolly Paton was right, it was a glorious day, the last hot Saturday of July, and even now at half-past nine in the morning there was no doubt that the great arc of blue beyond the girders and glass of the station canopy was in place for the rest of the day. Not only would the weather remain 'glorious' in contrast to the previous three years of washed-out seaside expeditions, but the tide would, for once, be in exactly the right place – that is, as far out as possible, and the children would be able to eat their picnic, paddle their feet and play their games, without fear of being swept away by the sea.

Mrs Reeves had a piece of paper in her handbag on which she had written down a list of songs to sing on the train and a list of games to play on the beach – three-legged races, team rounders, human croquet and beach cricket. Mrs Reeves was glad of the male presence of Mr Dobbs, not only to help with the rules of cricket which were only hazily sketched in Mrs Reeves' mind, but also as an influence on the boisterous little boys in the party, some of whom in Mrs Reeves' opinion did not come from well-disciplined homes. But then, Mrs Reeves reminded herself, was it not part of her Christian duty to foster such qualities in these poor, and rather common, children? 'Suffer the little children,' she murmured to herself but her words were smothered by the arrival of the King's Cross to Aberdeen Express train and Miss Fanshawe had to lay a detaining hand on Mr Dobbs' arm because he looked as if he was about to jump aboard.

Miss Terry was not quite as well-organized as Mrs Reeves; she had not made any lists at all, but she had brought some stories to read to the children, not the usual improving Bible tales she recounted rather wearily Sunday after Sunday, but a copy of a brand-new book, *Swallows and Amazons*, which her younger brother assured her was a 'jolly good adventure'. Although, as it turned out, the book would never be opened because instead Lolly Paton gave an animated, impromptu rendering of *Peter Pan* in which she cast all the children as Lost Boys and even managed to persuade the rather stiff Mr Dobbs to enact a lively Captain Hook, although Mrs Reeves flatly refused to play the crocodile and Miss Fanshawe sulked over the bottles of lemonade.

'I shall go and buy the tickets,' Mrs Reeves announced. 'There's no point in waiting until all the children are here, for there are bound to be latecomers and it will hardly do to miss the train.'

'Especially when we have had to arrive so very early,' Miss Terry said gravely and Lolly Paton pinched her in the waist so that they both had to stare hard at the huge florid station clock to stop themselves from laughing. An over-punctual child was already approaching the rendezvous, spotless in white from head to toe and her hair tied up in a baroque confection of ribbons.

Meanwhile, back in the Lowther Street household, the children hadn't even left the house, detained both by their natural tardiness and their mother, who had only recently realized that she'd forgotten to provide anything for the picnic and that Mrs Reeves had especially asked for everything to be delivered to the church hall the previous evening. In haste, Nell had thrown a batch of scones in the oven before it even reached the right temperature and refused to let Babs, Clifford and Bunty leave the house before the scones were done. Betty was laid up in bed, the last one of the family to succumb to a bout of whooping-cough that had driven Nell almost out of her wits. Ted was still deemed too young for Sunday School outings.

'We'll just go without – there'll be plenty of stuff there,' Clifford said, scuffing his toe impatiently against the kitchen doorpost.

'That's not the point,' Nell said, in a fit of irritation. 'What would they think?' and she pushed her hair back from her forehead as if she would have liked to erase her mind.

'What would who think?' Bunty asked, sitting on the kitchen linoleum, fumbling with the buttons on the straps of her shoes and biting her lip in concentration.

'Mrs Reeves – the people at your Sunday School, whoever—' Nell broke off to grab Ted who was stuffing something in his mouth and she had to wrestle with him to extricate a stone. Babs ran a hasty comb through her hair. 'Can we please just go!' she said anxiously. There were no ribbons for Babs and Bunty, their pudding-bowl haircuts hung lankly over their ears. Nor were there any white dresses. Babs was in an unbecoming sage-green smock and Bunty's best frock was a drop-waisted slub brown. 'The train goes at five past ten,' Babs said, 'and it takes a good half-hour to walk to the station—'

'Specially with Bunty in tow,' Clifford said glumly. Babs began to wail, 'And Mrs Reeves asked us to be there by twenty to ten—'

'It's twenty-five to now,' Clifford murmured, staring blankly into the back yard with the air of a condemned man who had begun to accept his fate.

'Be quiet, the pair of you!' Nell snapped. 'The scones will be out in a minute, you – Clifford, Babs, what's-your-name – get a cloth to put them in.' Babs pulled a green-and-white check tea-towel from a drawer and tried not to cry.

Nell took the baking tray out of the oven and tipped the pale scones onto the tea-towel. 'They needed to be in longer,' she said crossly.

'No, no – we've got to go,' Babs shouted, unable to squeeze her tears back any longer, and she picked up the cloth, knotting the corners together as she went and then ran out of the door after Clifford, who already had a head start on her. Bunty started to cry because she still hadn't got one of her shoes done up. Nell bent down and gave her a sharp slap on her calf before fastening up the shoe and Bunty hurtled out of the house after the other two.

'Come on!' Babs screamed to her from the front gate, reaching out a hand that barely made contact with Bunty's fingers before they were up and running, flying up Lowther Street and along Clarence Street. Bunty got a terrible stitch in her side as they clambered over the footbridge across the railway and moaned and hobbled down Grosvenor Terrace into Bootham, Babs screaming at her all the time to keep up. They shot over the Ouse on Scarborough Bridge, a train keeping them company up above. 'That's probably our train,' Babs gasped, almost falling down the metal steps and onto Leeman Road. Babs ran on after Clifford, but Bunty had to stop to get her breath and then limped feebly onto Station Road and just glimpsed Babs' green frock disappearing within the station portals.

Bunty could feel her thick petticoat sticking to her skin underneath the dress and the hot tears that were pricking her eyes uncomfortably. She was terrified out of her wits at the idea of being left behind and trotted gamely across the station concourse up to the ticket barrier, where the ticket collector stopped her with an imperiously raised hand and eyebrow. The station master had already blown his whistle, and the train, clearly visible on the platform beyond the barrier, had started to move, very slowly, and Bunty stared at it with tragic eyes. Then she spied Clifford, running for his life, and Bunty put her hand over her mouth and said, 'Oh,' as she watched her brother sprinting along the platform and yanking open one of the carriage doors before leaping on board and hauling Babs after him – Babs who was screaming Bunty's name, but whose foot was already on the step, and as she disappeared into the carriage she let go the bundle she was carrying and the green-and-white check tea-towel went fluttering like an escaped flag and its clutch of scones went rolling all over the platform and under the wheels of the train. An angry guard slammed the door shut as the train passed him, gathering speed all the while. Bunty glimpsed Mrs Reeves' bemused face through one of the windows and wondered if she would pull the communication cord when she realized that Bunty had been left behind.

But no, for the train whistled loudly, sending a flurry of pigeons from the rafters, and passed beyond the canopy and out into the blue morning. Bunty sobbed noisily as the train grew smaller and then curved away into nothing and a strange silence descended on the station, a silence full of wretched disappointment and yet at the same time oddly peaceful. It was broken by the heavy, clanging noise of something metallic being dropped and the ticket collector came out from his box and took Bunty's hand, saying gruffly, 'Shall we try and get you sorted out, young lady?' because Bunty was standing not only in a pool of tears but in a puddle of something more embarrassing.

It was quite some time before the station master could even get a name out of Bunty, who was gasping for breath in between convulsions of sobbing.

Bunty was put in the dubious care of a young porter who took her home on a tram, leaving her on Huntington Road to walk the rest of the way home. Bunty felt as if she had been in the company of strangers for hours and was looking forward to sobbing out her misery into a familiar pair of arms. But when she walked into the kitchen it was to meet a disturbing sight – her mother appeared to be in the middle of making a rice pudding (grains of white rice had scattered like little pearls all over the table) but was clearly not quite herself for the big two-pint enamel dish she used for milk puddings and egg custards was full to overflowing – yet Nell kept on pouring from the big blue jug she was holding so that the milk poured over the edge of the dish and splashed onto the table before flowing over the edge, like a white milky waterfall.

All the time this was happening, not only was Ted providing a wailing counterpoint upstairs but Nell was also talking to herself, sneering, biting kind of words that made her sound like a madwoman putting a curse on someone – although when Bunty listened she found that it was nothing more than an alphabetical recitation of the cake recipes in Nell's Dyson's *Self-Help* book – *Afternoon Tea Scones, Almond Paste Cakes, Bachelor's Buttons, Chocolate Sandwich, Coconut Rock Buns, Cream Cake, Feather Cake, Fluffy Cake, Genoa Cake*. Bunty crept out of the kitchen and sat on the bench in the yard. She'd been quite wrung out of tears by now and she sat quietly in the sun trying not to think about what the Sunday School would be doing in Scarborough. All the while Betty's sick cough hacked at her ears. When she looked over her shoulder, through the kitchen window, she could get a glimpse of Nell, grating nutmeg on top of the milk, not just the usual sprinkle, but the whole nutmeg – up and down, up and down on the grater and she only stopped when there was a dreadful bumping noise followed by screaming and Bunty supposed Ted had fallen downstairs again.

The following Sunday, Mrs Reeves gathered her exuberant brood around her skirts and allowed them to chatter on for a full five minutes about their wonderful outing and when they had finished she looked at Bunty and said, 'What a shame you missed our outing, Berenice. I hope it's taught you a lesson about punctuality, you missed such a lot of fun and games,' and then Mrs Reeves nodded at Adina Terry, who opened her big *Children's Illustrated Bible* and, with a small sigh, said, 'Today, children, we're going to read the story of the Good Samaritan.'

CHAPTER SEVEN

1960

Fire! Fire!

WE HAVE VISITED GILLIAN. SHE IS TUCKED UP, NICE AS ninepence, under a neat blanket of green turf that's like a card table. We do not play cards on it, not even a simple game of Snap. Bunty stuffs a bunch of jewel-bright anemones into a stone that has holes in it. It reminds me of the stone on Burton Stone Lane – a big, black boulder at what was once the city boundary where country folk left their wares when York was in the throes of the plague. Now our Gillian is as untouchable as a plague victim. We couldn't touch her even if we wanted to, unless we clawed away the turf and dug deep down into the cold, sour soil of the cemetery. Which we're not about to do, especially as we're both dressed in our favourite outfits for the visit, me in my tartan taffeta and Patricia in a plaid woollen skirt that's stretched over a stiff tulle-net petticoat in all the pastel shades that flying saucer sweets come in. Her flying saucer skirt creaks and rasps around her thin legs which are strapped into stockings and suspenders and a pantie girdle while her 'Junior Miss' bra, and the junior breasts lurking inside it, make wrinkled patterns under her pink Courtelle sweater. Her mousy hair is scraped back into a pony-tail that is tied with a pink satin ribbon. Sometimes it's hard to be a woman.

It would be pointless to dig anyway, for Gillian is not really here at all, but 'Safe in the Arms of Jesus'. That's what it says on her headstone –

Gillian Berenice Lennox
14th January 1948–24th December 1959
Beloved Daughter of George and Bunty
Safe in the Arms of Jesus

'It doesn't say anything about us,' I whisper to Patricia as Bunty produces a duster from her handbag and starts rubbing the gravestone. More housework.

'Us?'

'Beloved Sister.'

'Well, she wasn't, was she?' Patricia says reasonably and we are both immediately consumed by guilt for having thought such a thing. Come back, Gillian, all is forgiven. Come back and we'll make you our Beloved Sister. Bunty takes out the kitchen scissors and starts snipping away at the turf. What will she do next, hoover? Gillian's headstone is very plain and rather unexciting. I have been here before with my friend Kathleen and her mother to visit Kathleen's grand-father's grave and Kathleen and I played hide-and-seek amongst the gravestones. We particularly liked the ones with angels carved on them, either solitary and rather wan, or in pairs – one on either side, their wings hoisted protectively over the invisible inhabitant beneath. Kathleen and I spent some time pretending to be grave-guardian angels, using our blazers for wings.

Do you have to be dead to be safe in Jesus' arms? Apparently not. Kathleen, who has already introduced me to the exotic, blood-soaked interior decoration of St Wilfred's Catholic church, explains that we are all safe in His arms, especially the little children. Especially suffering ones, she adds. I think Patricia and I are suffering a good deal so this is good news. Furthermore, she tells me, He is a Lamb and we are washed in His blood (I swear you can *hear* the capital letters when Kathleen talks). I must admit I have some reservations about being washed in lamb's blood but if it's going to save me from the everlasting flames of hell – or Hell, as it sounds like a capital letter kind of place to me – then I suppose I can put up with it.

Mrs Gorman, Kathleen's mother, is always popping into church in the same way that Bunty might pop into the Ladies in St Sampson's Square when she's out shopping. We've just spent a Saturday morning – Kathleen, her mother and me – helping out at a Mile of Pennies in King's Square for the Junior NSPCC. I'm more than happy to help out – banking up good will and good deeds with the Lamb, for although He is meek and mild He is also (inexplicably) part of the trio that can consign you to the Inferno.

So, one minute we're meandering along Duncombe

Place discussing whether or not to go somewhere for a hot chocolate and the next we're ducking into church. Kathleen's mother dips her finger into the font at the entrance, crosses herself and bends one knee to the altar. Kathleen does likewise. What is the correct etiquette here? Do I follow suit and if I do will I be struck dead by God because I'm not a Catholic? Or by Bunty for the same reason? Neither Kathleen nor Mrs Gorman are looking, they're lighting candles, so I give the holy water a miss and drop a polite little curtsey in the general direction of the altar. 'Come and light a candle for your sister,' Mrs Gorman says, smiling encouragingly at me. The candles are lovely, creamy and waxy and as thin as pencils, all pointing upwards like holy signposts to some unknowable, mystical place where the Angel Gabriel and the Lamb and a host of white doves live on clouds. How will Gillian survive in such company? (She's probably bossing cherubs about already.) She's going to need all the help she can get so, with a slightly shaky hand, I light a candle and Kathleen's mother drops a sixpence in a box to pay for it while I try and look as if I'm saying a prayer.

I don't know about Gillian, but I certainly feel much better for lighting the candle; I can see that there is something to be said for all this ritual. Later, at home, I remove the Angel Chimes from the sideboard where they have been sitting anachronistically since Christmas – there is even some tinsel still lurking along the curtain rails – all evidence of the domestic careless-ness that ensued in the After Gillian era – 1960 AG. I place the Angel Chimes reverently on my pink Lloyd Loom bedside table and each evening I light the red candles and begin to devise prayers that will rise Lambwards like holy smoke.

The Angel Chimes have to be rationed as there are no more candles but not so my prayers and I pray so much – desperate, attention-seeking prayers to the Lamb – that I develop sore knees. My knees are so sore, in fact, that even Bunty notices it when we're out shopping for new shoes one Saturday. She became so annoyed at my shuffling cripple's gait that she stopped nagging me to keep up and asked me what the matter was (she's more mindful of her children now that she's lost one), with the result that now we're sitting in the doctor's waiting-room.

You could live in Dr Haddow's waiting-room, it's so warm and cosy, unlike Mr Jeffrey's the dentist whose waiting-room is cold and smells of dental antiseptic and toilet cleaner. Dr Haddow has a coal fire and leather chairs you can get lost in and on the walls are framed watercolours painted by Dr Haddow's wife. An old grandfather clock that has roses painted on its face ticks time away with a solid clopping noise, like horses' hooves – much nicer than the tinny noises our mantel-piece clock makes. A big polished table is loaded with an exciting assortment of reading matter from *Country Life* to old *Dandy*s. I prefer the *Reader's Digest*s. Bunty flicks through a *Woman's Realm* while I set about increasing my word power. I like going to the doctor, I think we don't go nearly often enough.

Dr Haddow is nice too and talks to you as if you're a real person even if Bunty answers all the questions on my behalf so that I'm left sitting there like a dumbstruck ventriloquist's dummy.

'So how are you, Ruby?'

'Her knees hurt.'

'And where exactly does it hurt, Ruby?'

'Right there,' Bunty says prodding a knee hard so that I squeal. 'What have you been up to, Ruby?' he asks, smiling genially at me. 'Saying too many prayers?' He laughs. 'I think it's just a bursitis,' he says finally, after a good many 'U-huhs' and 'Hmms'. 'A bursitis?' Bunty repeats in worried tones. 'Is that a parasite?'

'Nothing to worry about.'

'Nothing to worry about?'

'Housemaid's knee,' Dr Haddow explains. 'Housemaid's knee?' Bunty repeats, stuck in a fit of echolalia. She gives me a wary look as if I might be living a secret life, doing housework during the night when I'm sleepwalking. Sleephouseworking.

We come away with no medicine and no treatment advised other than to 'take it easy'. Bunty sniffs disparagingly at this idea but says nothing. Kindly Dr Haddow offers her another prescription for tranquillizers. 'You should take it easy too,' he says as he scrawls his pen across the prescription pad, leaving a trail of indecipherable, pale-blue ink that looks like *Arabian Nights'* handwriting. 'Time will heal everything,' he says, nodding and smiling (he's talking about Gillian's death, not my knee). 'I know God's been cruel to you, my dear, but there is a purpose to everything.' He takes his glasses off and rubs his pale-blue ink-coloured eyes, like a little boy, then he sits beaming at Bunty. Bunty is so soaked in grief and tranquillizers these days that there is a time-delay on most of her responses. Although she's looking blankly at the doctor, I know that any minute she'll turn nasty because she can't stand talk like this – God, taking it easy, et cetera – so I get up quickly and say, 'Thank you,' and tug at Bunty's hand. She follows like a little lamb.

We trudge home, past Clifton Green and along Bootham. The world is still locked in winter, the trees on Clifton Green are without any sign of leaf or bud, and form inky scrawls of black against a pale sky that is like grey sugar paper. A thin sleet begins to fall and I put up the hood on my duffle coat and, head down, hobble along Bootham behind Bunty like a little limping Eskimo child. It's a strange rule of life that no matter how quickly I walk I can never catch up with Bunty – slow or fast, she's always at least three feet in front of me as if there's an invisible umbilical cord between us that can stretch but never contract. No such piece of umbilical elastic binds Bunty and Patricia. My sister is free to stride fiercely ahead, linger sullenly behind or even occasionally shoot off in an alarming way up some side street.

My knees feel hot and sore despite the piercing coldness of the sleet. I pray to Jesus to provide a magic carpet to transport me home, but no such luck, and, as usual, my prayers seem to evaporate into the still air above the Vale of York. By the time we get back to the Shop there are frozen roses in our cheeks and little shards of ice in our hearts. Bunty thrusts her way in through the Shop door, setting the bell to clang frantically as if the Shop was about to be invaded, but she has no word of greeting so I call 'Shop!' on her behalf and George casts a look in my direction that speaks volumes of ambiguity. He raises a ginger eyebrow in Bunty's direction. 'So?'

'Housemaid's knee,' she says, rolling her eyes and making a little *moue* as if to say, 'Don't ask me.'

He asks anyway. 'Housemaid's knee?'

'A bursitis,' I supplement helpfully but they both ignore me. It's freezing cold in the Shop; the caged birds have their feathers all ruffled up and a hypothermic gleam in their eye as if they're collectively fantasizing about tropical climes. Why is it so cold? Why aren't the paraffin heaters lit? 'Why haven't you got the heaters on?' Bunty asks, casting a baleful glance at the nearest paraffin heater. 'It's freezing in here.'

'We've run out of paraffin, that's why,' George snaps, already struggling into his overcoat and big leather gloves. 'I was waiting for you to come back.' They're always waiting for each other to come back, it's like the Relief of Mafeking in the Shop sometimes. It's as if they can't both exist in the same space at the same time, *X = not Y* (or, to put it another way, *Y = not X*), or like the little men and women who live in weather-houses who never appear together at the same time, rain or shine.

George takes money from the till. 'I won't be long,' he says, heading for the door.

'Very likely,' Bunty mutters, suddenly finding herself stranded behind the counter yet again. 'I have Piles of Ironing to do!' she shouts as the door clangs shut behind George. 'Piles' is the collective noun for ironing – it doesn't come any other way for our mother.

I lean a hand on top of the cold speckled enamel of a heater, trying to wish it into life. I love the smell of the paraffin heaters, so warm and dangerous. 'Be careful,' Bunty warns automatically. In another life Bunty was related to Joan of Arc, constantly alert to the possibilities of fire. Perhaps she *was* Joan of Arc. I can just imagine her in control of a battalion of peasant soldiers, her cheeks pink with exasperation as she shouts orders at them while they shuffle and stare at their feet. And I can hear her at the end, as they put a burning brand to the faggots piled around her, *Be careful where you're putting that burning brand!*

Paraffin heaters are even more hazardous than stakes to witches, and they never occur in a sentence without a cautionary warning attached. None of us, neither Patricia, nor me, nor Gillian in her heyday, could be within five feet of one of the Shop heaters without being in danger of conflagration. The coal fire in the living-room is treated similarly and kept guarded day and night (lit or unlit); matches are *lethal*, of course; the burners on the gas cooker are alive and trying to grab you as you pass by; cigarettes are struggling to drop and smoulder – and as for spontaneous combustion! Well, it's just waiting to happen.

'Can I go upstairs?' I ask.

'No, not on your own,' she says, staring in an abstracted way at the Bob Martin display. This is so illogical it's not even worth combating – I am nine years old, I have been going upstairs on my own since I could walk. Since Gillian's death Bunty has been extra-sensitive to the dangers surrounding us – it's not only fire that we're under threat from, we are continually reassured of her maternal care for us by the stream of warnings that issue from her mouth – *Be careful with that knife! You'll poke your eye out with that pencil! Hold onto the banister! Watch that umbrella!* so that the world appears to be populated by objects intent on attacking us. I can't even have a bath in peace because Bunty flits in and out to check that I haven't slipped and drowned (*Mind the soap!*). Not so with Patricia, who locks, bolts and barricades the bathroom against Bunty. Our poor mother – can't bear us out of her sight, can't bear us in it.

Patricia suddenly clangs into the Shop, yelling 'Shop!' very aggressively, causing the Parrot to squawk with alarm. Patricia advances on it, making strangling movements in the air so that the Parrot tries to back off its perch. Over the years the Parrot has proved unsaleable so it has slowly evolved into the Shop Parrot – part of the fixtures and fittings – it resolutely refuses to talk and attacks anyone who goes near it. It has never even been graced with a name. Not even Polly. No-one treats it as one of God's little creatures, not even Patricia. Like me, it's become a kind of scapegoat. Scapeparrot.

'Mind that paraffin heater!' Bunty screams at Patricia as her coat flaps dangerously within two feet of the heater. Patricia turns to look at Bunty in disbelief. 'It's not lit,' she says, slowly and with great emphasis.

'That doesn't make any difference,' Bunty replies staunchly and busies herself with a tangle of dog leads, refusing to look at either of us because even she knows how ridiculous she's being. Patricia makes a disgusted face at her back and turns to go upstairs. 'Can I go upstairs with Patricia then?' I ask hastily, spying a means of escape. 'No!' they chorus in unison.

Bunty's edginess recedes after she's raked around in the depths of her handbag and come up triumphantly with her bottle of tranquillizers. Bunty's little helpers soon have her in a distinctly altered state and for a while she moves around the Shop like a twin-setted automaton, hauling out kittens, hamsters and mice for inspection and noisily ringing into the till the price of Pets until suddenly, in mid-sale, she clutches her forehead dramatically and announces that she's 'had enough' and has to go and lie down and rushes to the back of the Shop, only pausing long enough to push an enormous Belgian rabbit into my arms as she passes. 'Is your mother all right?' the surprised customer asks, relieving me of an equally surprised rabbit. 'Oh yes, she's just remembered that she's left a chip pan on the cooker,' I lie artfully. Very artfully, of course, as Bunty would no more leave a chip pan unattended than she would mix her whites with her coloureds on washday.

I have a busy morning and sell – two kittens (one tortoiseshell, one ginger), a very winsome puppy, two gerbils, a hamster wheel, three bags of sawdust, six pounds of biscuit mix, a dog basket, one gemstone cat collar (diamonds, fake), and the aforementioned Belgian rabbit which I claim as my sale because it was me that rang it into the till, not Bunty. I think I have a decided talent for this and I report my success very proudly to George when he finally comes back (paraffin-less, I notice) but he just looks at me blankly. Sometimes he seems to have the most enormous difficulty recognizing members of his own family.

I don't go completely without honour though, because five minutes later he produces a Milky Way from his pocket and gives it to me and then allows me to take all the rabbits out of their cages (one at a time, of course, or heaven knows what kind of rabbit chaos would have ensued). I stroke their long, velvety ears and bury my face in their plush fur, listening to their rapid, rabbity heartbeats. I think if Jesus were an animal he would not be a lamb but a rabbit, a big, furry, squashy chocolate-coloured rabbit.

'Where's your mother?' George says after a while. If he's going to encounter 'my mother' he'd better be reminded about the paraffin. 'Did you get the paraffin?' I ask innocently. He gives me another blank look. Not only do I appear to be a stranger but I don't even speak a language he recognizes. Ten minutes later he looks up from the till where he's been counting pound notes and says in amazement, 'I forgot the bloody paraffin!'

I make sympathetic noises.

He looks doubtfully at the Shop door, can he leave the weather-house unmanned? 'How can I go and get paraffin if your mother's not here?'

'I can manage.' 'No you can't.' Who does he think took all the money he's counting? It's not worth arguing, he can be so confrontational that he would swear black was white for the sake of an argument. Bunty would go further, claiming it wasn't a colour at all, but a piece of furniture or a banana. 'Go and get Patricia,' he says. 'She can mind the Shop.' My heart sinks a little at the words 'get Patricia'. Getting Patricia is invariably my job and it's a thankless task. As soon as I say to her, 'Daddy (or Mummy) wants you downstairs' a cloud of gloom settles around her head like a miasmic halo and she slouches unwillingly towards her summoner, blaming me all the while for this intrusion on her anchorite state.

I climb the stairs slowly and reluctantly, my bad knees complaining all the way. I pass Bunty's bedroom; I can see her sitting at her dressing-table, gazing into the mirror and doing a subdued version of her 'My Gillian, my pearl' routine as if she might be able to conjure Gillian back up from the depths of the mirror. She catches sight of my reflection walking past and gives a start as if she's just seen a ghost. But when she twists round to look she says, 'Oh it's only you,' in a flattened sort of voice. 'It's just me! Just Ruby!' I sing out in an inanely cheerful way as I hammer on Patricia's door.

'Go away!' she yells, so I open the door. 'Daddy wants you.' She's stretched out on her bed, arms folded across her sprouting chest and staring at the ceiling, rather like a thoughtful corpse. 'Go away,' she repeats without looking at me. I wait patiently for a while and then repeat my message. After another long period of silence has elapsed she finally turns her head slightly in my direction and says tonelessly, 'Tell him I'm ill.'

'What shall I say's wrong with you?' I know George will ask so I may as well have the answer ready rather than having to lumber all the way back up the stairs. Patricia returns her gaze to the ceiling and laughs mirthlessly. 'I have a sickness of the soul,' she declares in hollow, Gothic tones, closing her eyes and putting on the kind of sublimely bored expression that the Pre-Raphaelites were always demanding of their models.

'Shall I tell Daddy that?' I can just see his reaction if I say, 'Patricia can't come down, her soul's sick.' She laughs her Madeline Usher laugh and waves a thin, pale hand in the air. 'Tell him I've got my period – that'll shut him up.'

She's right, it does. 'Typical,' he says under his breath as if the menstrual cycle had been specifically designed to annoy him. 'Well, I'm going out anyway,' he says, swinging round the sign on the door which announces to the outside world that we're *Sorry we are closed even for Vetzyme*. When I'm sure he's gone I turn the sign back so everyone can see that we're *Open for Vetzyme* and spend a couple of pleasant hours selling and playing with Pets. I play catch and fetch with a peculiar looking white terrier (christened Rags by Patricia) that no-one ever wants to buy even though George keeps sticking it in the window with a big red bow round its neck. Patricia and I are desperate for someone to buy poor Rags because George keeps threatening to have him put to 'sleep', a euphemism if ever there was one. (Is Gillian only counterfeiting death? Is she really just asleep and proving very hard to wake up? She never was very good at getting up in the mornings.) Rags features heavily in my prayers. *Dear Jesus, Lamb of God, forgive me my sins and give us our daily bread. Make Gillian happy and give Rags a good home and I will never be bad again as long as I live. All my love, Ruby, Thy Kingdom Come, Amen.* That kind of thing.

I'm glad to say that all the Pets received a lot of attention from me on the afternoon of that fateful day; the kittens were fluffed up; the hamsters were allowed to run along the counter; I even attempted a conversation with the Parrot – it was suddenly clear to me where my destiny lay – I was going to be a Petmonger like my father before me. In a few years the sign above the door would no longer read 'G Lennox' but 'R Lennox' – here was my vocation! It will no longer matter that we're not allowed to have pets of our own (private, non-profit-making pets) because *all* the Pets will be mine one day. Dream on, Ruby.

George struggles through the door of the Shop,

an enormous can of paraffin in each hand which he deposits with a clank and a slosh next to the big barrel of sawdust in the corner of the Shop. Let's hope his cigarette doesn't jump over here!

'Careful!' Bunty warns as I enter the kitchen. She is making sausage, egg and chips for tea – a Health and Safety nightmare of a meal for a woman in her chemically sedated state. Her entire attention is concentrated on the chip pan to the detriment of the sausages which are smouldering nicely in their bath of smoking lard not to mention the eggs whose whites are turning into crackly black lace at the edges. I scuttle around the walls of the kitchen to get to the fridge for a glass of milk, staying well out of the way of the perilous pan. 'Tea's ready,' Bunty says, giving the chip basket a cautious little shake. (She'd be much happier if she had a fire extinguisher in her hand.) 'Get Patricia.'

'She's not very well,' I tell Bunty. She raises an eyebrow ever so slightly. 'It's her soul,' I explain.

'Just get her, Ruby, don't be clever.' They really *don't* want me to be clever, do they?

The rest of the evening is spent in quiet pursuits. George is out, as usual. Patricia stays in her room, also as usual. She is up to volume three of the library edition of *À la recherche du temps perdu*, which I see is about 'the metaphysical ambiguity of reality, time and death and the power of sensation to retrieve memories and reverse time'. Exciting stuff – but how can time be reversible when it gallops forward, clippity-clop and *nobody ever comes back*. Do they?

I am also in my room, playing Scrabble with myself while Teddy looks on forlornly, no longer able to join in now that he's too old for all that role-playing. Granny Nell is in bed where she spends a lot of her time these days. Bunty is down in the kitchen with only her Piles of Ironing for company.

When I've played three games of Scrabble with only minimal cheating I think it's probably time to go to bed. In the AG era, all the little comforting routines are lost. No-one checks I've brushed my teeth and washed my hands and face, nobody even checks that I've gone to bed at all, but I do, adhering to most of the BG routines and rituals. I say my prayers, kneeling on a pillow at the side of the bed. I pray fervently for Gillian to be very happy in Heaven and not be upset about being dead. The last of the advent candles are down to sticky red stumps but I light them anyway and watch as the gold angels bump and grind daintily against the bells, *ting-a-ling ting-a-ling*.

Meanwhile, down in the kitchen poor Bunty is forced to abandon the ironing with precipitate haste when she discovers what looks like Gillian's pink Viyella blouse nestling amongst the Pile (although actually it's only Granny Nell's big knickers). She clutches her forehead all the way up the stairs, swallows a double dose of sleeping tablets and drops into oblivion on her bed. I hear George come in much later, tripping and cursing his way up the stairs. Then the toilet flushes and the lights go out and I drift into the night on a raft of prayers and a few cheering choruses of 'How Much is that Doggie in the Window?' sung softly under the covers.

* * *

I'm dreaming about the end of the world, a common dream that takes many forms. This night the dream is about huge clouds that have boiled up in the sky and are turning into rabbits. The great rabbit-shaped clouds hang in the sky like Zeppelins (*see Footnote (vii)*) and somebody standing behind me says, *It's the end of the world, you know*.

And so it is in some ways. Downstairs the abandoned, forgotten iron was demonstrating its faults to the ironing board. Of course Bunty wasn't to know that the thermostat wasn't working properly and that while she's snoring in a ladylike way in her bed the iron just keeps getting hotter and hotter, scorching the cheerful red gingham cloth that covers the ironing board, a scorch that gradually grows as dark as our neglected tea-time sausages until the pad underneath begins to sizzle and burn. Then the flames find the wood of the ironing-board frame and are happy for a long time in a self-contained way, but then eventually the melting flex falls to the floor and finds the linoleum and one particularly energetic flame goes *whooooosh!* and stretches up and reaches the gay curtains that match the carbonized gingham pad and then there's no stopping it as it greedily gobbles up everything in its path – even the kitchen wallpaper with its pattern of fire-engine-red tomatoes and dancing salt-and-pepper pots.

But in the end even that isn't enough and the fire leaves the kitchen, popping its head out of the door and crossing the passage into the Shop where there are wonderful things to play with – paraffin, sawdust and the whispering, rustling noise of fear.

'Ruby! Ruby!'

I open my eyes quickly, yet it's not like being awake. The air is opaque and Patricia looks like a little old lady, veiled in smoke. There is a smell like burnt sausages. We have been swallowed by a great, grey rabbit-cloud. 'The end of the world,' I murmur to Patricia. 'Get up, Ruby,' she says urgently. 'Get out of bed!' She pulls back the covers and starts tugging me out of bed but I don't understand until she doubles up with a fit of coughing and splutters, 'Fire, Ruby, fire!'

We make our way rather unsteadily to the bedroom door and Patricia whispers, 'I'm not sure we can go out there,' as if she didn't want the fire to overhear, but she's not whispering – it's the smoke rasping her throat that's making her hoarse, as I discover when I try to speak. We open the door very cautiously as if all the fires of Hell were behind it, but there's only smoke, not even thick enough to obliterate Nell's bedroom door opposite. But when we try to leave my bedroom we immediately start to choke and have to stagger back inside, gasping and retching, hanging onto one another. We're human chimneys and it can only get worse, for the Red Horseman of the Apocalypse is already galloping up the stairs of the Shop.

Patricia starts pulling covers off the bed and stuffing them underneath the door; then she flings everything out of my chest of drawers until she finds two school blouses which she wraps round our faces so that we look like the Lone Ranger. In different circumstances this could have been fun. 'Help me,' she croaks from behind her outlaw gag, as she tries to push up the sash window but it's hopelessly stuck. I start to get hysterical and drop to my knees with a jab of pain and start praying frantically to the baby Jesus to save us from incineration. Patricia, more practical, grabs the Bambi-and-Thumper nightlight – once hers, now mine – and smashes it against the window, again and again, until she's broken all the glass. Then she takes the bedside rug and places it over the broken edges of glass on the sill (Patricia really paid attention at Girl Guides, thank goodness) and we both hang out of the window gulping in great lungfuls of cold night air. I think it's only then that I realize how very far away the Back Yard really is.

Patricia turns to look at me and says, 'It's all right, the fire brigade will be here soon,' knowing that neither of us believes this. For a start – who's called them? There is no sound of sirens, no sound of life at all in the street and the remainder of our family are probably little more than glowing cinders by now. Patricia's features are suddenly convulsed by a spasm of pain. She lowers her gag and wheezes, 'Pets. Someone's got to help the Pets.' We both know who that someone is (it doesn't seem to cross our minds that we should be saving our family).

'Here,' Patricia says, pushing something into my hands which, on closer inspection, turns out to be

Panda. Unseen, Teddy jumps up and down on the chest of drawers, frantically trying to catch our attention. Patricia swings herself off the windowsill and over onto the drainpipe in a very Robin Hood kind of way, pausing just long enough to say, 'Stay there, don't move!' in a manner inherited directly from Bunty. She cuts a truly heroic figure as she climbs down, wearing only her white broderie-anglaise baby-doll pyjamas and two big pink sponge cushion-roll curlers in her fringe. Half-way down she pauses and I wave encouragingly down to her. 'Stay there, Ruby, help will be here soon! I'll get the fire brigade.' I believe her, you could trust Patricia in a way that you could never trust Gillian; if it had been Gillian shinning down that drainpipe she would have forgotten all about me by the time she reached the ground. When Patricia's feet finally find the far-away concrete of the Back Yard she raises an arm, half-salute, half-wave and I respond with an exaggerated thumbs-up signal.

Within minutes the Back Yard is transformed from a deserted arena of death into a place of safety. There are firemen all over the place, intelligent as ants – unreeling hoses, putting up ladders, shouting reassurance. Soon a stocky, jovial fireman is perched outside my bedroom window, like a budgerigar up a ladder, saying, 'Hello, sweetheart – let's get you out of there, shall we?' and I am upside down over his shoulder and we are off down the ladder. I have to concentrate so hard on not dropping Teddy (did he really think I would forget him?) and Patricia's Panda that I don't even have time to pray for our deliverance. From my excellent bird's eye view I can see that the Back Yard is now buzzing with life. Patricia is there shouting encouragement; Bunty is screaming something incomprehensible, her mouth forming a perfect circle from which pours a river of glossolalia, while George, who is standing by her side, is shouting something to her (probably 'shut up').

Most peculiar of all is Nell, who is wandering around down there, wearing a navy straw hat like a Salvation Army bonnet without the ribbons (Blood and Fire!) and carrying her leatherette shopping-bag as if she was just off to the Petergate Fisheries and was trying to find out what everyone wanted. (We have been reduced from a 'one-of-each-six-times' family to a 'one-of-each-five-times' family. By as early as 1966 our incredible shrinking family will be down to a 'one-of-each-twice' unit. Plus scraps, of course.)

I realize with a little frisson of excitement that if everyone is down there, then I have been alone in a burning building! What a story I'll have to tell in later life. As we descend towards Bunty this thrill is displaced by a sense of guilt – might I, in some unknowing, ignorant way have caused the fire (I suddenly remember the unextinguished advent candles)? Did a sleepwalking Ruby unwittingly set a fire? I'm waiting for Bunty to say something like *I told you to be more careful!* but to my surprise she says nothing at all and pulls me towards her, wrapping me in the shelter of her dressing-gowned arms and, for once, the invisible cord between us shrivels and shirrs to nothing as we bridge the three-foot chasm. Patricia meanwhile has been wrapped in a grey blanket by a fireman so that she looks like an Indian brave by a (rather large) camp fire. She is weeping hysterically and uncontrollably and making horrible noises, partly due to smoke inhalation and partly due to the fact that she has witnessed the reeking, charcoaled insides of the Shop and smelt the unforgettable smell of toasted fur and feather (no lime tisane and madeleine for us in future years, but it was amazing what the smell of frying sausage could achieve).

But then a miracle occurs – a little black dog runs into the Yard, yapping itself silly, a limp, burnt ribbon dangling from its neck, and Patricia frees herself from the arms of the blanket and runs towards the dog. 'Rags,' she sobs deliriously. 'Oh Rags,' and hugs his singed, smoke-blackened body to her grimy broderie-anglaise. The household ghosts regard their own charred debris – the melted stained-glass panels, the blackened centurions' helmets, the frizzled periwigs, and raise a collective sigh of endurance. York has been scoured and destroyed by fire many times and they are not in the least surprised at going through another one.

Just as the Great Fire of London helped to purge the Great Plague, so the Great Pet Shop Fire helped to purge the death of Gillian. The fire was a purification, an ordeal that we survived and which allowed some change and renewal. For some reason, Gillian no longer hung quite so heavily on our consciences ('If she'd been alive,' Patricia reasoned with tortuous logic, 'she might have died in the fire, so she'd be dead anyway. Right?').

Our days of Above the Shop living are over, even though it's only the ground-floor that's really suffered and the rest of our home is merely greasy with soot. Nonetheless George is under an ultimatum and is down at the Leeds and Holbeck Building Society the next day securing a mortgage on the nice little semi. In a matter of only weeks we will be inspecting the newly-plastered, freshly-painted insides of the Shop, watching counters and display-stands being delivered while Walter questions George about the new line of business. 'Medical and Surgical Supplies?' he quizzes.

George is alive with entrepreneurial enthusiasm. 'Trusses, wheelchairs, hearing-aids, elastic stockings, walking-sticks – there's no end to it, Walter. There'll be stuff on prescription from doctors, folk sent here from the hospital, people off the street for stuff like Elastoplasts and Durex.'

'Durex?' Walter says speculatively. 'There'll be some brass in that. Trade price to friends, eh?' and they both double up with manly laughter.

'What *is* Durex?' I whispered to Patricia.

'I'll tell you later,' she whispered back, but she never did.

But that's all in the future. Now, a spring dawn creeps through the curtains as Patricia and I lie top-to-toe in Auntie Gladys' funny, lumpy, spare bed. (It seems that after every tragedy we must sleep together.)

Somewhere, crammed in between us, lie the sleeping, happy bodies of a dog, a panda and a bear. Unbelievably – or perhaps believably – George and Bunty agree that we can keep Rags for our very own, no longer an endangered Pet, but a proper family pet.

The sky is streaked with red as Pets' blood streams in the firmament. Flocks of budgies turn into angels with Technicolor wings and wheel across the sky. Perhaps in the Spirit World or Heaven, or wherever it is they have all gone, perhaps there, the Parrot will be given the gift of tongues and will be loved. I pray to the bloodstained, smoke-damaged Lamb to make everyone in Heaven very happy. Many things are uncertain but there is one thing we can feel sure about – this morning, the arms of Jesus are very full indeed.

Footnote (vii) – Zeppelin!

NELL AND LILLIAN STOOD AT THE FRONT DOOR AND waved goodbye to Tom. Rachel wouldn't stir herself from a chair to say goodbye to Jesus Christ himself. Tom was glad he didn't live with her any more, glad he had a wife now and a home of his own. He was lucky to have Mabel, she was the quiet devoted sort, a bit like Nelly. Lillian didn't have much time for Mabel, that's why he usually came to see his sisters on his own. He turned at the end of Lowther Street and could see them still standing there; they were great ones for saying goodbye that pair, and he waved his arms in a big semi-circle, like someone signalling with a flag, so they could see him.

They were worried about Zeppelin raids but Tom didn't think anyone would attack York. He reassured them with a lot of bravado, cocky talk about the Hun not having the stomach for fighting, how the war would soon be over and so on. He'd helped them fix their blackout blinds because they were worried about the chinks of light coming through, poor little Minnie Havis had been up in court for showing a light and was so ashamed she could hardly show her face. It seemed such a shame, especially when her young husband was at the Front.

Nell and Lillian had given him his tea, liver and mashed potatoes, and shown him a card from Albert – a grainy postcard of Ypres before the war. 'He says,' Lillian said, reading aloud, 'that they're having grand weather,' and Tom laughed because it was just like his younger brother to say something like that. Sometimes he caught Nelly looking at him as if to say she thought him a coward compared with Albert, but then both of them had always liked Albert best. Albert was everyone's favourite (except Rachel's, of course), and sometimes Tom felt jealous, but it never lasted, you couldn't have bad feelings about Albert, even when you tried. He wasn't so sure about Jack Keech though – the lad was a bit too clever for his own good, he wasn't right for Nell, too cocky – more Lillian's type really.

He was a coward himself though, that much he knew for certain. A woman had come up to Tom in the street yesterday and called him a 'slacker' and he'd gone bright red with embarrassment. Then another woman had come up, quite drunk, and said, 'That's right, lad, you keep out of t'bloody uniform,' and he'd gone even redder. Tom knew that the first woman was right, he *was* a slacker. He was a slacker because he was terrified out of his wits at the idea of going to the Front. When he thought about the war he had this funny feeling, as if his insides were liquefying. And he didn't want to leave poor little Mabel, he didn't know what she'd do without him. Tom's employer was a member of the Society of Friends and had gone up in front of the Board and managed to get Tom an exemption, saying that all his other clerks had gone off to the Front and he couldn't manage if his remaining one went as well. The Board gave Tom a six-month exemption but Tom knew there wasn't much chance of them renewing it. Maybe he could stand up before them and say he was a conchie, but he didn't have the guts for that either; everyone in the Groves knew what had happened to Andrew Brittan, the schoolteacher from Park Grove who was a conchie.

Tom walked home the long way because it was such a lovely evening. May was his favourite month, it made him think of all the hawthorn in blossom in the country. Tom and Mabel often cycled out to the countryside and Tom told his new young wife about being a boy in the Dales, and about his mother; he even told Mabel how awful he felt when his mother had died – something he never talked about with anyone else. Tom had a picture of his mother – it had been taken by a travelling photographer, a Frenchman, just before his mother died. He'd found the photograph, with all the others, on the morning their father told them their mother had died. The photographs were just lying on the kitchen table; his father was in such a state that he hadn't even noticed them. The one of Alice was in a beautiful frame, all chased silver and red padded velvet, and Tom took it and hid it under his mattress, because he wanted this parting gift just for himself. But later, when they were joined in a united front of grief against their frightening stepmother, Tom showed Lawrence and Ada the photograph, although no matter how they begged, pleaded and wept he would not hand it over. Now it stood proudly as the centrepiece on the oak-dresser in his front parlour and Mabel dusted it every day and often said, 'Poor woman,' which, if Tom happened to overhear, gave him a funny, tight feeling in his throat.

The sky above St Saviourgate was a dark indigo and he was walking with his head up, looking at it, when it seemed as if a bit of the sky – a darker bit – had detached itself and was moving overhead. He watched it, puzzled, and then he heard the noise of other people and saw them looking up, the same as him, and someone said in a hushed, awed voice, 'It's a Zeppelin!' and someone else said, 'Bloody hell!' A couple of women screamed and ran indoors but several people stood watching the Zeppelin in fascination. It hung there so mysteriously that no-one seemed to think it would drop any bombs – but then there was a deep THUD and Tom felt something vibrate right through his body as a great crack of light lit up the street and it made Tom think of Nell and Lillian and their blackout blinds. Then for a second it was completely quiet and nothing moved except for the smoke, billowing like a cloud. Then people started to scream and moan and Tom saw a man with half of his head gone and a foot lying in the road that matched the one on the end of the man's leg. A girl was cowering on the steps of the Methodist chapel, whimpering like an injured animal, and Tom went up to her and tried to say something comforting. When he bent down and said, 'Are you all right, miss?' she looked at his hand and screamed and pulled away from him and when Tom looked at his hand he understood why – there was no hand, just a stump of blue-grey shiny bone and some ragged bits of gristle. A soldier in uniform ran up to him and said, 'It's all right, lad, come on,' and got him to the hospital on the back of someone's cart.

The soldier gave him a drink of something from his hip-flask, and kept looking at him in a worried way. He'd seen plenty of men wounded but he'd never met one that laughed his head off about it.

The pain in Tom's hand was unbelievable, as if it was dipped in molten metal, but he didn't care. He'd never get sent to the Front now, he'd be able to stay with his sweet little wife, he'd be able to wave his stump in the face of anyone who dared call him a slacker.

Lillian and Nell sat on his hospital bed, one either side, and Nell pushed back a lock of hair from his face. He'd been brought to the hospital on Haxby Road – Rowntree's dining-block that had been turned into a hospital for men being brought back from the Front – and his sisters behaved as if he really was a wounded soldier. They both smiled at him and Lillian leant over and kissed him. 'Poor Tom,' she said softly, and Nell smiled and said, 'Our brave brother – wait until I write and tell Albert.'

CHAPTER EIGHT

1963

The Rings of Saturn

THE REMAINING FEMALE LENNOXES ARE TEETERING between the two worlds of innocence and experience. For me, this is symbolized by the Eleven Plus exam which I am about to sit and which will decide my fate for ever. For Nell it is the passage from life to death, and Bunty may, or may not, succumb to the charms of infidelity, and Patricia . . . Patricia comes into my bedroom one January tea-time to proudly declare that she's about to 'lose her virginity'.

'Do you want me to help you find it?' I ask absently, because I hadn't quite caught what she said.

'Don't be so clever,' she snarls and slams the door behind her. As I have, this very day, just failed the arithmetic paper in the mock Eleven Plus, this remark hits home cruelly and I stare at the abused bedroom door for a long time considering the possible paths my life is going to take. Will I follow my sisters – dead or otherwise – to Queen Anne Grammar School for Girls or will I be consigned to the scrapheap of

Beckfield Lane Secondary Modern? As well as my future, the bedroom door is also host to my new 'Ye Olde England' calendar, given to me at Christmas by Auntie Gladys. This ye olde England is not a country we're very well acquainted with in our family – page after page, month after month, of thatched cottages, distant spires, haywains and milkmaids. It is also a fund of useful titbits of information – how else would I know when 'Dominion Day' was? Or the anniversary of the Battle of Hastings? If only these things were a help with the Eleven Plus.

I rifle listlessly through Monday's *Look and Learn* without finding anything I want to either look at or learn. Despite having central heating in the light-and-airy pebble-dashed semi that has replaced the dark shadows of Above the Shop, Bunty refuses to turn on the radiators in the bedrooms because she thinks warm bedrooms are unhealthy. Patricia points out that hypothermia is unhealthy too, but once Bunty has her teeth in a belief then she's an absolute terrier with it. It's so cold in my bedroom that I can see my fingertips turning first pink and then blue and if I watch them much longer I suppose they'll turn purple and fall off. I don't get the chance to observe this interesting phenomenon because Patricia comes back in the room and says, 'Can I talk to you, or are you just going to be stupid?' Poor Patricia – she's so desperate for a confidante that she has to make do with me. For some weeks now she has been courted by Howard – an earnest, bespectacled twig of a boy from St Peter's, the expensive public school whose playing-fields back onto Queen Anne's hockey-pitch. He has been spying voyeuristically on Patricia on the hockey-pitch – she's a psychopathically deranged Right Wing – when he should have been boiling things in retorts, and he finally persuaded her, just before Christmas, to go out with him.

'I've decided to do it with him,' she says, making 'It' sound like a tooth extraction and, having missed the subject of the original conversation, I'm still not sure what 'it' might be. From the bottom of the ghostless stairs, Bunty starts shouting at Patricia but Patricia ignores her. Bunty keeps on shouting and Patricia keeps on ignoring. Who will wear out first?

Bunty.

'Howard's parents are going away next week-end,' Patricia says, 'so we'll do it then.' She sits on the end of my bed looking uncommonly light-hearted and I venture to enquire if she is in love with Howard.

Patricia snorts loudly. 'Come off it, Ruby! Romantic love's an outmoded bourgeois convention!' (They don't tell us that in *Look and Learn*.) 'But,' she adds reluctantly, 'it is nice to have someone who *wants* you, you know?'

I nod in sympathetic understanding, it must be very nice. We celebrate this rare moment of intimacy between us by putting on my latest EP, bought with a Christmas record token, 'Chubby Checker's Dancin' Party', and solemnly practise the Twist for a while, a dance at which we are no good at all – Patricia is too stiff and self-conscious and I just fall over – until we collapse from exhaustion, side by side, on the bed and contemplate the pristine woodchip of my ceiling, so sophisticatedly different from the cracked plaster and whitewash of Above the Shop. Patricia turns her head and says, 'I suppose you want me to take you to the pictures tomorrow?' Patricia asks this as if she's doing me a huge favour, whereas I know she's as keen as me to go and see *Kid Galahad* because one of the few things we have in common is our devotion to Elvis Presley. And, what's more, tomorrow, 8th January, is Elvis's birthday, an anniversary marked on the Ye Olde England calendar by a constellation of little red, hand-drawn hearts. It is me that Patricia invites to the Odeon, rather than Howard, because she knows that Howard would scoff throughout at our tender-hearted, blue-suede-shod hero.

She meets me from school, where I have just failed yet another mock arithmetic exam, and consoles me with meat patties from Richardson's and the information that some of the world's great heroes – Gandhi, Schweitzer, Keats, Buddha, Elvis – never passed the Eleven Plus, but then, as I glumly point out to her, they never sat it either. Patricia herself is sitting her O Levels this year but you wouldn't know it from the amount of time she spends on school work (none).

Kid Galahad cheers me up somewhat and the meat patties and the giant box of Poppets which we share in the dark go some way to compensate for the lack of anything to eat when we get home. Bunty is wilting these days, taking to her bed with alarming frequency, for no apparent reason, except that she is 'not feeling well'. She has begun to make strange, unwomanly pronouncements that would have given Auntie Babs the shivers. I have, for example, stumbled upon her in the bathroom, on her hands and knees, scrubbing out the toilet bowl with Vim and vigour, and witnessed her breaking off from this meditation to snap her rubber gloves off and snarl, 'I don't see why a house needs a wife – it's me that needs the wife!' Whatever next? Demanding the vote?

As I am due to sit the first part of my Eleven Plus the following Tuesday she pulls herself together to make Sunday dinner (lunch hasn't arrived in the north yet), a last supper of *roast lamb, butter beans, roast potatoes, mint sauce and frozen peas*. What a shame no-one thought to cook the peas! That's a joke – Patricia's, when she asks Bunty what we're having for dinner, and Bunty recites the above menu. I laugh uproariously at this because, as you can imagine, Patricia doesn't make jokes very often. Not at all, in fact, and I laugh even more, in a Laughing Policeman kind of way, because it would be an awful shame if the first time Patricia made a joke nobody laughed.

Both Patricia and Bunty glare at me. It is an ill-timed burst of humour on Patricia's part because she is not in the parental good books, having come in with the milk this morning. Presumably she was doing 'it' with Howard last night. Bunty is cross-examining her closely for evidence of recent debauchery but, to my eyes anyway, Patricia looks just the same today as she did yesterday. 'If I thought for one minute,' Bunty says, stirring the gravy furiously round the roasting-pan, 'that you had been—'

'Enjoying myself?' Patricia says, a supercilious expression on her face that's just asking to be erased with a slap. But no blow falls. Instead, to our alarm, Bunty starts to quiver like a half-set jelly; even the stiff curls on her head tremble like a tinsel halo on a coathanger-wire. She keeps on stirring the gravy, pretending that this attack of emotion isn't happening. A very surprised Patricia lets her guard fall and hesitantly asks, 'Is something wrong, Mummy?' This unexpected manifestation of compassion ('Mummy'!) drives Bunty over the edge and she snaps, 'Wrong? Only you – that's the only thing that's wrong with *me*,' and a furiously white-lipped Patricia shouts in her face, 'What a bloody cow you are!' and flees the kitchen. Bunty continues her tremulous gravy-stirring as if nothing had happened and without looking at me says, 'Shift yourself, Ruby, do something useful and get the plates.' It's only when she's dishing up the butter beans that look like pale little foetuses curled up on the 'Harvest' dinner plates that she finally dissolves, great tears falling down her cheeks like crystal pear-drops which I try to mop up ineffectively with a Kleenex. By the time we eat our Sunday dinner the gravy is congealed and the peas almost frozen up again. How on earth am I supposed to pass my 'Verbal Reasoning' paper on Tuesday when I see so little of it in the course of my everyday life?

The first part of the Eleven Plus seems suspiciously

easy. *Absent is to A x x x as P x x x x x x is to Here* and the composition is really quite enjoyable: Write about one of the following:

(A) A busy street scene
or
(B) A visit to the swimming-baths
or
(C) What you would do if you had Aladdin's lamp for the day.

And I choose to have Aladdin's lamp, long a favourite daydream, and am lulled into thinking that everything is going to be all right. Two weeks later I sit the arithmetic paper and I'm reeling with horror when I leave the jail-like depths of Fishergate School into which we have been herded to take the scholarship exam. My brain cells feel as if they've been on the rack all morning, tortured by questions like *How many stamps ½ in. by ¾ in. will cover a sheet of paper 6 in. by 8 in.?* and *A grocer mixes 4 lbs. of tea @ 3s. 6d. per lb. He sells the mixture @ 5s. per lb. What is his profit?* Who am I to know the answer to these questions?

'How was it?' Patricia asks, meeting me at the bottom of Fishergate School steps, but I'm far too distressed to speak. We walk along by the Ouse; it's so cold that the river has been frozen for a week and great broken slabs of ice are now cruising downstream. 'This is the coldest winter since 1947,' Patricia says dreamily. 'I've never seen the river frozen like this. It used to freeze nearly every winter in the olden days, did you know that?' Of course I don't know that – I know *nothing*. 'Why olden?' I ask, deciding to take a first step towards improving my knowledge. 'Why not just old? Or Olde?'

'Dunno,' she says with a shrug, and then, as we stand watching the frozen river and contemplating the olden days, a curious feeling rises up inside me, a feeling of something long forgotten. It has something to do with the cold and the ice and something to do with the water too. I try to concentrate on the feeling, to bring it to life, but as soon as I do it evaporates from my brain. It's the same feeling I have sometimes when I'm woken from sleepwalking and I know that there's something incredibly important which I've lost and have been looking for – something that's been torn out of me, leaving a hole inside – and that thing, whatever it is, has been tantalizingly within reach as if it were just around the corner, behind a door, or in a cupboard somewhere. Then I grow fully awake and have no idea at all what it is that I've been looking for.

'Are you all right, Ruby?' Patricia asks, but we are diverted by the approach of a pair of swans, balanced forlornly on their own private iceberg. We can hear the river crackling and cracking and watch as our steamy breath billows into the air. 'What are you doing here anyway?' I ask after a while.

'Truanting. Do you think those swans are all right?'

'Well, I would change places with them anytime,' I respond gloomily. 'At least the rest of their lives doesn't depend on whether they can do mental arithmetic.'

'And they can fly away if they want to,' Patricia nods sadly.

'And they have each other,' I add as the swans glide past us on their ice-float, their magnificent wings ruffled to protect them from the numbing cold. A shiver goes through me from top to bottom. 'The water looks so *cold*.'

'It is,' Patricia says with feeling and then she gives me a funny, sideways look and says, 'Ruby?'

'Mmm?'

'Do you remember—' and then she shakes her head and says, 'Nothing, it doesn't matter, come on – I'll wait with you at the bus-stop if you like,' and she turns her collar up against the wind.

My birthday is marked by a party, grudgingly given by Bunty to comfort me for the distress of the arithmetic paper. The party is not an unqualified success – a girl called Vanessa is violently sick after eating too many sardine sandwiches and someone knocks over a table-lamp during a vigorous Twisting session. The birthday cake is a great success though – a precedent-breaking, shop-bought one – Bunty *always* makes our birthday cakes, their defects smothered by buttercream and stuck with candles like martyred hedgehogs, but this year she's rebelled. Unlike Bunty's cakes, the one from Terry's bakery is exquisite – crisp, swan-white icing that's been sculpted into scrolls and waves and plumes of snow before being decorated with dainty pink sugar-roses. But was it worth George rushing out last minute on Saturday to buy it, uttering language that made even Patricia flinch? Was it worth Bunty being 'not very well' again and screaming at Patricia, 'You're not my child!' to which Patricia replies, 'Thank God,' and walks out of the house just before she's due to orchestrate me and my party guests in our first game of Charades. I hear her coming in much later that night, stomping up the stairs, causing Rags to bark and Nell to shout out in her sleep. I have left a slice of birthday cake for Patricia on her pillow, contrary to Bunty's strict instructions that she is never to be fed again.

I think if it were left up to Bunty, none of us would ever eat again. 'I'm cooked out,' she announces wearily, wrestling with a Fray Bentos steak and kidney pie tin. A further downturn in her condition is signalled by her languishing, Elizabeth Barrett-like, on the shaved moquette of the living-room settee. She says she's 'had enough' but she doesn't say what of. George perhaps. This depression is counterbalanced by an unusual buoyancy on Patricia's part, due, she tells me, to the Bohemian joys of sex which she and Howard are discovering together. This new hobby causes her to forget to revise for her mock O Levels and she fails them all dismally.

Bunty rallies a little for Shrove Tuesday – a day of 'feasting and merry-making' according to the Ye Olde England calendar. Not in our house, not at any rate after Bunty throws the fifth pancake at the kitchen wall instead of tossing it nicely back into the pan. It sticks on the wall for a few seconds and then slowly unpeels itself into a sticky blob on the floor like an extra from a science fiction film (*Killer Pancakes!*). It seems awfully symbolic somehow, especially as it was George's pancake. 'Well,' Patricia says with Bunty's smile stuck across her face, 'I was almost full anyway, weren't you, Ruby?'

'Just about,' I murmur and we slink out of the kitchen quickly before the frying pan whizzes through the air towards George's head.

An appropriate air of contrition is in the air on Ash Wednesday, but we know it won't last. Lent also marks the beginning of Nell's decline, taking to her bed permanently after the pancake fiasco and not even rising for Easter Monday. Somewhere in the middle of this, on Mothering Sunday, Bunty displays a blatant lack of mothering by locking Patricia out of the house, so that she's unable to creep in as usual at three in the morning. Patricia, not to be outdone, stands down below in the quiet suburban night-air, screaming, 'Bloody bourgeois pigs – come the revolution, you'll be first against the wall, Bunty Lennox!' which, not surprisingly, creates quite a stir in the neighbourhood. I think Patricia's enjoying herself and almost looks annoyed when I throw my front-door key down to her.

I myself undergo a traumatic visit to Mr Jeffrey's, the dentist, the day before Good Friday, resulting in the loss of three much cherished baby-teeth which I have been hanging onto as long as possible. Perhaps I do not want to leave my childhood behind. (On the other hand, perhaps I do.) Patricia very kindly exchanges the teeth for three sixpences and takes me to meet Howard in the Acropolis Coffee House. It is hard to believe that this awkward gawky person, peppered with acne, is responsible for the Bacchanalian heights which Patricia reports to me most Sunday mornings as I lie in my innocent bed listening to *Easy Beat*.

Easter weekend is marked by a flurry of family visitors to say goodbye to Nell who has just about 'had enough' of life by now. This premature wake also produces a flurry of Easter eggs. Auntie Gladys, Uncle Clifford and Adrian come as well as Auntie Babs (on her own, thank goodness) and Uncle Ted. Adrian is entirely grown up now (twenty) but is still living at home. He's just started on a hairdressing apprenticeship and is very handy around the house – setting the table for tea and picking up the teapot and saying, 'Shall I be mother?' to Bunty so that she looks shocked as no-one has ever offered before to swap this role with her (you can see she's tempted). Uncle Ted, standing behind Adrian, winks at George and puts his hand on his hip and takes a few mincing steps. George gives a great guffaw of laughter but when Uncle Clifford says, 'What's the joke?' shakes his head helplessly. Adrian has brought his dog with him – a timid wire-haired terrier that Rags tries to dismember.

Uncle Ted announces to the company that he has finally become engaged to his long-standing girlfriend, Sandra, and George says, 'Knocked up?' and all the women shout 'George!' disapprovingly at him. Bunty, getting down to the nitty-gritty, asks who the bridesmaids will be, while Auntie Babs looks smug because the twins are in great demand as bridesmaids. Even I would have to admit that they would probably grace a wedding a bit better than me and Patricia, for we are clumsy, slouching sorts of girls compared with Daisy and Rose. They are too busy, revising for their O-Level exams, to come and say goodbye to their grandmother. They are fifteen-going-on-sixteen and I haven't seen them for a long time. Patricia is sixteen-going-on-seventeen and a few of her Favourite Things are Howard, the Campaign for Nuclear Disarmament and the Beatles, who have rapidly taken over from Elvis in our fickle affections. (All his smouldering six-by-six, glossy, black-and-white photographs have come down off her wall and been replaced by the cheerful grins of the Fab Four. Poor Elvis.) Patricia manages to be rude to everyone – two aunties, two uncles, a cousin and even a dog, within the space of fifteen minutes (as I recall, something to do with her proposal to join the Communist Party) and I gain to the sum of three extra Easter eggs because everyone is so disgusted that they give me her eggs. But what profiteth it a girl if she gains three Easter eggs and loses her sister?

George and Uncles Ted and Clifford gather round the kitchen table with a bottle of whisky that Ted has brought and engage in an animated tri-partite discussion on a) whether or not George should build a patio at the back, b) the sight of our new neighbour, Mrs Roper, breast-feeding her baby in the conservatory next door, which elicits cries all round of 'Bloody Hell!' said half in admiration and half in disgust and c) the best route to Scotch Corner.

I scurry upstairs to seek refuge from this grown-up talk but up in Nell's bedroom an even worse scene is waiting for me. Bunty, Auntie Gladys and a captive Nell are spectating at a morbid women-only striptease show with Auntie Babs as the main attraction. She moves like a statue on a revolving dais and, turning to her audience, she peels back her navy blue cardigan and white blouse to reveal – on one side a pendulous, matronly breast, and on the other side – nothing, just a pucker of skin and scar tissue. Bunty and Auntie Gladys suck in air quickly, making mouths like stricken fish and Nell moans softly. I leave the room quickly. I haven't even learnt about *getting* breasts yet, let alone about losing them. I sit on the stairs pushing chocolate buttons from my Easter egg into the empty sockets in my mouth until eventually boredom propels me to go and find Patricia and secretly give her back the Easter eggs which are rightly hers.

Our new neighbours are Mr Roper, Mrs Roper and their children, Christine, Kenneth and the baby-David. Mr Roper – Clive – is an ex-RAF squadron leader who now has some kind of executive job with British Rail – exactly the kind of man my mother dreams about. And indeed, for several weeks after the Ropers move in at New Year, when Bunty is in her torpid phase, she lets fall a hail of remarks of the 'Why can't you be more like Clive Roper?' variety. These remarks stop with the upturn in Bunty's condition, somewhere around Whit, when she no longer needs George to be more like Mr

Roper because she is toying with the original model.

My friendship with Christine Roper is based solely on proximity – there is no escape from her. She's a year older than me and a particularly bossy girl, in some ways she is more like Gillian than Gillian was, except that she is very plain and Gillian was pretty (although it's only now that she's dead that I'm willing to say that). Kenneth, my junior by two years, is like a distillation of all the little boys that ever were, a kind of demonstration model – from the sagging socks to the half-sucked gobstopper in his pocket. He's annoying but harmless. Less so the baby-David, who dribbles from every orifice and is always red in the face from either screaming or doing his 'big jobs' to use Mrs Roper's inelegant phraseology. Mrs Roper (Harriet) isn't really my mother's sort. She's more like a squadron-leader than her husband – a big, raw-boned woman with an air of certainty about her – very loud and very English. You expect her to rummage around in her extremely untidy house and produce a lacrosse stick or a riding crop rather than the unprepossessing baby-David – or his accessory, a swollen breast, pumping with blue veins like a 3-D delta map.

I am both repelled and fascinated by this sight. I have never seen anyone breastfeeding before Mrs Roper (we aren't that kind of family). It also makes an unfortunate contrast to Auntie Babs' chest, now entirely shorn, as she lies looking paler than the sheet on her bed in St James' in Leeds where Bunty and I go on a cheap-day return one Saturday while Patricia stays at home to fast for India.

This was shortly after I witnessed, for the first time, Bunty and Mr Roper together. Bunty and I were in the Co-op mobile shop, lurking amongst the tinned milk puddings, trying to decide between rice and semolina, when Mr Roper bounded on board, looking for washing-powder – a new man ahead of his time. 'Well, hel-*lo* there!' he said to my mother. He was smartly dressed in cavalry-twill trousers, a dogtooth-check sports jacket and a cravat. Bunty handed over her purse to me so I could pay for our purchases and she could remain ensnared by Mr Roper at the back of the van. While I chanted our divvy number to the driver I could see, reflected in the windscreen, the vision of Mr Roper presenting, with a flourish, the red plastic tulip that was being given away with every packet of Daz.

I was there and, believe me, the woman who took that tulip off Mr Roper was not my mother; that woman was a giggling confection of girlishness – charming, playful, spirited, sort of Debbie Reynolds before Eddie Fisher left her.

I fear for my mother. She is entering murky, uncharted deep space where the meteorites shower unexpectedly down and the Rings of Saturn, as we know, are Deadly.

A little while after this, at the end of June, a miracle happens – George and Bunty receive a letter telling them that I will be going to Queen Anne Grammar School. Phew, as Uncle Ted would say. Patricia, on the other hand, has some grisly results in her O Levels. This is because she walked out of most of them early. (When asked why by a furious Bunty, she just shrugs and says, 'Dunno.')

As a substitute for the summer holiday that we're not getting this year because of Nell's imminent death, Patricia takes me and Kathleen to see the film instead. Patricia is not a Cliff Richard fan, she has recently come into the house holding aloft a little orange-and-white striped Decca forty-five. 'The Rolling Stones!' she says, a wild gleam in her eye. Subterfuge has been necessary to prevent Christine finding out about this event; she is trying to make herself a human wedge between me and Kathleen, and I keep expecting her to pop up between us and spoil things. No need, Howard does a good job of that, snorting with hilarity at Cliff, Una, Melvyn and the gang. 'Puerile!' he comments very loudly and then proceeds to do some bizarre biological things with Patricia while we munch our way haplessly through a box of peppermint creams. Because of them we have to sit in the back row and do not get a very good view of the screen.

Nell expires not long after this. Her last words to me were, 'Mind your boots, Lily!' (see *Footnote (viii)*) as she lay like a shadow in her bed. Her very last words of all (reported by Patricia, who by sheer chance was the only one in the room with her when she died) also lacked a certain lucidity, *'Shall I help put Percy's tea on now, Mrs Sievewright?'* We go and visit Nell in the funeral parlour. She is poor company. The funeral parlour is not what I had expected. I had hoped for something more frightening, more mystical like St Wilfred's – darkness, incense, organ music – instead of the well-lit tableau in front of us with its lemon walls, maroon curtains and the jardinières of plastic flowers that look as if they might have been given away with Daz. Kathleen, along for the ride, views it all suspiciously. 'No candles?' she whispers, astonished. Who will light poor Nell's journey into darkness?

Patricia has a bad cold and her eyes are red but I don't think it's Nell she's crying for. Our grandmother looks much the same dead as she had done in the last weeks of life, her skin a bit more yellow perhaps and an uncanny resemblance to Christine Roper's tortoise. I feel very sorry for her but also very guilty that I'm not wracked by grief the way we were when the Pets died.

The viewing is a leisurely affair, front row, no peppermint creams. 'Had enough?' Bunty asks after a while and we agree that we have. As we're leaving, Bunty turns to look back and after a slight pause says, 'That was my mother,' and the hairs stand up on the back of my neck, just like June Allyson's in *The Glenn Miller Story* on television the previous Sunday afternoon, because I knew, with the certainty of premonition, that one day I will say exactly the same thing.

The summer rolls on, vast oceans of nothing, punctuated by days playing with Christine. Mrs Roper is always asking us to look after the baby-David and we spend a good deal of time trying to lose him. A favourite game is Hide-and-Seek with him, where we Hide him somewhere – under a hedge in the garden or in the Ropers' potting-shed, and then go off to Seek something else – Rags, perhaps, or the tortoise. On one memorable occasion (signalled as 'Trafalgar Day' on my calendar), we completely forgot where we had left him. If it hadn't been for Rags, the baby-David might be in the airing-cupboard to this day.

On a hot, listless day in the middle of August, I wander into the garage looking for something – the dog's ball, the baby-David – who knows what? Instead I find Bunty and Mr Roper together again. I certainly look and learn something in the garage that day – the extraordinary medley of underwear Bunty hides from normal view, for example. In the hot, summer gloom of the garage I catch a glimpse of something nasty poking out from Mr Roper's cavalry-twill. Perhaps Bunty has finally found her instrument of martyrdom? You could certainly think so from the expression on her face. Mr Roper – now at full throttle – suddenly spies me out of the corner of his eye and the lunatic expression on his face changes to one of disbelief. 'Well, hel-*lo*,' he gasps, breathlessly. I say not a dicky bird and remove myself from the scene of the crime.

Perhaps George is vaguely aware that he is losing his wife to another man and that is why he decides to tempt her back with an exotic outing to a faraway place – the Chinese restaurant in Goodramgate. This is his first mistake, for Bunty does not like foreign food. She has not actually tasted any foreign food but nonetheless she knows she doesn't like it. His second mistake was to invite me and Patricia.

'Well,' Bunty says, sitting down at the table and staring at the red tablecloth, 'this is different.' Glowing red paper lanterns with golden tassels hang from the roof where you would expect normal lights to be. I point out the lanterns to Patricia and she smiles indulgently at me. High-pitched string music twangs plangently in the background. 'This place is decorated like a you-know-what,' Bunty says, nibbling suspiciously on a prawn cracker. She fishes a flower out of her little porcelain cup of jasmine tea and examines it critically in the dim crimson light. George orders for us – the *Three-Course Meal for Four* – prawn cocktail, beef chop-suey, sweet-and-sour-pork, chicken chow-mein, followed by tinned lychees and coffee. 'You've been here before!' Bunty says accusingly, and George laughs and says, 'Don't be daft.' But he obviously has because the waiter gives him an inscrutable wink.

George draws on his Shopkeeper's stock of small-talk to keep Bunty amused ('Well, how does this weather suit you, then? We'll pay for this sunshine, eh?') but Bunty is not seduced. 'How long are they going to take?' she demands impatiently after ten seconds. The prawn cocktail arrives, more lettuce than prawn; in fact it's hard to find any prawns at all in the jungle of leaves. 'I found one!' I say triumphantly, 'I've found a prawn!' and George says, 'Don't be clever, Ruby.' Patricia counts her prawns, putting them on the side of her plate where they lie like fat, pink commas. 'They're shrimp, not prawn,' she says, prodding them with a toothpick like an earnest marine biologist. 'Oh for heaven's sakes!' George says, 'Shrimp, prawn – does it matter?'

'It does if you're a shrimp wanting to reproduce,' Patricia says mildly, and Bunty says swiftly, 'We won't have any of that kind of talk, thank you, Patricia – it's to be expected from you, isn't it?'

The next course arrives. 'Chopsticks!' I say excitedly, twirling them in Patricia's face and she fends me off with a napkin. 'You don't expect me to eat with those, do you?' Bunty says, looking in amazement at George.

'Why not? Millions of Chinese do,' he says, scissoring his own ineptly in the direction of a strip of beef. Who would have known he was so cosmopolitan? Bunty lifts a limp and lanky beansprout from her plate. 'What is this?'

'Why don't we just eat?' Patricia says. She looks uncomfortable, even more pale than usual and rather edgy as if she can't sit still in her seat. The pallor of her skin begins to change dramatically, turning to a flushed prawn-pink and – just as Bunty holds up a bit of pork and says, 'What does dog taste like, do you think? Like this?' – Patricia begins to shake and return from rosy-red to snow-white before falling awkwardly off her chair.

'Well, at least now you know you're allergic to prawns,' I comfort her, as she lies stranded on her high, white hospital bed.

'Shrimp,' she reminds me and offers me a fruit gum.

* * *

There follows a frantic week of uniform-buying when Bunty realizes that I have to be kitted out from top-to-toe before the start of the new term. We have a uniform list from Queen Anne's which is quite frightening, not only for the bewildering number of articles of clothing I seem to need in order to attend grammar school, but also for the strictness of the uniform list's tone. Capital letters and underlining abound to warn the lax parent. For example – *Navy blue skirt, pleated or gored,* NOT STRAIGHT, *with pockets* or *navy blue tunic with pocket* although it does not explain why it is so morally imperative to avoid straight skirts. The configurations of shoes are also highly specific – indoor shoes, for example, should be *preferably with rubber sole and low heel.* (*Sling-back or toeless sandals may* NOT *be worn.*) *Clark's type sandal* is strongly advised. Curiously enough, the uniform list bears little relation to anything that Patricia wears – she frequently trips out of the house in a forbidden straight skirt and sling-back shoes, thereby confirming her moral delinquency, no doubt. This road is not for me, however, and Bunty and I trail from Isaac Walton's to Mrs Matterson to Southcott's on an endless quest for *navy blue pleated gymnastic shorts* of approved pattern *for games*.

I don't know why – probably because of her new-found skittishness in love – but these are some of the most pleasant times that Bunty and I have ever spent together. In between acquiring bits of uniform we rest up in cafés with our big paper bags. Bunty kicks off her shoes under the table in Betty's and devours a huge strawberry and meringue basket and looks almost happy.

I take to grammar school like a duck to water – the rigour of fifty-minute lessons, the discipline of the dinner queue, the petty alignments and re-alignments of new friendships – these are all a great release after the continual melodrama of home life. The only unnerving thing is how after every time any teacher reads out my name from a register they look up, slightly fazed, and say, 'Patricia's *sister*?' as if they've never imagined Patricia having a family. Luckily, no-one seems to remember Gillian.

Patricia, despite her poor exam results, is now an *habituée* of the Lower-Sixth Common Room and I rarely encounter her in the mellow oak of the corridors. When we do, she completely ignores me, which is rather galling, especially as other senior girls with new sisters in the school make a great fuss of them and show them off like pets to their friends.

Time trots, canters and gallops towards the end of term and I work hard at producing contour maps and diagrams of Roman central-heating systems and writing sentences in French – another language! The French teacher says I am a natural linguist and I practise the lovely new language of French at every opportunity. *Je m'appelle Ruby. Je suis une pierre precieuse.* Sometimes Patricia can be persuaded to converse with me but this makes Bunty paranoid because she thinks we're talking about her. '*Notre mère*,' Patricia remarks sweetly, '*est une vache, n'est-ce pas?*'

* * *

When I hear the news that Kennedy has been shot, I am the only person remaining seated at the dining-room table, listening to the news on the radio to distract myself from the fact that (in order of disappearance) Patricia, Bunty and then George have all abruptly left the table in the course of an argument which has escalated to proportions which made anything that has happened in the Lone Star State seem small by comparison. The incident has been sparked off by the packet of Featherlight that has turned up in Patricia's blazer pocket, unprotected – as it were – by the Sphinx emblazoned on her Queen Anne's badge and its encouraging motto, *Quod potui perfeci*.

Thereafter I spend a lot of time perfecting my Twist for the end-of-term party that the Sixth Form traditionally throw for First Formers. Patricia, never much of a party-goer, does not turn up but I am honoured by the Head Girl choosing me to lead off with her in a spirited Gay Gordons. After the sandwiches and jelly we play several games, including musical knees (the kind of game I imagine Mr Roper and my mother would be good at), and then dance to pop records, but alas, no Twist; instead people do shapeless, formless dances, their feet shuffling chaotically, their hands grasping at invisible ropes.

It doesn't really matter – I get a splendid end-of-term report, *Ruby works hard and is a pleasure to have in class,* which I wave first at Bunty, then George and finally

Patricia, none of whom show any interest, even when I sellotape it to the outside of my bedroom door.

The end of the year is turned into the Twilight Zone by the arrival of the freshly-bereaved Daisy and Rose on New Year's Eve. They sleep in Nell's now empty bed and are never seen to cry. Auntie Babs – hopefully reunited with her missing parts – has surely sent them a message from the world of Spirit, but if she has, they never divulge it. Bunty never stops going on about how well behaved the twins are but I think what she means by that is that they never speak.

I am in bed and asleep long before the bells but am woken by Patricia just before midnight, drunk, but eager to reminisce on the passing year. She has an almost empty bottle of Bristol Cream Sherry with her, from which she takes an occasional slug. I decline. She had planned to see the New Year in on the Knavesmire, in the back of Howard's old Zephyr, but they have had a falling out. 'He's decided he's going to be an accountant,' she says, the words an alcoholic slurry. She struggles to light a cigarette, an expression of disgust on her face.

'And what are you going to be, Patricia?' I ask cautiously. She blows out a stream of thoughtful smoke and knocks ash everywhere. 'Dunno,' she says finally, and then after a while, 'I think I'd just like to be happy.'

Of all Patricia's ambitions that somehow seems the most outrageous. 'Well,' I say to her, as the nearest church bells begin to welcome 1964, 'if I had Aladdin's lamp for the day, Patricia, that's exactly what you would be.' But when I look closely I can see that she's fallen asleep and so I remove the burning cigarette from her hand and carefully stub it out on the last picture of Ye Olde England calendar – a pretty thatched and timbered cottage with roses round the door and smoke curling from the chimney.

Footnote (viii) – New Boots

THE END OF THE BOER WAR! ALL DAY LONG THE STREETS had been full of people celebrating the news. By happy coincidence there was a great travelling fair visiting St George's Field and Lillian and Nell were hoping to visit its gas-lit stalls and experience the thrill of being amongst the crowds on such a patriotic occasion. Albert had gone fishing with his pal Frank, and Tom was already away from home, living in lodgings in Monkgate. Lillian was fifteen now and Nelly fourteen and both were working. Lillian was at Rowntree's in the packing department. When she'd first left school Rachel had made her go into service, but one morning Lillian had just stood there in the kitchen, her arms folded, her chin up, and said she wasn't going to skivvy for anyone. Nell had prayed every night that her sister would get another job soon because they needed new boots so desperately and Rachel said they couldn't have any until Lillian was bringing in a wage again. Their old boots were worn right through so that they could feel the pavement through their stocking-feet.

Nell earned hardly anything; she was apprenticed to a milliner in Coney Street and both girls had to hand over every penny of their wages to Rachel every week when she grudgingly gave them a few coppers back. They got their new boots before Lillian got her job because Lillian was so disgusted by the state of their boots that she'd gone out one day in her bare feet, and Rachel, her face red with fury, was finally goaded by embarrassment into giving them the money for new boots.

'Can we go to the fair after tea?' It was Lillian that asked, of course. Nell was so timid that she got Lillian to do all her talking if she could. Rachel looked right through Lillian and completely ignored her. 'Say "please",' Nell whispered in her sister's ear. Lillian screwed up her face, 'Please can we go to the fair after tea?'

'No.'

'Why not?'

'Because I said not,' Rachel said, looking from one to the other of them as if they were both idiots. Then she picked up a pile of clean laundry and walked out of the kitchen. Lillian picked up a wooden spoon from the kitchen table and threw it after Rachel's retreating back and to pay them back Rachel waited until they were both up in their room and then she turned the key in the door and locked them in.

They sat on their bedroom floor and laced up their new

boots. They were made of soft, black leather and were the most expensive boots they'd ever had. 'She'll find out,' Nell said, staring at the still unscuffed toes of her boots. 'I don't care,' Lillian said, jumping up and lifting the sash. They were still living in the house in Walmgate, a poky upstairs apartment in a slum courtyard. The yard beneath their bedroom window was dank and smelt of sewage and slimy green moss covered the paving-slabs. But in the middle, through a big, cracked hole in the stones, a lilac tree had taken root many years ago, its seed blown in from some pleasant town garden along the length of dark Walmgate. Its bark was rough and torn as if someone had taken the tines of a giant fork and scratched them down the trunk, but its blossom was as rich and heavy as any tree in a grander place. Last year, Lillian had reached out from their bedroom window and torn off a great branch of it and stuck it in an old jug in their room and the heady scent of lilac had cheered them for weeks.

Nell brushed Lillian's hair for her and tied her ribbons, then Lillian did the same for Nell. 'I'm sure the branches will break with our weight,' Nelly hissed as Lillian put one leg over the sill.

'Stop fussing, Nelly,' Lillian whispered back, one arm already grasping a branch. Lillian swung herself out and grabbed the trunk. 'Mind your boots, Lily!' Nell hissed as Lillian clambered down the tree. She stood at the bottom and said, 'It's easy, Nelly, come on.' Nell was already sitting on the window-sill, leaning out, but then she drew back; she'd never had a good head for heights and when she looked down she felt sick – although it wasn't so much the height that stopped her as the fear of Rachel's wrath if she found that they'd sneaked out like this after she'd expressly forbidden them. Nell shook her head miserably. 'I'm not coming, Lily.' Lillian cajoled and pleaded with Nell, but it did no good and in the end she said angrily, 'What a coward you are, Nelly! Well, I'm going even if you're not!' and she marched out of the yard and out of Nell's sight without a backward glance. Nell stood for a long time at the open window. The sound of people celebrating the end of the war drifted into the courtyard on the soft air of a May evening. Nell's tears had dried and the sky had grown a very dark blue and the first star was out before Lillian came back, her ribbons askew, her new boots scuffed and a grin of triumph on her face.

Nell opened the window for her and helped her climb back in over the sill. Lillian took a paper poke of toffee from her pocket and shared it with Nell. 'It was really grand, Nell,' she said, her eyes shining.

A wind got up in the night and it began to rain. Nell was woken up by the tapping of a branch of the lilac tree against the bedroom window. Nell lay with her eyes wide open in the dark, listening to Lillian's peaceful breathing next to her. Nell wished she was more like Lillian. The rain and the tapping grew louder and the wind wilder and Nell didn't think she'd ever get back to sleep.

CHAPTER NINE

1964

Holiday!

WE'RE OFF! NOT TO SEE THE WIZARD, BUT ON HOLIDAY. 'We're off!' I say enthusiastically to Patricia. 'Shut up, Ruby!'

Shutupruby, shutupruby. Honestly, you'd think that was my name in the World According to Patricia. She's busy drawing obscene anatomical diagrams on the misted-up insides of the car windows. It's cold and damp both inside and outside the car – a weather situation that doesn't seem a good omen for our impending holiday. The self-catering years (Bridlington, Whitby) are over and the exotic destinations lie ahead of us (Sitges, North Wales) beginning with, possibly, the most foreign location of all – Scotland!

What's more, we are travelling in convoy – or at least, in tandem – and there, at the head of our two-camel caravan, is the blue Ford Consul Classic of our friends and neighbours, the Ropers. Bunty could have been a real poker-fiend judging by her poker-face when George proposes this idea after a 'chat' with Mr Roper over the hedge-battlement between our suburban castles. Bunty and I are busy feeding the toaster with an assortment of bakery goods – crumpets, pikelets, tea-cakes and so on – when George tramps in from the garden, leaving mud everywhere, and says, 'I've been having a chat with Clive – what do you think about going on holiday with the Ropers this summer?' and quick as a wink, Bunty sticks her smile on and says, 'The Ropers?' as a tea-cake flings itself with dramatic timing out of the toaster.

'The Ropers,' I echo in horror, leaping to catch the tea-cake.

'Well, why not?' she says brightly, buttering the tea-cake and offering it to George. He declines and strides across to the kitchen sink and washes his hands. Bunty is obviously shaken because she doesn't even point out to him that he has left a trail of muddy footprints across her red and white vinyl tiles, like something from an Arthur Murray handbook. Or footbook. A more alert man would have realized instantly that he was being cuckolded.

Occasionally, Kenneth pops up in the rear-window of the Ropers' car, like an unlucky mascot, and makes a variety of faces – cross-eyed, tongue out, fingers in his ears – but the female Lennoxes stoically ignore him. Bunty, who's only too grateful that she's never had any little boys of her own, is baffled by Kenneth's behaviour, but George is not shy of pronouncing judgement, 'Bloody stupid little bastard.'

George hasn't got time for Kenneth's distractions

– he needs every ounce of concentration to keep up with the Ropers. We're terrified of losing sight of our squadron-leader because he's the only one who knows how to get to Scotland and every so often Bunty has a fit of panic and screams at George, *He's overtaking someone! Quick, quick – put on your indicator!* Woe betide any vehicle that gets between us and the Ropers, for it faces instant disintegration from Bunty's brainwaves.

Still, following the Ropers in this blind slavish fashion is infinitely preferable to being subject to Bunty's navigation which is either hit and miss – *B125, B126 – what's the difference?* or defensive – *How should I know what the sign said. You're the driver!* If she had an AA man on one shoulder and a spirit guide on the other she'd still get us lost, although at the moment Mr Roper doesn't seem to be doing a much better job, taking us spiralling around the suburbs of Carlisle like a plane on a death spin (see *Footnote (ix)*).

'What the bloody hell is he doing?' George splutters as we whirl round a roundabout that we've circled at least twice already. 'There's that fish and chip shop again!' Bunty says.

'And that garage – what's he playing at?' George shakes his head. 'I knew we should have come by Newcastle,' he says with the bitterness of hindsight.

'Well then, clever dick, if you thought that, you should have said something to him, shouldn't you?' I don't think it's very wise of our mother to defend her lover in public in this way. I cast a sideways glance at Patricia to see what she thinks but she's busy committing the Kama Sutra to the steamy window. Rather childish behaviour in my opinion (which is worth nothing, of course – I am under no illusion) but not as childish as Bunty's; she is demanding that George stop the car and let her out. It's amazing how an argument can escalate when you take your eyes off it for just a second.

'Oh, and what are you going to do –' George sneers, 'walk home from Carlisle?' But he doesn't get an answer because Mr Roper's indicator suddenly starts flashing and Bunty has to alert George to this fact. *'He's slowing down! He's stopping!'* she shrieks, and George applies the brakes so fast that my brain almost comes loose from its moorings. 'For God's sake,' Patricia says nastily to no-one in particular. Sometimes I would like to cry. I close my eyes. Why weren't we designed so that we can close our ears as well? (Perhaps because we would never open them.) Is there some way that I could accelerate my evolution and develop earlids?

George and Mr Roper have a hurried consultation on the pavement, turning the map this way and that until they come to some kind of agreement. Bunty fumes in the passenger seat, fulminating indiscriminately about the stupidity of both husband and lover. Christine puts her head out of the side window and waves. Two weeks with no time off for good behaviour in the company of Christine Roper is not a prospect to relish, she treats me like a slave – if we were in Ancient Egypt I would be building a pyramid for her single-handed. I wave back obediently. There's no sign of the baby-David, perhaps he's strapped to the luggage-rack.

We're off! again. 'When are we going to eat?' I ask plaintively.

'Eat?' Bunty asks in disbelief.

'Yes, eat,' Patricia says sarcastically. 'You know – eat, food, ever heard of it?'

'Don't talk to your mother like that!' George shouts into the rear-view mirror and Patricia sinks down in her seat so she's out of sight of the mirror and mutters, 'Don't talk to your mother like that,' again and again. Patricia now wears her hair in two thick curtains that hang drably down either side of her face – she has already discovered Joan Baez, ahead of the Top Ten, which I regard as very *avant garde* of her – and talks a lot about things like 'injustice' and 'racial prejudice' (in America, that is, we don't really have coloured people in York, to Patricia's disappointment. Every single face in assembly at Queen Anne's each morning is a pasty white. The nearest thing we have is Susannah Hesse, a very clever German girl on an exchange year. Patricia is always cornering her and asking her if she feels discriminated against). Naturally, Patricia has my complete support in her campaign against injustice, but George says she should pay more attention to her A Levels. She has recently 'chucked' Howard which may account for the appearance of a previously unmined seam of moodiness. Although it may just be a further refinement in her character.

We play 'Spot the . . .' for a while – Spot the red cars, Spot the telephone boxes – Spot anything really.

Somewhere south of Glasgow we leave the main road and stop at a hotel for lunch. Usually when we're out in the car we take a hastily-made picnic and eat it as we drive along, so this is indeed a sophisticated departure from the norm. Bunty preens herself before stepping out of the car; she is after all, about to have lunch in a hotel with her lover, which is quite a romantic thing to do, even with the drawback of two spouses and five children. Hang on a minute – there's something missing from this inventory, isn't there? I turn a puzzled face to Patricia. 'What did we do with Rags?'

'Rags?'

We both look at the back of our mother's head; she's peering into her powder-compact so we can see not only the back of her head but also bits of her face moving about in the little mirror. 'What did you do with Rags?' we chorus.

'The dog?' She's got her off-hand voice on – always a danger sign. 'Don't worry about him, he's taken care of.'

Patricia's suddenly very alert. 'What do you mean "taken care of"? Like Hitler took care of the Jews?'

'Don't be silly,' Bunty says in her don't-be-a-fusspot voice and paints on the dazzling smile of a scarlet woman. This conversation is fatally interrupted by George banging on the car window, telling us all to hurry up because we haven't got all day. 'Ah, but we have,' says Patricia. 'We have all day today, and then all day tomorrow and so it goes on until the crack of doom, believe me.'

'Oh, for heaven's sake, Patricia,' Bunty says,

snapping her compact shut. 'Just get a move on, will you?'

I will draw a veil over lunch, suffice to say that the 'Homemade Tomato Soup' was redolent with the savour of Heinz and that Bunty and Mr Roper exchanged a wide range of flirtatious looks – from prim to downright lustful – without apparently anyone apart from me noticing. Bunty and I have never talked about the fact that I have caught her *in flagrante* with Mr Roper in the garage, which I find quite understandable – after all, what could she say? Nor have I talked about it with Patricia, you can't talk to Patricia about anything any more, so I'm not sure whether or not she knows about our mother's adultery.

We scramble back into our old Wolseley, and we're off! A bit of a false start, as we pull up almost immediately (*Why is he indicating? Stop! Stop!*) so that Kenneth can vomit on the verge – an unattractive pink *mélange* which owes a lot to the tomato soup, but then finally we're off! again.

Unfortunately, our brains are still trying to digest lunch when we hit the outer circle of Glasgow, which must account for our erratic progress towards the inner circle, a hellish journey on which hope and good manners are both abandoned. 'I thought he was supposed to be a bloody RAF pilot,' George hisses with disgust as the Ropers' left indicator goes on – and then off – followed by the same behaviour from their right indicator – until we're weaving crazily along Sauchiehall Street as if we're harpooned onto Moby Dick rather than a 1963 Consul Classic. 'How did he find Dresden? He couldn't find his way round bloody Woolworth's.'

'Neither could you,' Bunty says, her lips moving like a pair of scissors. The real crisis occurs when we are separated by a traffic light at the top of Sauchiehall Street and Bunty lets out a wail of despair, *'We've lost them, we've lost them now!'* I think it's at this point that I decide to play dead. Patricia, I see, is already faking a coma.

Things improve a little on the other side of Dumbarton, a highway of tranquillity lies ahead of us until Crianlarich. Patricia entertains us by reading aloud from *Tristram Shandy*. Bunty shifts uneasily in her front seat because all eighteenth-century prose sounds smutty to her and she has trouble believing it's on Patricia's A-Level reading list. Every so often she glances behind to check we're not sniggering at something dirty – completely missing the Stone Age genitalia with which Patricia has adorned the rear window. Patricia seems to be quite obsessed by human biology.

Crianlarich passes in a blur of raindrops and it's only several miles up the road that we discover we've gone right when we should have gone left: *What's he doing? He's turning, he's turning!*

Where is Scotland? What is Scotland? Is it rain solidified into the shapes of houses and hills? Is it mist, carved into roadside cafés with names like The Crofter's Kitchen? (*Don't give that to the baby, Christine – he'll be sick. There – what did I tell you?*) Who knows? We are going to a place that sounds like it's called 'Och-na-cock-a-leekie'. The Ropers and our parents have been seduced by a brochure temptingly entitled 'Scottish Farmhouse Holidays' and their brains are awash with hot bannocks and griddle scones dripping with salty sun-yellow butter and thick porridge in a pond of cream, warm from the cow.

I've just fallen into a fitful doze on Patricia's uncomfortable, bony shoulder when we screech to a halt yet again. *What's he stopping for now?* 'Pit-stop!' Mr Roper yells, making helpless, apologetic gestures with his hands as 'Harriet' yanks the baby-David out of the car and holds him over the grass verge. A stream of liquid like weak tea emerges from his nether regions. 'I don't see why she has to put things like that on public display,' Bunty says with distaste. 'She [she means Mrs Roper] may have a posh accent, not to mention having been to boarding-school ('Send me,' mutters Patricia. 'Please.'), but really she's just a slattern.'

Slattern! What a wonderful new word. 'Slattern,' I murmur appreciatively to Patricia.

'Yes, slattern,' Bunty says firmly. 'That's what she is.'

'Not a slut like you then?' Patricia says very quietly. Loud enough to be heard, but too quiet to be believed. There is a starched silence for a while and then somewhere around Dalmally Patricia breaks it by embarking on the *Patricia Lennox Songbook,* which is full of songs about tender maidens, dead union officials, unfaithful lovers and a lot of people hanging their heads and weeping and wailing and generally having a great deal of 'trouble', which we rollick along to in fine spirit. We've just reached a wailing crescendo ('ve-ey-ey-ey-al') when Bunty's nerves finally snap (Had we not realized it was about adultery?) and she shouts, 'Shut up the pair of you!' and gives us cheese and onion crisps to prevent us singing any more.

The road grows narrower. The weather grows wetter. The air seems darker – although whether this is due to the evening or the rain, it's hard to tell. We plough slowly on through the gloaming, as if it was a tangible force slowing us down. We jolt gracelessly to yet another halt (*I don't believe it!*) and sigh as Kenneth trots off into a clump of gorse bushes, unbuttoning the flies on his grey flannel shorts as he goes. 'Why didn't he go when they stopped before? Doesn't she have any sense?' Bunty blows air out of her mouth like a carthorse. Christine gets out of the car and follows her brother into the bushes while Mrs Roper holds out the baby-David-teapot again. 'They went at the hotel, didn't they?' Bunty asks, snorting with incredulity at the slack state of the Roper bladders. (Ours, under Bunty's tutelage, are made of cast-iron.)

'It's not the destination that's important,' Patricia says in a dreamy way, 'it's the journey.' (She's reading *On the Road* as well as *Tristram Shandy* so it's hardly surprising that she's turning a bit zen.) But finally we're off! yet again, following the yellow brick road, or rather, a dubious single-track. 'Does this road have a number?' George asks, huddling over the steering-wheel to see better. 'I wish he'd put his bloody lights on!'

he adds, flashing his own headlights furiously.

Then a new hazard presents itself on the road without name or number – sheep! 'They're bloody everywhere!' George exclaims in horror. Bunty has to go on sheep alert (*There's one! Mind that one! That one's going to cross! Keep an eye on that one on the left!*)

Tired of *Tristram Shandy*, Patricia and I play 'Spot the . . .' again but really there isn't anything to Spot except for sheep.

Then disaster strikes – not as expected from the sheep slalom but a flat tyre on the Consul Classic. 'See!' George says triumphantly because Bunty's been rattling on for weeks about how nice the Ropers' car is compared to our own (which it is), but Bunty just tosses her head and says tartly, 'A flat tyre can happen to anyone.'

'That's the road of life for you,' Patricia says, the smile of the Buddha playing on her features.

Reluctantly, George gets out of the car and helps Mr Roper change the tyre – or rather Mr Roper changes the tyre and George hands him things, like a nurse assisting at an operation. Bunty also gets out and stands around observing George's incompetence with spanners and nuts and Mr Roper's manly grace under pressure. ('Well done, Clive!') All the while, Kenneth buzzes around with his arms out, pretending to be an aircraft, or a fixed-wing insect, or perhaps both. 'Thank God I've got girls,' Bunty says when she climbs back into the car (the only statement she ever produces indicating gratitude for our existence), and when George has sighed his way back into the driver's seat, we're off! again.

We are approaching our Mecca, there's no doubt about it; we pass through several 'Och-na-cockna' villages and finally arrive at the right one. We take a left turn, double back, take a right turn, double back again and take the original left. 'Oh fucking hell,' George says wearily as he executes yet another three-point turn, and Bunty flaps her hands at him in disgust. But then, at last, we're off! for the final time, splashing and rocking our way along a dirt track until we arrive in a muddy yard amongst a flurry of angry chickens. On one side is a long, low outbuilding, on another a dilapidated barn, and on the third is a big, square, grey-stone building – our Farmhouse. The Hammer Holiday from Hell is about to begin!

The occupants of the farm, our hosts for the next two weeks, are called von Leibnitz, which doesn't seem like a very Scottish name to me. Wouldn't we have done better to have chosen a Farm from the Farmhouse Brochure that was run by a McAllister, a Macbeth, a McCormack, a McDade, a McEwan, a McFadden – even a McLeibnitz – in fact anyone whose name began with a 'mac' rather than a 'von'? Mr von Leibnitz ('Heinrich'), we discover later on, was a German POW who was sent to work on the farm and stayed on, marrying the farmer's widow – Mrs von Leibnitz – or Aileen McDonald as she was before her husband died in North Africa and was substituted by the enemy. This, together with the fact that Mrs von Leibnitz came originally from Aberdeen, makes them a pair of total outsiders in

Och-na-cock-a-leekie, which perhaps accounts for their stern character. 'So it was old McDonald's farm then?' George jokes, on hearing this story, but is met with stony countenances from the von Leibnitzes. They have no sense of humour whatsoever – even Bunty has a sense of humour compared with our hosts. They have united Prussian gloom and Presbyterian dourness in an awesome combination. Spare and tall, straight-backed and solemn, they clearly regard holidaymakers as frivolous, weak creatures. Perhaps they're right.

There is a lot of fuss about bedrooms, reminiscent of the dilemma over taxonomies in the Spirit World. How will we be permutated? Boys with boys, girls with girls? Roper with Roper, Lennox with Lennox? And what of the adults – husband with wife? Or not? Mrs Roper dispatches us with efficiency, while Bunty exchanges lingering looks with Mr Roper. 'Shall I carry that for you, Bunty?' he asks soulfully, and, reaching for a suitcase, their fingers meet for an achingly long time, until, in fact, they are bodily separated by Patricia, barging up the stairs between them and grabbing the suitcase on her way.

Mrs Roper puts all the girls together in an attic bedroom that reeks of must, and Patricia makes a dive for the single bed, leaving me to share the double with Christine, who spends half of every night telling me to move up, even though I'm already sleeping on the edge, and the other half grinding her teeth and muttering in her sleep.

For our first breakfast, seated at a long, dark-oak table

in a gloomy, cold dining-room, we are served plates of lukewarm, salty porridge (to Patricia's dismay) with neither milk nor sugar, and afterwards a strip of bacon each and a little pile of cold baked beans. This is prison food, not holiday food.

'*Cold* baked beans?' Bunty puzzles.

'Maybe that's how the Scots eat them,' Mr Roper suggests, 'or the Germans,' he adds as an afterthought. I think it was at this moment that Patricia lurched from the table, informing everyone that she was going to be sick and indeed was as good as her word, throwing up before reaching the door ('Heinrich, fetch a clout – the lassie's boaked!') And she hasn't even eaten any breakfast yet! We have been on holiday less than twenty-four hours and three people have vomited already. How many more times will this happen? (Many.)

And from there it's downhill all the way. There isn't very much to do on the farm; you can look at the five cows, whose milk goes straight to the dairy, not to our porridge, and you can annoy the four chickens, whose eggs go straight into a tarred barrel of water-glass, and you can survey a couple of damp, rain-flattened fields of barley, but after that there isn't much left, apart from the sheep, scattered like little limestone outcrops over rolling, humpy hills of brown-green grass and bracken.

In the distance, over those hills and far away, at the outer barriers of the von Leibnitz property, is where the real Scotland seems to be (I have read *Rob Roy* and *Waverley* and *The Heart of Midlothian* in preparation for this trip), a swathe of purple and lilac rising up to the horizon and melting into the sky, cloaked on one side by a forest of bristling, bottle-green trees. 'Aye,' says Mr von Leibnitz, in a more forthcoming mood than usual, 'dat's partov di ancient Caledonian Vorest,' and my heart leaps because this sounds more like Scott's Scotland. ('It's funny, isn't it, that he was called Scott, when he *was* a Scot,' I venture conversationally to Mrs von Leibnitz when I'm abandoned to her care on Black Tuesday – of which more later, unfortunately – but she responds, 'You're a gey peculiar wee lassie, are you no?' because she doesn't read anything except *The People's Friend*.)

We are rather surprised to find that we aren't near the sea and there's quite a lot of discussion about whose fault this might be, Mr Roper's orienteering skills once more being brought into disrepute by George (and defended by his mistress). Several day trips are planned to visit not only the sea but other places of 'historic and architectural interest' – Mrs Roper has brought a guide-book with her – and our first expedition is to Fort William via the famous Glencoe. 'Why is it famous?' I ask Mrs Roper, who is peering at the guide-book in one hand while wafting one of the baby-David's dirty night-nappies in the other. 'A massacre,' she says vaguely.

'A massacre,' I tell Patricia.

'Oh good,' she says with relish.

'No, no,' I say hastily, 'an historical one,' but you can see from the look in her eye that Patricia isn't thinking about Campbells and Macdonalds but Ropers and Lennoxes. Or perhaps just Lennoxes.

A black cloud, both metaphorical and real, settles above our heads as we enter Glencoe. ('Aye,' Mrs von Leibnitz confirms later, 'it's an uncanny dreich place that Glencoe.') The hills rise, grim and threatening, on either side of us but we arrive safely *sans* massacre, and sample the delights of Fort William on a rainy day. We take immediate cover in another Kitchen, a 'Highland' one this time, which is full of people and pushchairs, sopping macs and dripping umbrellas, and a chrome Gaggia, hissing aggressively. The grown-ups, as they comically refer to themselves, have coffee in glass cups and saucers and Bunty smiles across the red tinfoil ash-tray at Mr Roper and says, 'Sugar, Clive?' holding out the stainless-steel pot as if it contained Aphrodite's golden apples and not brown-sugar crystals. 'Thank you, Bunty,' he says, locking his smile onto hers while the rest of us watch his spoon as if we're hypnotized, as he stirs it round and round and round and round and round and round until Mrs Roper says suddenly, 'You don't take sugar, Clive!' and we all wake up.

Patricia sips feebly at a glass of water, I have a cup of tea, Christine has milk, Kenneth has a Fanta and the baby-David is allowed a banana milk-shake which Mrs Roper pours into his baby-cup. The banana milk-shake is a sickly yellow colour that seems to owe very little to a bunch of Fyffes and it comes as no surprise to me when he dribbles most of it back up again after a few minutes. Patricia retires with precipitate haste behind a door marked 'Lassies' but everyone else, I'm glad to say, manages to hold their liquids down.

We discover that we've left the guide-book in Och-na-cock-a-leekie and wander the streets disconsolately, looking for something of architectural or historical interest, settling eventually on the Wee Highland Gift Shop where we buy many totally useless objects adorned with thistles and heather, although personally, I am delighted with my *Illustrated Pocket Guide to Scottish Tartans*, even if half the tartans are reproduced in hazy black-and-white. Foolishly, we buy sugar in large quantities – Whisky Fudge, Soor Plums (a Scottish delicacy, the woman in the shop tells us), Edinburgh Rock and long ropes of shiny liquorice. A sudden, painful August hailstorm prompts a group decision to abandon the Fort and we scamper back to the car park, and take the high road back to the Farmhouse.

On the journey back, we set about consuming our newly-bought confectionery in lieu of lunch and it isn't long before the Ropers' car is drawing up at the side of the road (*He's stopping!*) for the baby-David to splatter the remains of his banana-yellow vomit all over the grass verge and, two minutes after we're off! for the second time, it's our turn because the lassie's boaking again. Even the normally stalwart Mrs Roper has to 'take some fresh air' under the lowering skies of Glencoe. 'Poor Harriet,' George says, causing Bunty to look at him in speechless astonishment because he has never said 'Poor Bunty' in his life, but she never gets round to articulating this astonishment because Patricia moans gently and we have to *Stop!* again.

I commiserate with her, 'Nobody knows the trouble you've seen, Patricia.'

'Shutupruby.'

Not surprisingly, it is several days before we venture on another trip, but in the meantime there are other pastimes – we watch the cows being milked several times and Patricia makes quite a friend of one of the chickens. Then there are the evenings, which we pass in old-fashioned pursuits. There is a cottage piano, for example, very out-of-tune, on which Christine entertains us with her quirky versions of 'My Bonny Lies over the Ocean' and 'Home Sweet Home', a song whose popularity Patricia and I have never understood. Reading matter is supplied in the form of *Reader's Digest*'s condensed novels and a large black leather-bound Bible, big enough to sink a ship. We play the usual games of Snap, of course, and Mrs Roper teaches us all Piquet. A previous holidaymaker has left behind Cluedo so we play that a lot, but instead of releasing murderous impulses it just seems to intensify them. You can tell from this, of course, that there is no television *chez* von Leibnitz, freeing us to fully appreciate the delights of living in a family with a double nucleus.

We have several days of relative peace down at the Bottomless Loch. 'Bottomless?' Mr Roper queries. 'Aye, bottomless,' Mr von Leibnitz confirms. It's more of a pond really, nestling amongst the sheep-strewn hills like a lump of liquorice, its blackness suggesting that it might well be unplumbable. Mr von Leibnitz lends the holiday party some fishing-rods and Mrs Roper, Mr Roper and George stand at the edge of the loch twitching and flinching their rods but catch nothing. I suppose all the fish have drained away to Australia. Meanwhile, the baby-David wobbles and totters around like a large, annoying insect and Patricia sits huddled on the grass reading *Humphry Clinker* and giving the baby-David the evil eye whenever he comes near her.

Bunty glides around the loch, casting meaningful glances instead of bright, feathery little flies. Her romance is being seriously hindered by the presence of Mrs Roper, but despite this her loch-side perambulations bring her round and round again to Mr Roper. It's amazing how often, in the daily round, they collide with each other, fingers brushing as they reach for cups, bodies bumping as they try to pass through doors together as if Mr Roper is a magnet and Bunty a heap of iron filings.

Christine tries to involve me in a stream of games that she invents, all of which are based on the premise that we are horses. It's difficult to avoid playing equine games with her and the best I can usually manage is to gallop hell-for-leather towards the nearest hill and hope that she doesn't follow. Sometimes I escape successfully, especially if she becomes embroiled in some minor distraction (Oh, my God – *where's the baby?*) or gets inveigled into helping Kenneth test the bottomless theory (*Kenneth, get out of the water this minute!*). It seems to me that the easiest way to test this theory would be to simply throw Kenneth in.

I prefer to be as far away as possible from the loch. It creates a feeling of unease in me and if I get too near the edge I begin to think it's trying to suck me into its endless blackness. It reminds me of something, but what?

We have several fine days of weather together ('It cannae last,' Mr von Leibnitz says dismally, shaking his head, and Mrs von Leibnitz agrees, 'Aye, we'll suffer for it next week.') and traipsing across hill and dale to the loch isn't an altogether unattractive proposition. One afternoon, hot and bright, I gallop free of Christine, up to the top of the highest of the hills around the loch and, panting like a racehorse, throw myself down on the grass which is coarse and tickly like a straw mattress. Down below, the water gleams, fathomless and secretive, and the people buzz around meaninglessly. Far away in the distance, the wide horizon of heather meets a big, pale sky that's been swept clean of everything except for a buzzard, hanging like an augury, and I experience a moment of pure elation, like an unexpected gift, and the hole inside me – where something has been taken away – heals over and is filled. This rapture cannot last, of course, and I'm summoned down to eat our lunch (Mrs von Leibnitz packs us a picnic, always the same – potted meat sandwiches, over-ripe bananas, plain crisps and mint Yo-Yos), and by the time we walk home everything is the same as usual and my own bottomless loch of loneliness is back in place.

* * *

Patricia continues to be nauseous almost all the time but everyone else seems to be restored to equilibrium, so another adventure is planned for Monday, this time to Oban; it can't, after all, be worse than the trip to Fort William, Mr Roper laughs.

Familiar problems present themselves – we have to run an impressive sheep gauntlet, zig-zagging for nearly a mile behind one particularly insouciant beast (*Just run over the bloody thing!*) and Patricia pukes in the heather. 'What's wrong with you, Patricia?' Bunty glares at her.

'Is it your soul, Patricia?' I ask sympathetically.

'Shutupruby.'

As we descend into Oban we can see the sea, like the rim of the world, and the sky above, aqueous and translucent. We pass a piper standing – inexplicably – at the side of the road in full regalia (an Anderson kilt, I note) and he pipes us into Oban on a mournful, shivery pibroch. I could enjoy this holiday if they would just let me, but no, there is already talk of, 'A little boat trip – or should I say "wee" boat trip, ha ha – after lunch,' Mr Roper chuckles, accidentally rubbing against Bunty as we make our way to a restaurant in a hotel that has a tartan (McGregor) carpet. We all have fish and chips, except for Patricia who has one chip and turns greener than the water in the harbour.

The Mull ferry steams away like a *grande dame* as we struggle to board our own craft – the *Bonny Bluebell*, a tiny little thing, more coracle than boat. We find her below a sign that says, 'Trips Round the Bay', and underneath, 'Mr A Stewart – Proprietor', and George says, 'Donald, where's your troosers, hoots mon!' and Mr Stewart looks at him with a mixture of pity and disdain in his eyes.

What harm can there really be, I say to myself as I sit down, next to Patricia on a sea-sawing plank; the weather, after all, is fair, the bay relatively small. Then the motor goes prut-prut-prut and we're off! Bunty would never have set foot on this boat if she hadn't been blinded by love and she soon discovers her mistake because hardly are we out of the harbour when all the colour drains from her skin and she whispers, 'Oh, no.'

'What is it, Bunty?' Mr Roper's voice is full of earnest concern as he leans over towards her. Both Mrs Roper and George look up quickly at the intimate timbre of his voice, but Mrs Roper is immediately distracted by baby-David wanting to be a little teapot again. Not so George, who from this moment on is on his guard, watching the pair of lovers like a hawk.

As soon as we've chugged out of the harbour, the previously glassy-calm water seems to change – the water is ruffled by waves and it's not long before an alarming swell begins to develop. The forget-me-not blue of the sea grows claret-dark and trouble brews. Gusts of wind begin to batter and buffet the little boat and its jolly sailor occupants. 'Poor Bunty,' Mr Roper says as she heaves up her fish and chips over the side of the boat. I can understand how she feels because my own stomach is conducting the Highland Fling. Patricia slides down in her seat and I shuffle up to be nearer her. When I grasp her hand she responds without hesitation, squeezing mine hard, and we cling to each other in terror.

'It's just a wee squall,' Mr Stewart yells, which doesn't comfort any of us, especially not Mr Roper, who shouts above the wind, 'Wee or not, I don't think this boat is up to a squall, old chap.' I don't know whether it's the Anglo-imperialism in Mr Roper's tone or that our captain is an evolved species with earlids, but he turns a deaf ear and sails on into the storm. Mrs Roper is fully occupied with the baby-David who is damp and screaming, with Christine who is moaning and clutching her stomach and with Kenneth who is dangling over the side of the boat, apparently trying to plumb the sea with his own body. Mr Roper is not helping his wife at all, but has moved over to Bunty's side of the boat so that we're now listing dangerously, caught between the Scylla of George's jealousy and the Charybdis of Oban Bay.

And then – and this is dreadful – suddenly I begin to scream, a fearful scream of despair that rises up from the bottomless loch deep inside me, a place with neither name, number nor end. 'The water,' I sob into Patricia's neck, 'the water!' and she does her best, given the circumstances, to soothe me. 'I know, Ruby . . .' she shouts, but the wind carries away the rest of her words.

Whatever else it did, at least this lost child's cry seems

to have an effect on Mr Stewart, who, finally and with great difficulty, turns the boat round and heads back to the shelter of the harbour.

But we are not safe from the storm yet. That evening, Mrs Roper stays upstairs with Christine, for although everyone else recovers their land-legs, Christine does not. Mr Roper puts the baby-David to bed and then joins the rest of us downstairs for a game of Cluedo, sitting next to Bunty, and drawing his chair very close to hers. There is much giggling and accidental touching of hands until at a crucial point in the game George can stand it no longer. Miss (Bunty) Scarlet and the Reverend (Clive) Green collide one too many times in the hallways of Tudor Close causing George to throw his lead piping down and dash from the room. 'Well, really,' Bunty says, 'some people.'

Several dramatic things occur shortly afterwards, with the timing of a disagreeable farce. Miss Scarlet and the Reverend Green abandon the game after George's hasty departure and are next encountered together in the dining-room where, unable to contain himself any longer, Mr Roper is copulating with our mother on the dark-oak of the dining-table. I am drawn thither by George's war-hoop yell, 'Whore!' which, not unnaturally, also brings Mr and Mrs von Leibnitz to the scene of the crime. By this time, the offending couple are vertical and looking modestly decent, but I think we can all see the blazing scarlet letter 'A' branded across Bunty's beige turtle-neck sweater. George is making some rather feeble pugilistic gestures towards Mr Roper, who is looking flustered and angry, while Bunty is trying to look as if she isn't really there at all.

'Zair's a problem?' Mr von Leibnitz asks, stepping forward, and Mr Roper turns to look at him and growls, 'You stay out of this, you Nazi,' which, as you can imagine, doesn't go down too well with the von Leibnitzes. I look around for Patricia to see if she's going to stand up against this injustice and am surprised to see her leaning against the door-post, a rather twisted smile on her face. Seeking a scapeparrot, Bunty turns to her and says testily, 'Stand up straight, Patricia!' as if Patricia's deportment was the issue here. Patricia, in one of her greatest *non sequiturs*, smiles and shrugs and then says in a funny drawl, 'Actually, Mama, I just came down to tell you that I'm pregnant.'

Can anyone top that? Yes, Mrs Roper can. She flings herself into the dining-room like a tea-cake from a toaster, shouting, 'Help! Help! Someone call an ambulance!'

Well, it was only an appendicitis which isn't that bad, although my grandmother always said her first fiancé died from one. Nevertheless, dying or not, Christine is ferried by ambulance to Oban where the offending organ is swiftly removed. The next day we split into new combinations – Mrs Roper, George and Kenneth in Oban with the hospitalized Christine, while my mother, Mr Roper and the baby-David roam the hills searching for Patricia. They eventually find her at the Bottomless

Loch, mooching mournfully, a bit like Miss Jessel, amongst the reeds and sedge. I am in the company of Mrs von Leibnitz and together we make floury potato-scones and eat them warm in the kitchen by a singing kettle on the fire and discuss Scottish literature. 'Do you no have any relatives hereabouts then?' she asks, and I say yes, they're hereabouts, wandering on the hills, and she says no, she doesn't mean that, she means other Lennoxes, because Lennox, she informs me, is a Scottish name. I wrinkle my nose and say I don't think so because George and Bunty never stop going on about how they're Yorkshire born and bred (although, admittedly, there is a Lennox clan tartan in my *Illustrated Pocket Guide to Scottish Tartans*), generation after generation, time out of mind. Et cetera.

On Wednesday, we curtail our holiday and go home, leaving the Ropers to make whatever arrangements they want. The journey home is relatively plain-sailing. Bunty concentrates very hard on the map and the road signs in an effort to placate George – she's seen the error of her wandering ways. I suspect that after a day in his company, the prospect of the baby-David as stepson was enough to dissuade her from infidelity without the added incentive of Mr Roper's own misgivings ('Look, Bunty . . . poor Harriet needs me, you know . . .'). Not to mention the added prospect of grandmotherhood.

Patricia and I sleep most of the way home, although we wake up for a thoroughly nice meal in a restaurant on the road to Glasgow, which no-one regurgitates. The atmosphere in the car is the stunned, silent one that follows on great disasters. We leave Och-na-cock-a-leekie very early in the morning, giving the porridge and baked beans a miss, because George wants to get a head start on the sheep and traffic. We pull away from the farm in a thick, early-morning mist that muffles and baffles the normal world. As we approach the road with no name and number, at the end of the farm-track, I peer sleepily through the car window to catch a last glimpse of our Scottish Farm and am astonished to see the head and shoulders of an heraldic beast emerging from the mist like a trophy on a wall. He's only a few feet from the car but gazes at me with regal indifference. It's a stag, a huge monarch, with a great head of antlers, like something from a myth. I don't even bother prodding Patricia to tell her about him, because I know I must be dreaming. Somewhere just beyond the mist, there's our real Scottish holiday – and perhaps all the other holidays we never had as well.

I think Patricia must have been thinking on the same lines because later on, just as the mist clears and we're surprised to find ourselves half-way up an impressive mountain, she leans over to me and whispers, 'Do you remember Auntie Doreen?' and looks quite relieved when I nod and say, 'Of course I do.'

Patricia got a second holiday that year, staying in Clacton in a Methodist mother-and-baby home. When she came back, a mother-and-no-baby, she was a different person somehow. By that time, the Ropers had moved away and been replaced by a widow called Mrs Kettleborough. Bunty and George had decided to remain married and behave as if nothing had happened, which was something they were very, very good at. Patricia never went back to school, never took her A Levels, and she was so full of darkness that in some awful way it was quite a relief when she walked out one bright May morning and never came home again.

As for Rags – Bunty had given him to the RSPCA on St George's Field and he was still there when we came back from holiday, unwanted and about to go to the electric chamber. Patricia bought him back with her pocket-money and the last thing she said to me on the morning she left home was, 'You'll look after Rags, won't you, Ruby?' and I did, believe me, I did.

Footnote (ix) – In the Realm of Aire and Angells

EDMUND, BUNTY'S HANDSOME CANADIAN COUSIN, WAS the bomb-aimer on D for Dog. One of his other tasks was to help get the big four-engined Halifax in the air but after he'd helped Jonty Patterson by setting the flaps and locking the throttles he crawled away into his transparent nest in the nose of the plane and watched as the dark edges of Flamborough Head gave way to the sea, shining like polished jet in the moonlight.

He didn't usually spend a long haul down there, preferring to assist the navigator, Sergeant Wally Whitton, with his GEE Box, or annoy their easy-going radio operator, Len Toft, but tonight Edmund was in an odd mood.

He wasn't alone. The crew of D for Dog had a bad feeling about this flight. Yesterday one of the armourers had made a careless mistake and a trolley of bombs had blown a crater in the runway, taking a Halifax and half its crew with it. And now Taffy Jones, the flight engineer, had left behind the tarnished, bent St Christopher that they always fixed dangling from the perspex canopy and everyone had cursed him blackly on take-off. Wally Whitton told them to shut up and said scathingly they were a load of bloody foreigners because, apart from Taffy, a Welshman, naturally, D for Dog also had a Jock – Mac McKendrick, as rear-gunner and a Canuck – Edmund, for a bomb-aimer. 'Shove off, you Brummy prick,' Len Toft said amiably, and Jonty Patterson, their twenty-two-year-old pilot, flinched. This was only Patterson's second op as pilot of D for Dog – their previous pilot had whiplashed his neck in a wheels-up landing – and he was ill at ease with his experienced crew, some of whom, like Taffy Jones, were well into their second tour and could probably fly the plane better than he could. He never knew when they were joking and felt oddly ashamed of his public school education and ringing vowels. Only his sweet-tempered bomb-aimer treated him the same as everyone else.

Privately, his crew were more worried by their new pilot's flying skills than his social background. He was 'bloody useless in cloud' as Wally Whitton put it succinctly, a fact they'd discovered over Holland on their first trip with him and Taffy had to take the controls as they rocked and bounced through a big dollop of cumulo-nimbus – making their poor boy-pilot, who still only shaved once a week, go pink with shame.

When Wally Whitton made his cheerful xenophobic jibe no-one added that they'd been even more foreign until last week when Sergeant Ray Smith, their Aussie gunner in the mid-upper turret and a mild, cynical chap, had been blasted by gunfire from a Bf-109. The new gunner, Morris Dighty, a van driver from Keighley, was as nervous as a kitten. They could feel his jumpiness creeping down, spreading through the fuselage like a clammy fog.

'Well, our luck's run out,' Mac said miserably after they hauled the splintered Sergeant Smith out of his turret, because Mac and Edmund and the Aussie had chalked up eleven flights together and it had been one of the reasons why Edmund had resisted leaving this mixed bag and transferring to the Royal Canadian Air Force.

'We're on borrowed time now, Ed,' Mac muttered behind him as they did his pre-flight checks and Edmund cheerfully told him to go to hell. 'How was that nurse, Ed?' Taffy asked suddenly over the intercom and Wally Whitton swore hugely at him to 'Get off the effing intercom' and Edmund smiled to himself over the glassy, moonlit sea because 'that nurse' was OK. Doreen O'Doherty – sweet as maple syrup, with her big brown eyes that made Edmund think unkindly of a cow and her curly brown hair and her strangled Irish accent. Half the time he couldn't understand a word she was saying but she was softly accommodating, stumbling out with him from Betty's Bar and down to the blacked-out river, blacker than the North Sea, where she tasted like marzipan and felt like liquid caramel and whispered, *Oh, Eddie, you're wonderful, so you are—*

'Corkscrew starboard, go, go, go!' a voice – Mac's – screamed over the intercom and the heavy Halifax immediately dropped three hundred feet in the darkness and rolled and dropped again and then accelerated upwards to port and Edmund, from his bird's-eye position, could see a spurt of red tracer fire falling away into nothing. It was several seconds before anyone said anything, then Mac's voice says calmly, 'I think we lost him,' and Morris Dighty began to jabber incomprehensibly until they all told him to 'stow it'.

The solid density of the Dutch coast passed below them and they had no time to relax after their encounter with the Messerschmitt because now they had to be as alert as cats for the coastal defences. All remained dark and hushed around them as the big four-engined plane droned on like a grotesquely heavy insect. Although there were another four hundred planes on this stooge to bomb Krupps at Essen, D for Dog seemed to be the only plane up in the star-filled sky. And then, from nowhere, they were suddenly fingered by a blinding white light as a huge searchlight beam reached out from nowhere and grabbed them.

Dazzled, Edmund clambered out from the nose and swung himself up and hung on behind Taffy and Jonty Patterson. If there was one thing that made you feel more vulnerable than being trapped in a searchlight beam, it was being flat on your belly with your head poking into it. The beam was joined by others – up in his turret, Mac was keeping count of them, in a horrified kind of times-table – 'Thirty, thirty-five, thirty-nine, Jesus, forty-two, another five, Jeeesus!' and the voice of the normally affable Len Toft was yelling, 'Dive down it, Jesus, dive down it, you berk!' and there was another, fainter noise of someone being sick into their face-mask, which Edmund was sure would be Morris Dighty. Edmund looked behind him and could see, in the unnatural white of the searchlight, the faces of Len Toft and Wally Whitton, frozen like small animals of prey. Jonty Patterson came to life suddenly, screwing his eyes up against the light, and started a text-book pattern of evasive tactics – starboard climb, port dive, dive, dive, climb – diving more than climbing to keep the speed up in a desperate attempt to get into a part of the sky where the flak battery crew couldn't find them – for all the while the flak was coming up, *crump, whoosh, crump, whoosh* and occasionally a great thudding noise against the fuselage – and then suddenly, miraculously, they were out of the deadly light and back under the cover of night.

When Edmund looked at Jonty Patterson he could see him peering through the windscreen, his knuckles white from clutching hard on the controls and pearly beads of sweat stood out on his blanched face. 'Well done, skip,' a voice said over the intercom, too high-pitched with relief to be recognizable.

Wally Whitton's curtain flicked back as Edmund crawled into the back of the fuselage. 'Get us a coffee, Ed,' he said wearily. Edmund poured coffee for both of them and while Wally swallowed a Benzedrine, Edmund ate his way through a corned beef sandwich and returned to prone position in the nose. He wanted to think about home, about the farm in Saskatchewan. After he'd taken his English degree in Toronto he'd thought about staying in the city, maybe teaching or getting a job in journalism, but then the war had happened and now he thought it was funny because he would be willing to make any Faustian pact going if he could just go home again, go home again and lead a quiet life, work on the farm with his brother Nat, marry, raise children. If he ever had a wife he'd like her to be like his mother, strong and adventurous and pretty – not that he was likely to have a wife; he was pretty sure Mac was right, their luck had been used up. Edmund tried to imagine taking a girl like Doreen O'Doherty home with him – or perhaps one of his English cousins. What would Bunty be like if he took her to Canada, to the prairies that rolled on farther than the North Sea?

Edmund adjusted his bomb sight. 'Approaching the target now,' Wally Whitton's voice said in his ear. Light flak tracer was spraying everywhere in threads of red and orange and yellow like seaside lights. Searchlights were raking the sky and Edmund could see what looked like a Stirling, trapped in one of the beams. The Stirling couldn't escape its tormentor and a few seconds later it suddenly exploded into a bright red ball of fire that turned to pink and then finally to nothing.

There was a sea of light flak, tracer fire *zip-zipping* past D for Dog and Taffy Jones said, 'You need more height, skip,' although nothing would get them out of the way of heavier flak when it started coming up. Edmund could see Pathfinder flares burning below and a few incendiaries burning but mostly the target was covered in billowing smoke. 'Right, right, steady – right a bit, steady, left, left – steady—' It looked like they'd have to go round again. 'Sod,' someone said quietly over the intercom and then they were in the heavy flak. *Crump, crack!* A shell exploded near them and the whole aircraft yawned to port as if somebody had punched it through the sky and Edmund pressed the bomb tit and said, 'Bombs gone,' even though they had completely lost the target. He'd never done that before. He could hear the starboard engine vibrating obscenely and the big Halifax started bucking in the air. 'Well, so much for the photograph,' Willy Whitton said sarcastically and there was another enormous thud against the plane. 'What the hell was that?' Len Toft shouted and then metal splinters tore through the plane as a shell came up through the nose and missed Edmund by an inch before embedding its remaining shards in the lap of the flight engineer, Taffy Jones.

Another shell exploded near D for Dog making the plane bounce and Edmund was thrown forward into the nose through which freezing cold air was streaming. He had a sudden unsettling glimpse of land through the hole and scrabbled to pull himself away and into the cockpit. The smell of cordite hung everywhere and the plane was being buffeted around like a toy. 'Christ,' he said quietly when he saw Taffy Jones, shaking all over but staring blankly at the windscreen, pink bubbles frothing into his face mask; then the plane lurched into a dive just as a voice said, 'Help me,' and for a moment Edmund thought it was Taffy before realizing it was Jonty Patterson, half his face torn away by shell splinters so that he was speaking out of the corner of his mouth like a poor ventriloquist. 'I'll get the morphine,' Edmund said, but Jonty Patterson mumbled, 'No, no help me get her up.' It took the combined weight of both of them pulling back on the control column to get the plane out of the dive. By now D for Dog was vibrating along her whole length, juddering and shaking like Taffy Jones had been. Now, when Edmund looked across at him, he could see he was slumped, glassy-eyed.

On the intercom, Edmund heard Morris Dighty shouting, 'Baling out!' and at the same time Len Toft's voice saying, 'Sergeant Whitton's dead – and there's a great big bloody hole back here that he fell out of.' The starboard engine was whining malevolently and Jonty muttered, 'Turn it off,' with the good side of his face. Edmund tried to contact Mac in the tail but there was no answer. Len Toft appeared behind him. 'Christ,' he said when he saw Jonty Patterson's face and, 'Christ,' again when he saw the state of Taffy Jones. 'I think he's dead,' Edmund said. 'Can we get him out of here?'

'Let's just bloody bale out,' Len Toft said, and Edmund saw that he already had his parachute clipped on. The port engine was sounding rough now and the whole plane seemed to be trying to rattle itself to pieces. Mac's voice came suddenly over the intercom, 'What the bloody hell's going on?'

'Where've you been?' Edmund said. 'The intercom went dud.' 'Bale out,' Jonty Patterson said. He was gripping the central column and staring straight ahead; his lop-sided face looked ghoulish. There was blood on his legs as well and it suddenly struck Edmund that the boy was dying but when he reached out to touch him, Jonty Patterson just mumbled, 'Bale out.' Mac's voice came over the intercom, surreally calm, 'Can't bale out, my chute's shot to pieces.'

'Come forward, Mac!' Edmund shouted as the plane started to pitch into a dive. Jonty Patterson was fighting the controls but when Edmund looked back he could see that a hole had been blown through the side of the fuselage. 'I'm going,' Len Toft said, struggling towards the escape hatch. Mac made his way gingerly to the front of the plane. 'The port engine's on fire, and there's a hole big enough to put Wales in,' he said and then, 'Bloody hell, skip – what happened to you?' when he saw the shredded face of the pilot. 'Bale out,' Jonty Patterson said again. 'What about you, skip?' Edmund asked, clipping on his parachute. 'I can't move my legs – just bloody bale out, will you?' Jonty Patterson muttered and for the first time he suddenly seemed very grown-up.

'We're not leaving you.' Edmund had to shout now to be heard over the roaring noise of the plane. 'Come on,' Mac said, moving towards the escape hatch. 'He can have the posthumous medal; we can make it on one parachute, it's been done before.' The plane was diving steeply now and yellow flames were licking the inside of the fuselage. They had to fight against the centrifugal force that was trying to glue them into D for Dog. They heaved the upper half of their bodies out of the hatch and were immediately slammed by the wind so that they couldn't breathe. Edmund didn't think they would be able to get out and even if they did he didn't think they'd manage to fall free of the plane's superstructure. If the wind had allowed him to look aft he would have found no encouragement – there, Len Toft, or what remained of him, was entangled in his parachute, wrapped around the tail section. Nor did they register that the plane was now ablaze along the length of its wings or see the starboard ailerons hanging in rags. But they did know when the starboard engine suddenly tore away from the wing, because the dying plane tipped to one side and chuted Edmund and Mac McKendrick out of the hatch.

They fell, clinging to each other like face-to-face Siamese twins, and as they fell down the burning port wing a jagged piece of metal caught Edmund and ripped at his arm. The earth was coming up to meet them with unbelievable speed. The thick snow on the fields and the bright moon made everything as clear as daylight. In a panic Edmund yanked on the cord release with his good arm, but it meant he was no longer hugging Mac to his body and when the parachute canopy jerked them, Mac's arms were dislodged from around Edmund's neck and he fell soundlessly to earth, his arms and legs spread like a starfish as he plummeted.

Edmund floated down, feeling light-headed, almost euphoric, and found himself dreamily reciting poetry to himself. *Repaire me now, for mine end doth haste. I runne to death, and death meets me as fast.* The frozen fields below were glazed blue in the moonlight. Edmund had just a moment to consider how beautiful the world was before he went crashing through the tops of a copse of snow-laden fir-trees and into a deep, cold snowdrift.

He felt he had been asleep for hours under his chilly white quilt, although in fact he was unconscious only a few seconds. When he opened his eyes he saw two young boys and an old man standing around him. The old man had a shotgun and was pointing it at Edmund's head and the two young boys had sticks. Edmund closed his eyes and waited for the shot but the next thing he knew he was being carried, wrapped in his cocoon of parachute silk. The old man was speaking all the time in German and Edmund wished he knew what he was saying. He was in no pain; most of his blood had pumped out of his arm now and all he could think of was how peaceful he felt and wonder why he couldn't hear any noise from the burning plane flying over his head, like a huge firebird. D for Dog hit the ground two fields away with a massive *thud!* and *whump!* but Edmund didn't hear it, he was looking at the night sky above him, spread out like an astronomer's map. And then a wave of blackness crept slowly across the sky as somebody rolled up the map.

* * *

Doreen O'Doherty only found out about Sergeant Eddie Donner's death six weeks later when she tried to get a message to him through his station commander. Doreen cried herself to sleep that night. The station commander had been very nice to her on the phone when he said the crew had been lost (although in fact Morris Dighty was picked up and spent the rest of the war in a prison camp and is now retired and spends a lot of time on his allotment), and for a moment she'd wanted to confide in him, but then there wasn't much he'd be able to do. Doreen had only been with Edmund twice and couldn't really remember what he looked like at all, apart from what everyone remembered – the blond curls and the blue eyes. She could remember, however, how strong he felt when he held her and she could remember what his soft skin smelt like, a strange perfume of carbolic, tobacco and grass, and it did seem truly terrible that someone who had been so alive should now be dead and even more terrible that she should be carrying his child, and then she cried even more because she felt so sorry for herself. When the baby was born, Doreen O'Doherty had it adopted and moved to Leeds where she married a council workman called Reg Collier and found she couldn't have any more children.

When the woman from the adoption agency came to the maternity-home in York to pick up Doreen's child, Doreen consoled herself with the thought that it was the best thing for the baby and that she herself would have more babies one day that would make up for the gaping hole left inside her after she said goodbye to her tiny daughter. The woman from the adoption agency smiled as she took the baby from Doreen and said, 'What a little angel.'

CHAPTER TEN

1966

Wedding Bells

'SHOP!' BUNTY HAS TURNED HERSELF INTO A BAG LADY. She is carrying so many smart paper bags that she can't see where she's going and almost falls through the Shop door, dislodging part of the hearing-aid battery display as she sinks down with a grateful sigh into the nearest wheelchair and kicks off her shoes. 'It's murder out there,' she informs us. It's going to be murder in here when George finds out how much money she's just spent.

'What the heck have you been buying?' he asks as she fishes out a hat and sticks it on her head. The hat is pea-green satin and looks like a drum. George stares aghast at the drum-hat. 'Why have you bought that?'

'Don't you like it?' she says, swivelling her head round just like the Parrot used to. Her tone of voice indicates that she hasn't the faintest interest in whether George likes it or not. She conjures a pair of shoes from nowhere. 'Lovely, aren't they?' They're wickedly narrow with long stiletto heels, in the same shade of green as the hat. You know from looking at them that they'll be worn once and never again. She crams a foot into one of her new shoes with all the determination of an ugly sister. 'You could cut your toes off,' I suggest helpfully.

The number of as yet unplundered bags at Bunty's feet implies that she might have been buying things to wear in between the extremities of hat and shoes. She wrestles with a particularly large Leak and Thorp's bag – 'And . . .' Bunty says, like a magician's assistant, 'Ta-ra!' and produces a matching dress and coat in a slightly darker shade of soupy pea-green, in a heavy, artificial shot-silk. 'Why?' George asks with a pained look on his face.

'For the wedding, of course,' Bunty holds up the dress against herself, in a sitting position, like an invalid. She turns to me, 'What do you think?'

I sigh and shake my head in envy and longing, 'It's lovely.' (Extracts from Ruby Lennox's school report, summer term, 1966 – *Ruby has a real talent for acting . . . Ruby was the star of the school play.*)

'The wedding?' George is thoroughly baffled now. 'Whose wedding?'

'Ted's, of course, Ted and Sandra's.'

'Ted?'

'Yes, Ted. My brother,' she adds helpfully as George stares blankly at her. 'Ted and Sandra. Their wedding's on Saturday – don't tell me you've forgotten?'

'*This* Saturday?' George seems to be having a mild apoplectic fit. 'But . . .' he splutters and flounders, 'they can't get married this Saturday – it's the World Cup Final!'

'So?' Bunty says, weighting the one little syllable with a heavy mixed cargo of disdain, indifference and wilful misunderstanding, not to mention twenty years of marital antipathy. Even a Mandarin-speaking Chinaman would be floored by the subtleties of Bunty's intonation.

George is stunned. 'So?' he repeats, staring at her as if she'd just grown a second head. '*So?*'

This could go on for ever. I cough politely, 'Ahem.'

'Have you got a cough?' Bunty asks accusingly.

'No, it's just I have to get back to school . . .' It's a Monday lunchtime and Janice Potter has persuaded me to sign out with her (you can only leave school in pairs and you're supposed to stick like glue to each other in case you're raped, robbed or lost), so she can go to the Museum Gardens to smoke and snog with her boyfriend. Cast adrift at the gates, I have washed up at the Shop.

Bunty suddenly drops her bags and leaps from the wheelchair like a Lourdes miracle and says 'Mind the Shop!' to me and hustles a hapless George out to help her 'choose' (that is, pay for) a wedding present for Ted and Sandra.

And so, here I am, abandoned to mind the Shop – sometimes I feel like Bunty, a discomfiting thought, to say the least. Will I turn out like my mother? Will I be pretty? Will I be rich? I'm fourteen and already I've 'had enough'. Bunty was nearly twice my age before she started saying that. I'm an only child now with all the advantages (money, clothes, records) and all the disadvantages (loneliness, isolation, anguish). I'm all they've got left, a ruby solitaire, a kind of chemical reduction of all their children. Bunty still has to run through all our names until she reaches mine – 'Patricia, Gillian, P— Ruby, what's your name?' Luckily, I now know that all mothers do this as soon as they have more than one child – Mrs Gorman, Kathleen's mother, has to run through an astonishing litany of children – *Billy-Michael-Doreen-Patrick-Frances-Joe* – before she arrives at 'Kathleen-or-whatever-your-name-is.'

Being a Monday, business is slack so I occupy my time by deputizing for one of Bunty's prime functions – wrapping the Durex. I take up my position by the huge roll of brown paper that's bolted on to the wall behind the counter and patiently pull and rip, pull and rip, until I've got a good supply of big square pieces. Then I take the pair of 'Nurses' Surgical Steel Scissors – Best Quality' that are chained to the counter and set about cutting up the big squares into smaller squares, like a particularly dull *Blue Peter* demonstration. When I've done that I get out a new box of Gossamer from the storeroom at the back (which was once the dining-room) and wrap the individual packets of three, neatly folding and sellotaping each end of the little brown paper envelopes. Now the Durex can be handed over like gifts ('Here's one I prepared earlier'), rapidly and discreetly, to our valued customers. Not by me, of course. I have not yet managed to sell one packet while

I've been left in charge of the Shop; no-one seems keen to buy their rubber johnnies ('A planned family is a happy family') from a fourteen-year-old child, and when they charge into the shop, change at the ready, and see me, their eyes immediately shift to the nearest likely object and they shuffle out in dissatisfaction, clutching a packet of corn plasters or a pair of nail-clippers, and in this way I am probably personally responsible for a great many unplanned families.

I have wrapped an entire gross box of Durex and still they're not back. How long does it take to choose a present? Perhaps they've run away from home. I slump disconsolately into an electric wheelchair and push the control stick to 'Slow – forward' and trundle round the Shop pretending to be a Dalek, *I am a Dalek I am a Dalek*. For my Dalek gun, I use the dismembered dummy leg that models an Elastanet two-way stretch stocking and exterminate a stand of male urinals, a shelf of Dol's Flannel and two miniature Bakelite torsos, one male, one female, who face each other across the Shop – Greek and mutely tragic – displaying their little surgical corsets to each other.

Restoring the male urinals to their former positions – balanced on top of each other like a circus tightrope act ('And now the fantastic, death-defying, one-and-only Male Urinals!') – I think about how I miss the Pets. For one thing, they were a less embarrassing stock to carry. It's not just the contraceptives – the Durex, the mysterious jellies and foams and the Dutch caps – there's a high snigger factor to nearly everything we carry. The glass counter is full of jock straps and incontinence pads; there's a shelf full of prosthetic breasts like small conical sandbags, another of trusses that look more like something you'd put on a horse; then there are the colostomy bags and this month's special offer is on rubber sheeting, thick red stuff that George cuts from a heavy roll that smells like car tyres. They might have given some thought to the effect that this has on my social life. ('And what exactly do your parents sell, Ruby?')

I even miss the Parrot. It's hard to believe that this is the same Shop it was before the fire. I often go upstairs, into the empty rooms where we once lived, and try to call the past back. Above the Shop has fallen into a rapid decay – it's never really been put back to rights since the fire. Whitewash balloons off the ceiling where Patricia once slept and the bedroom I shared with Gillian has an odd smell in it, the aroma of something decaying, like a dead rat concealed behind the wainscot. It seems now as if Above the Shop was just a trick of lath and plaster and light – and yet sometimes, if I stand on the stairs and close my eyes, I can hear the voices of the household ghosts being carried hither and thither on a current of air. Do they miss us, I wonder?

Sometimes I think I hear the Parrot, a ghostly squawk echoing around the Shop. Sometimes I think I can hear it on the other end of the telephone, all the way out in Acomb. We don't only have telephone calls from spectral parrots, we also have calls from nobody at all, a mute phantom phoner who manifests himself as crackling static down the wires. When George answers these silent calls, he stares for a few seconds at the receiver as if it personally was to blame and then slaps it back down in the cradle and walks off in disgust. Bunty persists a little longer, trying to coax a response by repeating her normal phone greeting, 'Hello, this is the Lennox residence, Bunty Lennox speaking, how can I help you?' which is enough to put off all but the most determined caller and our poor spook is anything but robust. 'Mr Nobody again,' Bunty says, as if he was a personal friend.

But when I answer, I hang on for the longest time, waiting and hoping for a message. I'm sure it's Patricia on the other end of the phone – we haven't heard from her for well over a year and surely she'll be in touch soon. 'Patricia? Patricia?' I whisper urgently into the receiver, but if it is her, she doesn't answer. Your sister says not to worry would do (see *Footnote (x)*). Bunty must still expect Patricia home because she has left her room untouched, and as Patricia was not the tidiest of girls and her room was always littered with dirty clothing and food crumbs, it has by now taken on a Miss Havisham-air of decay and will probably soon revert to primordial slime.

Perhaps it isn't Patricia at all, but our Gillian, wandering in limbo and trying to phone home. But can spirits make telephone calls? Are there call-boxes beyond the veil? Do you need a coin or could she reverse the charges? Is it somebody else entirely? Perhaps I'll be able to corner Daisy and Rose at the wedding and get some satisfactory answers to these questions.

'Shop!' George says perfunctorily. 'There!' Bunty says, very pleased with herself as she winkles a china figure out of its box – a woman in a crinoline. 'It's called "The Crinoline Lady",' Bunty says, turning it this way and that to examine its porcelain flounces. George snorts, 'It looks like a toilet-roll holder.'

'That's exactly the kind of remark I would expect from you,' Bunty says, putting the offended Crinoline Lady back in her box. 'And you need a new tie for this wedding, in fact you can come out with me now and choose one.'

'No!' I wail, struggling back into blazer and beret, 'I have to get back to school.' The afternoon bell will have gone by now (*Late again, Ruby?*). George looks at me. 'Are you going to this wedding?' he asks suddenly.

'Oh, for heaven's sakes!' Bunty says, her eyebrows taking off in exasperation. 'She's the *bridesmaid*!'

'You?' George says incredulously.

'Me,' I confirm with a helpless shrug of the shoulders. I'm not insulted by his disbelief, I'm even more amazed than he is.

Not merely a bridesmaid, but chief bridesmaid, heading an unruly gaggle of miniature bridesmaids. They are all from Sandra's side of the family, but wedding etiquette decrees that she must have a representative of Ted's family in her train. When it came to choosing from the spear-side, however, Sandra was beset by doubt – all the potential bridesmaids on the groom's side are either corpses, runaways or spiritualists, none of whom, Sandra rightly judges, are fit to strew rose petals at her feet (although, disappointingly, no strewing takes place). Certainly, if I were in her shoes (white satin pumps, size 6) there would be something very unsettling about having Daisy and Rose at my bridal back. I am the default choice – she should have searched beyond blood-relatives and trawled the in-law pool – Lucy-Vida, for example, would make a quite splendid bridesmaid. Our cousin has been transformed from an ugly duckling into an extraordinary, mini-skirted swan, with Twiggy's make-up and Sandie Shaw's hair. Her white stockings cover her shapely, bony legs that are too long for the stiff Methodist pew in which they are imprisoned. Every so often the discomfort forces her to untwine and stretch them and when she recrosses them, twisting them round each other like two-ply wool, the minister trips over the words of the marriage service and his eyes glaze over.

The Methodist chapel on St Saviourgate is huge and cavernous, like a cross between a Masonic temple and a municipal swimming-baths. Apparently they're all Methodists on Sandra's side and there is an uneasy rumour circulating on 'our' side (we are already almost on a war footing) that this is going to be a 'temperance do'. The marriage service seems to be going on for ever and if it wasn't for the catacomb-cold of the chapel and the bad behaviour of my juvenile flock I could quite easily fall asleep on my feet, especially as, in lieu of breakfast, I downed two of Bunty's tranquillizers before posying-up. The little bridesmaids shuffle and giggle and bicker, drop their posies, yawn and sigh, but every time I turn round to glare at them they freeze into positions of ineffable goodness. It's like playing Statues and I'm just waiting for one of them to tag me so that I can knock it unconscious with the bride's heavy bouquet of scentless roses that I'm holding for her. I am in far too bad a mood of black adolescent bile to be in charge of small children and if I had known that this was to be part of my duties (this is my first wedding) I would have resisted even more fervently when Bunty begged me to accept the job.

The bride and groom, from the back anyway, display a remarkable similarity to the little figures on top of a wedding cake. The bride is in white and is reliably reported (by Ted) to be a virgin. Indeed, it is only my uncle's extreme sexual frustration which has finally driven him up this nuptial cul-de-sac. He has delayed getting married as long as possible – from his first Odeon date with Sandra to this final altar rendezvous has taken him eight years. When finally forced to set a date for the event by a touchingly romantic ultimatum from Sandra ('If you don't name the day they're going to be shovelling your brains up in Coney Street'), Ted put the date as far in the future as he could. How could he know then that 30th July 1966 would turn out not only to be the final of the World Cup, but that England would be playing – and not only that, but that she would be playing against our family's sworn enemy – the Hun!

The bridesmaids are in pale peach polyester-satin and

our dresses, like the bride's – big, round, puffy dresses with big, round, puffy sleeves – make us all into Crinoline Ladies. Our satin slippers are dyed to match our dresses, as are our carnation posies, and on our heads we wear artificial peach-coloured rosebuds on vice-like Alice-bands.

I stifle one yawn after another but unfortunately there is no stifling the deep embarrassing rumble that my stomach gives out every now and then – precipitating a rash of parrot-squawks and giggles from the bridesmaid clutch.

The minister asks if anyone has a good reason for the marriage not to go ahead and everyone looks at Ted as he is the most likely person to object, but he stiffens himself manfully and the service proceeds with only the slightest falter on the part of the minister as Lucy-Vida tries to pull her skirt down to cover her crotch.

My first wedding is turning out to be rather disappointing. When I get married it won't be a peach polyester affair. The church I get married in will be a very old one – they're two-a-penny in York, of course – perhaps All Saints on Pavement with its lovely lantern tower – or St Helen's – our very own Shopkeeper's church! The church will have the musty smell of old timbers and the stonework will be like Belgian lace and the windows will be jewelled lozenges of colour. The church will be illuminated by banks of tall white candles and all the pews and side chapels will be decorated with gardenias and trailing dark-green ivy and waxy-white lilies like angels' trumpets. My antique-lace dress will fall in drifts of snow and it will be garlanded and swagged with rose-buds as if the little birds who helped Cinderella dress for the ball had flown round and round me, nipping and tucking and pinning. There will be peals of bells ringing the whole time and I will be spotlighted by a single, dusty shaft of sunlight. The congregation will be drowning in rose petals and all the men will be in elegant morning dress (Ted has not even bought a new suit for the occasion). And there will be *no* bridesmaids.

One of the little polyester bridesmaids is scuffing the back of my shoe with her satin foot and another one is poking her nose and wiping the resultant slimy grey crop on her dress. I hiss at them to stop but they make faces back at me. Will this ever end?

At last, the bridal pair vanish into the vestry and someone plays Bach, very badly, on a tired organ while the divided congregation – his and hers – whisper frantically to each other about what they think of it so far. Finally, 'The Wedding March' bleats triumphantly and we sweep down the aisle while everyone grins like idiots at us, not so much from pleasure as relief. 'Flippin' heck, my bladder's killing me,' Auntie Eliza says to no-one in particular, as I pass by, while the extra-terrestrial floral pair swivel robotically in their pew so that their eyes can follow the bride who rejected them and Auntie Gladys can be heard sighing gratefully, 'Well, at least no-one fell over.'

The photographs on the steps of the church seem to take longer than the service and it's only when the next wedding party arrives and both sets of guests mill around outside the church and get mixed up, that any attempt is made to move on to the reception and the wilting bridesmaids are allowed to droop into the big black Austin Princess that's tied up with white ribbons in the street below. I sulk unattractively in the back of the car – I feel like Alice when she grew tall, a huge outsize girl crammed in amongst identical smaller ones. I've just fallen into a fitful and disturbing doze when we draw up at the hotel and are disgorged from our car. The 'do' is not temperance and the bar of the hotel in Fulford fills up rapidly as if we had just crossed the Sahara instead of York city centre.

My little flock scatters to the four winds and are hugged and congratulated by their respective parents for being so pretty, charming, cute, delightful and so on. I can't see George and Bunty anywhere but eventually I sight George across the room, talking to a plump woman dressed strikingly in a vivid royal blue two-piece underneath a vast red-and-white straw sombrero. On closer inspection, this turns out to be Auntie Eliza, a lipstick-smeared glass in one hand and an undelivered wedding present in the other. She pulls me to her bosom and deposits slurpy kisses all over both my cheeks and tells me how lovely I look. I'm about to congratulate her on wearing such patriotic colours on this day of national importance but she pushes the present into my hand and orders me to go and 'Put it on the pile – it's only tablemats,' and get her a plate of something from the buffet 'while I'm at it'.

The buffet, which occupies two long, cloth-covered trestles against the walls of an adjacent room, is, apparently, a departure from the usual sit-down tradition in Sandra's family. I know this because the female guests on the distaff side – mainly coutured in pastel crimplene – are in there, walking up and down the tables and discussing the buffet and its innovatory significance. They make funny noises like a cornfield in a high wind, *tsk-tsk, shu-shu, foo-foo* and hold their handbags high under their bosom like pantomime dames. 'It can't hold a candle to a real sit-down do,' someone says to a susurrating chorus of agreement. 'Remember our Linda's do – roast topside and all the trimmings?' 'And oxtail soup,' someone reminds her and they promenade another length of table, pointing to the flabby character of the ham slices ('They might at least have had a proper York ham'), and the anaemic egg sandwiches ('More salad-cream than egg') and regarding with suspicion the two waitresses employed to dole out such fare. They spy me with the present still in my hand and smile encouragingly. 'Present pile's over there, love,' one of them says, indicating another table laden with toasters in duplicate and Pyrex in triplicate, but luckily, no sign of any other tablemats.

I load a plate from the buffet for Auntie Eliza; she's the least fussy person I know, especially about food, so I pile it indiscriminately with everything on offer, except for the trifle which is as virgin and untouched as the bride herself under its veil of hundreds and thousands which have already melted into a rainbow smear.

When I get back to Auntie Eliza and my father they are at least three double gins the worse for wear and there is still no sign of their respective spouses – Uncle Bill and Bunty. How Auntie Eliza is going to manage a plate, a glass, a cigarette and my father is difficult to say so I act as her dumb butler, holding the plate for her which she attacks with admirable relish. 'They're a rum bunch, that Sandra's lot,' she says, nodding in the direction of the nearest crimplene-clad guest and taking a bite out of a mushroom vol-au-vent which immediately starts deconstructing itself everywhere. 'They all look like they've got pokers stuck up their arses,' she adds cheerfully, unaware that the bride's mother, a formidable woman called Beatrice – part-Soroptimist, part-Sumo wrestler – is well within earshot. George spots her advancing bulk and makes a visible effort to pull himself together. 'Hey-up,' he says, striving for diplomacy and failing miserably. 'Here's the mother-in-law.'

George is extricated from this situation by Ted, who is gesturing urgently to him from the door. I pick up scattered bits of vol-au-vent from the floor and then make my excuses and leave. My stomach is making alarming noises, so I head back to the buffet. I'm just wondering where all the male members of the party have disappeared to – there's hardly a man in sight and there surely hasn't been another world war while I wasn't looking – when I come across a tearful Lucy-Vida, a considerable proportion of her heavy black eye make-up streaked down her cheeks. She sniffs noisily and wipes her face with the purple feather boa that's draped around her neck. 'Biba,' she sighs tragically. 'I think you'd be better off with a Kleenex,' I offer, steering her away from the busy centre of the room and towards a row of spindly chairs behind the table that holds the wedding cake. The table is further adorned by the bridal bouquet and the bridesmaids' posies, as well as an assortment of good luck in the shape of black cats, silver horseshoes and bunches of white heather. Sandra's wedding cake is a mere two-tier hummock, whereas I shall have a towering five-tier Mont Blanc of carved and moulded snow and roses from Terry's.

We sit like wallflowers at an Assembly Rooms' ball, watching the other guests parade and parry while we whisper our secrets. Lucy-Vida's secret is a distressing one, to say the least. 'I'm only bloody knocked up, kid,' she blurts out, gazing blindly at the wedding cake, which is growing in my eyes, not in stature but in symbolic significance, for as she continues with her story it becomes clear that there is to be no cover-up of almond paste and royal icing for Lucy-Vida. ''E was only bloody married, wasn't 'e?' she says, the passion and betrayal still visible in her smudged eyes. She sighs heavily and sags farther into the uncomfortable chair. She's very pale, her lips as bloodless as a hungry vampire's. Perhaps she has been named for Lucy Harker, after all, although her pale visage might just be due to her make-up. Or her condition. She looks at her stomach and shakes her head in disbelief. 'And now I've got a bloody bun in t'oven!' After a few seconds of silent contemplation, she adds, 'Me dad'll kill me.'

'Never mind,' I try and comfort her. 'It could be worse,' but even though we furrow our brows and rack our brains, we can't come up with anything much worse than this. 'You're not going to Clacton, are you?' I ask, remembering what happened to Patricia only too well. Lucy-Vida looks at me doubtfully, 'Clacton?'

'To a mother-and-baby home, to have it adopted, like Patricia.'

She clutches her stomach protectively, and says fiercely, 'Not bloody likely!' and I experience a little pang of jealousy towards Lucy-Vida's unborn offspring. Although it could be hunger, in fact I feel quite dizzy from hunger, especially when I get up too quickly and offer to get Lucy-Vida something from the buffet. She blanches at the very idea and I stagger off, eager for a bridge roll, but have hardly negotiated my way round the wedding cake before I'm waylaid by a baleful pair of flower twins. 'So, Ruby?' one of them says coldly. This rather enigmatic question hangs in the air between us, gathering weight, while I try to think of a suitable reply. 'So,' I say lamely after a while. A slight toss of the head on the part of one of them reveals the under-chin freckle and identification gives me confidence so I borrow Bunty's smile (where *is* my mother?) and say brightly, 'Hello, Rose, how are you?' She smiles, a chilly gleam of triumph in her eye. 'I'm Daisy, actually, Ruby.'

'You've got the freckle,' I reply stoutly. 'I can see it.' The other twin takes a step nearer to me and tilts her chin to reveal an identical freckle. Horror! I want to lift up a fingernail and scratch at it to see if it's real, but I'm too much of a coward. I stare from one to the other in a state of serious confusion; I feel as if I've just stepped through the looking-glass and can't find a mantelpiece to hang onto.

'Are you enjoying being a bridesmaid, Ruby?' one of them – the one on the left – asks. It feels like a trick question, but I'm not sure what the trick is. 'Of course,' the other one says, as smoothly as a snake, 'people feel sorry for you. I expect that's why they chose you.'

'Sorry for me?' I repeat blankly, blinking at the novelty of this concept.

'Losing so many sisters,' the one on the right says with a dramatic sweep of her arm. 'To lose one,' the other twin says, 'might be considered careless . . .' '. . . but to lose three,' the other twin continues seamlessly, 'well . . . that's a bit suspicious, don't you think, Ruby?'

'Goodness, Ruby,' the other one says, tossing her melted-lemon-drop coiffure, 'what on earth did you do with them all?'

'Two sisters,' I reply faintly. 'I only have two sisters, and Patricia isn't lost, she's coming back.'

'Don't be so sure,' they say in perfect harmony, but by now I've already backed off to the other side of the room and go off in search of refuge. Out in the hallway I can hear a television blaring, *And it's Ball with the corner . . . Hurst . . . and a chance at goal* – and then a great uproar, both from the TV and the TV Lounge, and *It's all smiles in the Royal Box*. I open the door and peep in and amongst a smog of tobacco smoke and alcohol find most of the male members of the wedding party executing a tribal war dance, hallooing the name of Martin Peters. I would like to stay and watch but out of the corner of my eye I spy a twin and make a run for the Ladies.

Where, to my great surprise, I discover my mother, somewhat the worse for wear – her drum-hat dented, her feet shoeless, and quite astonishingly drunk. 'You're drunk!' I gasp at her. She gives me a bleary-eyed look and starts to say something but is overcome by an attack of hiccups.

'Breathe!' a voice says commandingly from one of the cubicles, followed by the sound of flushing water, and I wait with interest to see who is going to emerge. It's Auntie Gladys. 'Breathe!' she reminds Bunty again and Bunty obediently takes in a huge gulp of air and proceeds to choke on it. 'That should do it,' Auntie Gladys says, giving her a comforting slap on the back. But it doesn't and Bunty's hiccups recommence with a new vehemence. I offer to give her a fright but she declines with a weary gesture of her hand as if she'd already had quite enough frights. The decor of the hotel Ladies is pink and fluorescent, and three of its walls are unflatteringly mirrored. Bunty, sitting askew on a little boudoir-stool like a toadstool, is reflected to infinity in the mirrors – a disturbing vision of a mother who seems to go on for ever.

'Where are your shoes?' I ask, deciding to be practical in the face of all this tipsy emotion, but receive only a loud hiccup in reply. Auntie Gladys rakes in her capacious handbag and produces a little bottle of Mackintosh's smelling-salts which she wafts in front of Bunty's nose, causing her to gag and tilt alarmingly on the stool. 'She's all right,' Auntie Gladys says reassuringly to one of my reflected images in the mirror. 'She's just had a bit too much to drink; she was never a drinker your mother.' I volunteer to go and fetch a glass of water and as I leave the Ladies I can hear my mother muttering something that sounds very much like, 'I've had enough.'

The barman, who is very nice and rather handsome, puts a slice of lemon, two ice-cubes and a little parasol in the glass of water when I tell him that my mother isn't very well and gives me a Coke for free. My progress back to the Ladies is erratic. First of all I encounter Adrian who tells me he's got a new dog, a Yorkie, appropriately enough. 'It would be funny, wouldn't it?' I say, 'if only people in Alsace kept Alsatians, and only people in Labrador had Labs and the Welsh had Welsh terriers and the Scots had Scottie dogs – but then who would have poodles? And what kind of dogs would people in Fiji keep—' until Adrian says, 'Shut up, our Ruby, there's a good kid,' and lifts a strand of my lank and greasy teenage hair and makes a face. 'Who cut this, Ruby?' He shakes his head in distress. 'Still,' he comforts, 'at least, it's not as bad as their Sandra's.' Their Sandra's hair is appalling, a great towering bouffant confection that wouldn't look out of place at the court of the Sun King. There are probably birds nesting in it.

I've no sooner left Adrian than I'm suddenly

ambushed by a posse of Sandra's aunties who question me closely about Ted's family background. The crimplene Inquisition is very unhappy about the state of affairs at the reception which is now in its third hour without any sign of a toast or a cutting of the cake. It is only with the greatest difficulty that I extricate myself from this grilling and almost immediately trip over one of the small bridesmaids and utter an oath which turns the air as royal a blue as Auntie Eliza's outfit. There are several sharp intakes of breath from the Methodists as I resume my journey to the Ladies. *And it's a free kick to West Germany. One minute to go, just sixty seconds – every Englishman coming back, every German going forward*. The tension coming out of the TV Lounge is visible, like the smoke of gunfire. A terrible groan rises up from somewhere deep within the collective national unconscious, *Jack Charlton has collapsed, head in hands*. Every Englishman in the TV Lounge is also in a state of collapse and I hurry on my way, only to be confronted by a seething bride. 'Have you seen Ted?' she demands in a very vexed way.

'Ted?'

'Yes, Ted – my bloody, so-called husband!' Sandra twirls round, surveying the corridors of the hotel like a snapping crocodile.

'Where are they all?' she asks, a puzzled look on her face.

'All who?'

'The men.'

I watch with interest as enlightenment dawns slowly

on Sandra's face. She gives a little scream of frustration and stamps her satin foot. 'Bloody World Cup! I'll kill him, I will, I'll kill him,' and with that, she's off, lifting up her long white dress and steaming off, picking up her mother in her wake. I look around for Lucy-Vida because I've just thought of something worse than being pregnant and unmarried (being Ted) but there's no sign of her so I continue my progression to the Ladies, finally unhindered.

Two of the three cubicles in the Ladies are occupied and I bob down to check for Bunty's feet, shod or otherwise, and experience a frisson of alarm when I see that both cubicles are occupied by identical pairs of feet. A pair of voices speak, 'Who's that?'

'Just Ruby!' I shout, beating a hasty retreat.

I return the glass of water to the bar, or more specifically to the nice barman, but when I get there I find Adrian and the barman deep in conversation and although I perch as chirpily as a budgie on the bar stool next to Adrian I soon discover that they don't have eyes for anyone else. Feeling like a gooseberry, I wander off, gloomily twirling the little paper parasol.

There is a sudden commotion as all the men who had previously disappeared are suddenly herded back into the reception by Sandra and her mother. Beatrice remains by the door, standing guard, 'In the TV Lounge,' she says loudly by way of explanation to the rest of the wedding party. 'That's where they were – watching the football!' The commentary drifts in after them through the open door. *There's Ball running himself daft, there's Hurst – can he do it?* The men stand rooted to the spot, craning to hear, *He has done! – yes – no,* their faces twist in agony, *No, the linesman says no!* 'Fucking linesman!' Uncle Bill shouts and the crimplene relatives make dreadful noises as if they are suffocating. *It's a goal! It's a goal! Oh, the Germans have gone mad at the referee!* The men go mad at Sandra.

She's unaffected. 'Bloody World Cup,' Sandra says, her eyes like arrow slits as she turns to Ted in disgust. 'Aren't you ashamed, isn't your wedding day more important than the World Cup?'

Ted can't help himself somehow. Until this moment of his life lies have fallen from his lips like rain, but on this occasion, this very public, important occasion, we watch in horror as he drops, like a parachutist without a parachute, onto the hard rock of truth.

'Of course not,' he says. 'It's the bloody Final!'

Whack! goes Sandra's hand against his cheek. 'Steady on!' Ted says as she reaches for the nearest handy missile, which happens to be the bridal bouquet on the wedding-cake table. 'Sandra,' he whines in a feeble attempt at mollification but Sandra is white-hot now and all the silver horseshoes in the world aren't going to help Ted. 'We haven't had any speeches,' she screams at him. 'We haven't had any toasts, we haven't cut the bloody cake! What kind of a wedding do you call this?' *It's all over, I think – no, it's . . . And here comes Hunt . . .*

'You're just riff-raff!' Beatrice's voice booms out as she elbows her way towards her new son-in-law, handbag at the ready. Alarmed, Ted tries to back away but he almost trips over a small bridesmaid underfoot (they're like vermin) and in an attempt to avoid crushing her he loses his balance and lurches towards the table bearing the wedding cake. Everything seems to go into slow motion as Ted pitches and reels, his arms flailing like windmills, in a desperate attempt to regain his balance and avoid the irresistible, inevitable accident which we can see hanging before our eyes. The tiny bridal couple on top of the cake sway and totter as if they were sitting on top of a volcano. *Some people are on the pitch – they think it's all over—* Ted moans as his feet go under him and in one dreadful slapstick movement he falls, face first, into the wedding cake. *It is now!* A kind of strange sigh moves round the watching audience of guests as if now they can relax because at least they know that the worst possible disaster has happened and anything else cannot be as bad. (I'm not so optimistic.)

The strange silence in which we have been wrapped, broken only by the TV commentary, dissolves instantly and a great babble and squeak rises up from the wedding party. Beatrice's 'riff-raff' insult is just finding its target and, as it hits home, battle lines can be seen to form. 'Riff-raff?' Uncle Clifford says. '*Riff-raff?* Who are you calling riff-raff?' This is said to Beatrice, who barks back, 'You, you and all your family – that's who I'm calling riff-raff! Any objections?'

'I most certainly bloody have!' Clifford says, and looks around for support. His eyes rest naturally on his only son, who, unaffected by the combat-stations being taken up all over the room, is still deep in his engrossing conversation with the barman. Uncle Clifford's brow pleats. 'That's queer,' he says suspiciously, but is unable to elaborate on this judgement because Beatrice clouts him so hard with her handbag that his glasses fall off. Within seconds the place is in turmoil with people bashing and thwacking each other at random. I notice that George and Bunty – the two people who could teach them everything about finesse and technique – are absent from the fray. I feel I have no particular allegiance to either warring party, blood-ties or not, and I try and slip away unnoticed. For preference I would have exited on the buffet-room side as I have reached a state of near starvation, but it has been completely cut off by the skirmish between the immediate wedding party – Ted and his Best Man defending their corner against Sandra and all the little bridesmaids. 'Ruby!' Sandra shouts when she sees me. 'Come on, your place is over here with me!'

'No, it bloody isn't!' Ted yells at her. 'She's my niece!'

'She's my chief bridesmaid!' Sandra counters furiously, and a whole new fight develops about whose colours I should be supporting. I struggle to the exit on the TV Lounge side, losing my hair-band and a shoe in the process. I'm looking forward to the relative calm of the TV Lounge. For a second I'm not sure what it is I'm looking at but then the complex, struggling black-and-white heap in the middle of the floor, which at first sight resembles an epileptic penguin, resolves itself into something even more distressing – George and one of the buffet waitresses deep in sexual congress. 'Oh bloody, bloody Nora!' my father exclaims in the throes of ecstasy and collapses in a sated heap on top of her. Underneath him, the waitress looks like a squashed insect, arms and legs waving helplessly. She suddenly sees me and the look of horror on her face is well-nigh indescribable. She's struggling ineffectually to escape from my father but his dead weight remains slumped on top of her. I have never witnessed an orgasm before but even in my ignorance I feel that by now my father should at least be lighting a post-coital cigarette and sighing with satisfaction instead of lying there speechless. With one great heave, the waitress manages to push her way out from underneath and George rolls onto his back, open-mouthed and motionless. His last words seem to linger in the fetid air of the TV Lounge. I'm about to ask the waitress if by any chance her name actually *is* Nora when I think better of it. This hardly seems the right time and place for introductions. She, meanwhile, is struggling to adjust her uniform, never taking her eyes off George, a dreadful expression of dawning realization on her face. We both drop to our knees, either side of George, and look at each other in dumb horror – it is quite apparent to both of us by now that George is not in a stupor of satisfaction but is quite, quite dead. Kenneth Wolstenholme carries on regardless. *This great moment in sporting history as Bobby Moore goes up to get the World Cup . . .*

The waitress leans over and listens to his soundless chest. 'Do you know who he is?' she whispers, and when I say, 'He's my father,' she gives a little yelp of horror at the new ramifications that this adds to the scenario. 'I don't usually do this sort of thing,' she says helplessly, but whether she means casual sex with wedding guests or inadvertently killing them in the process, isn't entirely clear, and there's no opportunity to pursue this as Bunty suddenly appears in the doorway and we both flinch at the sight of her, now hatless as well as shoeless, and even more intoxicated than before. She stares in mute astonishment at the tableau in front of her. Poor George cuts an undignified figure, lying there sprawled on his back with his flies still gaping – but zipping them up doesn't really seem like an appropriate last rite. 'We think he's had a heart attack,' I say loudly to Bunty, trying to break through the haze of alcohol surrounding her. 'Can you call an ambulance?'

'It's too late for that,' the waitress says flatly, and Bunty gasps and lurches over towards him. 'Did you know him?' the waitress asks tenderly, her tenses already adjusted to the event. 'He's my husband,' Bunty replies, dropping down on her knees to join us and the waitress has to suppress another little yelp. 'I'll get an ambulance,' she says hastily and removes herself from the TV Lounge as swiftly as she can. 'We have to do something,' Bunty says agitatedly and, taking a deep breath, she leans over and starts giving George artificial respiration. Where did she learn this? *Dr Kildare,* probably. It's strange to watch her trying to give him the kiss of life – while he was alive I never saw her kissing him and yet here she is, now he's dead, kissing him with all the passion of a new bride. To no avail. Finally she sits back on her heels and gazes blankly at the TV screen which is by now an ocean of triumphant Union Jacks.

The funeral, held the following Friday, is like a negative of the wedding – many of the same guests, much the same food but, thankfully, a different church and hotel. It's a perfunctory sort of service. The duty vicar at the crematorium tells us what an 'upstanding member of the community' George was and what 'a loving husband and devoted father' he had been. Bunty, freed now to reinvent the past, quivers in agreement with this eulogy. Bad daughter to the last, I stare, dry-eyed and numb, as the coffin slides through the curtains and George disappears for ever. My mouth goes suddenly, uncomfortably dry at this point and my vision blurs into a thousand dancing spots. My heart starts knocking like a pile driver and I summon all my resources to suppress the rising tide of adrenalin-fuelled panic – this is my father's day, after all, and I shouldn't be spoiling it with my own drama. But it's no good, a wave of sheer terror sweeps inexorably over me and I don't even make it to the end of the row of chairs before passing out.

In the days following the funeral I find myself reliving the ceremony again and again. I am haunted by the vision of the coffin sliding beyond the doors like a ship being launched into nothing. I want to run after it, drag it back. I want to lift the lid and demand answers from my father to questions I don't even know how to ask.

* * *

On the night of George's funeral Bunty and I went to bed late. She was in the kitchen making Ovaltine when the phone rang and I said, 'I'll get it.' Bunty said, 'It's after midnight, it'll be Mr Nobody I expect,' but when I lifted the receiver in the hall I knew it would be George and I sat down on the stairs with the phone cradled against my neck, and waited for him to say all the things he'd never said. I waited for the longest time. 'Who is it?' Bunty asked, turning off the light in the kitchen and handing me a cup of Ovaltine. I shook my head helplessly and put the phone back in its cradle. 'Just Mr Nobody again.'

Footnote (x) – Lillian

AFTER THE WAR, LILLIAN GOT TAKEN BACK ON AT Rowntree's. To explain the existence of Edmund she passed herself off as a war widow and said her married name was Valentine. 'Valentine?' Nell screwed up her face in disapproval and Lillian thought how odd it was that sometimes Nell reminded her of Rachel. 'Well,' Lillian said, 'I thought if I was going to give myself a name it might as well be a pretty one.'

'Lily Valentine,' Frank said with distaste. 'It sounds like a music hall turn.'

'Well, I'm sure I'm sorry if it doesn't meet with your approval, Frank,' Lillian said sarcastically, and Frank thought how his uppity sister-in-law had it coming to her but his anger was deflected by Edmund, being jiggled on Lillian's hip, who giggled at him and reached out a finger so that, despite himself, Frank smiled and took the finger.

'I don't see what difference it makes anyway,' Nell said with a peevish look on her face. 'Everyone in the Groves knows you were never married. What must people think? I don't know how you can hold your head up when you go out on the street.'

'You'd rather I didn't go out at all, wouldn't you? What should I do – hide Edmund like a nasty secret?'

'It's not the bairn's fault,' Frank said, trying feebly to make peace.

'It might be something if you knew who his father was,' Nell said tartly and Frank's spirits sank. Why couldn't she just let the subject drop?

'I know who his father is all right,' Lillian said, and it would have been so much better if she'd just turned on her heel and marched out of the room the minute she said that rather than waiting an uncomfortable length of time staring Nell down.

When Lillian finally went upstairs with Edmund, Nell stomped off into the kitchen muttering darkly and Frank sighed; it was right what they said about two women in the house. He'd never seen a cross word between them before he and Nell were married; now they were on each other's nerves all the time. He felt like a man caught in a siege. He, for one, didn't want to know who little Eddie's father was. He'd never believed it was Jack; there was no resemblance at all – and Jack had been such a striking, handsome man, the kind that would coin a son in his own image; and whoever Edmund's father was he 'hadn't made much of an impression' on him. So said Rachel when he was born, after she'd been forced to accept the fact that her roof was sheltering a fallen woman. She'd even gone so far as to produce a photograph they'd never seen before – of Albert, sitting on Ada's lap. Lillian and Nell pored over the photograph, holding it right under the lamp and exclaiming at the uncanny likeness of the young Albert to the infant Edmund. But it was the image of their long-dead sister which excited them most for they had almost forgotten Ada and it was a dreadful shock to suddenly see her, pretty and beribboned and scowling at the photographer. Perhaps she knew he was about to steal their mother. Lillian, her eyes damp with tears, jerked her head out of the lamplight and looked accusingly at Rachel, creaking on her rocking chair in the corner. 'Have you got any more photographs hidden away?' and Rachel looked suddenly shifty but pretended to laugh and said, 'Don't be daft,' so that Nell and Lillian knew that she had more. They didn't find the rest of the photographs until after she was dead. Lillian went through all Rachel's things while Nell and Frank were on honeymoon and discovered the unframed photographs that Monsieur Jean-Paul Armand had taken. They finally had the full set – including the one Tom had of their mother – and in some small way the family was reunited. Later, just before Clifford was born, Lillian had these photographs framed at some expense.

She had wept for half a day over a photograph of her own infant self being cradled in Ada's arms (like a little girl with a doll), but when Lillian left the house on Lowther Street it was the photograph of Ada and Albert that she took with her because, of all the photographs, that was the one that aroused her tenderest feelings.

Sometimes Frank found himself wondering if Albert might have fathered Lillian's child; he could remember only too clearly how both sisters used to hang around Albert and joke that he 'was the only man in their lives'. But the idea of brother and sister together was so disgusting that Frank thought himself twisted to even think such a thing.

Lillian laid Edmund down in his little bed. His eyes were already half-closed, his long, pale lashes drooping on his cheeks. While she was at work she left him with a Mrs Hedge on Wigginton Road who doted on him so much that she played with him all the time and never let him sleep during the day. She was a widow who'd had three sons, all fine strapping lads, all taken in the war, and she rattled around now in her big end-terrace house like a lonely pea in a pod. Edmund, she said with a sad smile, gave her something to hold again.

Lillian had never even asked Nell to look after him. She didn't want to be beholden. It was bad enough being in the house with the pair of them. You would never think it was her house as much as Nell's. The minute she was married Nell behaved as if she and Frank were the rightful owners. Now that Nell was pregnant it was worse. Every week as her belly got bigger the more she seemed to seethe with resentment against Lillian, and the more stubborn Lillian grew.

'He's a natty dresser, our Frank,' Lillian said, slicing the top off Edmund's breakfast egg. They could see Frank out in the back yard pumping up his bicycle tyre before setting off to work. He had a job now in a gents' outfitters and was always turned out very smart. Lillian's attempts at pleasantry fell on stony ground. Nell was brushing the crumbs off the table, with the fancy electro-plated brush-and-pan set that Minnie Havis next door had given her as a wedding present. She was brushing around Edmund's plate with little short stabbing movements as if she'd like to brush him away as well. 'Why don't you just leave it, Nelly?' Lillian said mildly. 'And I'll do it when Eddie's finished.'

'Because breakfast's over with,' Nell said, avoiding Lillian's eye. 'But breakfast's *not* over with,' Lillian said, trying to sound reasonable even though she felt like pinching her sister. 'Edmund's only just started his and I'm going to make another pot of tea. Do you want a cup?'

'No thank you,' Nell replied self-righteously. 'I've had *my* breakfast.'

'I didn't know we had only one sitting like a cheap hotel,' Lillian said crossly.

'I wouldn't know about hotels – cheap or otherwise,' Nell said with an arch little smile on her face because it wasn't often she could think of a clever rejoinder to anybody.

Lillian ran out of patience and snapped unkindly, 'Don't try to be clever, Nell – it doesn't suit you,' and an angry Nell flicked the little horsehair brush so that it accidentally knocked one of the forget-me-not cups off the table and when she saw that it had broken she screamed and threw the brush across the room. Which set Clifford off crying upstairs and Nell wrapped her arms round her head so she couldn't hear him because he was the kind of baby who only stopped crying long enough to feed and was driving her to distraction; but it didn't stop her from hearing Lillian say, 'There goes that gurning baby of yours, does he never stop?'

Clifford was an ugly baby, especially when you saw him against Edmund – Edmund who was as placid a baby as a mother could wish for. Nell felt quite sick sometimes when she saw Lillian cooing and singing to Edmund as if he was a toy. 'That child is spoilt rotten,' she said to Frank. 'Heaven knows what he's going to grow up like.'

'He does well enough on it,' Frank ventured because he thought Edmund a 'great little chap'.

'She'll smother him with kisses one of these days, if you ask me,' Nell said. 'And what's more—' but whatever else she was going to say was interrupted because she accidentally stuck a nappy pin into one of Clifford's rare moments of peace and he went very red and started to scream and scream until poor Nell shook him before bursting into tears herself and exclaiming to Frank, 'I didn't know it was going to be like this.'

Lillian left the house in Lowther Street one fine hot July morning, striding up the road towards Rowntree's great red-brick land-going ship, and before she turned into Mrs Hedge's gate, she decided what she was going to do. She yanked on Mrs Hedge's bell-pull. Edmund, in her arms, pointed up into the summer-blue sky where a swift was climbing. 'Yes, it's a birdie,' Lillian smiled and held him close and smelt his delicious smell of milk and soap and sleep. She couldn't stand another minute in that house. They were such a small-minded pair, mealy-mouthed and small-minded, that's what they were, and if Lillian stayed with them she would shrink and tighten and Edmund would grow up suffocated, listening to Frank and Nell blethering on of an evening in the little parlour about the price of stewing-steak and the carrot-fly on Frank's allotment and how dreadful the Bolsheviks were. It wouldn't do. It wouldn't do at all. 'Well, here's my bonny young lad,' Mrs Hedge said, opening the door as they came up the short path. Edmund put out his arms and hung them round Mrs Hedge's neck and she placed a big kiss on his ripe apple-cheeks and Lillian said, 'I'm going to emigrate,' and all morning Mrs Hedge cried every time she looked at Edmund.

Lillian felt a reckless need to leave the future completely up to chance so she tore a piece of writing paper into neat squares and wrote all the possibilities she could think of on them – *New Zealand, Australia, South Africa, Rhodesia, Canada* – and then put them inside her best hat – a dark blue straw toque with a white silk camellia – then she closed her eyes and pulled out the future. Thus it was that one cool autumn day she left Liverpool, Montreal-bound on the *Minnedosa*, of the Canadian Pacific Overseas Service. Lillian, wearing the same best hat on her head, hoisted Edmund up high to say farewell to the country of his birth. On the quay,

Frank and Nell waved goodbye with big exaggerated arm movements so that Lillian could see them – Frank with one arm because he was holding Clifford aloft to say goodbye to his only cousin. Edmund wriggled and squirmed with excitement at the coloured streamers and the brass band playing and the overwhelming sense of something happening. Nell spoilt it all with her tears; from the lower decks Lillian could see her quite clearly, sobbing dreadfully. It broke Lillian's heart to see her sister like that and she wished that she could have left without a word, just slipping away in the night; perhaps if Nelly hadn't grown so cold she never would have left. When the ship began to slip away from the dock Lillian buried her wet face in Edmund's pudgy neck.

Lillian stayed for two years in Montreal, in the French district, living in one room above the baker's shop where she worked for a gentle, fat man called Antoine who begged her to marry him from the first week she was there. Lillian liked the friendliness of the neighbourhood, liked to hear little Edmund chattering away to his playmates like a native in French, and she loved the smell of baking bread that woke her up in the mornings, wafting up from the ovens below where Antoine was sweating. But in the end it seemed a pity to have come so far to end up in one little room and the baker's proposals were becoming tiresome and she was frightened that she might say yes. Having already left everything behind once it was easy to leave again and one day Lillian packed a small trunk and bought them a ticket on the Canadian Pacific, and when the booking clerk said, 'How far are you going, ma'am?' she didn't know what to say because she hadn't considered this question, so in the end she shrugged and said, 'All the way, please.'

Ontario rolled endlessly under the wheels of the train, mile after mile of water and trees so that it seemed that the whole vast continent must be made of nothing else, then, just as Lillian said to Edmund, 'I didn't know there were so many trees in the whole world,' the trees started to thin and the water to dry up and in no time at all the prairies began and the huge ocean of wheatfields lasted even longer than the trees and water of Ontario. As the train moved through Saskatchewan into Alberta in the night, Lillian sat up in the observation car and saw the moon hanging over the infinite prairies like a huge yellow lantern and thought of the house in Lowther Street. All the time that she'd been in Montreal Lillian had the feeling that she would get pulled back to England, but now as they travelled farther and farther from the east coast she realized she would never return, not to Montreal, not to England, and above all not to Lowther Street and she felt so guilty that she resolved to write to Nell first thing in the morning because all this time she had written nothing. But somehow she never managed to get beyond, *Dear Nell, How are you?* and eventually abandoned all attempt as they had passed through Calgary and suddenly a foaming green tract of glacier water was framed in the window of the carriage, like a coloured postcard. And then the mountains began.

They had to get off the train in Banff because Lillian couldn't bear any longer just to look at the Rockies and not taste and breathe them too. And right there on the station platform at Banff, she flung her arms wide and twirled round and round laughing out loud until Edmund was afraid she was going to fall on the track.

They stayed a whole week in Banff in a cheap little boarding-house and they hiked in the foothills of Sulphur Mountain and paid a man to take them in a dog-cart all the way to Lake Louise where they looked at the glacier and walked around the green lake, and Lillian might have stayed there for good, but in the end they boarded the train again because there might be something at the end of the line that would be even better.

In Vancouver, Lillian got a job in the post office and the sight of hundreds of letters passing over the counter every day made her feel dreadfully guilty again and she started several more letters to Nell. Once, she even got as far as enquiring whether Clifford had any brothers and sisters now, before tearing it up and throwing it on the fire, because why waste a letter when any day she might get restless again and leave and then Nell's reply would travel a whole continent and not find her and Lillian was too conscientious a postal worker to encourage lost letters. So she put it off again. Lillian thought that perhaps she'd written so many letters during the war that she didn't have any left inside her. In the end she sent a telegram, *I am doing well. Don't worry about me,* which hardly seemed adequate but was the best she could do.

After she'd sent the telegram off she suddenly remembered the telegram that had arrived telling them about Albert's death and worried that Nell would have a fit at the sight of another telegram, but by then it was too late and Lillian had other things on her mind anyway. She had agreed to marry a Saskatchewan farmer, a handsome widower who had travelled to Vancouver for a friend's wedding and had come into the post office for a stamp to put on a postcard to send to his mother back at the farm. 'She never gets any post,' he explained shyly. 'No-one she knows ever goes away. She's never been farther than Saskatoon.' Then Lillian said, 'Saskatoon?' and the conversation went from there, as conversations do, until Lillian's supervisor came over and said, 'Mrs Valentine, if I could just remind you that you are not paid to chatter,' so that Lillian had to suck in her cheeks to stop herself from laughing and the handsome farmer tipped his hat at her and smiled and walked away from the queue that had built up at her counter.

When Lillian left work in the early evening the streets were slick and shiny with rain and the lamps flared yellow giving her the melancholy feeling that always came with the rain and the dark. She'd just struggled to push up her umbrella when the farmer from Saskatchewan came out of the shadows and tipped his hat again, very politely, and said could he escort her home? She put her small hand on his broad arm and held the umbrella over both their heads (he was very tall) and he walked her all the way back to her lodging-house where the landlady, Mrs Raicevic, looked after Edmund after school. By then, Lillian had learned the farmer's name and she said, 'Edmund, this is Mr Donner,' and Pete Donner squatted right down and said, 'Hello there, Edmund, you can call me Pete.' Although he never did, preferring to call him 'Pop' almost from the day his mother married him.

Pete Donner was surprised at how quickly his new wife took to life on the farm; even that first harsh winter didn't get her down and in the summer she was up at sunrise, feeding their chickens and milking the cow and humming while she cooked breakfast for Pete and his farmhands Joseph and Klaus who lived in a big cabin beyond the vegetable patch. The railway ran right through the Donner property and once or twice the next summer he'd found her down by the track watching one of the great wheat trains that ran across the prairies in a never-ending chain of trucks. Secretly, he worried that she might just up and leave again, she had such a dreamy look on her face when she watched the trains go by. In the evenings of that summer they would sit together on the porch of the big, clapboard farmhouse under a summer moon that was like one of the fat squashes that his mother grew on the vegetable patch and Lillian told him about Rachel and Nell, and about Edmund's father and why she'd kept him a secret. Pete Donner grew afraid then because his wife seemed so strong and although nothing she told him about England made it sound as if she ever wanted to go back there, he still had to ask and she hooted with laughter and said, 'Don't be daft.' The following winter, at the age of thirty-six, she gave birth to a son, whom they called Nathan after Pete Donner's father.

Nathan looked nothing like his half-brother – the only feature they had in common was a bottom lip that pouted like a girl's and which had belonged to Ada and before that to her mother. The two boys were close and when Edmund was younger they talked all the time about how one day they would work the farm together, but when Edmund went away to university in Toronto to do an English degree Nathan fretted that he might not come back. When they got the news that he was missing in action Nathan went quite crazy for a few weeks because he couldn't imagine a future that didn't contain Edmund.

But the future came about anyway and in due course Nathan married and had two children. The eldest, Alison, qualified as a lawyer and moved to Ottawa to work in the government. Just after she left for university, Nathan was killed in an accident on the farm. Pete Donner had already died of lung cancer in the fifties. Alison always laughed and said she would never get married and never live on a farm again, but her younger brother, Andy, did both, running the farm after his father died and marrying a girl from Winnipeg called Tina.

That was 1965 and by then Lillian had moved out to Klaus and Joseph's old cabin that Andy had done up for her. She said she was getting ready to die but it took a long time, another ten years in fact, by which time arthritis had bent her into an awkward and uncomfortable shape.

Andy's wife, Tina, often came over in the evening to sit with Lillian. She'd had three little boys one after the other – Eddie, the eldest, named after Edmund, and then twins, Nat and Sam, and now a fourth one was on the way. She joked that she only came to see Lillian to get away from her noisy children, although both of them knew that wasn't true. Lillian liked Tina better than anyone – she was a statuesque girl with clear eyes and blond hair that she scraped back in a ponytail most of the time so you could see how strong the bones in her face were. In the summer she had freckles all over as if she'd been splattered with gold paint but in winter her skin went as white as milk and she had so much energy that sometimes it seemed to spill out of her and get left behind when she'd gone back up to the farmhouse. It seemed to Lillian that, like Albert, Tina contained more light inside her than most people.

One morning in spring, when Tina was heavily pregnant with her fourth and last baby, she looked out of the kitchen of the farmhouse and saw smoke rising up from the cabin. She shouted to Andy's mother, who lived with them, to mind the boys and set off in a lumbering run to the cabin, but when she got there she found Lillian feeding a brazier with paper from a cardboard box at her feet. A scrap of charred paper flew up from the fire and floated on the breeze to land at Tina's feet. She picked it up and read, *I've been meaning to write,* but the rest was burnt away.

'I'm clearing out before I die,' Lillian shouted cheerfully to her.

'I hope you're not planning to go before this baby's born,' Tina said disapprovingly, but Lillian just laughed and said, 'Don't bet on it.' Then she stoked the brazier with more paper and smiled against the sharp spring sun and said, 'I've lived too long anyhow and when I'm dead I'll be with my children and that's the only place a mother really wants to be,' and Tina laughed and said, 'Not always.'

When Lillian had finished they went inside the cabin and Tina made them both hot chocolate. Lillian said, 'I've got something I want to give you,' and took the photograph that always sat in its pretty silver frame on her dresser and put it into Tina Donner's hands. Tina had been often moved by the poignancy of this photograph of dead siblings – her own brother had been killed in a childhood accident – and she had to squeeze back the tears when Lillian gave it to her, not just because the dead children made her sad but because she knew it meant that Lillian wasn't kidding when she said she was going to die.

When Tina got up to leave she patted her stomach and said, 'I just know it'll be another boy, I wasn't meant to have girls. What shall I call him, d'you think?' and Lillian thought for a while and said, 'Why not call him after Edmund's father?'

* * *

Tina Donner cried her eyes out at the funeral service and people said it was heartening to see a young woman so close to an old lady, although it was mainly the old ladies who said that. 'I really loved her,' Tina said, shaking her head, and Andy Donner put his arm round his wife and said, 'I know, honey.' They laid on a great spread back at the farm and people said they hadn't seen so many people together, not even at a wedding. The funeral tea was a cheerful affair because, after all, Lillian had been very old and compared to most people she'd had a pretty good life. And there was a new baby to celebrate in the Donner house as well and Andy Donner raised a glass and toasted his grandmother and his sister Alison raised one as well, to the new baby, Jack.

CHAPTER ELEVEN

1968

Wisdom

MY FUNERAL IS A VERY MOVING OCCASION. MY COFFIN rests in the aisle of a beautiful old church – Holy Trinity, Goodramgate with its box-pews and pack-saddle roof – and is surrounded by grieving mourners. Birdsong floats in through the open door, through which can be seen a magical vista of green hills and English woodland, unfolding as far as the eye can see, and then a little bit farther. The open coffin is strewn with heavy-scented lilac and branches of snowy hawthorn so that I look like the Queen of the May. People tiptoe up to me and gaze reverently at my alabaster skin and raven hair – hair that in death has mysteriously grown darker and more luxuriant so that its curlicues of gleaming jet tumble over my lavendered coffin pillow. 'She was so beautiful,' a mourner murmurs, shaking his head in wonder. 'And so misunderstood,' someone else says. 'If only we had realized how incredibly special she was.' 'And don't forget how talented,' another voice adds, and the people standing around the coffin nod to each other in regretful agreement.

The church is filled, not just with friends and family, but even people I have never known – an admiring Leonard Cohen and a soulful Terence Stamp, for instance. In the background, Maria Callas sings *'J'ai perdu mon Eurydice'*. Bunty sits at the end of the pew, shaking her head in contrition – 'Perhaps if she hadn't been swapped at birth this would never have happened,' she says softly to Mr Belling, who is sitting next to her—

'Ruby!' Mr Belling says, startling me dreadfully so that I almost fall off my bed. 'Your mother and me thought we'd take a run out to Castle Howard. You don't want to come with us, do you?' He pats his little fat stomach, full of Bunty's Sunday chicken, and looks at me anxiously in case I jump up in eagerness to inspect Vanbrugh's arches and astragals. I raise my hand, limp and dismissive, 'No, you go, I'll just stay here,' for I have learnt from experience that three's a crowd on these occasions. At the beginning, when I was a novelty to Mr Belling ('Sweet sixteen'), he was prepared to make an effort towards me. Now he doesn't regard me as sweet at all but an unfortunate by-product of Bunty that he has to put up with. Only last week I went with them to Knaresborough to visit Old Mother Shipton's Dropping-Well and found myself quite surplus to requirements. They twitterpated away to each other while I moodily surveyed the eccentric array of articles left to drip-drop dry at the soothsayer's well, everyday objects turned into stone by the limestone water – teddy bears, a boot, an umbrella, a dishcloth. Afterwards we sat outside a pub called the World's End and over half a beer-shandy and a 'cheese 'n onion' sandwich, Mr Belling looked at me morosely and asked, 'How long until you leave home then, Ruby? Eh?'

I return to my corpse meditation on the ceiling. (How like Patricia I have become!) I am practising Millais' *Ophelia* for when the River Foss recovers from its unseasonably low level. I have tested its depths and found it sadly wanting – wading out into its murky-dark channel, only to find it hardly reached the hem of my Etam mini-dress. Lacking pebbles, not to mention cardigan pockets to put them in, I had to resort to clutching a brick, discovered amongst the maze of tree roots along the bank. Could a person drown in such shallow water? Ever the optimist, I tried to squat down on the muddy river-bed and force myself to drown – but, as luck would have it, a noisy, enthusiastic spaniel upset this plan. It would be much easier to drown in the Ouse, but it's a broad, brown river and nowhere near as romantic as the Foss – especially the dank stretch beyond the gasworks where the very air is green and choked with rush and reed and pond weed and brave little yellow flag irises.

I can hear Mr Belling's Rover revving noisily in the drive and then crashing away in a spurt of gravel. He will probably buy Bunty afternoon tea out somewhere and then bring her home and she'll come in the house laughing and saying, 'Now, now Bernard I'm a respectable widow-woman, you know,' and he'll pinch her bottom and say, 'Not for long, Bunty.' I suppose I should be grateful that she's not being courted by Walter, who had a very good try, tempting her with slabs of liver, loins of lamb and even, on one occasion, a naked, shiny-pink rabbit that looked like something from a pornographic magazine. (I have seen one – I have also found out what a Durex is for. These are the days of my lost innocence.) Needless to say, we did not eat the rabbit and Walter has been vanquished by Bunty's Prince Valiant – Bernard Belling, who has a plumbing supplies business somewhere in the nether regions of Back Swinegate. His warehouse is like a cathedral dedicated to sanitary ware – serried ranks of lidless toilets gleaming in the half-light like secular fonts and stacks of martyred tapless sinks, their amputated u-bends bandaged in sticky brown paper.

Mr Belling is nearly bald and wears things he calls 'slacks' topped off with Val Doonican sweaters and he's constantly telling me what a wretched life my 'poor mother' has had. Bunty runs the Shop now, with the help of a school-leaver called Elaine. 'Fancy,' Bunty says, 'Elaine's your age and yet she's got a steady boyfriend and is saving up for her bottom drawer.' So, more alarmingly, is Kathleen, who has recently become engaged to a boy called Colin from Archbishop Holgate's Grammar School who is hoping to go into his father's ironmongery business. Kathleen wears her diamond engagement ring on a chain round her neck, hidden under her school blouse.

Kathleen and I mull over the contents of her bottom drawer. What does she have in it? Four Irish Linen tea-towels, a basket-weave lampshade and a set of stainless-steel cake forks. Is this enough to found a marriage on? I buy her a chopping-board to boost the drawer's contents.

'She's a very sensible girl,' Bunty says. 'You don't want me to go to university then?' I ask her. 'Yes, yes, of course I do,' she says, flustered. 'Your education's very important, obviously.' But really you can tell that she'd rather I would just get married and belong to someone else.

'What is the point of a bottom drawer?' I question Kathleen. 'To save things for the future,' she says promptly.

What would I put in my bottom drawer if I had one?

I'm in the grip of Sunday afternoon lethargy, lying on my bed, incanting over and over again the battles of the Peninsular War – *Vimeiro, Corunna, Oporto, Talavera de La Renna, Ciudad Roderigo, Badajoz, Salamanca* – like a magic spell, but to no effect as I cannot remember a single one after five minutes, which is a pity because my O Levels begin next week. I wonder if my results will be as bad as Patricia's were. Where is Patricia? Why doesn't she come and rescue me from this stultifying life?

I give up my revision and wander downstairs to the kitchen where I make myself a piece of toast and eat it lying on the living-room carpet where the sun, coming through the patio doors, is baking-hot. I bask for a while like a lizard taking in heat then fall asleep and when I wake up again, feel quite disorientated. I try to recite my prepared oral for French but cannot remember a word of it beyond, *'Paris – une ville très belle et intéressante.'* As for German and Latin, good-at-languages Ruby cannot string a single sentence together. Even English, my native tongue, can get the better of me sometimes and when I try to speak in class I find my syntax all jumbled and my vocabulary turned into gobbledegook.

Beyond the patio window, out in the garden, I can see a neighbourhood cat stalking a thrush which is plucking a worm from a bed of petunias, blithely unaware of its approaching nemesis. I crawl over to the patio door and bang on it to alert the thrush. The cat stops in its tracks and the thrush flies off, snapping the worm in half as it goes. And then a curious thing happens – I keep on banging on the glass, very hard with the side of my hand because what I want to do – what I have a sudden, overwhelming urge to do – is to smash the glass and saw my wrist against the broken edge, backwards and forwards, backwards and forwards, like Lockwood did to poor Cathy's ghost – until the blood pumps out, smearing the clear view of the patio and the tidy flower beds beyond. The glass is double-glazed and won't break, but I still keep on hammering – although, unlike Cathy, I think I want to be let out, rather than in.

Why does nobody notice how unhappy I am? Why does nobody comment on my bizarre behaviour – the recurring bouts of sleepwalking that still erupt from time to time, when I wander the house, indeed very much like a little ghost-child, one that is searching futilely for something it's left behind in the corporeal world. (A toy? A playmate? Its heart's desire?) Then there's the inertia – lying lifelessly on my bed for hour after hour, doing nothing and apparently thinking nothing either. (Bunty thinks this is normal behaviour for a teenager.) Worst of all is the panic – since the first attack at George's funeral, I've lost count of how many times I've had to run from cinemas, theatres, libraries, buses, dinner queues, department stores. The symptoms of panic are terrifying – my heart feels as if it's on the brink of exploding, my skin turns pale and clammy when my blood drops to my shoes – all of which, naturally enough, leaves me in fear of imminent death. If somebody made a television programme about me and ran it at a time when Bunty would be certain to be watching – instead of *This is Your Life*, for example, so it wouldn't look too out of place, by the time the credits were rolling she'd be shaking her head and tut-tutting and saying, 'That child needs help,' but because I'm under her nose, eyes and feet, she doesn't seem to notice.

Perhaps it is all part of growing up, a tormented rite of passage, a dark valley of adolescent shadows, a wretched hormonal cataclysm, a teenager of sorrows, a—

'Ruby!' Mr Belling's face is a cartoon of amazement as he comes round the back of the house and catches sight of me trying to smash the glass. He wrenches open the patio door. 'What on earth are you doing, Ruby?' he asks, trying his best to sound stern and paternal. 'Trying to escape,' I reply grimly.

'Just ignore her, Bernard!' Bunty says, sweeping through the open patio doors. 'She's too clever for her own good – she takes after her sister.'

'Which one of the many children that you've lost would that be?' I ask sarcastically and am rewarded with a stinging slap on the cheek from Bernard which makes me bite deeply into my bottom lip. 'Thank you, Bernard,' Bunty says to Bernard, and then to me, 'Long past time somebody put you in your place, milady!' and then she turns back to Bernard with a smile, 'Shall I open a tin of salmon?' and off they go into the kitchen leaving me too white and shocked to speak. I curl up into a little ball of misery on the carpet and watch as, instead of a tear, a single drop of blood falls from my lip onto the beige Wilton and darkens to a colour which is not to be found on the normal spectrum. The only sympathy I get is from Rags, who pushes a cold, wet nose into my hand.

What would I put in my bottom drawer? – I would put only sharp objects, the clean lines of broken glass, the honed steel of paring knives, the tiny saw-teeth of bread knives and the soothing edges of razor blades. I weigh knives in my hands like strange comforters. Soon, Bunty will probably discover me on one of my nocturnal wanderings with a huge knife dripping blood onto my nightdress. (What would she say? 'Get back into bed,' probably.)

At the top of the Minster Tower you are almost in the realm of angels, so high that the town laid out below is like a street map that fades away at the edges into the Vale of York and beyond, to the north, the hazy rise of the Howardian Hills and to the east the Wolds like a mirage. On a day like this, when the sky is a limpid blue and the only cloud is a wisp of chiffon in the distance, it's easy to be in love with the world. What would I put in my bottom drawer? I would put the horizon, and some snatches of birdsong, the blossom-like snow in the garden of the Treasurer's House and the white ruined arches of St Mary's Abbey below, like petrified lace.

What would it be like to fall? To go down, down, down, to plummet like a stone down into the little landlocked sea of the Dean's Park below, to splash into the green grass like a stricken bird? If you lean over the parapet far enough, as far as a gargoyle water-spout, you can feel the force of gravity tugging at you, inviting you to taste the air—

'Ruby!' Kathleen's anxious little face appears sandwiched between the crenellations – 'Come on. We're going to miss the afternoon bell!' We scamper back down the spiral stone stairs at a dizzying pace and run all the way along Bootham back to school and fling ourselves into our allotted desks in time to 'Turn over and begin' our Latin Unseen—

Theoxena counsels her children to commit suicide rather than suffer death at the hands of the King – 'Mors,' inquit, 'nobis saluti erit. Viae ad mortem hae sunt . . .' Somewhere in the distance is the noise of a cricket match on St Peter's playing fields and the smell of freshly-mown grass comes in on a faint breeze through the open windows. *Cum iam hostes adessent, liberi alii alia morte ceciderunt.* How can life be so sweet and so sad *all at the same time*? How? A ragged little cheer goes up from the cricket field. Judith Cooper whacks a wasp with her examination paper. Just out of my reach, there is understanding. Somewhere just out of reach – hidden on a high shelf, under a floorboard – there is the key. And what will the key open? Why the lost property cupboard, of course.

The Lost Property Cupboard theory of life is a relatively recent development in my philosophical quest for understanding. It has come about, no doubt, because all this year Kathleen and I have held the onerous office of lost property cupboard monitors and every Thursday afternoon at four o'clock we open up the lost property cupboard which is situated in the corridor of the New Block, which also houses Domestic Science, as well as the less domesticated sciences of physics, chemistry and biology. The school rules dictate that four o'clock on Thursday is the *only time* we are allowed to open the cupboard and requests outwith that hour are met with professional indifference from myself and my fellow monitor. At that hour, people (that is schoolchildren, for no member of staff has ever lost anything to our knowledge – an eloquent comment on the carelessness of youth) can examine the cupboard's innards for their errant belongings. If they find what they're looking for – the most commonly lost articles are pens, partnerless gloves and hockey boots – they must sign their name on a list which we give them and then they are given their wandering things back, so that they can become found property.

There are fearsome consequences for children who do not reclaim their property – ownership is easy to trace as it is compulsory to have Cash's woven name tapes sewn into everything we possess, including our bras, and the insides of our shoes, boots and plimsolls must be marked with indelible marker pen. Constant random checks are done to make sure we are tagged properly. (Did anyone ever dare to look down the back of Patricia's blouse, I wonder?) At least if I ever suffer amnesia they will know what name to call me. The owners of unclaimed property have their names written down on another list which is read out in assembly on the last Friday of every month by Miss Whittaker, the headmistress, and the penalty for offending criminals is that they must stand throughout assembly while the rest of us sit. This public humiliation does little to deter people and the lost property cupboard remains full to overflowing with abandoned things. Sometimes it is so full that when we unlock it everything falls out on our heads and we are driven to restoring property to people secretly just to get rid of the damn stuff. Perhaps soon we shall have to arrange clandestine midnight openings of the cupboard and hope that hitherto reluctant children will be attracted by the cloak-and-dagger nature of the operation.

This is my Lost Property Cupboard theory of the after-life – when we die we are taken to a great Lost Property

Cupboard where all the things we have ever lost have been kept for us – every hairgrip, every button and pencil, every tooth, every earring and key, every pin (think how many there must be!). All the library books, all the cats that never came back, all the coins, all the watches (which will still be keeping time for us). And perhaps, too, the other less tangible things – tempers and patience (perhaps Patricia's virginity will be there), religion (Kathleen has lost hers), meaning, innocence (mine) and oceans of time – Mr Belling and Bunty will find a lot of time in their cupboard. Mr Belling is always sitting at the wheel of the Rover, parked in the driveway, looking at his watch and fuming, 'Do you know how much time we've lost waiting for you, Ruby?' On the lower shelves will be the dreams we forgot on waking, nestling against the days lost to melancholy thoughts (if they paid dividends Patricia would be rich). And right down at the bottom of the cupboard, amongst the silt and fluff and feathers, the pencil shavings and hair swept up from hairdressers' floors – that's where you find the lost memories. *Deinde ipsa, virum suum complexa, in mare se deiecit.* And perhaps we can sign our names and take them home with us.

I have had a terrible scene with Mr Belling. He came round on Tuesday evening to take Bunty to see a touring production of *Showboat* at the Theatre Royal, but Bunty was still upstairs fussing over what dress she should wear, so I showed him into the lounge and he sat down and said, 'Why don't you offer me a little drink, Ruby?' and I said, 'Why don't you get it yourself?'

and he said, 'What a rude little madam you are,' and I said, 'And I don't like you either,' and he said, 'You're going to get what's coming to you, one of these days, Ruby Lennox,' and I said, 'Oh, yeah, what's that – love and affection?' and he said, 'Your poor mother's given you everything but you're just an ungrateful little bitch!' and I screamed at him, 'You don't know anything!' and then he put his face just two inches from mine and shouted at me—

'Ruby! Ruby Lennox! Where are you going?' Miss Raven's voice screeches from the invigilating desk. There's a spatter of applause from the cricket match. 'Ruby,' Kathleen whispers as I stride past her, 'Ruby, what's wrong?'

'Where are you going, Ruby?' Miss Whittaker shouts at me as I stalk underneath the oak plaques hung around the Old Hall inscribed with the names of head girls and scholarship winners in gilded lettering – 'Ruby! You're supposed to be in Latin!' and she tries to do a rugby tackle on me but I dodge and weave and finally fling myself out into the warm, breezy air and march along to Clifton Green. And perhaps also in the Lost Property Cupboard, I think to myself, to pass time as I walk home, there I will find my real home, the one where a fire always twinkles in the hearth and a brass toasting-fork hangs ready and a kettle sings on the hob and the battered old armchairs are pulled up into a cosy circle and my real mother's needle flashes in the firelight as she plies it, in and out, in and out, and begins her story, the story of how her real child, the blood-red jewel, was replaced in the cradle by a changeling—

'You stupid fucking girl! Why don't you look where you're going!' A furious, red-faced, ugly man rests his hand on the horn of his car, his face disintegrating in hatred while a queue of traffic builds up behind him, horns honking. I put two fingers up at him and gain the safety of the pavement and stride on, past the Homestead and over the new bridge that spans the flat and unromantic Ouse.

The house is cool and quiet. Bunty redecorated everything and bought new furniture with George's insurance money so that now there's hardly anything left that is evidence of the past, of other lives. There's nothing of Patricia. Bunty has finally decided she isn't coming back and has given all her things away, the only thing I managed to salvage was her panda, and sometimes I daydream about how pleased she will be when I hand it back to her, just when she thought that everything had gone for ever. It was surprising how easy it was for Bunty to eradicate George, not a sock nor a cigarette end remains. I imagine that when I am gone she'll have a good cry and then hoover up every last skinflake and make a cup of tea.

Three o'clock chimes unevenly on the clock, my great-grandmother's clock. It's never been the same since the fire and I'm surprised that Bunty hasn't got rid of it for jumble, but then the workings of Bunty's mind are as mysterious to me as the workings of the clock, or time itself.

I go upstairs and make a little nest at the bottom of the airing cupboard, out of clean towels that smell of fresh air and soap powder, and like a small mammal turn round and round in my little burrow until I have made it comfortable and then with only an occasional gurgle from the immersion heater for company unscrew the top of the bottle of tablets, cramming them into my mouth like a greedy duck, in case I should fall asleep before I've taken enough.

Down, down, down. I hurtle down through space and time and darkness. Sometimes I accelerate and I can feel the centrifugal force strapping the organs to the inside walls of my body. Down and down towards the stars that are twinkling at the end of the world and I pass a voice that's saying 'Aye, bottomless,' but the words are drowned by a great rushing and roaring noise in my head that's like all the oceans of the world coming into confluence. Then, thankfully, I slow up and start to float as if attached to an invisible parachute. Now that I've slowed down I can make out strange objects in the darkness, things petrified in stone and dolls and spoons, and when I see something that looks like a Mobo horse carved in marble I gasp in delight because I had quite forgotten him. A disembodied stag's head leaps out from the darkness and it opens its mouth to speak, like the horse's head in *The Goose Girl*, and says, 'Well, hel-*lo* there,' before disappearing again.

Down and down, floating like thistledown, passing Patricia's panda and Gillian's Sooty and Granny Nell's old Ekco radio and I realize with a little thrill of delight that I must be in the Lost Property Cupboard – not the school one, but the great metaphysical one. Soon I'll reach the bottom and find my lost memories and then everything will be all right.

Someone thrusts a companionable paw into my hand and I turn my head and see Teddy smiling sadly at me. 'It's the end of the world, you know,' he says, and, overjoyed, I say, 'Oh, Teddy – you can speak!' and he says, 'In the Lost Property Cupboard all animals can speak,' and I'm so happy for him but then his face darkens and he says, 'Watch out for the Rings of Saturn, Ruby! Don't forget they're—' but then his paw slips out of mine before he can say anything else and suddenly I begin to accelerate again – horribly – so that my brain feels as if it's being stretched and pulled from my skull on a thread of elastic and dreadful pains shoot along all the nerves in my arms. Great multicoloured sunbursts explode on either side of me and the faster I move towards the stars at the end of the world, the more they recede and I grow afraid that this is a journey that will go on for ever and I search my mind for the terrible thing I must have done to deserve such a punishment.

Then out of the darkness, like something from the Ghost-Train ride in Scarborough, looms Mr Belling's angry face and he starts to shout at me but I can't hear any words until suddenly, very loudly right in my ear, his voice booms, 'Your poor mother's given you everything but you're just an ungrateful little bitch!' and I put out my hands to fend this vision off but he will keep on speaking, 'You're a wicked, wicked girl,' and I try to shout, 'No!' because I know what he's going to say next but I can't speak and suddenly I can't breathe either and dreadful noises start to issue from my mouth, the noise of a drowning person, drowning on air, and Mr Belling's apparition hurtles down the well of time with me so that I have to put my hands over my ears to shut out what I know he's going to say – but I can't block out his voice which is repeating over and over again, 'You killed your own sister, Ruby! You killed your own sister!'

'I ask you – what kind of a little girl would do that?' he shouted, a trickle of angry spittle appearing at the corner of his mouth, and from the top of the stairs Bunty's voice sang out, 'Are you ready, Bernard? It's curtain up at half-past seven!'

'I know all about you, Ruby,' Mr Belling hissed. 'Your mother told me everything!'

'I did not kill my sister!' I hissed back at him. 'She was run over,' but he just gave me this horrible kind of leer and said, 'I don't mean that one, you stupid little girl, I mean your twin sister!' and with these extraordinary words he turned on his heel and left the room. Then I heard Bunty shouting from the hallway, 'We're off to the theatre now, Ruby, we'll see you later!' and the front door slammed and the Rover drove off.

My own twin? My own twin? What on earth was he talking about? It was a curious thing because although part of me was totally baffled by this statement, another part could hear alarm bells going off and my skin felt as if centipedes were crawling over it. I ran upstairs to Bunty's bedroom and poked about on the top shelf of her fitted wardrobe amongst the shoe-boxes in which she kept her large collection of unworn shoes, until finally I found what I was looking for, the shoe-box with no shoes inside, the one that she kept crammed with the bits of paper that made our lives official and random objects that couldn't find a home anywhere else but somehow couldn't be thrown away. I sifted my way down through medical cards, log books, insurance certificates, a broken earring, an old ration book, the silver locket (see *Footnote (xi)*), mortgage papers, a mouldy-looking paw, an old theatre programme, a plastic ring from a cracker. After a while I got down to George's will and his death certificate, to Patricia's O Level certificates from the JMB (now Bunty will have two daughters who are academic failures), to Bunty and George's marriage certificate, Gillian's death certificate, and then all the birth certificates, held together with a rubber band – *Berenice Eileen, George Arthur, Patricia Vivien, Gillian Berenice, Ruby Eleanor*. And Pearl's.

There I had it – Pearl. *Pearl Ada Lennox*. Born in Fulford Maternity Hospital on – incredibly – the same day, of the same month, of the same year as – me. The 8th of February 1952. I read Pearl's birth certificate over and over again and then compared it with mine, looking from one to the other endlessly as if eventually they would explain themselves. But there was only one explanation – 'Pearl Ada Lennox' really was my twin sister. I could feel a dreadful, threatening pulse beating in my stomach, yet I had no recollection of this sister, could bring no image to mind. I had a strange surge of memory – as if caught in a photographer's flash – of alphabet cards in a horseshoe – a pig, an elephant, an apple, a rabbit, a lemon, but nothing more. Perhaps, like Elvis's twin, Pearl died at birth – perhaps we were Siamese twins and she had to die for me to live and that was what Mr Belling meant. But somehow I didn't think so. I raked down through the papers in the shoeless shoe-box until finally, right down at the bottom, I found what I was looking for – another death certificate, this one made out for 2 January 1956.

Cause of death – drowning. It made me think of *The Tempest* and *those are pearls that were his eyes* or pearl fishermen diving for oysters in the Southern China Seas, but it didn't make me remember anyone called Pearl and it certainly didn't make me remember a twin sister.

Did I drown my own sister? Could such a thing be possible? I couldn't even drown myself. I opened the silver locket and there again were the two pictures of me as a baby that I had found once before in Bunty's bedside table and it took me a long time, staring hard at the twin images in the diptych, to realize that one of them wasn't me at all, but my sister. I stared and stared until my eyes ached trying to work out which one was me and which one wasn't. But if one of them was the false Ruby and the true Pearl, I couldn't for the life of me say which.

I put all the papers back in the shoe-box and closed the door of the wardrobe. By the time Mr Belling brought Bunty home I was already in bed and was feigning sleep when Bunty looked in on me as she usually does these days – to check if I'm still breathing, I suppose. But then something made me change my mind and I sat bolt upright in the bed so that she gave a little scream as if I was a zombie suddenly getting up from its grave. I switched on my bedside light and waved the silver locket at her. 'Why have we never talked about this?' and Bunty's silence was frightening because I didn't know what it contained. Finally, I heard her swallow, nervously and say, 'You forgot.'

'I *forgot*? What do you mean, I forgot?'

'You blacked it all out. Amnesia,' Bunty said shortly. She still managed to sound slightly irritated, even when telling me these momentous, earth-shattering things. 'Dr Haddow said that was probably for the best – after what happened.' Half of her had already disappeared round the door but something stopped her from leaving. 'We all thought it was for the best,' she added. 'After all, nobody wanted to be reminded about what happened.'

'But you can't just blot something like that out,' I yelled at her. 'You can't just pretend somebody never existed, not talk about them, not look at photographs—'

Bunty had slipped even farther round the door so that she was little more than a hand and voice. 'There *are* photographs,' she said. 'And, of course we talked about her; it was you that blotted her out, not us.'

'It's always *my* fault, isn't it?' I screamed, and then a

silence fell between us that stretched out and expanded and took on a strange watery kind of substance, trapping us until I dropped the question that couldn't be avoided any longer into the pool of silence and felt the ripples moving outward. 'How did I kill my sister?' The ripples reached Bunty and she sighed. 'You pushed her in the water,' she said flatly. 'It was an accident, you didn't know what would happen, you were only four years old.'

'An accident?' I echoed. 'Bernard Belling talked about it as if I was a cold-blooded murderer—' My mother had the grace to sound annoyed, 'Well, he shouldn't have been talking to you about it—' She hesitated. 'At the time, I did blame you, but of course it *was* an accident . . .' Her voice trailed away and then finally she said wearily, 'It was a long time ago, there's no point in bringing it all up again,' and she finally managed to disappear behind the bedroom door.

But a few minutes later she came back and sat on the end of my bed. Then she took the locket from me and opened it up and sat for a long time without saying anything. 'Which one?' I said finally. 'Which one is Pearl?' and she pointed to the photograph on the left and said, 'My Pearl,' and began to cry.

Oh no, here we go again – down, down, down – into the dark backward and abysm of time. Will it ever end? There goes Sweep holding onto Denise, followed by Daisy and Rose's doll's house, and I think to myself, Ruby and Pearl, Ruby and Pearl, the jewel twins, and immediately see the witch's treasure chest from *Hansel and Gretel*, overflowing with opals the size of duck eggs, rubies like hearts, diamonds like ice-floes, emeralds like glacier-lakes, sapphires like pieces of the summer sky and pearls – huge, iridescent globes of pearls stranded together in great ropes, tumbling down the sides of the treasure chest, and I reach out my hand and try to grab onto a rope of pearls but my fingers slip along the smooth spheres and I plunge on, through a hail of pins and a shower of buttons like meteors, past an invisible Eamonn Andrews saying, 'Ruby Lennox – This is Your Life!' and then the Parrot squawks, right next to my ear and, given the gift of speech by the Cupboard says, 'Shutuprubyshutupruby.'

Then just blackness, a profound deaf-dumb-and-blind darkness that goes on for ever and ever and ever as I dive down like a diver fishing for pearls until – *Flash!* There's a light ahead and I think, *The Light of the World*, and know that I must be coming to the bottom of the Cupboard. In the middle of the light there's a little figure and the closer I get the brighter she gets, standing, like Botticelli's Venus, in a great, gleaming shell made of mother-of-pearl, pale and opalescent, and I can almost touch the figure now, the one who is my twin, my double, my mirror, wreathed in smiles, saying something, holding out her little arms to me, waiting for me, but I can't hear anything at all except for a clock chiming in my head *four, five, six* and the sound of something whimpering and scratching at the door; then there is more blackness, blackness like a woolly shroud, blackness that's trying to get inside me, stuffing itself into my mouth and nose and ears like a thick, black fleece and I realize that I am being buried alive and the earth is raining down on my coffin and coming in through tiny little cracks. Cracks of light—

'Ruby?' In one of the light-cracks is a pair of lips and slightly yellow teeth, an eye-tooth that glints gold and the mouth is saying something over and over and with the greatest effort I concentrate on the shape that the lips make until I realize with some surprise that they're saying my name. 'Ruby.'

'Ruby? How do you feel now, Ruby?' and the mouth smiles and pulls back and I can see a funny-looking woman, quite old, with plaits wound round her ears like headphones and spindly gold spectacles hanging round her neck. I can't speak, my throat feels as if it's been washed with gravel and my head is throbbing. I squint my eyes up against the sunlight which is pouring through the hospital window and spilling onto the green linoleum in big geometric pools. 'Hello, Ruby – I'm Dr Herzmark, and I'd like to help you, is that all right?'

Dr Herzmark's room is always very hot and stuffy. I think she keeps it like that on purpose to make you sleepy. She has cakes in her drawer, strange sticky cinnamon cakes and syrupy lemon buns, and pours bitter coffee which I drink to stay awake. Or I suck on one of the knobbly brown sugar cubes like pale compressed sand that she has in a bowl on her desk. Then, in her funny German accent, she says, 'Do you want to lie down, Ruby?' because she never tells me, only asks me, and then she covers me with a blanket – dark blue with red stitching like a horse blanket, and says, 'Now then, Ruby, I want you to imagine that you're wrapped in one of the colours of the rainbow and start counting down from ten . . .' and every time I try to choose a different colour to see what it feels like and I can tell you that red is the colour of rubies, of course, and orange makes you feel as if you are full of light. That yellow makes you feel fizzy as if you've breathed in sherbet lemons, and that green is the smell of summer grass after rain (a melancholy colour). Indigo is the colour of magic and violet tastes of flowery cachous. Red, orange, yellow, green, blue, indigo, violet. *Rowntree's Of York Give Best In Value*. From Dr Herzmark's window you can smell the factory and the scent of strawberries because this is the time of year they make the strawberry jellies. 'I like the smell of cocoa best,' I murmur. And Dr Herzmark says, 'Mmm,' in a very foreign, expressive way.

And what about blue? Blue is the colour of memory. And all the prettiest flowers – bluebells and hyacinths and the tiny starry forget-me-nots in Uncle Tom's field, but not today because it's the middle of winter and they're covered in snow. It's the second of January 1956 – and this is the first time that patient Dr Herzmark has managed to take me back to this fateful day, and yet suddenly here I am, sitting at Uncle Tom's dining-room table in his cottage in Elvington on a dutiful New Year family visit. His wife, Auntie Mabel, is saying to Bunty, 'It *is* lovely to see you,' and she turns to Gillian and Patricia and says, 'Are you looking forward to going back to school after the Christmas holidays?' and Patricia says, 'Yes,' and Gillian says, 'No.' Uncle Tom turns to George and says, 'I thought the road might be blocked – it was a real white-over last night,' and George says, 'I know. We had quite an adventure getting here.'

Auntie Mabel has put on an unseasonable salad for our dinner and even the sight of the round lettuce leaves and pale icy green cucumber discs is enough to make you shiver and I say, 'We had a tongue salad,' to Dr Herzmark and laugh and tell her about Gillian tucking into the thick slice of cold tongue that Auntie Mabel has just carved – from an ox tongue that she has pressed herself especially for our visit. Gillian takes a big bite and, swallowing quickly (I think in a former life she died of starvation), she says to Bunty, 'Why can't we have this? I like it,' and then watching Auntie Mabel carving another piece, adds, 'What is it?' Auntie Mabel smiles, 'Tongue, Gillian.'

Gillian's forehead creases in a little frown as she digests this information – both literally and otherwise – and she repeats the word, 'Tongue,' to herself and then 'Tongue,' again, feeling the word on her own tongue as it touches her palate, more uncertainly this time, before laying down her knife and fork and staring at half a tomato on her plate. Patricia laughs cruelly at the expression of discomfort on Gillian's face and Pearl joins in even though she doesn't know what Patricia's laughing at. Pearl likes to laugh, she is all light and sunshine to my dark brooding. 'That's enough,' Bunty says because the sound of laughter worries her, touching some deep, unhealed part of her soul. 'You can play in the snow after dinner,' George says. 'We put your wellingtons in the boot.'

'And make a big snowman?' Pearl asks excitedly, and Uncle Tom laughs and says, 'You can take some coal from the scuttle for his eyes.'

'That's enough,' I say abruptly to Dr Herzmark. Because it tears something inside me to see Pearl so clearly in my mind and know that she's so utterly beyond reach. Dr Herzmark says, 'Another day, Ruby,' and offers me a piece of toffee cracked from a slab. When I hold it up to the light, the sun shines through it like amber and the smell of strawberries follows me all the way home.

Bunty and Auntie Mabel are buttoning us into duffle-coats and scarves and mittens. Pearl and I have little woollen bonnets – mine is red, hers is blue – with white pom-poms on top. Pearl is so excited by all the snow that she paddles her feet up and down impatiently and can hardly stand still long enough to get her wellingtons on. 'Stand still, Pearl!' Bunty says, thrusting a boot awkwardly onto her foot. Bunty finally decides that we all have enough clothes on and Auntie Mabel opens the back door and we stream out into the cold, our voices ringing like bells in the clear air. 'Mind you don't go near the duck pond!' Auntie Mabel shouts after us as we flounder in the virgin field and her words echo across the whiteness.

'That's enough.'

'Another day then,' Dr Herzmark smiles. 'Did you see the tanks in Prague on the news?'

'Awful,' I agree, munching my way through a Russian caramel. A siren sounds from the roof of Rowntree's and we both start but Dr Herzmark says, 'It's only a fire drill.'

Auntie Mabel might as well have said, 'Mind you go straight to the duck pond,' because as soon as we're in the field we make a bee-line for the big pond where Auntie Mabel's ducks and geese congregate. We have held the little egg-yolk yellow chicks in spring and taken home the huge blue duck eggs that look so beautiful and taste so horrid but we have never seen the duck pond in winter before and for a second we all pause and look in astonishment because it is a magical place, a frozen icescape of sparkling white and all the snow-covered trees on the island in the middle look as if they would chime if you shook them, like trees in a fairy story. The duck pond is so full of winter water that it has flooded out onto the field and in places you can look through the glassy ice at the edge and see the green grass below.

A few geese waddle at the edges of the pond while one or two ducks are swimming in lazy circles moving a slurry of ice crystals around on the surface of the water to stop it from freezing, but most of the birds are ice-bound on the little island in the middle and set up a flurry of quacking and honking when they see us approaching. 'Oh, we should have brought some bread!' Patricia wails. Gillian yelps with delight when she finds a solid sheet of ice at the far side of the pond, banging her foot on it like a demented Disney rabbit. 'Be careful, Gillian,' Patricia warns and wanders off, walking a pair of ducks around the pond. Pearl rushes after Gillian, jumping up and down as she watches our sister perform the miracle of walking on water. Gillian has nearly reached the island when the ice gives a frightening *Crack!* and moves a little so that you can see the edges of it where it dwindles away and becomes liquid again, thanks to the ducks' marathon swimming efforts. Pearl has already got both feet on the ice and Gillian is laughing and shouting at her, 'Come on! Come on, don't be a coward! Cowardy-custard Pearl!' because she knows that's the one way to goad Pearl into doing things. I shout at Pearl to come back and Gillian is furious with me, yelling, 'Shut up, Ruby! You're just a big baby!' and I look round wildly for Patricia, but she's disappeared behind a clump of frosted trees and I can't see her. Pearl has walked nearly half-way out onto the ice and I can actually see it moving, with a slight see-saw motion, and I begin to cry. All the time Gillian continues to shout, 'Come on, come *on*, Pearl!' when all of a sudden the ice that Pearl is standing on tilts and I watch in horror as she simply slides off as if she'd been tipped on a chute and slips into the water, quite slowly and feet first, and as she drops into the water her body twists round so that she's facing me and the last thing I see is her face, stretched in horror, and the last words she ever says, before the black water claims her, hang on the freezing air, forming ice-crystals of sound long after the little white pom-pom on her hat has disappeared.

All I can do is stand there with my mouth open wide, one long, unwavering scream of hysteria coming out of it, and although I'm aware of the dreadful ululating noise that's coming from inside me, and aware of Gillian on the island screaming at Patricia to hurry up and Patricia herself sprinting round the pond towards us, despite this cacophony – joined now by all the geese – all I can really hear are Pearl's words which have found a home inside my skull, creating dreadful ricocheting echoes – *Ruby, help me! Ruby, help me!*

Patricia dives into the water and comes up again almost immediately, retching with the cold, her stringy hair plastered to her head, but she blinks like a strange amphibian and forces herself under the water again. By this time the commotion has reached not only Uncle Tom's cottage but the neighbouring farm as well and people seem to come running from everywhere churning up the smooth white snow. Someone drags a shivering, blue Patricia out of the water and wraps her in a rough, dirty jacket and carries her away and one of the farm labourers wades confidently into the water but has to start swimming almost straight away, gasping with shock, because the duck pond is unexpectedly full.

But Pearl has floated away under the ice somewhere and refuses to be found. It is only several hours later when the men have brought hooks and long sticks to fish for Pearl, that she agrees to come out of hiding. One of the men, big, with pocked skin and a heavy jaw, carries her in his arms, holding her away from his body as if she was something immensely fragile and important, which she is, of course, and all the way across the trodden snow of the field his body judders with the sobs he's trying to suppress.

And my heart is breaking, breaking into great jagged icy splinters. I breathe in big noisy gulps because I'm drowning on air, and if I could cast a spell to stop time – suspend it for ever and ever, so that the cobwebs grew over my hair and the ducks stopped in the middle of their circles and the feathers lay still on the air, drifting through time for ever – then I would do it.

Pearl's limp little body is laid on the kitchen table but Auntie Mabel shoos us out of the room and across the passage to the front parlour. Patricia has already been dispatched to hospital. Gillian sits in an armchair and stares at her feet. The parlour smells of camphor and old wood. The only sound is the ticking of a carriage-clock which chimes the quarter-hours with a tinkling carillon. I don't feel up to sitting in a chair and curl up instead in a little ball behind the sofa and I lie there, quite numb, hearing – not Pearl's dreadful words – but Gillian's.

As Patricia was dragged out of the pond, screaming and kicking, desperate to get back into the water and find Pearl, Gillian remained stranded on the island (they fetched a little rowing-boat eventually to get her off). As the men began their search for Pearl, Gillian jumped up and down like a savage in a story book, executing her own personal tribal dance. Terrified that she'd be blamed for what had happened, she pointed at me and screamed until her lungs gave out, 'It was her, it was her, it was her. Ruby pushed her in, she pushed Pearl in the water. I saw her! I saw her!' and I just stood there, dumbstruck, staring at the frozen grass under the ice, where a long white feather from one of Auntie Mabel's geese had found a cold nest.

'All right?' Dr Herzmark asks, holding me like a baby and rocking me back and forwards. And after a while I grow quiet and we sit in a strange companionable fashion, listening to the *whizz whizz* of bicycle wheels as Rowntree's day-shift goes home; then she hands me a Lyons chocolate cupcake from her drawer and I peel the stiff pleated silver cup off it. 'My mother really did blame me. She packed me off to her sister in Dewsbury because she couldn't bear to look at me.'

'Because you reminded her of Pearl, not because she hated you,' Dr Herzmark suggests.

I shrug. 'Both, I suppose. Poor Bunty – losing two children. And poor Patricia too; we expected her to do something, to save Pearl. And she couldn't. And poor Gillian too,' I add with some surprise. 'If anyone was to blame it was her. And she's dead. And poor Pearl because she's dead too.'

'And so,' Dr Herzmark says with a smile, 'shall we go through every person in the world, dead or alive, and say "poor so and so" and "poor so and so" and will we ever come to "poor Ruby"?'

And I try the words out to feel how they fit, 'Poor Ruby', but hardly have they formed in my mouth before I am crying and crying until I almost drown in my own pool of tears.

I have been to the world's end and back and now I know what I would put in my bottom drawer. I would put my sisters.

Footnote (xi) – The Wrong Life

ALICE, SITTING IN A SHAFT OF SEPTEMBER SUNSHINE IN her rocking-chair in the kitchen of the cottage, nursed the newly-christened Eleanor. Baby Nell had fallen asleep at the breast and Alice herself was dozing miserably, quite unable to face the unwashed clothes, unfed children and unsatisfied husband that comprised her lot in life.

She was thinking, in a glumly metaphorical way, that she felt as if a great stone had been laid on her breast-bone and she was being slowly suffocated by it, like one of the martyrs of old, although – a godless woman at the best of times – she couldn't work out what on earth she was suffering *for*.

She listened, in a sleepy, abstracted kind of way, to the *creak-creak* of a cart and heard the dog barking its alarm. She knew it added up to something but for the life of her she couldn't remember what and then she heard that peculiar voice saying something to one of the children – *Bonzjoor* – so that she almost dropped the sleeping baby as she buttoned up the front of her dress in dismay. Jean-Paul Armand! He darkened the door majestically and then invited himself to sit at the kitchen table, saying many extravagantly sentimental things about the small, mousy baby almost lost in the depths of the big wooden crib. ''Appy muzzair!' he said in his exotic accents. 'What a pity ze little one missed having 'er photograph taken!' On the matter of the photographs, Alice's mind was working furiously – had she put her signature to an agreement? Committed herself to paying money she could not possibly find? (Her entire material wealth could be measured by six silver sixpences in a tea-caddy on the mantelpiece.) How could she possibly know the answers to these questions when her mind was a permanent sieve of maternal amnesia?

From a large black leather Gladstone, Monsieur Armand produced the fruits of his work. He had framed three of the prints to demonstrate to his customer how much she needed to pay the extra cost of framing in order to display her progeny to the best advantage – although one of the framed photographs (framed, it has to be said, in a much more expensive frame than the other two) was Monsieur Armand's own personal favourite and not of her progeny at all, but the one of Alice hiding her fertile bulk behind the *chaise-longue* and pouting enigmatically at the camera.

Belle, he murmured appreciatively, pushing the sepia portrait across the pine table. Alice regarded it in-differently, but she stretched out a hand to gather in the photographs of her children – they seemed much more attractive somehow when frozen into immobile poses and her eyes grew slightly moist at the sight of them and she sniffed quietly. Monsieur Armand produced an enormous (clean) silk handkerchief from one of his many magician's pockets and handed it over with a flourish so that Alice was able to blow her nose in a rather unladylike way. She got up abruptly from the table after the nose-blowing and fetched the tea-caddy savings bank from the mantelpiece, opened the lid and in a melodramatic gesture emptied the contents onto the table, scattering the coins over the images of her children. 'There,' she declared tragically. 'That is my entire worldly wealth. I am at your mercy,' she added and promptly burst into tears.

Monsieur Armand was momentarily at a loss – he frequently had customers unable to pay, indeed he'd got into the habit of expecting it, but none of them was usually so histrionic, so emotional, so, well – foreign – about it and it was several seconds before he collected himself together and reached for her slim little hand across the rustic table. 'Dear lady,' he said. 'Dear, dear lady, you must not upset yourself, I will not take your money.' Alice was startled. She could not recollect anyone having said this to her before; generally the only thing people ever did was to take the money from her purse and she regarded Monsieur Armand suspiciously. 'What will you take then?' she asked, holding her chin high in defiance in case he bartered for her virtue. 'Nothing, dear lady – I want nothing but you 'appy will.' The schoolmistress in her moved to correct his grammar but was overcome by his unexpected kindness which primed the pump for a torrent of weeping and wailing from her until Monsieur Armand began to grow quite worried for her sanity.

All this had not gone entirely unnoticed and Alice's three-dimensional offspring were now hovering silently on the threshold. 'Mother,' Ada ventured, 'is summat up?' and Alice sobbed even louder at the rural accents of her eldest and best child, especially when compared with the rococo exotica of Monsieur Armand's vowels.

Eventually emotions were quieted and children dispersed and Monsieur Armand himself made ready to remount his *creak-creaking* chariot. 'I feel,' he said, tapping his left breast, 'I feel in my 'art, dear lady, your un'appiness, your grief. You—' Here he swept his arm around to indicate both the farm cottage and the entire county of Yorkshire – 'You were not meant for this 'orrible life!' Alice, still red-eyed from sobbing, nodded her head in mute agreement as he had just voiced her own thoughts exactly. His ancient pony, trapped between the shafts of the equally ancient cart, arched its neck and snorted and, under cover of his transport's restlessness, Monsieur Armand bent down so that his thin lips were only an inch from my great-grandmother's ear and his whiskers tickled her cheek. What passed between them in this intimate moment? An invitation to disaster, loss, hair-tearing grief and downright ruination which my silly great-grandmother misread completely as an opportunity for her true nature – so stifled and suffocated by drudgery and penury – to escape and fly free. 'I wait,' said Monsieur Armand, 'at the end of the track – at midnight. I wait all night for you to come to me and run away to a better place.'

'*Shall* wait,' Alice was driven to correct his tenses. 'Or possibly, in this case, "will".'

'Whatever.'

Later that afternoon, if you had been watching, you might have seen Alice high up, aloft in the hay loft, its upper doorway framing her spreadeagled figure, standing like Pythagorean woman and contemplating the height/weight implications of a fall. She had dressed herself suitably in black for the occasion, an ancient grosgrain, spotted with rust on the frills, and she gazed down at the ground below with a certain kind of wretched delight that would not be manifest again in our family until the advent of Patricia.

However, even a woman in Alice's mental condition was capable of calculating that the fall would simply not be long enough or hard enough to guarantee much beyond a broken limb – an injury which would merely make her life much worse rather than affording any kind of escape, so she was really not too put out when Ada appeared down below, her pretty pouting mouth agape in horror. 'What yer *doing*, Mother?' she shouted, and her mother, a black, rusty angel, merely sighed and shrugged her shoulders as if to say she really didn't have the slightest notion what she was doing.

Later still, after they had suppered on an unappetizing potato and cabbage stew and squabbled and pinched and pulled and generally frayed Alice into a tattered heap, the children were shepherded reluctantly upstairs, and Alice dropped into a weary sleep in her chair by the empty grate until Frederick crashed into the house, so much the worse for drink that in the dark kitchen he started at the sight of his wife in the rocking-chair and said, 'Who's that?' and looked as if he might attack her until she lit a candle and said, 'It's me, you daft fool,' and he said, 'Oh aye,' and collapsed on the settle.

Alice squinted in the flickering candlelight at a wet, red patch on his arm. 'Been fighting again?' she asked with very little interest, and Frederick stared at the blood for a few seconds trying to recollect how he had come by it and then snorted and said, 'Some great stupid lummox in cart at t'end of t'track – I fell into it.'

His wife offered no word of sympathy, she was in too thrilled a state of shock; she had quite forgotten Monsieur Jean-Paul Armand – the potato and cabbage stew, the attractions of suicide, the demands of children – these things had all conspired to drive him from her aerated brain. Frederick tripped his way up the stairs and fell – she knew without needing to observe – into a deep, deep alcohol-saturated sleep.

Alice remained downstairs, arguing with herself about the future by the light of a melancholy tallow candle. What were her alternatives? Certainly she could kill herself – this possibility still exerted a considerable attraction despite the aborted attempt earlier in the day.

But what of the consequences? Wouldn't the lives of her children be riddled henceforth with horror, scandal, guilt? Would they not be better off if they woke up in the morning and discovered that their mother had simply disappeared into the night rather than waking up to discover her body splattered all over the yard or foaming at the mouth from fly-paper poisoning? The 'better place' offered by Monsieur Armand would undoubtedly be a course beset with problems and surprises but surely it was better than death by her own hand?

And having come to this conclusion it was only a matter of minutes before she was packing a small bag and giving poor little Nelly a last cuddle. Then she kissed the soft, damp foreheads of Ada, Albert and Lillian, lingering long enough to stroke Albert's golden, downy cheek and suppress a sob, and to take her mother's little silver locket from her neck and slip it under Ada's pillow. Ada moaned in her sleep and brushed her mother's farewell kiss away with her hand. There were no goodbyes, though, for poor Lawrence and Tom as they slept up in the attic where the floorboards were all creaks and Lawrence was such a light sleeper that Alice decided not to risk it. She lived to regret this unmotherly omission, but then she lived long enough to regret more or less everything. Her very last act was to take off her wedding-ring and lay it on the pillow next to her drunken husband's snoring head. When he awoke to find it there the next morning in place of his wife, he understood, with an insight quite unusual for him, that she was gone for good.

Alice found Monsieur Armand waiting patiently at the end of the track and he showed no surprise when she clambered up beside him and said, 'Right then,' which seemed somewhat uninspiring words with which to embark on a new life.

Monsieur Armand, anxious at the prospect of being pursued by an angry husband, made straight for the north and the pair settled, or tried to settle, in Glasgow for a while. But although Monsieur Armand managed to scrape by as a travelling photographer he didn't seem to have the same luck once he was ensconced in a stationary studio, and certainly Glasgow was awash with photographic studios at the time and could get by perfectly well without the addition of Monsieur Armand's talents. With the failure of this venture they uprooted themselves within a year. By this time, certain doubts had begun to display themselves in Alice's heart but nonetheless she was willing to decamp the country and travel to Marseilles, Monsieur Armand's native town, on the understanding that it would be a short visit after which they would come back to Yorkshire and – well, she didn't know quite what followed the 'and' of this sentence, but somehow or other she would work out how to get her children back. She did, of course, have the photographs, because Monsieur Armand still had the plates and she was able to persuade him to print up a whole new set for her when they were in Glasgow, which she made him frame in expensive tooled-leather travelling frames that closed securely, enabling Alice to hug her children – fixed for ever in time – to and fro across the Continent.

Things did not go according to plan and the sojourn lengthened into years. Almost immediately on returning to Marseilles, Monsieur Armand made the unfortunate mistake of sinking every penny they had into a disastrous business venture. He was a man with no judgement in business affairs, as the Glasgow enterprise had demonstrated, and if Alice had known what he was doing she would have put her foot down and saved them from what followed – Monsieur Armand's conviction for bankruptcy. He was even jailed for a short time and his poor wife was left destitute. (They had married bigamously with startling ease – although by now, Frederick was dead so technically Alice was a widow.) For a time Alice was even reduced to taking in washing, rubbing soap bars on the sullied linen of the bourgeoisie of Marseilles, and bitterly questioning a non-existent God as to whether this was really what he had intended for her.

When Monsieur Armand was released from prison, still surprisingly cheerful, another misfortune befell them in the shape of a bout of pneumonia to which Alice succumbed, leaving her weak and exhausted for many months afterwards. In between nursing his wife Monsieur Armand managed to earn a little money from his itinerant photography (knocking on doors was one thing he was good at) and eventually took her to the country to convalesce. Alice would have preferred to remain amongst Marseilles' urban squalor rather than be buried in a pastoral idyll again, but, for once, Monsieur Armand was insistent. Then the money ran out again so that they were stranded in the country for quite some time just as Alice had feared and then when they returned to the city several more setbacks followed of the kind that Alice had come to expect, and so it went on.

On the morning of Alice's forty-seventh birthday, she got out of bed, flung back the shutters on the bedroom window to reveal a flood of clean sunshine and, looking out of the window rather than at the inert Gallic shape under the bedclothes, declared to Monsieur Armand that she had absolutely and categorically had enough and that they had to return to England to recover her children *that very instant* even if she had to sell her body on the streets in order to raise the fare. Monsieur Armand mumbled something to the effect that she would only be able to sell her body if her lips were sewn together, forcing her to hurl both jug and washbasin at the bed.

Unhappily, this was also the fine summer's morning that Archduke Franz Ferdinand and his wife set off to drive through the streets of Sarajevo, thus setting in motion a train of events which would conspire to keep Monsieur Armand and his wife in France for another four years.

During the war, Alice had a curious experience, the kind that other people might have taken as evidence of some mental disturbance; but she was so used to feeling disturbed that she didn't think this at all and came to the even more outlandish conclusion that it demonstrated the existence of God. This transformatory experience occurred in 1916, on the night of 1 July, when Alice was woken suddenly from a very deep sleep. When she opened her eyes she saw a figure at the end of her bed – an angel, or at least an apparition that conformed to her idea of what an angel should look like – gauzy white robes, snowy wings, incandescent halo, golden curls, forget-me-not blue eyes – and she waited for it to speak to her but it, or rather he – for it was clearly a male figure – did not speak, but simply smiled and raised a hand heavenward in a gesture remarkably like that of the cheap plaster statues of saints and madonnas and Christs with which France was infested. Then it vanished. Next morning, Alice scoured every corner of the room to see if any angelic remnant had been left behind but there was nothing, not even a feather; but his fleeting presence had been enough to convert Alice to Catholicism and she became quite zealous, as all good converts do.

However, the bead-counting and candle-lighting did nothing to stop Alice's search for her abandoned children and the second that the armistice rang out over Europe she packed Monsieur Armand onto a train bound for Calais. She began her search in the logical place – the little cottage she had left behind so hastily thirty years ago – only to find that, this time, it was her children who had vanished into thin air. Several families had lived in the cottage since Rachel and the one presently incumbent knew nothing about any

Barkers who might have once been there. Down in the village – where her reappearance caused something of a stir – the older inhabitants remembered the family quite clearly – Ada's death, Frederick's death, Rachel's baby, Lawrence's disappearance – these events were narrated dispassionately to Alice. It was, after all, a very long time ago, although not unfortunately to Alice who took these blows in anguish. And where had they decamped to? Here there was only a general shaking of heads. For the life of them no-one could remember.

Monsieur Armand and his wife caught a train at the nearest railway station, heading for Whitby as Alice conjectured that Rachel might well have behaved like a homing pigeon, and for the entire journey she raved about Rachel coming to take her place and wept at the death of Ada and agonized over Lawrence's disappearance until Monsieur Armand dearly wished that he had never set eyes on his wife. Frazzled, unravelled and fat, she was driving Monsieur Armand into an early grave, in Monsieur Armand's opinion. Neither her temper nor her spirits improved with their arrival in Whitby where Alice spent several gaunt and dishevelled weeks traipsing up and down the narrow little streets like a demented woman asking every passer-by if they had ever heard of a Rachel Barker or a Rachel Storm (which was the name Rachel was born with, appropriately enough). She darted down every yard, calling out the names of her lost children, *Tom, Albert, Lillian, Nelly,* but they did not answer her call. In the evenings she was to be found standing on top of the West Cliff staring mournfully out to sea like the mother of a drowned sailor, before coming back to the cheap rooms they had rented to curse Jean-Paul Armand and the day she met him. After one of these tirades, when she had hit him on the head with a vase, he changed into his pyjamas and lay down on the thin, tired mattress of their double bed and closed his eyes with a sigh, never to open them again.

Now a widow twice over, Alice continued her search everywhere she could think of – Scarborough, Hull, Leeds, Bradford, Middlesborough; she even tried her own birthplace of York, the last place she expected Rachel to have chosen. All Alice's own relatives were dead by this time and she knew no-one in York so she stayed only a couple of weeks before resuming her quest elsewhere, never knowing that she had passed Nell with Clifford, Babs and Bunty in tow, in Davygate, and not even noticed them. Finally she washed up in Sheffield, quite penniless, living in a terrace slum and taking in, not washing but other people's children, the irony of which was not lost in her.

My great-grandmother died, an old lady surrounded by her photographs and a collection of plaster saints, in 1940 during one of the worst wartime raids on Sheffield. She was pulled out from a pile of rubble the next morning by a policeman and an air-raid warden and, held protectively against her body, they found an old-fashioned photograph of five children. The glass on the photograph wasn't even broken. The policeman took it tenderly from her dead hands and said, 'Ee, they'll be sad when they hear how their old mam died.' (He was a sentimental man, too sentimental for the job he'd had to do that night.)

Coincidentally, the bombing of Sheffield had been witnessed by the eldest survivor of that photograph – Tom, a man who was under the impression that his mother had died fifty-five years previously, and who was visiting a pal in Doncaster. On a long, meandering journey back from the pub they climbed a hill to watch the raid, clearly visible even from that distance. 'By 'eck,' his pal said, 'that's Sheffield burning, lad,' and then, 'Poor folk,' and then, 'Sod Hitler!' But Tom just shook his head sadly and felt grateful that he wasn't in Sheffield that night.

CHAPTER TWELVE

1970

Broken English

KATHLEEN TRIES THE IRON BED IN THE CONDEMNED CELL for size.

'How is it?'

'Pretty uncomfortable. You'd think they'd give condemned people a mattress or something.' We are in the cell where Dick Turpin spent his last night, sans mattress. I lie down next to Kathleen on the hard black iron slats. 'Mattressless – do you suppose that's a word?'

'Dunno,' Kathleen shrugs, a difficult thing to do on an iron bed. We've just finished our A-Level exams and are filling the empty time by behaving like tourists, spending the morning in the Castle Museum amongst the stuffed horses and fire buckets, muskets and period shops that make up the past. Once, I had a dream about the Castle Museum – it was the middle of the night and I was the only person in the museum and while I watched everything came to life – the fires flamed up in the Victorian fireplaces, the delicate eighteenth-century harpsichords began to play, all on their own, and a carriage-and-four began to trundle along one of the cobbled streets. The secret museum at night was much more interesting than the daytime one where visitors keep shuffling into Dick Turpin's cell and disturbing the peace.

'I've had enough,' Kathleen says, suddenly rising from her condemned bed. 'Let's go and get an ice-cream.'

Outside the museum we wander aimlessly around the grassy mound on which Clifford's Tower sits, eating our 99s and breathing in the smell of new-mown grass. My head is still buzzing with Racine and Schiller and the mystifying questions on the European History paper, but Kathleen has her mind on different things. 'Why don't we work in a hotel for the summer?'

'A hotel?'

'Mm. I think it would be good for us to get some experience before we get on with the rest of our lives.' (Only when Kathleen says it, it sounds like The Rest Of Our Lives.)

'Some experience of what exactly?'

Kathleen looks bemused. 'Well . . . anything, I suppose.' Kathleen isn't going to university, she's joining the Civil Service. I have been offered a choice of university places to do a degree in modern languages and I've chosen one of the farthest away on the map (Exeter) and if there had been a university in the Scilly Isles then I would have applied there. After Dr Herzmark returned the past to me, free of obscure fears, things returned to much how they had been before – I took my O Levels at a second sitting and for a while Bunty treated me as if I was a delicate piece of china, but before long we had more or less settled back into our old ways, apart from the absence of Bernard Belling who made a hasty exit from our lives after my flirtation with the world of Spirit. I have surprised myself with how dutiful I have been, but then I am all the daughters of my mother's house now, and it does put you under a certain obligation. On tedious Christmases or harrowing birthdays I have cursed Patricia for wriggling so successfully out of her responsibilities.

Now that I'm going to university Bunty has begun to take a bit more interest in my academic progress and talks about me in that sickly way that other mothers do – *Did you know that my daughter's got a place at university?* – the very same way in fact that Mrs Gorman, Kathleen's mother, does – *Did you know my daughter's getting married to a very nice boy?*

We climb the steps to Clifford's Tower and walk round its white quatrefoil walls. Suddenly set free from everything that has previously imprisoned us (school) we are in a strange, listless limbo. We stare down into the courtyard below. In the twelfth century hundreds of Jews locked themselves in here and burnt themselves to death rather than face the mob outside, baying for their blood. Now its clover-shaped walls are open to the blue sky but the air is still tainted with the scent of immolation and it makes me uneasy. There's too much history in York, the past is so crowded that sometimes it feels as if there's no room for the living.

We wander aimlessly across St George's Field and down to the river. Here, the Vikings once established their trading capital but there is no river trade any more and the big old warehouses stand empty now.

My immediate future (Exeter) appears to be more dependent on my A-Level results than Kathleen's does, as The Rest Of Her Life looks as if it will be defined by marriage to Colin. I'm not at all sure that Mrs Gorman is right in her judgement of Colin – he doesn't seem a particularly 'nice boy' at all to me and I think Kathleen is making a big mistake. In these circumstances helping her to get some 'experience' seems like the decent thing to do and so I say, 'Why not?' in that careless way people do when they're not aware that they're making momentous, fateful decisions.

I thought Kathleen meant a hotel in York, or perhaps London, where we have been only once, on a school trip – both Kathleen and I are keenly aware of how hopelessly provincial we are – so I was quite taken aback when she informed me that she'd found jobs for us as chambermaids in The Royal Highland Hotel in Edinburgh.

'Edinburgh?'

'Yes, Edinburgh, you know – history, culture, the Castle, the Festival, anything, *something* . . .'

So I have come to Scotland a second time and if I knew how long I was going to stay (for ever) I expect I would do some things differently – bring more clothes, for example. But I know nothing; my future is a wide-open vista, leading to an unknown country – The Rest Of My Life.

The first surprising thing about Edinburgh is that we have arrived here without going over the Forth Bridge. I'm still waiting for it to appear beneath our wheels when the train draws up alongside the platform at Waverley. Kathleen is busy hauling down suitcases from the luggage-rack and worrying about getting left on the train, but I'm in my seat puzzling over the disappearance of the Forth Bridge. I'm not as bothered as Kathleen is about getting off; I would be quite happy to stay on the train and find out where it's going (*Haymarket, Inverkeithing, Kirkcaldy, Markinch, Ladybank, Cupar, Leuchars, Dundee, Arbroath, Stonehaven, Aberdeen*).

The second surprise is that Edinburgh is all hills. York is a flat town where the air hangs quietly and the sun sets behind houses, not horizons.

We hover uncertainly in the foyer of The Royal Highland Hotel which smells of roast meat and rice pudding. The Royal Highland is really an amalgamation of several houses on a sweeping New Town crescent. This transformation has been cobbled together with veneered plywood and concealed light fittings like a trick box. A figure glides out from nowhere and speaks in a foreign accent which I recognize (Scottish), 'Hello gurruls, I am Marjorie Morrison, the housekeeper, and I hope you'll be using the back door in future.' Marjorie Morrison is as thin and as straight as a pencil. She has widowed eyes and black braided hair and looks like a near-relation of Mrs Danvers.

Once we have been shown to our room in the attic, Kathleen begins to unpack methodically but I clamber up the chair and stick my head out of the little window in the roof into the evening sunlight and breathe deeply. The attic window is better than the camera obscura on the Royal Mile will be, for a panorama of Edinburgh shimmers below in silvery watercolours, stretching far away to the Salisbury Crags and the Pentland Hills.

Being a chambermaid turns out to be housework under a different guise, much of which seems quite unnecessary to me. I can never polish up my mirrors the way Kathleen can or get my baths free of their grainy deposits. My Hoover clogs up, my sheets wrinkle, my coathangers disappear – clearly I have not inherited the housework genes from Auntie Babs and Bunty. I spend a lot of time dozing on unmade beds in empty rooms, contemplating the uneven, beige plaster on the walls of the Royal Highland and listening for the approach of Marjorie Morrison's sharp little heels. If this is 'experience' then I'd rather skip it and get on with The Rest Of My Life.

Edinburgh, when I venture onto its streets, is both exotic and friendly at the same time – but I must explore its charms alone for – astonishingly – I have lost Kathleen. Almost as soon as we arrive she appears to completely forget about The Rest Of Her Life with Colin and takes up with a student called Martin who is working as a porter for the summer at the same hotel. Martin wears wire-rimmed spectacles and a purple grandad vest and a skimpy ponytail that Marjorie Morrison insists he has cut, threatening him with a little pair of silver scissors dangling from a chain at her waist. Martin is studying electronic engineering and is heavily into drugs and Marshall McLuhan and if you searched the length and breadth of the country you couldn't find anyone less like hapless, ironmongering Colin. I make friends with two Irish girls working as waitresses for the summer. Niamh and Siobhan are also waiting for The Rest Of Their Lives to start, but are a poor substitute for Kathleen.

But my future is still as promising as railway tracks. I don't know that I am doomed by Janet Sheriff, our history teacher who fell in love at the beginning of our A-Level History course and forgot to teach us large chunks of the European syllabus. Only when we were sitting our exam did we discover that there had been terrible battles and bloody revolutions of which we knew nothing.

In the evenings, Niamh and Siobhan and I sit in Benedetti's, an Italian café off Leith Walk which seems warm and inviting with its red Formica-covered tables and steaming chrome machines. The Benedettis themselves are living opera, a brooding and melodramatic Italian family in which relationships are indecipherable – an endless succession of grandmothers and sisters and cousins replacing one another behind the counter, all of them tossing mysterious words at one another like flowers. Sometimes behind the counter there is a beautiful boy with green eyes and black-satin hair tied back with a shoelace so that you can see that his cheeks are as sharp as knife blades. His nut-brown skin looks as if it will smell of olives and lemons. This is Gian-Carlo Benedetti and you would never think from looking at him that he would turn out the way he does.

On the walls of the café are hung posters of Pisa and Lucca and Barga, posters with pictures of huge quattrocento towers and blue Tuscan skies and sometimes when old Mr Benedetti is in charge and waiting idly for custom he stands and looks at these posters with a faraway look in his eye and I know he's thinking about home (*see Footnote (xii)*). Later, when we have the chip shop in Forfar, we too will have one of these posters on the wall and sometimes when Gian-Carlo Benedetti is waiting for the fat to reach the right temperature I catch him gazing at it with the same vacant expression. But by then I know he isn't thinking anything at all and I scream at him in Italian, in words that sound as if they are embroidered with blood.

Kathleen and I phone up Queen Anne's to get our exam results and discover that we have both failed our History A Level. A curtain falls across the wide open vista that was my future – all of a sudden I have no idea what's going to happen to me. *Que sera sera* says Kathleen with a smile and a shrug. She doesn't care – she's in love with Martin.

But it's not to be. Colin must have sensed that Kathleen was re-ordering The Rest Of Her Life for he comes storming up to Edinburgh, hammering on the bell in reception and calling down Marjorie Morrison's wrath on his head. He shuts himself up with Kathleen in a linen cupboard until he's talked her round and within a matter of hours they are back on the train to England. I see them off at Waverley and watching the tail-light of their train disappear into the darkness I wish Kathleen a happy future, but, unfortunately, I know that it takes more than wishes to secure that.

Her subsequent grudge against Janet Sheriff, our history teacher, will be greater than mine, for it is, after all, Miss Sheriff's amnesic love life which is directly responsible for our failing our History A Level and for Kathleen joining the Civil Service at clerical rather than administrative grade, which in turn will result in her bottom drawer expanding on credit. This will put pressure on the marriage and lead to Colin drinking, losing the family business, going bankrupt before he's forty and shooting the family dog. So in a way I was lucky that all that happened to me was that I married Gian-Carlo Benedetti and ran the chip shop in Forfar.

Martin is heartbroken and leaves Edinburgh the next day. We will keep in touch sporadically for the next few years. Martin will get into computers and move to California and I think it's safe to say that poor Kathleen has just made the wrong decision.

A week or so later, I'm staring vacantly out of the window of Room 21, when Marjorie Morrison sweeps in and glares at the twin beds I've just finished making. 'Your pillows,' she declares, 'look as if they have been in the Battle of Vienna!' But this statement produces in me, not contrition, but a storm of helpless weeping and I collapse on one of the poorly-made beds and in between hiccuping sobs I tell her woefully that I have never heard of any Battle of Vienna. Perhaps sensing that my grief comes from a deeper source than mere ignorance of military history, Marjorie Morrison bends her stiff form and sits next to me on the bed and like an awkward, angular insect, unfolds her arms and puts them gingerly around my heaving body. 'Lennox,' she muses after a while, 'you must have Scottish blood in you, dear.' Over her scrawny, musty shoulder I notice for the first time a watercolour hanging on the wall of the Forth Bridge, its blood-rust girders dark against a blue sky. 'No,' I say, weeping and shaking my head. 'No, I don't think I do.'

The Irish girls are packing, getting ready for grape-picking in France; they invite me to go with them but I decline. I try to wash away my torpor by climbing Arthur's Seat. It's a soft, gentle evening and when I reach the top I can see bridges and water and hills in abundance and above my head wheels a flock of satin-black birds making prophetic patterns in the air and when I walk into Benedetti's the beautiful boy, who will indeed smell like olives and lemons, looks up from the floor he is sweeping and smiles hugely at me and says, *Ciao, come sta?* And later that night, when the café is closed, he proposes to me over a seething *cappuccino* in dreadful, halting English. I wilfully misinterpret all the signs and believe that a magnificent kind of destiny has revealed itself to me (unaware then the reason he asks me is because he is only a distant cousin Benedetti and about to be deported – this faint kinship is the reason why we can't have the café in Kirriemuir or the ice-cream parlour in Dundee and must make do with the fish-and-chip shop in Forfar).

On my way back to the Royal Highland I ring up Bunty from a call-box outside Princes Street Gardens, surrounded by midnight revellers from the Festival. She answers wearily and I can almost see her blue rollers and pink hair-net. 'It's just Ruby!' I shout down the phone at her. 'Guess what – I'm getting married!' The shocked silence that greets this news goes on for ever – at least until my money runs out. 'I've found someone who wants me at last!' I yell into the phone, but it has already gone *beepbeepbeepbeepbeep* and my words fall into nothing. 'Congratulations, hen,' a man says as I come out of the phone-box. 'I hope you'll be very happy,' and I must make do with his whisky-laced epithalamium for the only person we invite to our hasty register-office wedding is Marjorie Morrison and we have to borrow a witness from the previous wedding. Bunty refuses to speak to me for over a year and I am horrified to find that I miss her.

And so I married Gian-Carlo Benedetti and finally found the Forth Rail Bridge. I crossed the Forth and then the Tay and found out what would have happened if I had stayed on the train (*Haymarket, Inverkeithing, Kirkcaldy, Markinch, Ladybank, Cupar,*

Leuchars, Dundee) and in doing so condemned myself to some truly wretched years in which Gian-Carlo Benedetti's charms melt into the air along with his fine cheekbones and radiant smile. Not only that, but he grows unattractively plump on all the chip-fat and acquires such a taste for *grappa* that sometimes I think about throwing a match at him to see if he'll ignite like a well-doused Christmas pudding.

Once I caught a train to Cardenden by mistake. I was on the way to Forfar (it was near the end of my marriage to Gian-Carlo Benedetti) and the train was in the wrong place, alongside the number 17 platform at Waverley where the Dundee train should have been, and the guard was already slamming the doors and raising his whistle when I ran up, one small, nut-brown child under each arm, their black curls bobbing as I ran and jumped aboard. The train had meandered through half of Fife before I realized we were going the wrong way (my state of mind was not good at the time). When we reached Cardenden we got off and waited for the next train back to Edinburgh. I was very tired and if Cardenden had looked more promising I think I would have simply stayed there. And if you've ever been to Cardenden you'll know how bad things must have been.

That was just before I had a phone call that took me by surprise. 'Eez the phone – yours!' Gian-Carlo Benedetti shouted (his English had improved very little under my uxorial tutelage), but when I picked up the phone I was greeted by a familiar silence – it was Mr Nobody. 'Well, you haven't called for a long time,' I reprimanded him, but there was no answer, no word, no heavy breathing, no breathing at all in fact, and I listened to the silence very carefully in case it was a message in itself and discovered that it had a soothing quality, like listening to the sea in a shell, full of invisible rhythms and waves and I might have sat listening to that silence for ever but then my caller from the ocean floor suddenly spoke – a hesitant, 'Hello?' and the mysterious noise of spiritual ether resolved itself into antipodean static as the voice repeated, 'Hello? Hello? Ruby?' It was not Mr Nobody, nor some long-distance mermaid, it was Patricia. 'Where *are* you, Patricia?'

There's an odd, contorted noise, like someone learning to laugh, 'Australia!' she shouted. 'I'm in Australia, Ruby!' (Forfar paled into insignificance compared to the lengths Patricia went to remove herself from the family's broken circle.) 'You couldn't have got much farther away, could you, Patricia?' I chastised her, but she just made that funny noise again.

Not long after that phone call, when I was loading the ever-open mouth of the tumbling potato-peeling machine, I experienced a personal epiphany – looking up from a peeled pile of misshapen King Edwards I saw a tremendous flash of blue light and every hair stood up on my head for a second. The potato-peeler had blown itself up and in that electric moment I had seen everything clearly – I was leading the wrong life! This wasn't my life – it was someone else's and the sooner I found the right one the better, judging by the murderous look on Gian-Carlo's face when I told him about the peeling machine. 'You've got the wrong wife,' I muttered to him over the pile of potatoes I had to peel laboriously by hand. I waved the potato-peeler at him. 'I know, without a shred of doubt that this is not what I'm supposed to be doing.' I am the goose girl, I am the true bride, I am Ruby Lennox still.

I left the next morning, early, long before Gian-Carlo was awake. I took nothing with me except the little nut-brown girls, putting as much distance as I could between me and whoever's life it was I had been falsely inhabiting. We rapidly became connoisseurs of time-tables – British Rail, Bluebird coaches and eventually a huge Coastlines ferry that sailed us away to Ultima Thule, and in our first summer, during the endless Shetland nights, I would stand guard, watching over the sea to make sure that the black heads bobbing on the waves belonged to the seals and not to the vengeful Benedettis.

Once Patricia and Bunty and I had become three points on a far-flung family triangle our relationship was closer. We all went together to Australia – Bunty, myself, and the two nut-brown children, whose names were (and still are, of course) Alice and Pearl. Bunty spent the entire flight worrying that our plane would be shot down by an Argentinian Exocet – it was 1982 and we were in the middle of the Falklands War, and Alice had to hold her hand for most of the flight. We landed on Australian soil unscathed and Patricia introduced us to her new life – a white clapboard house with a fig tree in the garden in an affluent Melbourne suburb. She was married to a mild-mannered Jewish dentist several years older than her and they had two children, Ben and Naomi, and when we arrived she had just graduated from veterinary college. 'Your dreams have come true then, Patricia,' I said to her, but she said she couldn't remember having any dreams. I think she'd forgotten the past.

Patricia had become a Buddhist and meditated every morning at sunrise underneath her fig tree. It was almost impossible for us to believe that this person, glowing with sun and energy, could possibly be Patricia. But it was.

Under the pale skies of the southern hemisphere Bunty is a changed person too; she even allows Louis to probe delicately amongst her fillings and tidy up her bridgework. Surrounded in the sun by her four half-English grandchildren she relishes this sudden role as the Lennox matriarch and I feel sorry for her when I return her to the semi in Acomb and leave her behind there. ('She could always come and live with you, Patricia,' I say cheerfully to my sister as we're waiting to board our Qantas flight, and the look on Patricia's face is worth waiting fifteen years to see.)

This was in the future, as was The Rest Of My Life – but that's another story (*Ruby 2 – The Sequel, What*

Ruby Did Next!) and so when Gian-Carlo Benedetti says in his broken English, 'Ruby – I will marry you yes?' I nod my head and, unable to think of any other answer, say, 'Why not?' and for seven years, three months and eighteen days I am the oddly-named person, Ruby Benedetti, before I am restored, courtesy of the Court of Session in Edinburgh and the even more oddly named Lord Ordinary, to my true self and I am Ruby Lennox once more.

Footnote (xii) – 1914 Home

LAWRENCE TUGGED AT THE WHISTLE ON THE LITTLE PUFFER as it approached the wooden pier. The captain of the boat, a grizzled, kindly man called Robert Jenkinson, was yelling in his pidgin Portuguese to one of the Mission Church brothers on the pier and Lawrence laughed. The old man had been plying up and down this tributary of the Amazon most of his life but he still couldn't speak the lingo. Lawrence could, Lawrence delighted in the lilting cadences of this strange Portuguese language. 'You have a gift for it, Lawrence,' Father Domingo had said and Lawrence had felt ridiculously proud.

Once the boat was moored they began unloading their cargo – flour, coffee, paraffin, candles, fish hooks, ink, sugar, heavy flat bolts of calico and half a dozen wyandottes. Beyond the pier, in a wide swathe of cleared trees, the new Mission Church rose white and straight-edged. But it was not as inviting as the natives' huts – spindly open platforms with thatches over them.

Lawrence would stay in one of them tonight, friendly faces, a supper of fish and rice and *farinha* and a night spent fighting off the river mosquitoes.

When he'd hauled the last sack onto the Brothers' cart, Lawrence stopped for a rest. He sat on the pier, his back against a strut, and rolled a cigarette.

It was late afternoon and the sun was hotter than it had been all day, glinting like gold amongst the many different greens of the vegetation on the river bank. The water in the river was a gleaming, shining black, like polished coal. Lawrence inhaled deeply on his cigarette and breathed in the river smell of fish and rotting vegetation and heat.

Lawrence was thinking about home. He thought about home a lot these days – the cold, northern home of his childhood. The plain fields and clean, bare hills where the plants and animals had to struggle to grow and survive, where fertility was something that had to be worked at and not something that swamped everything in a hot, steamy stew. Lawrence pulled at the front of his thin cotton shirt and bellowed it in and out to try and cool himself. He'd been happy here for a long time, but all of a sudden he was stricken with the desire to go home – at least for a visit if nothing more.

He thought about his sisters, Lily and Nelly, and wondered what kind of women they had grown into. He thought about his brothers, Tom and Albert, and the evil Rachel, and he thought about his pretty dead sister, Ada. But most of all he thought about his mother, whom he'd seen running away, a ghost among the shadows of the night.

He had been out at the privy that night, the result of a dreadful potato and cabbage stew his mother had cooked for tea, and he'd been about to cross the yard back into the house when he'd seen Alice slipping out of the door, fully clothed in her rusty black dress, a short travelling cape and a bonnet. In her hand was a small Gladstone. What was his mother doing with bag and bonnet at three in the morning? Lawrence tried to follow to find out, but he was in his bare feet and the track was laid with sharp stones. His mother, fully shod in her little black boots, moved swiftly, lightly, and Lawrence had the curious impression that she was floating a few inches above the track. She disappeared over the brow of a hill and by the time Lawrence had stumbled to the top all he could see was the black cart, blacker than the night itself, trundling off with his mother's bonneted silhouette sitting aloft next to the Frenchman.

When he woke next morning he thought it must have been a dream for his father said his mother was dead. 'I saw her,' he said later to Ada (white-faced, with blue cups of grief under her eyes from sobbing her heart out).

'Saw 'er?'

'On t'Frenchman's cart.'

'You mun seen her ghost, Lawrence. Mother wouldn't leave us,' his sister said, and Lawrence thought no, she wouldn't do that.

Lawrence threw his cigarette stub into the black water where it sizzled for a fraction of a second and made him feel suddenly hot. He ran a handkerchief round the back of his neck to mop up the sweat. Lawrence still saw his mother in dreams sometimes – her lovely blond curls, her little white teeth, pointed like a cat's. When he dreamt about his mother he always woke up afterwards feeling happy, as if he had warm sugar in his veins, and then he remembered she'd gone and he could weep, did weep sometimes, unmanly, racking sobs that made him feel ashamed.

'I'd like to go home,' he said to Robert Jenkinson, who was walking along the pier towards him with a bottle of whisky in his hand. The captain sat down next to Lawrence and passed him the bottle and laughed. 'Home, you don't want to be going there lad, there's a war coming.'

Lawrence took a silver coin from his pocket and threw it as high as he could. A bird shrieked in the jungle and a streak of primary-coloured plumage flashed amongst the creepers and vines and Lawrence suddenly realized how much he wanted to see a lapwing rise or a lark sing its way towards heaven in the pale blue sky above the hills of home. The silver coin fell through the air, turning over and over and winking as it caught the sun. Lawrence reached out his hand to catch the coin and slapped it over onto the back of his other hand. He held it out for Robert Jenkinson's scrutiny. 'Home,' Lawrence said. 'I shall go home.'

CHAPTER THIRTEEN

1992

Redemption

I'VE COME BACK TO DISPOSE OF THE REMAINS OF MY mother, a task made more complicated by the fact that she isn't dead yet.

'She's lost her personality,' Adrian whispers as he opens the front door. 'She's nothing like her old self.' Well, surely any change can only be an improvement? Adrian has been holding the fort for the last few days while I have travelled back to York. Come home, although this is not my home any more.

'Any word from your Pat, then?' Adrian says cheerfully, mixing up scrambled eggs in a bowl. He is perfectly at home in Bunty's kitchen, while Bunty herself is now an exile from her own kingdom. She's sitting at the table arranging and rearranging knives and forks but somehow she can't get them into the pattern that she wants. She looks surprised when she sees me and asks, very politely, 'Who are you?' (When I arrived she welcomed me with open arms and a big kiss which was how I knew this wasn't really my mother any more.) I give her a bright reassuring smile (her smile) and say, 'It's just Ruby.'

'Patricia's fine – I haven't told her about any of this,' I say, waving a hand vaguely while Bunty looks at me with an interested smile on her face, as if I was a small child doing a charming party-turn.

Adrian offers to stay on for a few days and I gratefully accept. He has his own salon now and lives with an architect called Brian. They have a dog, a chihuahua called Dolores, that Adrian has brought with him. In these circumstances Adrian is the next best thing to a sister – he's quite happy to trail round nursing-homes with me, poking into their toilets and bedside lockers, and he flits round the house in Bunty's second-best pinny doing the housework with a lighthearted touch that would have galled my mother if she'd been herself. But she isn't.

Bunty's prognosis, according to the young Dr Haddow, who is a less genial version of his father, is thus – she will grow steadily more demented, but will probably live a long time because she's got a remarkably sound constitution. So that's all right then. 'Demented?' Bunty echoes with a puzzled little frown, and Dr Haddow and I smile stoutly and pretend we didn't hear her.

'Who *was* that man?' Bunty asks when he's gone. Much of her confusion centres on people's identities, as if she'd suddenly become a keen sceptical empiricist. Sometimes she knows who I am and sometimes she doesn't, and because I find this fascinating I spend a good deal of time asking, 'Do you know who I am?' One day when I'm doing this, Adrian, jaunty yellow duster in one hand, chihuahua in the other, looks at me shrewdly and says, 'Do you know who you are, Ruby?' (I do, I'm Ruby Lennox.)

Our days together speed past, eaten up by housework, shopping, cooking, little trips to the park. Bunty and I stroll around immaculately clipped bowling-greens and sit on benches wistfully watching small children being pushed on swings and she'd be quite happy to stay there all day but when I say, 'Come on, it's time we were getting home,' she gets up obediently and trots by my side.

The evenings are spent in a companionable kind of domesticity, discussing where would be the best place to incarcerate Bunty, working our way through stacks of nursing-home brochures that all seem to have *rooms with modern facilities* and *pleasant views*.

Bunty's replacement personality is a much nicer model than the old one. Her lost self, incapable of enjoyment, would have balked at the amount of time we waste every day. I've waited forty years to play with my mother and now at last we spend long sunny afternoons in an endless state of make-believe on planet Alzheimer. In her confusion, Bunty has her whole family round her skirts again and, being the only corporeal child available, I must understudy for them all, prepared to answer to *Pearl, Gillian, Patricia* (sometimes even *Ruby*). Gillian is still Bunty's favourite, I notice. (*Shall I make your favourite pudding for tea, Gillian? Would you like to come shopping with Mummy, Gillian?* and so on.) It's most peculiar to be surrounded by my invisible sisters and sometimes when I walk into a room it surprises me with its emptiness.

I leave Bunty in the living-room unsupervised for a few minutes one afternoon and when I come back in the room she's in the middle of a billowing cloud of grey dust, emptying the Hoover-bag onto the living-room carpet. 'What on earth are you doing?' I ask her, but she just looks at me with a serene smile and says, 'I'm scattering your father's ashes, of course.'

'Did he want them scattered in the living-room?' I ask her as I pick my way gingerly across the carpet (for the life of me I can't remember what we did with them after his cremation). I can feel something sticking to the soles of my feet and wonder if it's little bits of my father. Later when I've hoovered George back up again, Bunty accosts me with a puzzled little frown. 'You haven't seen my mother have you? I can't find her anywhere.'

'I think this might be the one,' I whisper to Adrian as we drive up in front of an impressive neo-Gothic pile. 'The one what?' Bunty demands – she has developed the hearing of a bat as if to compensate for the percolation of cells from her brain. 'How would you like to have a little holiday here, Auntie Bunty?' Adrian asks, giving her a smile in the rear-view mirror. Bunty says nothing; perhaps she knows it's a trap, but when I finally find the nerve to turn round and look at her she is smiling happily to herself. Our inspection of Silverleas is a satisfying one. No scent of disinfectant or boiled cabbage around the gleaming mahogany of the huge entrance hall – only lavender polish and the smell of warm baking. 'This is lovely, isn't it?' I say enthusiastically to Bunty and she nods in agreement. 'Lovely – how long are we booked in for?' We investigate the bedrooms, both single and shared, with their matching bedspreads and curtains and good quality carpets, and the lounges where there are newspapers and board-games and the kitchens where the food looks delicious and you really would think it was a quite good hotel (somewhere between two and three stars) if it weren't for the encounters with the residents – like the two little old ladies, joined at the hip and shopping basket, who tell the matron in very earnest tones that they can't find mattress-ticking *anywhere* and I'm all set to take them round more shops to look for some, but Adrian lays a restraining hand on my arm.

When it's time to leave, Bunty is reluctant to go but Adrian promises her that we'll be coming again and then she can stay for longer. The matron shakes our hands warmly but her voice drops to a murmur as Bunty starts down the steps. 'But do please remember,' she says, 'that Silverleas can only take people who don't need nursing care, so if your mother became ill in some way we wouldn't be able to keep her here.'

'That's all right,' I tell her cheerfully. 'My mother has a remarkably sound constitution.'

* * *

'Shall we get you all trim and ship-shape for your visit then?' Adrian smiles, rubbing her head with a towel. He pulls out a pair of scissors from his trouser pocket and twirls them impressively around Bunty's damp head. I notice how thin her hair is now. She has liver spots on the back of her hands and a funny red mark at the corner of one eye as if a cat's claw had caught her. I'm suddenly overwhelmed with pity for her and I loathe her for making me feel like that.

When we approach Silverleas for our final delivery Bunty seems less keen on the idea. She has already had a fit of near-hysteria as we crawled through York's permanently bottle-necked traffic, under the delusion that we were hopelessly late for a train we were trying to catch, and as we drive past the station and leave it behind she sets up a formidable wail.

We have to coax her out of the car and the nearer we get to the huge, baronial front door, the slower her footsteps become. As we start on the flight of stone steps she clutches my hand suddenly and for the first time I realize that she's smaller than me. I can still remember when she was twice as tall; now she's like a doll. How did she shrink so fast? My step falters. I'm not sure I can do this. Perhaps I could take this new doll-mother home with me and look after her, at least for a while?

'Don't even think it,' Adrian mutters under his breath, but anyway the matron already has Bunty's arm and is leading her along the corridor to her room with its modern facilities and pleasant views. Just before she disappears she turns and waves sadly, like a child on its first day at school. 'That was my mother,' I say with a sigh, and Adrian laughs rather grimly and says, 'She still is, our Ruby, she still is.'

When we visit Bunty the next day, however, she seems happier and tells us that the room service is wonderful. 'How big a tip do you think I should leave?' she asks, a worried little frown creasing up her features. We take her for a walk around the grounds, Dolores snapping at our ankles. Silverleas is set in a parkland of beautiful trees – weeping elms and Spanish walnut, glossy holly bushes and clumps of brooding yew. It is sheltered here and spring flowers sprout everywhere. The grass rolls out of view, green and fresh, and it strikes me that this is an excellent place to play horses and it's almost a shame that Christine Roper isn't here because I think it's the kind of game I'm ready to play now. We pause in our promenading and take a seat on one of the many sturdy benches presented by grateful people. Our bench is in memory of *Fred Kirkland 1902–1981* and all three of us sit formally on Fred's bench – straight backs, hands clasped on knees – and gaze at a little group of fritillaries, bobbing and waving in the gentle breeze like fairies' skirts. 'Would you like to stay here?' Adrian asks, and Bunty's whole body twitches like a startled rabbit's.

'Stay?' she echoes quietly. 'For ever?'

'Well,' I demur, 'perhaps not for ever . . .'

'Why can't I go home?' Bunty says, looking from one to the other of us in a rapid, panicky way that makes me wish I was anywhere but here. 'Why can't I go home?'

* * *

Adrian and I are eating sandwiches in front of the television, Bunty's television-snack trays perched on our knees. We're watching the *Antiques Roadshow*, with the religious intensity of people who've got nothing better to do. Tomorrow we'll have to start packing the house into boxes and disposing of everything. It seems strange to be getting rid of everything when Bunty isn't dead but there's nothing she has a use for any more. Then the phone rings.

Perhaps it will be Mr Nobody. It's not, it's the matron of Silverleas telling me that Bunty has had a stroke.

'How did she shrink so much?' Patricia is awe-struck by the change in Bunty. The three of us – Patricia, me and Adrian (four if you count Dolores who is stuffed inside Adrian's jacket) – sit around Bunty's hospital bed and talk in subdued whispers. Patricia got on the next flight when she heard about Bunty's imminent demise. Bunty's bed is in a side room of the new District Hospital, having been promptly ejected from Silverleas after her stroke (she did not, after all, leave a tip). A cerebral haemorrhage, not big enough to kill her, but enough to send her spinning deeper into limbo. Her tea has come and gone, uneaten, the leftovers picked at by Dolores.

The night-shift sister, Sister Blake, pops her head round the door, and asks us if we're all right. Sister Blake's tone of voice – solemn and supportive –

combined with the way we've been side-lined off the ward – suggests that Bunty is not expected to last much longer, and when the sister's gone we debate whether we should go home tonight or not. I draw the curtains at the window, curtains that have big colourful shapes on them as if we were in the children's ward. Bunty's room overlooks the Scarborough line and a short diesel train toots as it passes below. Patricia and I decide to go and ask Sister Blake if she knows the details of Bunty's terminal timetable. It's after nine o'clock and the last straggling visitors have gone and the lights have been dimmed. We find Sister Blake and a student nurse in one of the six-berth wards soothing a tiny old man who is trying to throw himself out of bed with remarkable determination. Sister Blake and the student struggle with the cot-sides while the old man, no bigger than a schoolboy, keeps up a stream of ferocious invective against them.

'I think she's busy,' Patricia says doubtfully. 'Let's go for a walk,' and we wander off around the maze of new staircases and corridors, arm in arm like the walking wounded whom we see perambulating in their dressing-gowns during the daytime. They are all safely tucked up now, as are the little electric trains that buzz along with the meal-trucks in tow. We walk along corridors with plate-glass walls beyond which we can see ducks roosting around a concrete pond, lit by small floodlights. The slight hum of a motor vibrates softly in the air as if the hospital was a huge ship ploughing confidently through the darkness. We sit for a while in reception in the big vinyl chairs and watch the revolving doors before going outside and taking a turn around the empty visitors' car-park, laid out like a huge hop-scotch. We're only a few hundred yards from where Bunty was born. And now she's dying. Farther up the other side of the road we can see the lights blazing on Rowntree's factory – that other great ocean-going liner.

When we get back to Bunty's bedside Sister Blake is there, holding one of Bunty's hands while Adrian holds the other. Adrian gives us a worried look and Sister Blake says softly, 'I think she's taken a turn for the worse.'

Our bedside vigil lasts all night. When you're waiting for death, instead of being surprised by it (as we usually are in our family), it can take a long time to come. Sister Blake (Tessa) is in her late forties and has two grown-up sons called Neil and Andrew. Neil is married and has a new baby daughter called Gemma. We know these things (and many other things) about Sister Blake for we swap stories over Bunty's living corpse. With her tired blue eyes and fading blond curls, Sister Blake looks like a plump and weary angel.

'I never knew my real mother,' she says in a low voice. 'I was adopted. Not knowing your real mother, it sort of nags at you, you know?'

Patricia flinches and asks, 'Didn't you try to find her?' and Sister Blake says, 'Oh yes, I did, but she was dead by then. She came from Belfast, that's all I know about her really, except she was a nurse too, that's funny isn't it? I was a war-baby.'

'We were all war-babies,' Patricia says enigmatically.

'She's hanging by a thread,' Sister Blake whispers, and we all watch Bunty's face with a curious inten-sity. I don't think I have ever looked at my mother so much as I have looked at her this night and now that I come to study her I feel as if I have no idea who she is. Patricia is watching this stranger in the bed with an oddly ferocious expression on her face and I am reminded for a second of the old Patricia.

There is a dull feeling inside me that is growing all the time. I had expected something different from Bunty's rite of passage – I had expected her to have some meaningful last words, pearls of wisdom, a death-bed confession ('I am not your real mother') but now I recognize the disappointing truth – she's not going to say anything, not even goodbye.

'I think she's gone,' Sister Blake says quietly and it's just as well we have a nurse with us, because none of us would ever have realized Bunty was dead, so quietly has she slipped behind the veil. I wish I was the kind of daughter who could rend her clothes and tear her hair out but I'm not, and neither is Patricia, who is sitting by the bedside with a kind of stunned look on her face as if the last thing she was expecting from a death-bed was death itself. Adrian is crying, and the only one who seems to have any idea how to behave on these occasions is Sister Blake, who gently smooths the sheets and touches Bunty's forehead as if she were tucking in a small child frightened of the dark. I am gripped by a wholly inappropriate urge to shake Bunty back to life and make her be our mother all over again – but do it better this time.

'Well, that's over with,' Patricia says, as we sit back in the taxi that's taking us away from the hospital. York speeds by in the flickering frames of the taxi windows. 'You know, Ruby, we loved her really.'

'Did we? It's not what I would call love.'

'Maybe not, but it's love just the same.' I check Patricia's face to make sure she's not looking smug or sentimental when she says this, but she's not, she's looking quite troubled, so I refrain from kicking her. Perhaps she's right. Perhaps my concept of love – as wide as the sky – isn't big enough to encompass Bunty's autistic mothering.

Patricia and I hold broad black ribbons either side of the coffin and pretend that we're lowering it into the grave. The other ribbon-bearers in this symbolic act are Uncle Ted, Uncle Clifford, Adrian and Lucy-Vida. The handful of dry soil hitting the coffin-lid makes me twitch. There's something dark and primitive about burying someone in the ground. I half expect Bunty to push the lid off in irritation and sit up and say to us, 'You should be careful, you could bury someone alive like that!' But she doesn't. Patricia and I have had a considerable debate about whether Bunty should be cremated or buried and finally, perhaps because we still had memories of the Shop fire, we decided on burial. Now I'm not so sure. I really don't think she would like it here. If only there was a pair of angels to raise their blazer-wings over her.

The graveside business is cursory, as was the funeral service. Bunty has hardly been inside a church since she left St Denys' Sunday School so the vicar of the local church doesn't put himself out too much. Despite our advice to the contrary, he insists on calling her Berenice throughout so I keep having the uneasy feeling that we're burying the wrong person.

Afterwards we go back to the house. Adrian has spent all morning making sandwiches and quiches and a fruit cake, and a newly-divorced Kathleen circulates round the house with trays of food, like a waitress, her mascara smudging under her eyes because she can't stop crying. She's crying about her divorce from Colin, not my mother, but not knowing that several people mistake her for a grieving daughter. The true daughters remain uncomfortably dry-eyed. There's an odd emptiness at the heart of Bunty's funeral, it's like being at a party without the noise and without waiting for something to happen, because it already has. The person at the centre of it all is missing.

I had thought that when she died it would be like having a weight removed and I would rise up and be free of her, but now I realize that she'll always be here, inside me, and I suppose when I'm least expecting it I'll look in the mirror and see her expression or open my mouth and speak her words. 'Well, you know, Ruby,' Patricia says, picking at the slice of broccoli quiche on her plate, 'people are given the mother they need for a particular incarnation.' But then she shrugs helplessly because neither of us can think why we needed Bunty.

'Do you believe in that stuff? Karma and all that?' Lucy-Vida asks. We're sitting on the stairs, sharing a bottle of wine with Lucy-Vida, twisting out of the way occasionally to let people pass to go upstairs to the bathroom. 'Patricia's a Buddhist,' I tell her. 'I'm coming back as a cat,' Lucy-Vida says, stretching out one of her ridiculously long, feline legs so that the hole in her black tights, shored up with shocking-pink nail varnish, suddenly expands and sends a ladder shooting up under her skirt. She has four children now but only her eldest is with her today. Wayne is a strapping twenty-five-year-old with thighs like York hams and is proudly wearing his army uniform. This is the very same Wayne that Lucy-Vida was pregnant with at Sandra's wedding and makes an unfortunate contrast to Sandra's two weedy boys, Dean and Todd. Sandra has put on a lot of weight in the intervening years and is throwing most of it about. 'Bossy cow,' Lucy-Vida remarks mildly as Sandra bellows at Uncle Ted.

Uncle Bill is dead but Auntie Eliza, who is waiting for a hip replacement, hobbles around on two crutches with Wayne carrying her glass and lighting her cigarettes. 'Game old bird,' Adrian says, dishing up quiche. Disappointingly, Daisy and Rose do not come to the funeral. It is some time since anyone has seen either of them – neither have married and they live together in a high-rise block in Leeds and Auntie Gladys says that they never go out of the house. 'They must go out some time,' Sandra says dismissively, 'or how would they eat?' (But Daisy and Rose probably don't need to eat.) 'Nah,' Wayne says, 'Mum sent me to check on them last year – they think aliens are talking to them through the television.' He screws a finger into the side of his head. 'Totally fucking barmy!' and Lucy-Vida slaps him hard on the other side of his head and says, 'Language, Wayne!'

In the kitchen, Brian, Adrian's lover, is wearing Bunty's pink rubber gloves and washing up for all he's worth. Uncle Clifford, his teeth removed, is sitting at the table eating a piece of pork pie, and holding forth on the subject of repatriating the 'blacks', to Africa preferably, and Brian nods and smiles in the tolerant way of people who know they can go home whenever they want and never have to see you again.

'Well,' Auntie Gladys says as she leaves, 'that was a right good send-off; your mother would have enjoyed it.'

'No she wouldn't,' Patricia says, closing the front door behind the last funeral guest. 'She hated things like that.'

We spend the next few days attending to post-funeral business, putting the house on the market, sending off insurance policies and bagging clothes up for the PDSA shop. We go through the jewellery and the photographs, dividing them up between us. I get my great-grandmother's photograph, the one that Tom had, and the silver locket; Patricia takes the clock, and

– after some hesitation – the rabbit's foot, which she plans to bury in the garden.

The day before she leaves we go for a long walk around the heart of York; the Minster overlooks us wherever we go. There won't really be anything to bring us back to York now – perhaps we'll never come here again. It seems like a fake city, a progression of flats and sets and white cardboard battlements and medieval half-timbered house kits that have been cut and glued together. The streets are full of strangers – up-market buskers, school parties and coach parties and endless varieties of foreigner.

We walk under the long wooden sign for Ye Olde Starre Inn that stretches from one side of the street to the other. The Roman *via praetoria*. The whole place has been turned into an upmarket shopping-mall; there are no more Richardson's and Hannon's, no more Walters and Bernards, no more barbers and bakers or stained-glass makers – it's like one big, incredibly expensive souvenir shop.

Slowly and inevitably we make our way to the Shop. It's ten years since Bunty sold up and now the premises are occupied by an expensive men's clothing store; a rail of Harris tweed hangs where the rabbit cages once were; a carousel of silk ties has taken the place of the Parrot. There isn't a single timber or floorboard or pane of glass that is recognizable, not an atom or molecule remains. Upstairs, in Above the Shop, there is now a café – a 'tea-room' – and Patricia and I spend a long time debating whether or not we should go up there. But eventually we do, and sit at a lace-covered table and drink fantastically-priced tea in exactly the same spot where our television set used to stand. 'Spooky or what?' Patricia says with a shiver.

There are more tables on the next floor and on our way out we loiter at the foot of the stairs for a long time but neither of us is able to even put a finger on the banister-rail. The tinkle of spoons on saucers and the polite murmur of foreign voices, American, German, Japanese, floats down the stairs. I close my eyes. If I concentrate I can just hear an older murmur, equally foreign but less polite – Latin, Saxon, Norman-French. They are all still here, swishing and clanking. And then the most extraordinary thing happens – the building begins to shake as if a small earthquake has the Vale of York in its grip. The street itself vibrates and all the delicate cups and saucers rattle and clatter on the tables of the tea-room. From one of the newly-genteel lace-curtained windows I can see a wild scene in the street below – the stomping, disciplined marching of thousands of feet as a Roman army marches up from the river, through the *porta praetoria* and along the street. The plumes on the centurions' helmets tremble, the standard bearers hold their standards proudly aloft. And there at the front, burnished and gleaming in the sun, is the magnificent brass eagle of the great Ninth Hispana. Perhaps if I watch them I will see where they disappeared to, but at that moment a waitress drops a jug full of milk and the Ninth Legion is reduced to a fading echo of footfalls. 'Ruby, Ruby!' Patricia gives me a little shake. 'Ruby, what are you staring at? Come on, it's time to go.'

We collect ourselves on the street outside. 'That was horrible,' Patricia says, over the noise of an *al fresco* string quartet on the pavement. 'A tea-room, for heaven's sakes.' The string quartet come to a tasteful crescendo and people throw money into an empty violin case. But not us, we scurry away, past St Helen's, the Shopkeepers' church, along Blake Street and towards the Museum Gardens, chased all the way by the teasing, cruel chatter of the household ghosts.

In the Museum Gardens, now entirely free to the public – no sixpence needed – we pick our way through the peacocks and squirrels and tourists that litter the grass and make our way down to the path by the river and walk the length from Lendal Bridge to Queen Anne's and back again. We pause at the foot of Marygate and watch a train crossing Scarborough Bridge. The water level in the Ouse is very low for this time of year, exposing the different strata of earth and mud which line it. Everyone has left something here – the unnamed tribes, the Celts, the Romans, the Vikings, the Saxons, the Normans and all those who came after, they have all left their lost property – the buttons and fans, the rings and torques, the *bullae* and *fibulae*. The riverbank winks momentarily with a thousand, zillion, million pins. A trick of the light. The past is a cupboard full of light and all you have to do is find the key that opens the door.

And finally to our last farewell – the cemetery. We buy

bunches of spring flowers from a stall in the Newgate Market and replace the withering wreaths on Bunty's still unmarked mound with daffodils. We leave fat yellow tulips for Gillian, a few rows away, but for Pearl we bring lilies, white as new snow. Pearl's grave is in the midst of a whole knot of children, tiny gravestones poking up like broken baby teeth in one corner of the cemetery. Like Gillian, Pearl is 'Safe in the Arms of Jesus'. Both Patricia and I agree that this is somehow highly unlikely and, anyway, we prefer the idea that she is inside the skin of another life now – perhaps the robin that flies from headstone to headstone as we walk towards the gate, stopping every so often to wait for us to catch it up. Although the way it cocks its head on its shoulder suggests the Parrot. A breeze ruffles the grass in the cemetery and moves the clouds faster across the stretched canvas of sky above. Patricia lifts her face up to the pale sun so that for a second she looks almost beautiful. 'I don't think the dead are lost for ever anyway, do you, Ruby?'

'Nothing's lost for ever, Patricia, it's all there somewhere. Every last pin.'

'Pin?'

'Believe me, Patricia, I've been to the end of the world. I know what happens.' The breeze turns suddenly chilly and we turn up our coat collars and link arms as we pick our way amongst the sleeping dead.

We part on York station, in a suitably dramatic thunderstorm. Patricia isn't going straight back to

Australia, her family and her veterinary practice will have to wait for her return, for she is off on a quest – to find her own lost child, the one she parted from so long ago in Clacton. We have counted up the years, 'Just think, Patricia – you might be a grandmother and not even know it,' and Patricia makes that funny noise again, which I now know is laughter. She's carrying our great-grandmother's clock (her finally-retrieved panda cushioning it) in Nell's ancient leatherette shopping-bag, trying not to unbalance its insides, but by the time she finally gets back to Melbourne it will have stopped for good.

Patricia embraces me on the station platform. 'The past is what you leave behind in life, Ruby,' she says with the smile of a reincarnated lama. 'Nonsense, Patricia,' I tell her as I climb on board my train. 'The past's what you take with you.'

I am about to retrace my journey, take in reverse the train, plane and two boats that brought me to York. I have a life to go back to. I have been away long enough. I'm going back to far away Shetland, beyond which there is nothing but sea until the northern ice-cap. I belong by blood to this foreign country. I know this because Patricia (of all people) has paid someone to draw up our family tree – a huge, chaotic arboretum that has brought to light the true Scottishness of the Lennoxes. Patricia has taken this thirst for genealogy farther and has been busy writing to the sawn-off branches – corresponding with Auntie Betty's daughter,

Hope, in Vancouver and Tina Donner, a half-cousin by marriage, in Saskatchewan. Tina came over last year and in York she discovered Edmund Donner's name scratched in the famous mirror, downstairs in Betty's café, just next to the ladies' toilets. Tina Donner came up to visit me as well, bringing with her a copy that she'd had made of Lillian's photograph of Ada and Albert, the one that she took with her on the *Minnedosa*'s Atlantic crossing so many years ago. My copy sits in its frame on my desk and I like to look at it and wonder about my links with these people. Monsieur Armand's photographs are scattered around the world now – with Hope, with Tina, with Patricia. Adrian has one of Lawrence and Tom with baby Lillian, but I have the one of Alice – the foolish mother, the missing wife, the woman lost in time.

Those little nut-brown girls, my own Alice and Pearl, are grown up now. They are both at university, one in Glasgow, one in Aberdeen, and I live on my own, on an island where the birds outnumber the people. Where I live you can find the red-throated diver and the eider duck, the curlew and the plover. There, there are puffins and the black guillemots, ravens and rock doves, nestling on the summer cliffs while above the moorland rise the merlin and the great skuas.

And there I am too. And what became of me? For a living I translate English technical books into Italian, so my marriage to Gian-Carlo Benedetti was not entirely wasted. I enjoy this work, methodical and mysterious at the same time. I can lay claim to be called a poet too – I have had good reviews for my first volume of poems

– published by a small press in Edinburgh, and any day now I intend to begin work on a grand project – a cycle of poems based on the family tree. There will be room for everyone – Ada and Albert, Alice and Rachel, Tina Donner and Tessa Blake, even the contingent lives of Monsieur Jean-Paul Armand and Ena Tetley, Minnie Havis and Mrs Sievewright, for they all have a place amongst our branches and who is to say which of these is real and which a fiction? In the end, it is my belief, words are the only things that can construct a world that makes sense.

I have caught the slow train that stops everywhere – Darlington, Durham, Newcastle, meandering its way along the Northumberland coast to Berwick. As we cross the Tweed the air seems to lighten and the sky begins to dry a little and, like a watermark, the pale sheen of a rainbow welcomes our train over the border. I'm in another country, the one called home. I am alive. I am a precious jewel. I am a drop of blood. I am Ruby Lennox.

HUMAN CROQUET

Kate Atkinson

'Wonderfully eloquent and forceful . . . brilliant and engrossing'
Penelope Fitzgerald, *Evening Standard*

Once it had been the great forest of Lythe – a vast and impenetrable thicket of green. And here, in the beginning, lived the Fairfaxes, grandly, at Fairfax Manor, visited once by the great Gloriana herself.

But over the centuries the forest had been destroyed, replaced by Streets of Trees. The Fairfaxes have dwindled too; now they live in 'Arden' at the end of Hawthorne Close and are hardly a family at all.

But Isobel Fairfax, who drops into pockets of time and out again, knows about the past. She is sixteen and waiting for the return of her mother – the thin, dangerous Eliza with her scent of nicotine, Arpège and sex, whose disappearance is part of the mystery that still remains at the heart of the forest.

'Vivid, richly imaginative, hilarious and frightening by turns'
Cressida Connolly, *Observer*

9780552996198

EMOTIONALLY WEIRD

Kate Atkinson

'Funny, bold and memorable'
The Times

On a peat and heather island off the west coast of Scotland, Effie and her mother Nora take refuge in the large mouldering house of their ancestors and tell each other stories. Nora, at first, recounts nothing that Effie really wants to hear, like who her father was – variously Jimmy, Jack, or Ernie. Effie tells of her life at college in Dundee, the land of cakes and William Wallace, where she lives in a lethargic relationship with Bob, a student who never goes to lectures, seldom gets out of bed, and to whom the Klingons are as real as the French and the Germans (more real than the Luxemburgers). But strange things are happening. Why is Effie being followed? Is someone killing the old people? And where is the mysterious yellow dog?

'A truly comic novel – achingly funny in parts – challenging and executed with wit and mischief'
Meera Syal, *The Express*

'Sends jolts of pleasure off the page . . . Atkinson's funniest foray yet . . . it is a work of Dickensian or even Shakespearean plenty'
Catherine Lockerbie, *The Scotsman*

9780552997348

NOT THE END OF THE WORLD

Kate Atkinson

'Moving and funny, and crammed with incidental wisdom'
Sunday Times

What is the real world? Does it exist, or is it merely a means of keeping another reality at bay?

Not the End of the World is Kate Atkinson's first collection of short stories. Playful and profound, they explore the world we think we know whilst offering a vision of another world which lurks just beneath the surface of our consciousness, a world where the myths we have banished from our lives are startlingly present and where imagination has the power to transform reality.

From Charlene and Trudi, obsessively making lists while bombs explode softly in the streets outside, to gormless Eddie, maniacal cataloguer of fish, and Meredith Zane who may just have discovered the secret to eternal life, each of these stories shows that when the worlds of material existence and imagination collide, anything is possible.

'I can think of few writers who can make the ordinary collide with the extraordinary to such beguiling effect . . . left me so fizzing with admiration'
Observer

'Exceptional . . . sharp, witty and completely compelling'
Daily Mail

'An exceptionally funny, quirky and bold writer'
Independent on Sunday

9780552771054

CASE HISTORIES

Kate Atkinson

'Not just the best novel I read this year
but the best mystery of the decade'
Stephen King

Cambridge is sweltering, during an unusually hot summer. To Jackson Brodie, former police inspector turned private investigator, the world consists of one accounting sheet – Lost on the left, Found on the right – and the two never seem to balance.

Jackson has never felt at home in Cambridge, and has a failed marriage to prove it. Surrounded by death, intrigue and misfortune, his own life haunted by a family tragedy, he attempts to unravel three disparate case histories and begins to realize that in spite of apparent diversity, everything is connected...

'An astonishingly complex and moving literary detective story . . .
the sort of novel you have to start re-reading the minute you've finished it'
Guardian

'Triumphant . . . her best book yet . . . a tragi-comedy for our times'
Sunday Telegraph

'Part complex family drama, part mystery, it winds up having more depth and vividness than ordinary thrillers and more thrills than ordinary fiction . . . a wonderfully tricky book'
New York Times

9780552772433

ONE GOOD TURN

Kate Atkinson

'Very funny . . . that rarest of things – a good literary novel and a cracking holiday read'
Observer

It is summer, it is the Edinburgh festival. People queuing for a lunchtime show witness a road-rage incident – a near-homicidal attack which changes the lives of everyone involved: the wife of an unscrupulous property developer, a crime writer, a washed-up comedian. Jackson Brodie, ex-army, ex-police, ex-private detective, is also an innocent bystander – until he becomes a murder suspect.

Stephen King called *Case Histories* 'the best mystery of the decade': *One Good Turn* sees the return of its irresistible hero Jackson Brodie. As the body count mounts, each character's story contains a kernel of the next, like a set of nesting Russian dolls. Everyone in the teeming Dickensian cast is looking for love or money or redemption or escape: but what each actually discovers is their own true self.

'The most fun I've had with a novel this year'
Ian Rankin, *Guardian* (Books of the Year)

'Delivers everything a good book should have. It's a fantastic detective story and a wonderful piece of writing . . . has taken the crime genre to another level'
Daily Express

'Thrillingly addictive . . . quite unique in her ability to fuse emotional drama and thriller'
The Times

'A detective novel packed with more wit, insight and subtlety than an entire shelf-full of literary fiction'
Marie Claire

9780552772440

WHEN WILL THERE BE GOOD NEWS?

Kate Atkinson

'Genius . . . insightful, often funny, life-affirming'
Sunday Telegraph

In a quiet corner of rural Devon, a six-year-old girl witnesses an appalling crime. Thirty years later the man convicted of the crime is released from prison.

In Edinburgh, sixteen-year-old Reggie, wise beyond her years, works as a nanny for a G.P. But her employer has disappeared with her baby, and Reggie seems to be the only person who is worried. Across town, Detective Chief Inspector Louise Monroe is also looking for a missing person, unaware that hurtling towards her is a former acquaintance – Jackson Brodie – himself on a journey that is about to be fatally interrupted.

'Funny, bracingly intelligent . . . Kate Atkinson is that rarest of beasts, a genuinely surprising novelist'
Guardian

'An exhilarating read. Her wry humour, sharp eye and subtle characterisation are a constant joy'
Daily Mail

9780552772457